SYDNEY HARBOUR HOSPITAL: LEXI'S SECRET

MELANIE MILBURNE

WEST WING TO MATERNITY WING!

BY
SCARLET WILSON

MILLS & BOON

SYDNEY HARBOUR HOSPITAL: LEXI'S SECRET

BY
MELANIE MILBURNE

First published in Great Britain 2012
by Mills & Boon, an imprint of Harlequin (UK) Limited.
Harlequin (UK) Limited, Eton House, 18-24 Paradise Road,
Richmond, Surrey TW9 1SR

© Harlequin Books S.A. 2012

Special thanks and acknowledgement are given to Melanie Milburne
for her contribution to the *Sydney Harbour Hospital* series.

ISBN: 978 0 263 89170 6

Harlequin (UK) policy is to use papers that are natural, renewable
and recyclable products and made from wood grown in sustainable
forests. The logging and manufacturing process conform to the
legal environmental regulations of the country of origin.

Printed and bound in Spain
by Blackprint CPI, Barcelona

**Welcome to the world
of Sydney Harbour Hospital**

**(or *SHH…* for short—
because secrets never stay hidden for long!)**

Looking out over cosmopolitan Sydney Harbour, Australia's premier teaching hospital is a hive of round-the-clock activity—with a *very* active hospital grapevine.

With the most renowned (and gorgeous!) doctors in Sydney working side by side, professional and sensual tensions run sky-high—there's *always* plenty of romantic rumours to gossip about…

Who's been kissing who in the on-call room? What's going on between legendary heart surgeon Finn Kennedy and tough-talking A&E doctor Evie Lockheart? And what's wrong with Finn?

Find out in this enthralling new eight-book continuity from Mills & Boon® Medical™ Romance—indulge yourself with eight helpings of romance, emotion and gripping medical drama!

Sydney Harbour Hospital
*From saving lives to sizzling seduction,
these doctors are the very best!*

Sydney Harbour Hospital

Sexy surgeons, dedicated doctors,
scandalous secrets, on-call dramas…

Welcome to the world of Sydney Harbour Hospital
(or *SHH*… for short—because secrets never stay hidden for long!)

In February new nurse Lily got caught up
in the hotbed of hospital gossip in
SYDNEY HARBOUR HOSPITAL: LILY'S SCANDAL
by Marion Lennox

And gorgeous paediatrician Teo came to single mum Zoe's rescue in
SYDNEY HARBOUR HOSPITAL: ZOE'S BABY
by Alison Roberts

In March sexy Sicilian playboy Luca finally met his match in
SYDNEY HARBOUR HOSPITAL: LUCA'S BAD GIRL
by Amy Andrews

Then in April Hayley opened Tom's eyes to love in
SYDNEY HARBOUR HOSPITAL: TOM'S REDEMPTION
by Fiona Lowe

This month join heiress Lexi as she learns to
put the past behind her in May…
SYDNEY HARBOUR HOSPITAL: LEXI'S SECRET
by Melanie Milburne

In June adventurer Charlie helps shy Bella fulfil her dreams—
and find love on the way!—in
SYDNEY HARBOUR HOSPITAL: BELLA'S WISHLIST
by Emily Forbes

Single mum Emily gives no-strings-attached surgeon Marco
a reason to stay in July:
SYDNEY HARBOUR HOSPITAL: MARCO'S TEMPTATION
by Fiona McArthur

And finally join us in August as Ava and James
realise their marriage really is worth saving in
SYDNEY HARBOUR HOSPITAL: AVA'S RE-AWAKENING
by Carol Marinelli

And not forgetting Sydney Harbour Hospital's legendary heart surgeon
Finn Kennedy. This brooding maverick keeps his women on hospital
rotation… But can new doc Evie Lockheart unlock the secrets to his
guarded heart? Find out in this enthralling new eight-book continuity
from Mills & Boon® Medical™ Romance.

A collection impossible to resist!

These books are also available in eBook format
from www.millsandboon.co.uk

CHAPTER ONE

IT WAS the worst possible way to run into an ex, Lexi thought. There was only one parking space left in the Sydney Harbour Hospital basement car park and although, strictly speaking, she shouldn't have been parking there since she wasn't a doctor or even a nurse, she was running late with some things for her sister, and it was just too tempting not to grab the last 'Doctors Only' space between a luxury sedan and a shiny red sports car that looked as if it had just been driven out of the showroom.

She opened her door and winced when she heard the bang-scrape of metal against metal.

And then she saw him.

He was sitting in the driver's seat, his broad-spanned hands gripping the steering-wheel with white-knuckled force, glaring at her furiously when recognition suddenly hit him. Lexi saw the quick spasm of his features, as if the sight of her had been like a punch to the face.

She felt the same punch deep and low in her belly as she encountered that dark brown espresso coffee gaze. Her throat closed over as if a large hand had gripped her and was squeezing the breath right out of her. Her heart pounded with a sickening thud, skip, thud, skip, thud that made her feel as if she had just run up the fire escape of a towering skyscraper on a single breath.

It was so unexpected.

No warning.

No preparation.

Why hadn't she been told he was back in the country? Why hadn't she been told he was working *here*? He clearly was, otherwise why would he be parking in the doctors' car park unless—like her—he had flouted the rules for his own convenience?

OK, so this was the time to play it cool. She could do that. It was her specialty. She was known all over the Sydney social circuit for her PhD in charm.

She shimmied out of the tight space between their cars and sent him a megawatt smile. 'Hi, Sam,' she said breezily. 'How are things?'

Sam Bailey unfolded his tall length from the sports car, closing the driver's door with a resounding click that more or less summed up his personality, Lexi thought—decisive, to the point, focussed on the task at hand.

'Alexis,' he said. No "How are you?" or "Nice to see you" or even "Hello", just her full name, which nobody ever called her, not even her father in one of his raging rants or her mother in one of her gin-soaked ramblings.

Lexi's winning smile faded slightly and her hands fidgeted with the strap of her designer bag hanging over her shoulder as she stood before him. 'So, what brings you here?' she said. 'A patient perhaps?'

'You could say that,' he said coolly. 'How about you?'

'Oh, I hang out here a lot,' she said, shifting her weight from one high heel to the other. 'My sister Bella's in and out for treatment all the time. She's been in for the last couple of weeks. Another chest infection.

She's on the transplant list but we have to wait until it clears. The chest infection, I mean.' Lexi knew she was rambling but what else could she do? Five years ago she had thought they'd had a future together. Their connection had been sudden but intense. She had dreamed of sharing her life with him and yet without notice Sam had cut her out of his life coldly and ruthlessly, not even pausing long enough to say goodbye. Seeing him again with no notice, no time to prepare herself, had stirred up deeply buried emotions so far beneath the surface she had almost forgotten they were there.

Almost...

'Sorry to hear that,' Sam said making a point of glancing at his silver watch.

Lexi felt a sinkhole of sadness open up inside her. He couldn't have made it clearer he wanted nothing to do with her. How could he be so...so distant after the intense intimacy they had shared? Had their affair meant nothing to him? Nothing at all? Surely she was worth a few minutes of his precious time in spite of the different paths their lives had taken? 'I didn't know you were back from wherever you went,' she said. 'I heard you got a scholarship to study overseas. Where did you go?'

'America,' he said flatly.

She raised her eyebrows, determined to counter his taciturn manner with garrulous charm. 'Wow, that's impressive,' she said. 'The States is so cool. So much to see. So much to do. You must've been the envy of all the other trainees, getting that chance to train abroad.'

'Yes.' Another frowning glance at his watch.

Lexi's gaze went to the strongly boned, deeply tanned wrist he had briefly exposed from the crisp, light blue business shirt he was wearing. Her stomach shifted like a pair of crutches slipping on a sheet of cracked ice. Those wrists had once held her much smaller ones in a passionate exchange that had left her body tingling for hours afterwards. Every moment of their blistering two-week affair was imprinted on her flesh. Seeing him again awakened every sleeping cell of her body to zinging, pulsing life. It felt like her blood had been thawed from a five-year deep freeze. It was racing through the network of her veins like a flash flood, making her heart hammer with the effort.

Her gaze slipped to his mouth, that beautiful sculpted mouth that had moved against hers with such heart-stopping skill. She still remembered the taste of him: minty and fresh and something essentially, potently male. She still remembered the feel of his tongue stroking against hers, the sexy rasp of it as it cajoled hers into a sizzling hot tango. He had explored every inch of her mouth with masterful expertise, leaving no corner without the branding heat of his possession.

And yet he had still walked away without so much as a word.

Lexi lifted her gaze back to his. Encountering those unfathomable brown depths made her chest feel like a frightened bird was trapped inside the cage of her lungs. Did he have any idea of the hurt he had caused? Did he have any idea of what she had gone through because of him?

She swallowed in anguish as she thought of the heart-wrenching decision she had made. Would she ever be able to summon up the courage to tell him? But, then, what would be the point? How could he possibly understand how hard it had been for her back then, young and pregnant with no one to turn to? She hadn't felt ready to become a mother. A termination had seemed the right thing to do and yet...

'I have to get going,' Sam said, nodding towards the hospital building. 'The CEO is expecting me.'

Lexi stared at him as realisation slowly dawned. 'You're going to be working here?' she asked.

'Yes.'

'Here at SHH?'

'Yes.'

'Not in the private sector?' she asked.

'No.'

'Do you ever answer a question with more than one word?'

'Occasionally.'

Lexi gave him a droll look but inside she was screaming: *This can't be happening!* 'Why wasn't I told?' she asked.

'No idea.'

'Wow, that's two.'

'Two what?' he said, frowning.

'Words,' she said. 'Maybe we can work on that a little. Boost your repertoire a bit. What are you doing here?'

'Working.'

She mentally rolled her eyes. 'I mean why here? Why not in the private system where you can earn loads and loads of money?' *Why not some other place where I won't see you just about every day and be reminded of what a silly little fool I was?*

'I was asked.'

'Wow, three words,' Lexi said, purposely animating her expression. 'We're really doing great here. I bet I can get you to say a full sentence in a month or two.'

'I have to go now,' he said. 'And, yes, that's five words if you're still counting.'

She lifted her chin. 'I am.'

Sam looked into those bluer than blue eyes and felt as if he had just dived into the deepest, most refreshing ocean after walking through the driest, hottest desert for years. Her softly pouting mouth was one of those mouths that just begged to be kissed. He could recall the dewy soft contours under his own just by looking at her. He could even remember the feel of the sexy dart of her tongue as it played catch-me-if-you-can with his. Her platinum-blonde hair was in its usual disarray that somehow managed to look perfectly coiffed and just-out-of-bed-after-marathon-sex at the same time. He felt the rocket blast to his groin as he remembered having her in his bed, up against the wall, over his desk, on a picnic blanket under the stars…

Stop it, buddy, he remonstrated with himself.

She had been too young for him before, and in spite of the years a world of experience separated them now. She was still a spoilt, rich kid who thought partying was a full-time occupation. He was on a mission to save lives that were dependent on transplant surgery.

Other people had to die in order for him to give life to others. He was *always* aware of that. Someone lost their life and by doing so he was given the opportunity to save another. He didn't take his responsibility lightly. He had worked long and hard for his career. It had defined his life. He had given up everything to get where he was now. He could not afford, at this crucial time in his journey, to be distracted by a party girl whose biggest decision in life was whether to have floating candles or helium balloons at a function.

He had to walk away, just as he had before, but at least this would be his choice, made of his own free will.

'You dented my car.' It was not the best line he could have come up with but he had just taken delivery of the damned vehicle. To him it just showed how irresponsible she was. She hadn't even looked as she'd flung open her door. It was just so typical of her and her privileged background. She had no idea how hard people had to work to get things she took for granted. She had been driven around in luxury cars all of her life. She didn't know what it felt like to be dirt poor with no funds available for extras, let alone the essentials.

Just take his mother, for instance. Stuck on a long transplant list and living way out in the bush to boot, his mother had died waiting for a kidney. His working-class parents hadn't had the money to pay for private health cover. They hadn't even had the money to afford another child after him. He knew what it felt like to want things that were so out of your reach it was like grasping at bubbles, hoping they wouldn't burst when your fingers touched them. In his experience they always burst.

Lexi was another bubble that had burst.

'You call that a dent?' Lexi bent over to examine the mark on the door.

Sam couldn't stop his gaze drinking in the gorgeous curve of her tiny bottom. She was all legs and arms, coltish, even though she was now twenty-four. It didn't seem to matter what she wore, she always looked like she had just stepped off a catwalk. Her legs were encased in skin-tight black pants that followed the long lines of her legs down to her racehorse-delicate ankles. She was wearing ridiculously high heels but he still had a few inches on her. The hot-pink top she had on skimmed her small but perfectly shaped breasts and the ruby-and-diamond pendant she was wearing around her neck looked like it could have paid off his entire university tuition loan.

She smelled fabulous. He felt his nostrils flaring to breathe more of her fragrance in. Flowers, spring flowers with a grace note of sexy sandalwood, or was it patchouli?

She suddenly straightened and met his eyes. 'It's barely made a mark,' she said. 'But if you want to be so pedantic I'll pay for it to be fixed.'

Sam elevated one of his brows mockingly. 'Don't you mean Daddy will pay for it?' he asked.

She pursed her mouth at him and he had to stop himself from bending down and covering it with his own. 'I'll have you know I earn my own money,' she said with a haughty look.

'Doing what?' he shot back. 'Painting your nails?'

She narrowed her blue eyes and her full mouth flattened. 'I'm Head of Events at SHH,' she said. 'I'm in charge of fundraising, including the gala masked ball to be held next month.'

Sam rocked back on his heels. 'Impressive.'

She gave him a hot little glare. 'My father gave me the job because I'm good at what I do.'

'I'm sure you are,' he said. *After all, partying was her favourite hobby.* 'Now, if you'll excuse me, I have a meeting to get to.'

'Is this your first day at SHH?' Lexi asked.

'Yes.'

'Where are you living?'

'I'm renting an apartment in Kirribilli,' he said. 'I want to have a look around before I buy.'

A small frown puckered her smooth brow. 'So you're back for good?' she asked.

'Yes,' Sam said. 'My father's getting on and I want to spend some time with him.'

'Is he still living in Broken Hill?' she asked.

'No,' he said. 'He's retired to the Central Coast.'

Sam was surprised she remembered anything about his father. It didn't sit well with his image of her as a shallow, spoilt little upstart who had only jumped into bed with him as an act of rebellion against her over-bearing father.

That had really rankled.

Damn it, it *still* rankled.

Their red-hot affair had only lasted a couple of weeks before her father Richard Lockheart had stepped in and told him what would happen to his career if he didn't stop messing with his baby girl. To top it all off, it turned out she was six years younger than she had told him. It had been a jolting shock to find the young woman he had been sleeping with had only left high school the year before. Nineteen years old and yet she had looked and acted as streetwise and poised as any twenty-five-year old.

Sam had told her things during that short affair he had told no one else. Things about his mother's death, like how hard it had been to watch her die, feeling so helpless, his father's endless grieving, his own dreams of making a difference so no one had to go through what his family had suffered. For once in his life his emotional guard had come down and it had backfired on him. Lexi had used him like she used her social standing to get what she wanted. He had almost lost everything because of her puerile, attention-seeking little game.

When it came down to it, it had been a choice between relocating or sitting back and watching his career implode. To a working-class trainee who had lived on Struggle Street for most of his life, Sam knew that the well-connected and powerful Richard Lockheart could have done some serious damage to his career. He hadn't taken those threats lightly. He had been lucky enough to be able to switch to the US training programme, and while it had cost him a packet, it had been the best thing he'd ever done. He had worked with some of the world's leading transplant surgeons and now he was considered one of the best heart-lung surgeons on the planet. Everyone back home had believed he had transferred on a scholarship and he hadn't said anything to contradict the rumour. Interestingly, neither, it seemed, had Richard Lockheart.

The appointment to SHH had been timely because he had been keen to come home for a couple of years. He missed his homeland and his father. The man was the only family he had. It was time to come home and put the past behind him.

Lexi was a part of his past but she had no place in his future. He had been captivated by her beauty and her alluring sensuality. But her party-girl mentality had been at odds with his career-focussed determination back then—just as much as it was at odds with it now. He couldn't afford to be distracted by her. Even though the eleven-year age gap was no longer such an issue he didn't want anything or anyone—particularly not red-hot little Lexi Lockheart—derailing his career plans.

Lexi flicked a strand of hair away that had drifted across her face. 'How will I contact you?' she asked.

Sam's brows snapped together. 'About what?'

'About your car,' she said, with another little mocking quiver of her eyelids. 'About the dent you need a magnifying glass to see.'

'Forget about it,' he said.

'No, I insist,' she said, taking out her mobile. 'I'll put you in my contacts.' Her slim, beautifully manicured fingers poised over the data entry key.

And that's when he saw it.

The diamond engagement ring on her finger seemed to be glinting at him like an evil eye, mocking him, taunting him.

Engaged.

He felt his throat seize up.

Lexi was engaged.

His mouth was suddenly so dry he couldn't speak. His chest felt as if someone had backed over it with a steamroller. He couldn't inflate his lungs enough to draw in a breath. His reaction surprised him. No, damn it, it shocked the hell out of him. She was nothing to him. What did it matter if she was engaged? It wasn't as if he had any claim on her, certainly not an emotional one. He didn't do emotion. He didn't even like her, for goodness' sake. She was an attention-seeking little tramp who thought bedding a boy from the bush was something to giggle about with her vacuous, equally shallow socialite girlfriends. Good luck to the man who was fool enough to tie himself to her.

Lexi looked up at him with an expectant expression. 'Your number?' she prompted.

Sam reluctantly rattled it off in a monotone he hardly recognised as his own voice. He had changed his number five years ago as a way of completely cutting all ties. He hadn't wanted her calling him or texting him or emailing him. He didn't want that soft sexy voice purring in his ear. It had taken years to get the sound of her voice out of his head.

Engaged.

Sam wondered what her fiancé was like. No, on second thought he didn't want to know. He'd bet he was a preppy sort, probably hadn't done a decent day's work in his life.

Lexi was engaged. Engaged!

It was a two-sentence chant he couldn't get out of his head. Cruel words he didn't want to hear.

'Do you want mine?' she asked, tucking another wayward strand of platinum-blonde hair away from her face with her free hand. It had snagged on her shiny lip gloss. He guessed it was strawberry flavoured. He hadn't eaten a strawberry in five years without thinking of the taste of her mouth.

He blinked. 'Your...er what?'

'My number,' she said. 'In case you want to contact me about the repairs?'

Sam swallowed the walnut-sized restriction in his throat. 'Your car isn't damaged.'

She looked at him for a moment before she closed her phone and popped it back in her bag. 'No,' she said. 'It's made of much tougher stuff, apparently.'

Sam's gaze kept tracking to her ring. It was like a magnet he had no power to resist. He didn't want to look at it. He didn't want to think about her planning a future with some other nameless, faceless man.

He didn't want to think about her in that nameless, faceless man's bed, her arms around his neck and her lips on his.

'You're engaged.'

He hadn't realised he had spoken the words out loud until she answered, 'Yes.'

'Congratulations,' he said.

'Thank you.'

Sam's gaze tracked back to the ring. It was expensive. It suited her hand. It was a perfect fit. It looked like it had been there a while.

His chest cramped again, harder this time.

He brought his eyes back to hers, forcing his voice to sound just mildly interested. 'So, when's the wedding?'

'November,' she said, a flicker of something moving over her face like a shadow. 'We've booked the cathedral for the tenth.'

The silence crawled from the dark corners of the basement, slowly but surely surrounding them.

Sam heard the scrape of one of her heels as she took a step backwards. 'Well, I'd better let you get to work,' she said. 'Wouldn't be good to be late for your first day on the job.'

'No,' he said. 'That might not go down so well.'

The silence crept up to his knees again before he added, 'It was nice to see you again, Alexis.'

She gave a tight smile by way of answer and walked off towards the lift, the sound of her heels click-clacking on the concrete floor striking totally unexpected and equally inexplicable hammer blows of regret in Sam's heart.

CHAPTER TWO

LEXI got out on the medical ward floor with her heart still racing. She had to control her spiralling emotions, but how? How was she supposed to act as if nothing was wrong?

Sam was back.

The shock was still reverberating through her like a dinner gong struck too hard. Her head was aching from the tattoo beating inside her brain.

Sam was back.

She drew in a calming breath. She would have to act as if nothing was wrong. It wouldn't do to reveal to everyone how shocked she was by his appointment. Had no one told her because they were worried how she would react or because they thought she wouldn't even remember him? And how could she ask without drawing attention to feelings she didn't want—*shouldn't want*—to examine?

'Hi, Lexi,' one of the nurses called out to her. 'I just bought my tickets for the ball. I can't wait. You should see the mask I bought online. It's fabulous.'

Lexi's face felt like she was cracking half-dry paint when she smiled. 'Great!'

The ball was the thing she was supposed to be focussed on, not Sam Bailey. It was the event of the year and she was solely responsible for it. It was no secret that some people at SHH were sceptical over whether she would be up to the task. Rumours of nepotism abounded, which made her all the more determined to prove everyone wrong. The proceeds she raised would go to the transplant unit for the purchase of a new state-of-the-art heart-lung bypass machine. Government funding was never enough. It took the hard work of her and her fundraising team to bring to the unit those extras that made all the difference for a patient's outcome.

And her older sister Bella was one of those patients.

Lexi pushed open the door of Bella's room, a bright smile already fixed in place. 'Hi, Bells.'

'Oh, hi, Lexi...' Bella said, her voice sagging over the weight of the words.

Lexi could always tell when Bella had just finished a session with the hospital physiotherapist. She looked even more gaunt and pale than usual. Her sister's thin, frail body lying so listlessly on the bed reminded her of a skeleton shrink-wrapped in skin. She had always found it hard to look at her older sister without feeling horribly guilty. Guilty that she was so robustly healthy, so outgoing and confident...well, on the surface anyway.

She knew it was hard for Bella to relate to her. It put a strain on their relationship that Lexi dearly wished wasn't there but she didn't know how to fix it. Everything Bella did was a struggle, but for Lexi no matter what activity she tried she seemed to have a natural flair for it. She had spent much of her childhood downplaying her talents in case Bella had felt left out. She'd ended the ballet lessons she'd adored because she'd sensed Bella's frustration that she could barely walk, let alone dance. Her piano lessons had gone the same way. As soon as it had become obvious Bella hadn't been able to keep up, Lexi had ended them. It had been easier to quit and pretend disinterest than to keep going and feel guilty all the time.

But it wasn't just guilt Lexi felt when she was around Bella. It was dread. Gut-wrenching, sickening dread that one day Bella was not going to be around any more.

The Lockheart family had lived with that fear for twenty-six years. It was as if the looming shadow of the Grim Reaper had stepped uninvited into their family, and for years had been waiting on the fringes, popping his head in now and again when Bella had a bad attack to remind them all not to take too much for granted, patiently waiting for his chance to step up to centre stage for the final act.

Everyone knew Bella would not reach thirty without a lung transplant. The trouble was getting her healthy and stable enough to be ready for one if a donor became available.

And then there was the waiting list with all those desperately sick people hoping for the same thing: a suitable donor. It was like a weird sort of live-or-die lottery. Even being a recipient of a healthy lung meant that some poor family somewhere else would be mourning the loss of the person they loved.

Life was incredibly cruel, Lexi thought as she put on her happy face for Bella. 'I've brought you a surprise.'

Bella's sad grey eyes brightened momentarily. 'Is it that new romantic comedy everyone is talking about?' she asked.

Lexi glanced at the portable DVD player her sister had on her tray table. Bella was addicted to movies, soppy ones mostly. The shelves the other side of the resuscitation gear held dozens of DVDs she had watched numerous times. 'No, it's not out until next month,' Lexi said. She put the designer shopping bag she'd brought on the bed beside her sister's frail form. 'Go on,' she urged. 'Open it.'

Bella opened the bag and carefully took out the tissue-wrapped package inside. Her thin fingers meticulously peeled back the designer-shop logo sticker keeping the edges together. Lexi was almost jumping up and down with impatience. If it had been her receiving a package the tissue paper would have been on the floor by now in her haste to see what was inside. But Bella took her time, which was sadly ironic really, Lexi thought, when time was one thing she had so little of.

'What do you think?' she asked as Bella had finally unwrapped the sexy red lacy negligee and wrap set.

Bella's cheeks were about as red as the lacy garments. 'Thanks, Lexi, it was very kind of you but…'

'You need to break out a little, Bells,' Lexi said. 'You're always wearing those granny flannel pyjamas. Passion-killers, that's what they're called. Why not live a little? Who's going to notice in here if you wear something a little more feminine?'

Bella's cheeks were still furnace hot. 'I'm not comfortable in your type of clothes, Lexi. You look stunning in them. You look stunning in anything. You'd turn heads wearing a garbage bag. I'll just look stupid.'

'You don't give yourself a chance to look stunning,' Lexi said. 'You hide behind layers of old-fashioned drab clothing like you don't want to be noticed.'

'Don't you think I get enough attention as it is?' Bella asked with a flash of her grey eyes. 'I have people poking and prodding me all the time. It's all right for you. You don't have to lie in here and watch the clock go round while another day of your life passes you by. You're out having a life.'

There was a little tense silence, all except for the squeak of a nurse's rubber-soled shoes in the corridor outside as she walked briskly past.

Lexi felt her shoulders drop. 'I'm sorry,' she said. 'I just thought something bright would cheer you up.' She began to collect the lacy items from Bella's lap.

Bella put her hand out to stop her taking away the negligee set. 'No, leave it,' she said on a heavy sigh. 'It was sweet of you. I'll keep it for when I'm better.'

The unspoken words *if I get better* hung in the air for a moment.

Lexi summoned up a smile. 'Actually, I only bought it because there was a two-for-one sale. You should see the little number I bought myself.'

'What colour is it?'

'Black with hot pink ribbons.'

'Are you saving it for your wedding night?' Bella asked.

Lexi averted her gaze. 'I'm not sure…maybe…'

'Have you heard from Matthew?'

'I got an email a couple of days ago,' Lexi said. 'It's hard for messages to get through. His team are building a school in a remote village in Nigeria.'

'I think he's amazing to be volunteering over there,' Bella said. 'He could have just as easily stayed at home in the family business.'

'He'll come back to the Brentwood business once he's done his bit for humanity,' Lexi said.

'It's nice that you're both are so passionate about helping others,' Bella said.

'Yes… ' Lexi dropped her gaze again. 'Oh, and before I forget…' She rummaged in another bag and took out the latest editions of the fashion magazines Bella loved and spread them like a fan on the tray table. 'You should check out page sixty-three in that one. There's a dress design just like the one you drew last week, only yours is better, in my opinion.'

'Thanks, Lexi,' Bella said with a shy smile.

There was the sound of a firm authoritative tread coming down the corridor.

'I bet that's your doctor,' Lexi said, rising from the end of the bed where she had perched. 'I'd better vamoose.'

'No, don't go,' Bella said, grabbing at Lexi's hand. 'That will be the transplant surgeon. You know how much I hate meeting people for the first time. Stay with me? Please?'

There was a cursory knock at the door and then a nurse came in, followed by a tall figure with shoulders so broad they almost filled the doorway.

Lexi felt her stomach hollow out and her heart did that hit-and-miss thing all over again. Could this really be happening to her? What twist of fate had led Sam to be her sister's surgeon? She'd thought he'd planned to be a renal transplant surgeon. She hadn't for a moment suspected he would be Bella's doctor. It would be even harder to avoid him now. There would be ward rounds and consultations in his rooms, follow-ups if the surgery went ahead. Lexi was the one who mostly ferried Bella around. How was she going to deal with being confronted with the pain of her past on such a regular basis?

'Bella,' the nurse said cheerily. 'This is Mr Sam Bailey, the heart-lung transplant surgeon newly arrived from the US. We're very lucky to have someone of his calibre working for us. And lucky you, for you are his very first patient at SHH. Mr Bailey, this is Bella Lockheart.'

Sam held out his hand to Bella. 'Hello, Bella,' he said. 'How are you feeling?'

Bella blushed like a schoolgirl and her voice was nothing more than a soft mumble. 'I'm fine, thank you.'

'And this is Lexi Lockheart,' the nurse continued with a beaming smile as she turned to where Lexi was standing. 'You'll see a lot of her around the place. She's a tireless fundraiser for SHH. If you have spare cash lying around, watch out. She'll be on to you in a flash.'

Lexi cautiously met Sam's gaze. How was he going to play this? As strangers meeting for the first time? Surely he wouldn't acknowledge their previous relationship, not in a place like SHH where gossip ran as fast as the wireless broadband network, sometimes faster. His professional reputation could be compromised if people started to speculate about what had happened between them in the past.

He put out his large, capable hand, the same hand that had once cupped her cheek as he'd leant in to kiss her for the first time, the same hand that had skimmed over and held each of her breasts, the same hand that had stroked down to that secret place between her thighs and coaxed her into her first earth-shattering orgasm. Lexi slowly brought her hand to his, trying to ignore the way his warm palm sent electric zaps all the way to her armpit and back.

'How do you do?' he said in his deep baritone voice.

So it was strangers, then. 'Pleased to meet you, Mr Bailey,' she said, keeping her expression coolly polite. 'I hope you settle in well at SHH.'

'I'm settling in very well, thank you,' he said, his

eyes communicating with hers in a private lock that made her flesh tingle from head to foot.

She slipped her hand out of his and stepped back so he could speak to Bella. Her hand fizzed and tingled and she shoved it behind her back as she watched as he interacted with her sister with a reassuring mix of compassion and professionalism.

'I've been going over your history in a lot of detail, Bella,' he said, 'especially your lung function over the last couple of years. I guess I don't have to tell you that there's been significant deterioration.'

Bella's grey gaze looked shadowed with worry. 'Yes, I've been admitted to hospital more often with chest infections and it takes longer and longer to clear things up. I've only just started to improve and I've been in here almost three weeks.'

Sam gave an understanding nod. 'I've looked at your latest CT scans and lung function studies. The lungs are very scarred. That's making them stiff, so it's no wonder you're struggling to breathe when you exert yourself or when you get even a minor infection.'

Bella bit her lip and dropped her gaze to the magazines on her tray table. It was a moment before she looked up at Sam. 'Am I getting to…to the end? How much time do I have left?'

Sam gave her thin shoulder a gentle squeeze. 'We're getting to the stage of needing to do a lung transplant within the next couple of months. I've started the active search for a matching transplant donor. If we find one we need to move straight away before you get another bout of pneumonia. We could find a donor in a day, a week or a couple of months. I'm afraid that longer than that and the chances get worse of keeping you well enough to survive the surgery.'

Lexi listened with dread, feeling like a ship's anchor had landed on the floor of her stomach. It was such a massive operation. What if it didn't work? What if poor Bella died on the operating table or soon after? So much of it seemed up to chance: the right donor; whether Bella was well enough at the time to be the recipient; whether she would survive the long operation. So many factors were at play and no one, it seemed, had any control over any of it, least of all Bella.

Bella must have been thinking the very same thing as she said, 'What are my chances of coming through the operation?'

Sam was nothing if not professional and knowledge-able and encouraging in his manner. 'With modern anti-rejection therapy there's better than an eighty-five per cent chance that you'll survive the surgery and live a good-quality life for the next ten years. After that there's not much data, but expectations are that anti-rejection management will continue to improve and that you could end up living a fairly normal life.'

'You're in good hands, Bella,' the nurse said. 'Mr Bailey is considered one of the world's leading heart-lung transplant surgeons.'

Sam acknowledged the nurse's comment with a quick on-off smile as if he was uncomfortable with praise. Perhaps he was worried about operating on someone to whom he had a connection, Lexi thought. Not that he had ever met Bella before, but he had been intimately involved with Lexi. Clinical distance was paramount in life-and-death surgery. A surgeon could not afford to let the pressure of a relationship, no matter how distant or close, interfere with his clinical judgement. She hoped her involvement with him in the past wasn't going to complicate things for Bella.

'I'll keep you informed on things as we go along, Bella,' Sam said. 'You'll stay in the medical ward until your health improves. If a donor becomes available and you're healthy enough, we'll move you across to the transplant unit. Otherwise we'll send you home until something comes up.'

'Thanks for everything, Mr Bailey,' Bella said blushing again. 'I really appreciate you taking me on.'

Sam smiled and gave Bella's shoulder another gentle touch. 'Hang in there, Bella. We'll do all we can to get you through this. Just try and keep positive.'

He gave Lexi a brief impersonal nod as he left with the nurse to continue his rounds.

Lexi didn't even realise she was holding her breath until Bella looked at her quizzically. 'It's not like you to be so quiet when there's a handsome man in the room,' she said.

Lexi felt her face heating and tried to counter it with an uppity toss of her head. 'He's not that handsome.'

Bella raised her brows. 'You don't think? I thought you had a thing for tall muscular men with dark brown eyes.'

Lexi gave a dismissive shrug. 'His hair is too short.'

'Maybe he keeps it short for convenience,' Bella said. 'He's in Theatre a lot. Any longer and it would get sweaty under the scrub hat during long transplant operations.'

Lexi made a business of folding each sheet of the tissue paper into a neat square, lining them up side by side on the bed.

'He's got nice eyes, don't you think?' Bella said.

'I didn't notice.'

'Liar, sure you did,' Bella said. 'I saw you blush. I've

never seen you blush before. That's my specialty, not yours.'

'It's hot in here,' Lexi said, fanning her face for emphasis. 'How do you stand it?'

'Did you notice his hands?' Bella asked.

'Not really...' Lexi remembered how those hands had felt on her body. How they had lit fires under her flesh until she had been burning with a need so strong it had totally consumed her. Those hands had wreaked havoc on her senses from the first moment he had touched her. She opened and closed the hand he had taken in his just minutes ago. The tingling pins and needles feeling was still there...

'He wasn't wearing a wedding ring,' Bella said.

'Doesn't mean he's not involved with someone,' Lexi said, feeling a tight ache in her chest as she pictured his partner. Would she be blonde, like her, or brunette? Or maybe a redhead like Bella. Would she be a doctor or nurse? Or a teacher perhaps? A lawyer? 'Dad's got a new girlfriend,' she said, to change the subject.

'Yes, Evie told me.'

'I haven't met her yet.'

'I don't know why he bothers introducing them,' Bella said with an air of resentment. 'None of them stay around long enough for us to get to know them.'

'Dad's entitled to have a life,' Lexi said. 'It's not like Mum's ever going to come back and play happy families.'

'You always defend him,' Bella said irritably. 'You never let anyone say a bad word about him.'

'Look,' Lexi said, hoping to avoid the well-worn bone of contention between them. 'I know he's not perfect but he's the only father we have. The only parent when it comes down to it. Mum's not much use.'

'Maybe Mum couldn't handle Dad's philandering,' Bella said. 'Maybe it wasn't just because I was sick. Maybe she was left on her own too much and couldn't cope. Maybe she wouldn't have left if he had offered her more emotional support.'

Lexi knew Bella felt terribly guilty about the breakdown of their parents' marriage. Her illness had taken its toll on everyone, but their mother had been the first to abandon ship, taking the contents of the drinks cabinet with her. Miranda Lockheart flitted in and out of their lives, not staying long enough to offer any stability or support but just long enough to remind them of what they had missed out on.

But blaming their father was not something Lexi had ever felt comfortable doing. He had always been there for her. He was her stronghold, the person she looked up to, the person she craved approval from more than any other.

'Dad has always tried to do his best,' she said. 'He was meant to be a father, not a mother. He couldn't do both.'

Bella gave a weary sigh. 'One day you're going to find out that Dad has clay feet. I just hope I'm around to see it.'

Lexi shrugged and then tried another subject change. 'Have you had any other visitors?'

'Phone calls or texts mostly,' Bella said with a despondent look on her face. 'People get sick of visiting after the first week. It happens every time. Maybe it'll be different once I've had the transplant…'

Guilt struck at Lexi like a closed fist. 'I'm sorry I didn't get in yesterday,' she said. 'Matthew's mother wanted me to look at wedding-cake designs. Her sister has already made the cake. Now we just have to decide on the decoration. Matthew wants something traditional but I was thinking we could so something more along the lines of…'

Bella was frowning as she looked into space. It was as if she hadn't heard a word of what Lexi had been saying. 'Sam…' she said. 'Sam. It's really been bugging me. Why does that name sound so familiar?'

Lexi felt her stomach drop again. 'Sam's a popular name.'

'I know but it's more than that,' Bella said, frowning in concentration. 'Bailey. Sam Bailey. Bailey. Sam Bailey.'

Lexi closed her eyes. *Please, no.*

'Oh. My. God.'

Lexi winced as she opened her eyes to see Bella's saucer-like ones staring at her. 'Wh-what?' she choked.

'It's him, isn't it?' Bella asked. 'It's the same Sam Bailey. The Sam Bailey you had that naughty little teenage fling with that made Dad almost blow a fuse. Oh. My. God.'

'Will you please keep your voice down?' Lexi hissed.

'It's not like you'll be able to keep it a secret,' Bella said. 'Not for long and certainly not around here. People have long memories and they just love a bit of juicy gossip. You'd better let Matthew know. You don't want him getting into a flap about an ex-lover turning up out of the blue.'

Lexi turned away to look out of the window, crossing her arms over her body as if that would contain the pain that was spreading like an ink spill through her. Was she deluded to hope no one would remember their past connection? Who else would link their names and start the gossip all over again? How would she cope with it a second time?

No one knew about the baby.

No one.

At least that secret was safe.

But everything else was out there for everyone to pick over like crows on a rotting carcass. All the intimate details of her brief relationship with Sam would be fodder, grist for the mill of gossip that SHH was renowned for. She would be painted as the Scarlet Woman, the scandalous Lolita who had lured Sam away from his studies at the most pivotal moment in his career.

'Lexi?'

Lexi pulled in a breath and faced her sister. 'It was five years ago,' she said. 'Hopefully no one will even remember what happened back then.'

Bella looked doubtful. 'I still think you should tell Matthew.'

'I will tell him,' Lexi said, breaking out into a sweat. 'I'll tell him it was a stupid little fling that meant nothing.'

Bella chewed at her lip for a moment. 'Is this the first time you've seen Sam since you broke up?' she asked.

'No, I ran into him in the doctors' car park on my way to see you,' Lexi said, raking a distracted hand through her hair. 'That'll teach me for breaking the rules. I won't park there ever again. Cross my heart and—' She stopped and gave Bella an apologetic grimace as her hand dropped back by her side. 'Sorry, bad choice of words.'

Bella continued to look at her with a concerned frown on her face. 'You're not happy about seeing him again, are you?' she said.

Lexi lifted her shoulders in a couldn't-care-less manner. 'It's always a little difficult running into ex-partners. It's part of the dating life. Once a relationship ends you don't always end up the best of friends.'

'Not that I would know anything about the dating life…' Bella said as she fiddled with the edge of the sheet covering her thin little body.

Lexi sighed and reached for Bella's small, cold hand. 'You're being so wonderfully brave about all this,' she said. 'If it was me I'd be terrified.'

'I *am* terrified,' Bella said. 'I want what you have. I want a life. I want to one day get married and have babies.'

Lexi felt her insides clench like the snap of a rabbit trap. That aching sadness gripped her every time she thought of the baby she could have had if things had been different. It was ironic that Matthew was keen to start a family as soon as they were married. His parents were excited at the prospect of becoming grandparents. But she had come to dread the topic every time he raised it. It wasn't the only thing she argued with him about. Her lack of interest in sex had become a huge issue over the last few months of their engagement. Matthew's trip abroad, she suspected, were his attempts to make her heart grow fonder in his absence. She didn't have the heart to tell him it wasn't working. She missed him certainly, but not in the way he most wanted her to.

'I'll be the only Lockheart sister left childless and lonely on the shelf,' Bella continued to bemoan.

'Is Evie seeing someone?' Lexi asked feeling a little piqued that she hadn't been told by Evie herself. 'I was under the impression there's been no one since she broke things off with Stuart…what was it? Two years ago?'

'I heard one of the nurses talking about Evie and Finn Kennedy,' Bella said.

Lexi laughed. 'Finn Kennedy? Are you out of your mind? He's the last person I would have picked for Evie. He's so grumpy and brooding. I don't think I've ever seen him smile.'

'He's very kind to patients,' Bella said in his defence. 'And he's smiled at me lots of times.'

'In my opinion Finn Kennedy has a chip on his shoulder that it'd take an industrial crane to shift,' Lexi said. 'I hope to goodness Evie knows what she's doing. The last thing we need in the Lockheart family is another difficult person to deal with.'

There was a small silence.

'Has Mum been in to see you?' Lexi asked.

Bella's shoulders slumped a little further as she shook her head. 'You know what she's like…'

Lexi gave Bella's hand another little squeeze. 'I wish I could change places with you, Bells,' she said sincerely. 'I hate seeing you suffer… I hate the thought of losing you.'

Bella gave her a wobbly smile. 'I guess that's in Sam Bailey's hands now, isn't it?'

CHAPTER THREE

IT WAS a week later when Lexi ran into Sam again—
literally. She was coming out of the hospital cafeteria
with a latte in one hand while she texted a message on
her phone in the other when she rammed into his broad
chest. It was like stepping into a six-foot-two brick wall.
The coffee cup lid didn't survive the impact and the
milky liquid splashed all over the front of Sam's crisp
white shirt.

He let out a short, sharp expletive.

Lexi looked up in horror. 'Oops, sorry,' she said. 'I
didn't see you. I was…um, multitasking.'

He plucked at his shirt to keep it away from his chest.
'This is a busy hospital, not a social networking site,'
he said.

Lexi put up her chin. 'If you had looked where you
were going, you could've avoided me,' she shot back.

'You could've burned me,' he said.

'Did I burn you?'

'No, but that's not the point.'

'It is the point,' she said. 'There's no damage other
than a stained shirt, which I will take full responsibility for.'

He gave her a mocking look. 'You mean you'll hand
it to one of the Lockheart lackeys to launder for you?'

Lexi ground her teeth as she looked up at him. Why today of all days had she worn ballet flats? He seemed to tower over her and it put her at a distinct disadvantage. She was faced with his stubbly chin and had to crane her neck to reach his chocolate-brown eyes. 'I'll see to it that your shirt is returned to you spotless,' she said.

'I can hardly take it off and give it to you in the middle of the busiest corridor of the hospital,' he pointed out dryly.

'Then we'll have to arrange a handover time,' she said. 'What time do you finish today?'

He scraped a hand through his hair. 'Look, forget about it,' he said. 'I have my own laundry service.'

'No, I insist,' Lexi said. 'I wasn't looking where I was going.'

'I'm sure you have much better things to do than wash and iron my shirt,' Sam said.

'Like paint my nails?' she said with an arch look.

He shifted his mouth from side to side. 'OK, round one to you,' he said. 'I had no idea you were so actively involved in raising funds for the unit.'

'I did tell you I was Head of Events.'

'Yes, but I didn't know you had been responsible for raising over five hundred thousand dollars last year.'

'I'm going to double that by the end of this year,' Lexi said. 'You can make a donation if you like. I'll give you the website address. You can pay online. All donations over two dollars are tax deductible.'

Sam was starting to see why she had been chosen for the job. Who could resist her when she laid on the Lockheart charm? She looked especially gorgeous today. She was several inches shorter than usual. But she still smelled as delicious as ever. That intriguing mix of flowers and essential oils teased his nostrils. She was dressed in grey trousers and a loose-fitting white cotton shirt with a camisole underneath that hugged her pert breasts. She had dangling earrings in her ears; they caught the light every now and again, making him think of the sun sparkling on the ocean. It had been her brightness that had attracted him like a moth to a flame all those years ago. He had been drawn to her bubbly nature; her positive outlook on life was such a contrast to his more guarded, introverted approach. She had flirted with him outrageously at a charity dinner held by her father in honour of the hospital. Sam hadn't re-alised who she was at the time, and he often wondered if he would have taken things as far as he had if he had known she was Richard Lockheart's youngest daughter. He couldn't answer that with any certainty, even now.

Put simply, she had been utterly irresistible.

With her stunning looks, charm and at-ease-in-any-company personality, he had temporarily lost sight of his goal. He had compromised everything to be with her because that was the effect she'd had on him.

But finding out the truth about how she had used him had made him cynical and less willing to open his heart in subsequent relationships. He dated regularly but commitment was something he avoided. Friends of his were marrying and having families now but he had no plans to join them any time soon. He didn't want to end up like his father, loving someone so much that he couldn't function properly without them.

His gaze drifted to Lexi's sparkling engagement ring. He felt a ridge come up in his throat as he pictured her walking down the aisle towards that nameless, faceless man. She would be smiling radiantly, looking amazingly beautiful, blissfully happy to be marrying the man she loved.

Engaged.

The word was a jarring reminder.

Lexi was engaged.

The three words were a life sentence.

Sam gave himself a mental shake. 'I'll get my secretary to make a donation on my behalf,' he said. 'Now, if you'll excuse me…' He pushed against the fire-escape door with his shoulder.

'There is a lift, you know,' Lexi said.

'Yes, I know, but I prefer the exercise.'

She glanced at the lift again before returning her gaze to where Sam was holding the fire-escape door open. She gave him a tight little smile that had a hint of stubbornness to it and brushed past him to make her way up the stairs. He felt his body kick start like a racing-car engine when her slim hip brushed against his thigh. It was probably not deliberate as there wasn't a lot of space to spare. She went ahead of him up the stairs, another bad idea in spite of it being chivalrous on his part. He got a perfect view of her neat bottom and long legs as she made her way up. He tried not to think of those long legs wrapped around him in passion and that beautiful hair of hers flung out over his pillow.

He had lain awake for the last week, sifting through every moment he had spent with her five years ago. From the very first second when her blue gaze had met his across that crowded room he had felt the lightning strike of physical attraction. It had rooted him to the spot. He had felt like a starstruck fan meeting their idol for the first time. He had barely been able to string a few words together when she approached him. Whatever he had said must have amused her for he remembered the tinkling bell of her laugh and how it had made his skin lift in a shiver.

They had left the gathering together and they had barely surfaced from his tiny flat for the next two weeks. For the first time during his career he had neglected his studies. The thick surgical textbooks had sat on his desk opposite his bed, staring at him in a surly silence. And he had pointedly ignored them while he had indulged in an affair that had been so hot and erotic he could hardly believe it had been happening to him. The physical intensity of it had surpassed anything before or since. He had relished every moment with Lexi in his arms. She had been an adventurous and enthusiastic, even at times playful lover. He suspected she'd had a fair bit of experience, perhaps much more than him, but they hadn't talked about it. Looking back, he realised she hadn't said much about herself at all, even though he had tried to draw her out several times. In hindsight he could see why she had been so reluctant to reveal herself to him emotionally. There had been no emotional commitment on her part. She had simply wanted to create a storm with her father and had used him to summon up the thunderclouds.

'Why did you pretend we didn't know each other last week when you were visiting Bella?' Lexi asked, stopping in mid-climb to look back at him over her shoulder.

Sam almost ran into the back of her. He felt the warmth of her body and got another delicious waft of her perfume. 'I didn't think it was wise to advertise the fact that we'd once been involved,' he said.

'Not good for your career?' she asked with one of her pert looks.

He frowned up at her. 'It has nothing to do with my

career. I wasn't sure if your sister knew about us. I'd not met her before. I was playing it safe for your sake.'

'She wasn't at the dinner where we met,' Lexi said. 'But she remembered the dreadful fallout after my father found out we were seeing each other.'

Sam's frown deepened. It had niggled at him a bit that he had never actually seen or spoken to her after her father had approached him with that ultimatum. For the last five years he had just assumed she had run back to the family fortress at her father's bidding. Her little show of rebellion had achieved its aim. She had got her father's attention back solely on her. Back then, Lexi had struck Sam as the type of girl who would never do anything to permanently jeopardise her prized position as Daddy's Little Girl. She would go so far and no further. It was her way of working things to her advantage, or so he had thought.

But what if things hadn't been quite the way her father had said? Lexi had implied on his first day at SHH that she'd had no idea he had gone to the States. Why hadn't she been told where he had gone? Why hadn't she asked? Or had her father deliberately kept her in the dark, perhaps forbidding her to mention Sam's name in his presence, like some sort of overbearing aristocrat father from the past? Was it deluded of him to hope she had invested more in their relationship than her father had suggested? Was it his male pride that wanted it that way instead of feeling like some sort of cheap gigolo who had served his purpose and now meant nothing to her? Had never meant anything to her?

'Your father is well-known for his temper,' he said. 'I hope it wasn't too rough a time for you back then.'

A flicker of something moved over her face but within a blink it was gone, making him wonder if he had imagined it. She gave her head a little toss and turned and continued walking up the fire escape. 'I know how to handle my father,' she said.

Sam followed her up another few steps. 'Why didn't you ask him where I'd gone?' he asked.

He saw her back tighten like a rod of steel before she slowly turned to face him at the fire-escape door. 'Here's the fourth floor,' she announced like a lift operator.

'Why didn't you ask your father, Lexi?' he asked again.

Her blue eyes clashed with his, a spark of cynicism making them appear hard and worldly. 'Why would I do that?' she asked. 'I had a new boyfriend within a few days. Did you really think I was pining after you? Give me a break, country boy. You were fun but not that much fun.'

Sam ground his teeth as he joined her on the landing, conscious of the tight space and the warmth coming off both of their bodies from the exercise. Lexi's breathing rate had increased slightly, making her beautiful breasts rise and fall behind her camisole. He allowed himself a brief little eye-lock but then wished he hadn't. She was temptation personified. He had never wanted to kiss someone more in his life. Did she know she was having this effect on him? How could she not? He was doing his best to disguise it but there was only so much he could do. He was a red-blooded male after all, and she was all sexy, nubile woman.

He thrust the door open out of the fire escape and nodded for her to go through. She walked past him, this time not touching him. He felt the loss keenly. His body ached to feel her, to touch her, to bring her close against him, to feel every part of her respond to him as she had in the past. It frustrated him that she still had that power over him. It wasn't supposed to be like this now.

Engaged.

Lexi was engaged.

For heaven's sake, why wasn't his body getting the message?

'Is this your office?' she asked as she came to a frosted glass door halfway along the corridor.

'Yes.' He stood at the door, pointedly waiting for her to leave.

She peered past his shoulder. 'Aren't you going to show me around?' she asked.

'Alexis,' he began. 'I don't think—'

'I want your shirt,' she said with a determined look in her blue gaze.

I want your body, Sam thought. He let out a ragged breath. 'I guess I can hardly see patients wearing this,' he said. 'I'll put on some scrubs.'

Lexi followed him into the suite of rooms he had been assigned. He wondered for a moment if she was going to follow him all the way into his office but she perched her neat bottom on one of the seats in the currently unattended reception area and idly leafed through a magazine.

Sam came out wearing theatre scrubs and handed her his shirt. Lexi took it from him and tried to ignore the fact that it was still warm from his body. She wanted to hold it up to her nose to smell his particular male smell but she could hardly do that in front of him. It was perhaps a little foolish of her, sentimental perhaps, but she had never forgotten his wonderful male smell. He hadn't been one for using expensive aftershaves. He had smelt of good clean soap and a supermarket-brand shampoo that had reminded her of cold, crisp apples.

Lexi put the magazine down. 'Look, all other things aside, I just wanted to say thank you for all that you're doing for my sister.'

'It's fine,' he said, his granite face back on. 'It's what I do.'

The silence stretched and stretched like an elastic band pulled to its capacity.

Lexi couldn't stop looking at him. It was as if her gaze was drawn by a force she had no control over. She longed to know what was going on behind the un-readable screen of his dark eyes. Was he thinking of the time they had spent together? Did he *ever* think of it? Did he regret walking away from her without saying goodbye? Why had he gone so abruptly? She had thought he was different from other men. He had seemed deeper and more sensitive, more emotionally available. Or had that all been a ploy on his part to get her into his bed as quickly and as often as he could? It had certainly worked. She had held nothing back from him physically. Emotionally she had been a little more guarded because she'd been worried about revealing how insecure she'd felt as a person. She'd known how unattractive that was for most men. He, like all the other men she had met, had been attracted to her as Lexi the confident and outgoing party-loving social butterfly. She hadn't felt comfortable revealing how much of an act it had been to compensate for the deep insecurities that had plagued her. How being surrounded by people had stopped her thinking about how lonely she'd felt deep inside. She had wanted to wait until she was a lit-tle more confident that their relationship had a future before she revealed that side of herself. But he clearly hadn't been thinking about *their* future. His sights had been solely focussed on his own.

'Alexis.' There was a note of warning in his voice.

'Please don't call me that,' she said. 'I know why you're doing it but please don't.'

He turned and walked behind the reception desk, the action reminding Lexi of a soldier going back into the trenches. He fiddled with the computer for a moment before he spoke in a casual tone that belied the tension she could see in the square set of his broad shoulders. 'I didn't realise you hated your name so much.'

'I don't hate my name,' she said. 'It's just I can't get used to you calling me anything but Lexi.'

He stopped fiddling and turned, his gaze colliding with hers. 'Will you stop it, for pity's sake?'

'Stop what?' she asked.

'You know damn well what.'

'I don't know what.'

His hands went into fists by his sides. 'Yes, you do.'

'You mean acknowledging you?' she asked, coming to stand in front of him. 'Stopping to talk to you in the corridor or on the fire escape? Treating you like a person, that sort of thing?'

'You probably staged the coffee thing to get me alone,' he bit out.

Lexi glared at him in affront. 'You think I would waste a perfectly good double-strength soy latte on you?' she asked.

His frown closed the gap between his chocolate-brown eyes. 'That shirt cost me seventy US dollars,' he said through clenched teeth.

She put her hands on her hips. 'If that's so then you need some serious help when you go shopping, country boy,' she tossed back.

'What's that supposed to mean?'

She gave her head a toss. 'Call me if you want a style advisor,' she said. 'I have connections.'

He glared at her broodingly. 'You think I need help dressing?'

No, but I would love to undress you right now, Lexi thought. She reared back from her traitorous thoughts like a bolting horse suddenly facing a precipitous drop. What on earth was the matter with her? Her fiancé was working hard in a remote and dangerous part of a foreign country and here she was betraying him with her wayward thoughts about a man she should have put out of her mind years ago. 'Yes,' she said. 'You need to buy quality, not quantity. That shirt is not stain-resistant. For just fifty dollars more you could have bought a stain-and crease-resistant one.'

'Oh, for heaven's sake,' he said as he rubbed at the back of his neck. 'I can't believe I'm even having this conversation.'

Lexi headed for the door. 'I'll get this non-stain-resistant, non-crease-resistant shirt back to you as soon as I can but if the stain doesn't come out don't blame me.'

'Careful not to break a fingernail doing it,' he muttered.

Lexi stomped back behind the reception desk, right into his body space, eyes glaring, cheeks hot with anger. 'What did you say?' she asked.

He looked down at her from his height advantage, dark eyes glittering, jaw clenched, mouth flat. 'You heard.'

She stepped forward half a step and stabbed a finger at his rock-hard chest. 'I might be just an empty-headed party girl with nothing better to do than paint my nails in between organising the next shindig, but this unit, your unit, would not be able to do even half of what it does without my help,' she said. 'Maybe you should think about that next time you want to fling an insult my way.'

Suddenly the distance Lexi had been so determined to keep between them had closed significantly. She felt a current of energy pass from his body to hers. It was like receiving a pulse of high-voltage electricity through her fingertip. She felt it run all the way up her arm until her whole body was tingling. She felt the shockingly traitorous drumbeat of desire between her thighs. It was a primitive pulse she could not control. The proximity of his hard male body had jolted hers into a state of acute feminine awareness. She could feel every pore of her skin dilating in anticipation. The hairs on the back of her neck rose and danced. A shiver ran down her spine and then pooled at the base, melting her bones and ligaments until she wasn't sure what was keeping her upright. She looked into his eyes, those gorgeous sleep-with-me-right-now-and-be-damned-with-the-consequences eyes and her heart gave an almighty stammer.

He felt it too.

The air was vibrating with the heat of their past sexual history. Every moment she had spent in his arms seemed to have assembled and joined them in his office. Every steaming kiss, every smouldering slide of a hand over her breasts or thighs, every blistering caress that had left her senses spinning like a top.

Every heart-stopping orgasm.

She quickly pulled her hand away from his chest, stepping back blindly. 'I—I have to go...'

She was almost out of the door when he spoke. 'Aren't you forgetting something?'

Lexi turned back, her heart beating like a humming-bird's wings as she met his dark satirical gaze. In his hand was his stained shirt. She hadn't even registered she had dropped it. She stalked back over to him, her mouth set in a grimly determined line. She tried to pluck it from his hand but his other hand came from nowhere and came down on hers, trapping her.

Her breath stopped.

Her heart raced.

Her stomach folded when she looked at his darkly tanned hand covering her lighter-toned one.

Her flesh remembered his. It reacted to his. It flared with heat under his. She could feel the nerves beneath the surface of her skin twitching to fervent life. She could feel the blood galloping through her veins like rocket fuel.

She could feel her self-control slipping.

She moved her fingers within the prison of his, her fingernails scraping him in her panic to be free. 'L-let me go,' she said, but to her shame her voice sounded weak and breathless, nothing like the strident, deter-mined tone she had aimed for.

His eyes held hers in a sensual tussle that made her spine tingle. It seemed like endless seconds passed with them locked together, hand to hand, eye to eye. But then his fingers momentarily tightened before he finally re-leased her.

She stepped back, almost falling over her own feet, flustered and flushing to the roots of her hair. 'How dare you touch me?' she said, rubbing at her hand as if he had tainted her. 'You have no right.'

His eyes glinted smboulderingly. 'I hate to quibble over inconsequential details but you touched me first.'

'I did not!'

He pointed to his chest. 'Right here,' he said. 'I can still feel the imprint of your fingernail.'

Lexi swallowed as his eyes challenged hers. Her heartbeat sounded in her ears, loud and erratic, her breathing even more so. 'You're exaggerating,' she said. 'I barely touched you.'

'One way to find out.'

Her eyes widened as his hand went to the hem of his scrub top. 'What are you doing?' she said hoarsely.

The door behind Lexi opened and a middle-aged woman came sailing in. 'Oh, sorry,' she said. 'Am I interrupting something?'

'No!' Lexi said.

'Not at all, Susanne,' Sam said with an urbane smile. 'Miss Lockheart was just leaving.'

'I don't think I've met you properly before,' Susanne said, offering a hand to Lexi. 'I'm Sam's practice manager, Susanne Healey.'

Lexi put on a polite smile but her voice sounded wooden when she spoke. 'Nice to meet you, Susanne.'

'How are the plans going for the masked ball?' Susanne asked.

Lexi crumpled Sam's shirt into a ball against her chest. 'Fine… Thank you…'

Susanne swung her gaze to Sam. 'I suppose you've offered your yacht to Lexi for the silent auction, have you?'

'Er…no, I—' Sam began.

Susanne swung her gaze back to Lexi. 'You should get him to donate a cruise around the harbour in it,' she said. 'It'd be so popular. Everyone loves a harbour cruise and his yacht is gorgeous. I saw it down at Neutral Bay marina with my husband on the weekend. You could have a champagne lunch. You'll get heaps of bids. Think of the money it'd raise. I'll even put my name down right now. What do you think should be the opening bid?'

Lexi faltered over her reply. 'I—I don't know…two hundred dollars per couple?'

'How does that sound, Sam?' Susanne asked.

Sam spoke through lips that barely moved. 'Fine.'

'You'll have to buy tickets for the ball now, Sam,' Susanne prattled on. 'You can't miss the hospital's most important event of the year. But you must bring a partner. We can't have you dancing all by yourself, can we, Lexi?'

Lexi met Sam's gaze with a flinty look. 'I'm sure Mr Bailey will have no shortage of dance partners,' she said, 'even if he has to borrow someone else's.'

'I wouldn't steal anyone who wasn't already on the make,' he said with an indolent smile.

Lexi felt her cheeks go red-hot but she refused to be the first to look away. She put all the hatred she could into her glare. Her whole body seemed to be trembling with it as it poured out of her like flames leaping from the top of a volcano.

Luckily Susanne had been distracted by the ringing of the phone. She was now sitting behind the reception desk, scrolling through the diary on the computer screen as she spoke to the person on the other end of line. 'No, that should be fine,' she said. 'Mr Bailey is consulting in his rooms that day… Do you have a current referral from your GP? Good. Yes, I'll squeeze you in at five-fifteen.'

Sam raised a dark brow at Lexi. 'You want to continue this out here or take it somewhere a little more private?'

Lexi's eyes flared and her chest heaved with impotent fury. 'Do you really think I would come running back to you at the crook of your little finger?' she snarled at him in an undertone. 'I'm engaged. I'm getting married in less than three months' time.'

His eyes pulsed mockingly as they held hers. 'Is that little reminder for you or for me?' he asked.

'For you, of course,' Lexi said, and swung away, her head high, her cheeks hot, her heart thumping and her stomach an ant's nest of unease, for somehow, even though he hadn't answered, she suspected he'd had the last word.

CHAPTER FOUR

Sam was still sitting at his desk, absently rolling his pen between his fingers, when Susanne announced on the intercom the arrival of Finn Kennedy, the head of department. 'Send him in,' he said.

The door of his office opened and a tall, imposing figure strode in. Even if he hadn't already been aware of Finn's history Sam was sure he would still have been able to tell he had served in the military from the imperious bearing the man exhibited. There was something about the harsh landscape of his face, the commanding air, the take-no-prisoners demeanour and the piercing but soulless blue eyes that spoke of a long career spent issuing orders and expecting them to be obeyed without question.

Brusque at the best of times and reputedly intimidating to many of the junior staff, Finn was a no-nonsense, show-no-emotion type. But Sam had often wondered if Finn's aloofness had less to do with his personality and more to do with the fact that he had lost his brother while they had both been serving overseas. Finn never spoke of it. If he felt pain or grief or even guilt, he never showed any sign of it.

With a solid background in trauma surgery Finn had retrained to become a highly skilled cardiac surgeon.

His formidable manner didn't win him many friends amongst the staff at SHH but his reputation as a dedicated cardiac surgeon was legendary. Unlike most of his colleagues, Finn usually managed to distance his private life from the gossip network. But in the week Sam had been at SHH he had heard rumours of something going on between Finn and Evie Lockheart, Lexi's oldest sister, who was an A and E doctor. But if the rumours were true and Finn was having an affair with Evie, judging from his crusty demeanour, it wasn't going particularly well.

Sam rose from the behind the desk to offer him a hand but Finn waved him back down. 'How are you settling in?' he asked as he sat down in the chair opposite.

'Fine, thanks,' Sam said. 'Everyone's been very welcoming.'

'Accommodation all right?'

'Yes. Thanks for that contact,' Sam said. 'I'm using the same real estate firm to track down a property for me to buy.'

'The press will want an interview,' Finn said. 'You OK with that?'

'Sure,' Sam said. 'I've already spoken to a couple of journalists who've called. They want a photo opportunity but I'm not sure the patient I have lined up is suitable. Bella Lockheart doesn't strike me as the outgoing type.'

Finn grunted. 'Might be her last chance for the spotlight.'

'I hope it's not,' Sam said. 'I'd like to bring her forward on the waiting list but she's got a chest infection. It's a wait and see, I'm afraid.'

Nothing had showed on Finn's face at the mention of the Lockheart name. 'What are her chances?' he asked.

'She needs a transplant within in the next couple of months,' Sam said. He left the rest of the ominous words hanging in the silence.

Still no flicker of emotion on Finn's face.

'We do what we can, when we can, if we can,' Finn said. He rubbed at his arm and then, noticing Sam's gaze, dropped his hand back down to rest along his bent thigh. 'That rumour true about you and the other sister?' he asked.

Sam stiffened. 'What rumour is that?'

Finn's penetrating gaze met his. 'Word has it you and Lexi Lockheart had a thing going five years ago.'

Sam unlocked his shoulder to give a careless shrug. 'We spent a bit of time together, nothing serious.'

Finn gave him a measured look. 'Did her old man have anything to do with you switching to the US training programme?'

Sam frowned. 'What makes you ask that?'

'Just joining the dots,' Finn said. 'You and young Lexi got it on and then a couple of weeks later you were gone. Makes sense that someone had a gun to your head.'

'The truth is I had thought of studying overseas,' Sam said. 'I just wasn't planning to do it right there and then.'

Finn gave a chuckle. 'I'd like to have seen Richard Lockheart's face when he found out you were sleeping with his youngest daughter.'

'It wasn't a great moment in my life, that's for sure,' Sam said wryly.

'I'm surprised he approved of her fiancé,' Finn said. 'I thought no one was ever going to be good enough for his baby girl.'

Sam swung his ergonomic chair back and forth in a casual manner. 'You know much about her fiancé?'

'Met him at a couple of hospital functions,' Finn said. 'Nice enough chap. Comes from bucketloads of money but he's currently doing a stint with Volunteers Abroad. You see the rock on her finger? He made a big donation to the hospital the day the engagement was announced.' He gave a grunt of amusement. 'Hopefully he'll double it once they're married.'

Sam felt his chest tighten but he forced a smile to his lips. 'Let's hope so.'

'There's a drinks thing organised for Wednesday night at Pete's Bar across the road for you to get to know some of the other departmental staff,' Finn said. 'Just another excuse for the staff to get hammered if you ask me, but you might as well put in an appearance. Half-price Wednesdays are a bit of an institution with the registrars.'

'I got the email about it the other day,' Sam said. 'I'll definitely pop my head in the door.'

Finn stood. 'Right, then,' he said. 'I'm off home. It's been a long day and tomorrow's probably going to be no better.'

Sam stood looking out of the window once Finn had gone. The sun was sinking in the west, casting the city in a golden glow. He had missed that iconic view in the years he had been away. Just knowing it would be there waiting for him to come back had helped quell any momentary feelings of homesickness. But the view had changed, or perhaps his memory of it had.

It just wasn't the same.

On Wednesday evening Sam had been caught up with a particularly tragic case and had spent the extra time explaining the sad prognosis to the patient and his young family.

When he came out to the reception area after dictating the letter to the patient's GP, Susanne drew his attention to a wrapped parcel sitting on the counter. 'That came for you a little while ago.'

'What is it?'

'A shirt,' Susanne said, eyes twinkling. 'From Lexi Lockheart.'

Sam took the package, keeping his expression blank. 'Thank you.'

'She said the stain didn't come out so she bought you a new one,' Susanne said.

Sam frowned at his receptionist's intrigued expression. 'She spilt coffee on it when she bumped into me,' he explained. 'She offered to launder it for me.'

'A little bird told me you and Lexi dated a few years back,' Susanne said, leaning her chin on her steepled fingers.

'Your little bird is wrong because we never actually went out on an official date,' he said, leafing through a pile of correspondence. 'Our entire affair was conducted in private.'

Susanne's pencilled eyebrows lifted. 'I sense some angst between you,' she said. 'That little scene I came in on the other day…'

'Susanne,' Sam said sternly as he put the letters down on the desk, 'I need you to type my letters and schedule my theatre lists and organise my diary for me. I do not need you to speculate on my private life. That is totally off-limits, understood?'

Susanne nodded obediently. 'Understood.'

He was almost out of the door when he stopped

and turned to look at her. 'Who was the little bird?' he asked.

Susanne made a buttoning up motion with her fingers against her mouth. 'I promised not to tell. Guide's honour.'

'Oh, for heaven's sake,' Sam muttered and left.

The bar was full and loud with the buzz of conversation and thumping music when Sam finally arrived. He wove his way through the knot of people, saying hello to those he recognised from previous introductions and stopping to greet those who introduced themselves.

Evie Lockheart was one person he remembered from his training years. But as she had been a couple of years behind him in med school they hadn't really socialised. She moved through the crowd and offered a slim hand to him with a polite but contained smile. 'Welcome back to SHH,' she said. 'I'm not sure if you remember me. I'm Evie Lockheart from A and E. You came to a trainee doctor dinner thing my father held a few years ago.'

Sam took her hand as he returned her smile. Did she also remember he'd only had eyes for her knock-'em-out-gorgeous youngest sister that night as well? And had she been a witness to the fallout Lexi had alluded to? 'Of course I remember you,' he said. 'Nice to see you again.'

'I believe you're doing a great job of looking after my sister,' Evie said.

'Um…pardon?'

Evie smiled to put him at ease. 'I understand patient confidentiality, Sam, but under the circumstances, given we're colleagues, I think it's OK for you to discuss Bella's treatment with me.'

Oh, that sister, Sam thought. 'We're working on getting her well enough to receive a donor lung,' he said. 'She's getting better but finding a match is the next hurdle.'

'We've heard very good things about you,' Evie said. 'Mind you, my father wouldn't have approved your appointment unless he thought you were the best.' She gave him a hard little look. 'Not after what happened between you and Lexi. Talk about World War Three. I thought Dad was going to disown her. I've never seen him so furious with her. I was very worried about her. She took it very hard.'

Sam kept his expression impassive but inside he was reeling. 'Lexi seems very settled now,' he said.

'Yes,' Evie said. 'It's a good match. Matthew is lovely. He's just what Lexi needs. He comes from a very stable family.'

'A very rich family, or so I've been told,' Sam said.

'Mega-rich,' Evie said taking a sip of her drink. 'But unlike some of the silver-spoon set, they're good with it. They support a lot of charities. I think that's why Matthew and Lexi hit it off so well. They have a lot in common.'

Sam wondered what Lexi's fiancé would say if he found out about the tense little scene in his office the other day. Perhaps Lexi was feeling a little frisky with her man away for weeks, if not months, on end. She wasn't the celibate type. She was far too sensual for that. Sam had all the blisteringly hot memories of her to vouch for that.

Finn sauntered over with a glass of single malt whisky in his hand. 'So you finally managed to extricate yourself from the mother ship?' he drawled.

'Yes,' Sam said. 'It's been one of those days. Why is the last patient of the day always the hardest?'

'It's always like that,' Evie said, deliberately turning her body away from Finn as if his presence annoyed her.

Finn's lip curled at the all too obvious snub. 'So how is Princess Evie this evening?' he asked.

Evie gave him an arctic glance over her shoulder. 'There's a new barmaid on tonight, Finn,' she said. 'You might want to see if she's free later on.'

'Maybe I'll do that,' Finn said with a smirk.

The air was crackling with waves of antagonism. It was pretty clear Finn and Evie had something brewing between them but Sam wasn't sure exactly what it was. He had noticed Finn's hand trembling slightly as he brought his drink up to his mouth. He didn't want to think about what had caused that slight tremble. Was that what that arm rub had been about the other day? he wondered. Was that why Evie was so prickly and guarded around him? Did she suspect something but wasn't game enough to put her name and reputation on the line in outing Finn? It was a tough gig reporting a senior colleague and most junior doctors would think twice about doing it.

Being new at SHH would make it equally difficult for Sam. He hadn't been around long enough to be certain but even so, calling out a colleague for suspected alcohol abuse would be nothing short of career suicide. He would only do it if he had enough evidence to prove it was actually the case. There could be any number of contributing factors: extreme tiredness, for instance. He had experienced it himself after long operations and too many nights on call. His whole body had started to quake and tremble with exhaustion. Those symptoms could so easily be misconstrued, and if he was wrong it would have devastating consequences professionally.

Finn Kennedy looked like the overworked type. His piercing blue eyes were bloodshot, but the damson-coloured shadows beneath them could just as easily suggest a man who was not getting enough sleep rather than a man who was consuming too much of the demon drink. But, then, who could really know for sure?

'You haven't got a drink,' Finn said. 'What would you like?'

'It's OK,' Sam said. 'I'll make my way over now and grab something soft.' He smiled to encompass them both. 'Nice to chat to you.'

Sam was soon handed a drink by one of the registrars and drawn into their circle. He did his best to answer some of the questions fired at him but the whole time he felt strangely disconnected. It was as if his body was standing there talking to the small group surrounding him but his mind was elsewhere. Lexi was just a few feet away. There was a faint trace of her perfume in the air and every now and again he could feel her gaze on him.

'What about harvesting organs?' one of the junior interns asked. 'Do you have to travel to different hospitals to do that?'

'Sometimes, but not to harvest the actual organs I will end up using,' Sam said bringing his attention back to the group in front of him. 'As you know, it's impossible to transfer someone on a ventilator. It's easier for us to go to them once the family has come to the decision of turning off life support. We notify the recipient once the match has been made and then swing into action. There's a lot of co-ordination and co-operation between campuses.'

After a while the conversation drifted into other areas so Sam moved away from the bar to circulate some more. He had only taken a couple of strides when a cluster of people separated and he came face to face with Lexi.

There was an awkward silence.

'Thanks for the shirt,' Sam said gruffly. 'But you shouldn't have bothered.'

'I underestimated the efficacy of my laundering abilities,' she said. 'No matter what I did, the coffee wouldn't come out.'

'You should've just sent it back to me,' he said. 'You didn't need to buy such an expensive replacement.'

'It wasn't expensive. I got it in a half-price sale.'

Another tense little silence passed.

'You know, if you don't want to donate a cruise on your yacht, you don't have to,' Lexi said with a frosty look. 'I have plenty of other people more than happy to donate items much better than yours.'

Sam felt his back come up. 'I didn't say I didn't want to donate it.'

She rolled her eyes in disdain. 'You weren't exactly super-enthusiastic about it.'

Sam frowned at her. 'What did you want me to do? Cartwheels of excitement down the corridor?'

'I didn't even know you had a yacht.'

He threw her a cutting glance. 'Pardon me for the oversight,' he said. 'Would you like a list of the things I currently own?'

She glowered at him. 'I'll need to inspect it at some point,' she said. 'I can't allow it to be used if it's not suitable. I have to consider the public liability issue.'

'Fine,' Sam said. 'Inspect it. I'm sure you'll find it comes up to your impeccable standards.'

'How many people can you fit on board?' she asked.

'I could push it to ten but eight's probably the max for comfort.'

'And what sort of lunch do you plan on offering?' she asked, looking at him in that haughty manner of hers that seemed to suggest she thought he would think a sausage wrapped in a slice of bread and a can of beer would do the job.

Sam stared at her plump, shiny mouth. He couldn't seem to drag his gaze away. She was wearing lip gloss again. He wondered if it was the same one she used to wear. 'Strawberries...'

A tiny frown appeared between her ocean-blue eyes. 'Just...strawberries?' she asked.

Sam had to give himself another quick mental slap. 'Champagne and caviar,' he said. 'You know the sort of deal. Good food, fine wines, gourmet food.'

'I'll look into it and get back to you,' she said. 'What's your boat called?'

'*Whispering Waves,*' he said. 'It was already named when I bought it.'

'So it's big enough to sleep on?' she asked.

'It sleeps six,' he said, suddenly imagining her in the double bed beside him, rocking along with the waves. His body stirred as the blood began to thunder through his veins.

He had to stop this—right now.

'I didn't know you were into sailing,' Lexi said. 'You never mentioned it when we...you know...'

'I'd never even been on a yacht before I went to the States,' Sam said. 'I got invited to crew for a friend over there. We did some races now and again. I really enjoyed being out on the water so I decided to buy my own vessel. I had it shipped over before I came back.'

'Do you intend to race over here?' she asked.

'I'm not really into the competitive side of things,' he said. 'I just enjoy the freedom of sailing. I like being out on the water. It's a very different environment from a busy hospital.'

Lexi readjusted the strap of her bag over her shoulder, her gaze drifting away from his. She was aware that people would wonder what they were talking about for so long. 'I'd better let you get back to socialising.'

'You can probably tell I hate these sorts of gatherings,' Sam said. 'I'm not one for inane chitchat.'

'You just have to get people to talk about themselves,' Lexi said. 'Everybody will say what a great conversationalist you are, but really they're the ones doing all the talking. Believe me, it never fails to impress.'

He tilted his mouth in a mocking smile. 'Does that come from Lexi Lockheart's *A Socialite's Guide to Charming a Crowd*?'

Lexi gave him another wintry look. 'It comes from years of experience talking to people with over-inflated egos,' she said, shifting slightly to one side so one of the residents could make their way past juggling glasses of beer.

'What's going on between your sister and Finn Kennedy?' Sam asked, before she could step any further away.

Lexi looked at him in surprise. 'What? You've heard something too?'

'Not as such,' he said. 'But you've only got to look at them together to see something's going on. They're like two snarling dogs circling each other.'

'So you think that's attraction?'

'I didn't say that,' he said.

'But you think it's a sign.'

'They either hate each other's guts or they can't wait to fall into bed with each other,' he said.

'So that's your expert opinion?' Lexi asked with a cynical look.

He took another sip of his drink before he answered. 'You know what they say about hate and love and the two-sided-coin thing.'

'I think he's totally wrong for her,' she said, frowning.

'Why's that?'

'He's emotionally locked down,' she said emphatically. 'He can't give her what she wants.'

'And you know exactly what she wants, do you?'

Lexi pushed her lips forward as she glanced at her oldest sister. Evie was glaring at Finn, her mouth tight, her eyes flashing as he leaned indolently against the bar with a mocking smile on his handsome face. Lexi frowned as she turned back to Sam. 'I think she wants what every woman wants,' she said. 'She wants a man who loves her for who she is, someone who will protect her and support her but not crush her.'

His brows moved closer together over his eyes. 'You think Finn would crush her?'

'He's got a strong personality,' she said.

'But so does Evie.'

'You sound as if you know her personally.'

'I don't,' he said. 'I've only exchanged a few words with her, but I've heard she's one of the best A and E doctors this hospital has ever seen. I've heard she's ambitious but compassionate. Not unlike Finn.'

'So you think they'd be a perfect match for each other?' Lexi asked with an incredulous look.

He gave a noncommittal shrug. 'I think they should be left to sort out their differences without the scrutiny or judgement of others,' he said.

'That won't be easy in a place like SHH,' Lexi said, chewing at her lip as she thought of what people would make of her and Sam talking at length. If it hadn't been for his wretched shirt and his wretched yacht, she wouldn't have had to speak to him at all.

'Yes, like most hospitals, it's a bit of a hotbed of gossip,' he said. 'I'm surprised people can find the time to work at their jobs when they're so busy spreading rumours.'

'I didn't realise people would talk so much. I didn't realise anyone would even remember that we…' She grimaced. 'I hope it's not too embarrassing for you.'

'It will blow over,' Sam said. 'But to tell you the truth, I'm not sure we could've been any more discreet back then. We kept pretty much to ourselves. I don't think we left my flat for the first ten days. Perhaps if we hadn't ventured out for that take-away meal at the end of our second week, our affair might have gone unnoticed.'

Lexi wondered if he had ever thought about that full-on time over the last five years, the burning-hot lust that had burned like a wildfire between them. The days and nights of passion that had only been interrupted by the necessities of existence—water, sustenance and the minimum of sleep. They had been in such perfect tune with each other physically. It hadn't seemed to matter that they hadn't really known each other. Their bodies had done the talking for them. Each kiss and caress, each stroke of his tongue and each stabbing thrust of his body had revealed to her the truly passionate man Sam was underneath that cool, clinical facade he presented to the world. There was a streak of wildness in him that she suspected few people ever glimpsed. She wondered with a pang of jealousy if he had been like that with anyone else.

She looked into the contents of her glass again as the silence stretched and stretched. 'I shouldn't have lied to you about my age.'

'I shouldn't have believed you,' he said. 'You were too young for me, not just in years but in experience.'

Lexi brought her eyes back to his in surprise. 'So you knew all along?' she asked.

He frowned at her look. 'Knew what?'

She moistened her lips with the tip of her tongue, her gaze slipping away from his. 'Never mind,' she said, wondering if it was her imagination or was every eye in the room on them right at that point? She glanced nervously over her shoulder but everyone was chatting amongst themselves, apart from her sister Evie who was giving her the eye: the older, wiser, big sister look that said, *Be careful.*

Sam glanced at her empty glass. 'What are you drinking?'

'It's all right,' she said. 'I can buy my own drinks.'

'I'm sure you can, but I'm going to get myself a mineral water so in order to be polite I thought I'd ask if you would like a fresh drink.'

She let out a little breath. 'I'm drinking lemon, lime and bitters.'

He hiked up one brow. 'Nothing stronger?'

'I like to keep my head together at things like this,' she said. 'No one likes to see a drunken woman making a fool of herself, be she young or old.'

Sam had heard on the hospital grapevine about Lexi's mother's issue with alcohol. It seemed the burden of taking care of the chronically ill Bella for all those years had led Miranda Lockheart straight to the drinks cabinet. Gin had been her choice of anaesthesia. Sam had met many parents who had done exactly the same thing. He didn't judge them for it. He felt sorry for them. Sorry that there weren't enough supportive people in their life at that point of crisis to help them through without the crutch of other substances.

He brought their drinks back and handed Lexi hers. 'Your sister hinted at the reaction your father had to our affair,' he said. 'She said he almost disowned you. And that it was a very bad time for you. Is that true?'

Lexi looked at her drink rather than meet his penetrating gaze. 'I'd rather not talk about it.'

'Your father was furious with me,' Sam said after a moment of silence. 'He threatened to derail my career. I knew he had the power and the contacts to do it. It wouldn't have been the first time a trainee has been bumped off the training scheme. I decided to transfer my studies. The way I saw it, it was a case of leave or fail. I figured it was the only way to keep myself on track for qualifying. But I didn't realise he had directed his anger at you too. That hardly seems fair when I had already taken responsibility for everything that had happened.'

Lexi felt her heart give an almighty stumble. Could it be true? Had her father threatened him? Was that why he had disappeared without a trace, without even saying goodbye to her? She thought of how furious her father had been with her when he had discovered she had been involved with Sam. It had been the first time she had been on the receiving end of his wrath and it had totally crushed her. She had always been the one who pleased him. It was her role in the family: Daddy's little girl.

Evie was the academically gifted one, the mother substitute who had taken on all the responsibility of looking after the family after their mother had left. The nannies and au pairs their father had organised had had nothing on Evie. She was the go-to sister, the one who had always made sure they got everything they needed.

Bella was the middle one, the chronically sick and incredibly shy child who had not been expected to live past her early twenties, if that. Their father had made it more than clear that he felt repulsed by Bella's sickness and her shyness was another strike against her. He thought it brought shame to the family name to have a daughter who blushed and could barely string two words together in the company of anyone outside the family.

Growing up without a mother on hand, Lexi had idolised her father. She had come to realise that deep down she was terrified he too might leave if she didn't please him. Being a social butterfly was her way of feeling needed. She loved being surrounded by people, and parties were a perfect place to showcase her talent at working a room. Even as young as five she had been able to pass around plates of canapés like an accomplished hostess four times her age. And it had only got better as she'd grown into young womanhood. She had lapped up her father's approval with every event or party she had helped him organise. His praise had been like an elixir she'd needed to survive. It had been the only way to feel close to him.

Maybe Sam was making it up, maybe it wasn't true. Her father would never have gone that far, would he? The memories, long buried deep inside her, bubbled to the surface—her father's fury, how long it had taken her to get back into his good books, what she'd had to do to prevent him finding out about the baby... Suddenly, it felt like she had been betrayed by him in the most devastating way.

Her teeth sank into her bottom lip as she looked up at Sam's face. She had to know. 'Did my father really threaten to end your career?' she asked.

Sam's expression was impossible to read. 'It's not important now, Alexis,' he said. 'It wouldn't have worked out between us anyway. I was too career-oriented to give you the time and attention you needed. It was just a crazy lust-driven fling. I should've had better control.'

Lexi felt a choked-up feeling at the back of her throat as she looked up at him. If only she had known what had been at stake for him. If only she had known he hadn't really had a choice but to leave. It was so heartbreaking to think about what could have been if only she had known what had gone on between him and her father.

Her chest rippled with a spasm of pain. Would their baby have had his dark brown eyes and light brown hair, or would it have had her blue eyes and blonde tresses? Would it have been a girl or a boy? If things had been different, their baby would be in preschool now. He or she would be learning to recognise letters, making friends, finger painting, making things with Play-Doh: all the innocent things of childhood.

Lexi had made her decision based on what she had known at the time and it had been the hardest thing she had ever done. She had been so frightened of her father's reaction to the news of her pregnancy. She had felt so unprepared for the responsibilities of motherhood. She hadn't been able to talk to anyone about it. She had hidden it from everybody. She hadn't even told her sisters. Not even Evie, who would have surely helped her and guided her. Instead, she had booked herself into a clinic, miles away in the outer suburbs where her name wouldn't be connected with the powerful and influential Lockheart name. She had stoically faced the impersonal removal of Sam's baby, but on the inside she was devastated that she'd had to make such a harrowing decision. The bottomless well of sadness over that time never seemed to ease, no matter how hard she tried to put it behind her.

Lexi was aware that they were still in the bar surrounded by people but she had never felt so utterly alone. It was like a glass wall was around her, a thick impenetrable wall that had locked her inside with her sorrow.

'Why do you keep calling me Alexis?' she asked. 'I don't understand why you can't call me Lexi like you used to do.'

An irritated frown carved deep into his forehead. 'You know why,' he said. 'We need some distance.'

'How much distance do you want?' she asked. 'I'm based at the hospital and I'm not leaving just because you've flown back into town. You can't pretend it never happened, Sam. It did and nothing you do or say will ever change that.'

The strong column of his throat moved up and down as if he was trying to swallow a boulder. 'Don't do this, Alexis,' he said. 'Don't try and pretend our fling was something it wasn't. You only got involved with me to get back at your father. An act of rebellion, he called it.'

Lexi looked at him with tears burning like acid at the back of her eyes but only sheer willpower prevented them from appearing, let alone falling. Could this possibly get any worse? As if her father's threats against Sam hadn't been enough. Had her father really said that, lied like that? How could the parent she had adored for as long as she could remember deliberately sabotage her relationship with the man she had thought might be the only one for her? It was a devastating blow to see her father in such a light. He had put his own interests ahead of her happiness. What sort of parent did that to their child? 'Is *that* what he told you?' she asked.

He closed his eyes briefly as if this was all a horrible dream and she would disappear when he opened them again. 'I don't want to cause trouble between you and your father,' he said. 'Our relationship wouldn't have lasted either way. We had nothing in common. We were on completely different pathways.'

'You being Mr Ambitious and me being an empty-headed social butterfly with no aspirations beyond shopping and partying?' she asked, emotion bubbling up inside her like scalding lava.

He raked a hand through his hair in a distracted manner. 'Alexis…' He caught her glacial look and amended on an out breath, 'Lexi… '

'You think I didn't have aspirations?' Lexi said bitterly. 'You have no idea. Do you think I didn't want to do well at school and go to university? I could have achieved way more than I did but how could I do that to Bella? Tell me that, country boy. I had a sister two years older than me who ended up in the same class as me at school. She had to stay back because of her illness. How could I outshine her? How do you think that would have made her feel? I had to play down my talents so she could feel good about herself for just a few moments each day. I wanted to do well but she was more important. So don't talk to me about my lack of ambition. Sometimes there are situations that require sacrifice, not ambition at the cost of those you love. I chose the former, so shoot me.'

It was a great exit line and Lexi used it. She pushed past the knot of people blocking the exit and stumbled out into the street. But home was the last place she wanted to be. She wasn't ready to face her father after this evening's revelations.

Right now she desperately needed to be alone.

CHAPTER FIVE

SAM was walking along the corridor after finishing a ward round on the following Monday afternoon when he saw Lexi coming towards him. As soon as she saw him she swiftly turned on her heel and started walking quickly back the way she had come.

'Lexi, wait,' he said, increasing his strides to catch up. 'Can I have a quick word?'

She stopped and turned, sending him a hard little glare. 'I'm on my way to visit Bella.'

'Bella's resting,' he said. 'I've just been in to see her. She's having some oxygen to boost her levels. Just give me a couple of minutes, OK?'

She let out a long hissing breath. 'All right, if you insist.'

'I insist,' Sam said. 'But not here in the corridor.' He pushed open the door of the on-call room and waited for her to go in.

Lexi brushed past him with her head at a haughty angle. 'This had better not take long,' she said.

'It won't, I promise.'

Sam closed the door and allowed himself the luxury of sweeping his gaze over her. She was breathtakingly beautiful, dressed in corporate wear that on another woman could have looked conservative and boring but on her looked absolutely stunning. The prim white blouse hugged her breasts and the narrow skirt teamed with high heels gave her a sexy secretary look that was distinctly distracting. Her perfume drifted towards him as she folded her arms across her body and a tendril of hair escaped from the neat chignon she had fashioned at the back of her swan-like neck. Everything about her fired his blood to fever pitch. It was impossible to be in the same room as her and not want to take her in his arms and kiss her senseless.

His body remembered every contour and curve of hers: her sensual mouth and the way it had fed so hungrily off his; her soft hands with their dancing fingertips that had set his skin on fire; the way her long, slim legs had wrapped around his waist as he'd plunged into her hot moistness; the way her body had gripped him tightly as if she'd never wanted to let go; the way her hips had moved in time with his, her breathing just as frantic as his own gasps; the way her platinum-blonde hair had spread like a halo around her head in the throes of passion; and the way she had gasped his name, her body convulsing in ultimate pleasure, triggering his own cataclysmic release. No matter how hard he tried he couldn't remove the memory of her touch from his mind, much less his body. She wore another man's ring but, heaven help him, he still wanted her.

She tapped her foot on the floor impatiently. 'Well?'

Sam let out a long breath. 'Lexi, I owe you an apology. I should've come to see you before I left for the States. It was wrong of me to just up and leave like that. I didn't think about your end of things at all. I just believed what your father said about you and left it at that. I realise now that I should've at least listened to your side.'

Her blue eyes were still hostile, the set of her shoulders stiff with tension. 'Is that all?'

'No, it's not all,' Sam said. 'I took on board what you said about the sacrifices you've made to protect Bella.'

She didn't move or speak, just stood there watching him silently, accusingly.

Sam took another breath and slowly released it. 'I should've realised the adjustments you've had to make,' he said. 'I know more than most how the squeaky wheel gets the oil in families and how other siblings can feel left out or isolated as a result.'

'Fine,' Lexi said. 'Can I go now?'

Sam frowned. 'You're not making this easy on me.'

Her eyes hit his like blue diamonds. 'Why should I?'

'You're right,' Sam said, letting his shoulders down on a sigh. 'Why should you?'

He was still trying to get his head around this new Lexi. Not the party girl but the young woman who loved her sister so much that she put her own interests to one side. It went against everything she had told him about herself back then. During their short fling she had laughed off his comments about her lack of ambition. She had said how much she loved the social circuit, how all she had time for was fun, not boring old stuffy studying. Those had been her exact words. He had thought at the time it was such a waste given that he'd had to work so hard to get to medical school.

Unlike Lexi, he hadn't gone to a fee-paying school with the best resources on hand. He had toughed it out in the bush in between helping his father run their drought-ravaged sheep property. He had missed days, sometimes weeks of school to help nurse his mother through the last stages of her kidney disease. Catching up with his studies had been an added burden eclipsed by worry about his mother's declining health and the quiet desperation he'd seen in his father's sun-weathered face whenever he'd looked at his wife lying listlessly in the bedroom of the rundown homestead.

Hearing Lexi say she had deliberately sabotaged her educational achievements to protect her sister was something that had touched Sam deeply. It had made him take pause. He had not realised what a compassionate person she was. Her shallow party-girl persona was a clever artifice for a sensitive young woman who clearly suffered a lot of survival guilt. She had thrown herself into fundraising for SHH, but what else would she have secretly loved to have done? What dreams and aspirations had she put to one side in order to protect her sister from feeling inadequate?

It was part of his job to deal with the families of transplant patients. He understood the dynamics, the sometimes tricky family situations that fed into the patients' outcomes, whether they liked it or not. He wanted to do a good job on Bella, not just because she was Lexi's older sister but because she was a deserving recipient of a lung donation. But even more than that he wanted to make sure Lexi got her chance to shine. Operating on her sister could well be the most important transplant he had ever performed.

Sam looked at her standing there with a mutinous expression on her beautiful face. Anyone seeing her now would assume she was a sulky spoilt brat but he felt like the scales had been removed from his eyes. He could see the hint of vulnerability in her ocean-blue gaze and the almost imperceptible quiver of her bottom lip, as if she was holding back a storm of emotions. 'Why did you get involved with me?' he asked. 'Why me and not someone else?'

'It wasn't an act of rebellion,' she said. 'It was nothing like that.'

'Then what was it?'

She unfolded her arms and used one of her hands to brush back her hair. 'I can't explain why,' she said. 'It just…it just happened.'

Sam watched as she moved restlessly to the other side of the room, her arms folded protectively across her body. Her cheeks were a delicate shade of pink as if the memory of their time together unsettled her more than she wanted to admit. Her saw her beautiful white teeth sink into the soft fullness of her bottom lip. It was one of her most engaging habits, one he suspected she was largely unaware of. It gave her a look of innocence and guilelessness; the potent mix of sexy woman and innocent girl was totally captivating.

'At the pub the other night you said something that's been niggling at me ever since,' he said. 'What was it you thought I'd always known about you?'

Lexi kept her gaze out of the range of his. 'It doesn't matter now…'

But of course he wouldn't leave it at that. 'It was when I mentioned that we'd been worlds apart in years and experience,' he said. 'Tell me, Lexi. What was it you thought I'd always known about you?'

She pressed her sandpaper-dry lips together. Her throat felt tight, too tight even to swallow. Her stomach was churning so much she could hear it rumble in the prolonged silence. Why had she even mentioned it? What was the point of going over this now?

It was over.

They were over.

She was moving on with her life.

Or trying to…

'Lexi?'

His commanding tone summoned her gaze. 'I didn't just lie about my age,' she said on an expelled breath.

His gaze never wavered; it remained rock-steady on hers, but the darkness of his eyes seemed to deepen another shade. 'What else did you lie about?'

She moistened her lips in order to get them to move again in speech. 'Actually, it wasn't really a lie, not an outright one. It was just that I didn't quite tell you the truth.'

Sam's forehead became a map of frowning lines. 'The truth about what?'

Lexi took a breath and then released it in a rush. 'I was…I was… You were my first lover.'

His face looked as if it had just received an invisible slap. She saw him flinch, every muscle contracting, his eyes widening and his mouth opening and closing as if he couldn't quite locate his voice. *'What?'*

'I was a virgin.' Lexi bit her lip. 'At least technically I was…'

'Technically?' he asked. 'What the hell is that supposed to mean?'

She pulled in another uneven breath. 'I'd had boy-friends in the past,' she said, 'lots of them actually. I just hadn't…you know…done it…gone all the way…'

Sam raked his fingers through his hair as he paced back and forth. 'I can't believe I'm hearing this.' He stopped to glare at her furiously. 'Why on earth didn't you say something?'

'Because I knew if I'd said something you wouldn't have slept with me.'

'You're damn right I wouldn't,' he said. 'What were you thinking, Lexi? You were just a young girl. We had so much sex over those two weeks.' His throat moved up and down over a tight swallow. 'Did I…did I hurt you?'

She shook her head vigorously, perhaps too much so.

'Lexi?' He barked her name at her.

'All right, all right,' she said, her eyes rolling in defeat. 'Just a little bit but it was fine after the first—'

'Oh, dear God,' he said, rubbing a hand over his face.

Lexi stalked to the other side of the room. 'You're making such a big deal out of this,' she said. 'I had to lose my virginity some time. At least it was with a considerate lover. It could've been a lot worse.'

He glared at her again. 'How much worse could it have been? I thought I was sleeping with an experienced party girl who knew all the rules,' he said. 'Now I find out she was an innocent virgin.'

'Not so innocent,' Lexi put in.

He held his head in both of his hands and groaned. 'No wonder your father was ready to nail me to the floor.'

'My father didn't know I was still a virgin,' she said. 'It's not exactly something you discuss over the dinner table.'

'No, but it *is* something you discuss with a potential sexual partner,' he pointed out.

'Not when you're having a meaningless, short-term fling,' she threw back.

He stilled. Not a muscle moved. He was like a statue, frozen. 'So,' he said finally in a voice undergirded with steel. 'Let me get this straight. You just wanted a meaningless short-term fling and I was the handiest candidate. Is that right?'

'No…'

'For heaven's sake, Lexi,' he said bitterly, his voice a harsh rasp of anger. 'You nearly cost me my career. I almost lost everything because of you. Do you realise that? Did you even think about what the consequences would be?'

Lexi turned away from his thunderous expression, her arms going back across her body, tightening like a band to hold herself together. He was a fine one to talk about consequences. He hadn't had to face the biggest consequence of all. 'It wasn't like that,' she said.

'What was it like, damn it?' he asked.

She let out a shaky breath. 'When we met…I felt something.'

'Lust.' There was no mistaking the disdain in his voice.

She threw him a look. 'Not just lust. Before you came along I didn't feel ready for a relationship, not a sexual one at least. But it was different with you. From the first moment we met…'

His eyes hardened to chips of ice. 'Don't,' he said, a warning thread of steel in his tone.

'Don't what?'

'Don't try and dress up what we felt for each other as anything other than what it was,' he said. 'I know it's not the most romantic fact in the world but sometimes sex just happens because of instinct. Chemistry. Animal lust.'

'It wasn't like that for me,' Lexi said quietly.

'Well, it was like that for me,' he snapped back.

Lexi turned away again, not willing to let him see how much he had hurt her. She had hoped…foolishly hoped that he had felt something for her back then, but their brief relationship had meant nothing to him.

She had meant nothing to him.

She had just been another name in his little black book. It was deluded of her to have expected anything else. His career was his priority. It had been back then and it still was now. She had been a temporary distraction that he deeply regretted. The breathtaking magic of their relationship that she had revisited so many times in her mind was an illusion, a flight of fancy on her part, romantic nonsense that had no place in the cold, hard world of reason. Emotion clogged her throat, a cruel strangulation of regret and recriminations. Tears were so close she had to blink to stop them from falling. The tattered remnants of her pride would not allow her to cry in front of him.

She made a move for the door. 'I have to go…'

'Hang on a minute,' Sam said. 'We haven't finished this discussion.'

Lexi slung the strap of her bag over her shoulder from where it had slipped. 'I think we have, Sam. There's nothing more to be said.'

'Wait.'

He caught her arm on the way past, his fingers like a metal band around her wrist as he swung her back to face him, the sudden movement sending a shockwave through her body.

The skin on her wrist sizzled as if he had branded her with his touch. His long, strong fingers were like fire. They burned through the layers of her skin, setting nerves into a crazy, maniacal dance. She felt the strength of his grasp as she tried to pull away and her heart started to pound like a faulty timepiece.

She breathed in the scent of him, the hint of aftershave overridden by the sexy musk of late-in-the-day male. She could see the pinpoints of stubble on his jaw and her fingertips tingled as she remembered how it felt to stroke that sexy regrowth with her own soft skin.

Her lips, too, remembered how it felt to move over

that bristly surface. She wanted to do it now, to remind herself of how he tasted. She wanted to feel her tongue lapping at his skin the way she had in the past.

Lexi looked into his dark, mesmerising eyes and it was like looking into them for the very first time. She felt the same electric shock rush through her, making every single pore of her body acutely aware of him. The raw physicality of it terrified her. It shocked her that her body could want one thing while her mind insisted on another.

Her leg wasn't supposed to be moving forward half a step to bring her body up against the rock wall of his.

Her breasts weren't supposed to be pressed against his chest, the nipples already tightly budded with desire.

Her pelvis wasn't supposed to be anywhere near his, certainly not flush against him and shamelessly responding to the hard ridge of his growing arousal.

Her inner core was pulsing with a longing that felt so intense, so rampantly out of control it was like a fever in her blood.

It was wrong.

Forbidden.

Dangerous...

She dropped her gaze to his sexily sculpted mouth. It was suddenly just a breath away from hers as if her lips had drawn his down through a force of their own. She could see each of the fine vertical creases in his lips, the masculine dryness an intoxicating reminder of how it felt to have his mouth possess her soft, moister one. She could feel the mint-fresh breeze of his breath as it skated across her lips. It was like a feather teasing her, stirring every sensitive nerve until she thought she would go mad if he didn't cover her mouth with the heated pressure of his to assuage the spiralling need.

His mouth moved infinitesimally closer.

Lexi felt his erection, so thick, so powerful and so wickedly tempting against her. She pulled a breath into her lungs but it felt as if she was hauling a road-train along with it. All she had to do was step up on tiptoe and press her mouth to his…

'If you don't step back right now I'm going to do something I swore I wouldn't do,' Sam said in a deep, rough burr that sent a shiver down her spine.

'Why don't *you* step back?' Lexi asked, not because she wanted to win this particular battle but more because she couldn't get her legs to work right at that moment.

'Don't do this, Lexi,' he said, still staring at her mouth, his breath a warm caress on her lips, his body still hot and heavy and aroused against hers.

Lexi felt the hammering of his heart beneath her palm where it was resting on his chest. Its pace was just as hectic and uneven as hers. His hands were gripping her by the upper arms, his warm fingers scorching her flesh. She felt the battle raging in the pulse of his blood, pounding through his fingertips, the war between holding her tighter and letting her go. 'You touched me first,' she said. 'You grabbed my arm.'

'I know,' he said in a gravelly voice. 'It was wrong. I shouldn't have touched you. I don't want this complication right now.'

'So step back.'

His glittering eyes seared hers for a pulsing moment. 'You're enjoying this, aren't you?' he said. 'You're enjoying the fact that you still have this effect on me.'

'You want me to step back?' she asked with a pert look. 'Then let go of my arms.'

His fingers loosened but he didn't release her. 'When I'm good and ready,' he said. And then he brought his mouth down slowly, inexorably towards hers.

Lexi knew she should have moved. She knew she should have pushed against his chest and put some distance between their bodies. She knew she should not have just stood there waiting for his mouth to come down to hers. She knew it, but in that moment she was trapped by her own traitorous need to feel his lips against hers just one more time.

As soon as his lips met hers she felt the electric shock of it through her entire body. It travelled from the sensitive surface of her lips to the innermost core of her where that deep ache of longing was flexing and coiling. Hot pulses of need fired through her as her lips felt the subtle pressure of his. He kept the kiss light at first, experimental almost, as if he was rediscovering the landscape of her lips. It started with a brief touchdown of hard, cool lips on her softer ones. A barely touching brushstroke and then another. He raised his mouth off hers a mere fraction but her lips clung to the rougher surface of his. He pressed down again, slightly harder this time, his lips moving against hers in a gentle exploration.

But then it all changed.

That one searching stroke of his tongue against the seam of her mouth made the kiss became something else entirely. Lexi opened to his command, hungrily feeding at his mouth, brazenly playing with the stab and thrust of his tongue. It was a kiss of passion, of unmet desires, frustration and, yes, maybe even a little bit of anger thrown in for good measure. She tasted the wonderful familiarity of him, a hint of mint, good-quality coffee and that unmistakable maleness she had missed so very much. His tongue was roughly masculine against the softness of hers, stirring in her deep yearnings for the physical completion she had only felt with him.

Being back in his arms felt so right, so perfect, the chemistry so hot and electric it was making her blood hum in her veins. He drew her even closer by placing his hand in the small of her back, a touch full of intimacy and deliciously primal in its intent. She felt the rigid heat of him against her, the unmistakable swelling of his hard male body in response to hers. It was a breathtaking feeling to be back in his embrace, to experience the way her body fitted against the contours of his as if made specifically for him.

His kiss deepened even further as he gave a low growl deep in his throat, and the hand at her back pulled her even closer while his other hand cupped the back of her head, his broad fingers splaying in her hair. Every nerve ending on her scalp fizzed at the contact, sharp arrows of pleasure darting through her from the top of her head to her toes. She had to step up on tiptoe to kiss him back and the movement brought her breasts up against his chest, the friction so wonderful she pressed herself even closer. Below her waist she could feel the hard male ridges of his body, the stark difference that made him so male and her so female.

His mouth continued its sensual assault on hers—hot, moist, urgent, masterful and unbelievably thorough. She kissed him back with all the longing she'd had locked away inside her for five long, heartbreaking years. It was like unleashing a wild beast, and once let loose the unrestrained desire could not be subdued or tamed. Her tongue tangled with his, teasing, flirting and then darting away as he came in search of her. It was a cat-and-mouse game, a battle of wills, a war between two strong opposing forces.

The hand he had placed at the small of her back shifted to cup her bottom. The pressure of his hand drew her pelvis so close to his she felt the complete outline of his potent erection. She felt her stomach drop like an out-of-control elevator as he moved against her. This was what she remembered so well about him. The way he took charge physically, the way he left her breathless with longing, the way his body told her all she needed to know about what he felt about her.

He still wanted her.

Lexi could feel her mouth swelling from the prolonged kissing. She didn't care. She didn't even care that she tasted a hint of blood. She didn't know if it was hers or his. She didn't want the kiss to end. She linked her arms around his neck, her fingers exploring the thick pelt of closely cropped light brown hair on his head.

No one kissed her like Sam did. It was a sensual assault that made her whole body sing and hum with delight. His kiss was erotic and daring, demanding with that edge of hungry desperation in it that suggested he was only just managing to keep control.

Meanwhile, her own control had slipped way out of her grasp. She knew kissing Sam was wrong while she was wearing another man's ring, she knew it and yet she couldn't stop herself responding to the intoxicating magic of his mouth on hers. It was like a drug she knew was forbidden and dangerous but craved anyway. She didn't care about the moral consequences right now. Now was about feeling the red-hot passion Sam incited in her body. Her flesh was tingling and crawling with the need for more of his touch. Her breasts were aching for the caress of his lips and tongue. Her feminine core was pulsing a primal beat that was reverberating throughout her body. It was an unstoppable desire, a longing for the sensual high of passion that she knew he alone could give her. She pushed against him shamelessly, her mouth locked to the bruising pressure of his, wanting more, needing more, aching for more.

Sam suddenly wrenched his mouth off hers, his hands dropping away from her as if she had burned him. 'That should never have happened,' he said, breathing heavily, the fingers of one hand scoring through his hair in agitation.

Lexi took a moment or two to reorient herself. Her senses were spinning so much she felt as if she had just stepped off a merry-go-round that had been going way too fast. Guilt made her go on the attack. 'You started it.'

'You should have stepped back,' he scolded.

She gave him a challenging look, still not ready to accept the total blame. 'Why didn't *you* step back?'

He let out a stiff curse. 'I told myself I wasn't going to do this,' he said, dragging his hand down over his face until it distorted his features. He dropped his hand and glowered at her. 'We should never have got involved,' he said. 'Not then and certainly not now.'

'Who said anything about getting involved?' she said, waving her hand in front of his face. 'I'm engaged, remember?'

The ringing silence was accusing.

Lexi glared at him, directing the anger she felt at herself onto him instead. 'Do you really think I would become involved with you again?' she asked. 'I'm not that much of a fool. You might be happy spending your life passing from one bed to another like a game of musical chairs, but that's not for me. I want stability and certainty.'

'So you picked the richest man in your circle and got yourself engaged to him,' Sam said with a cynical look.

'You don't have any idea of what I want or who I am,' Lexi flashed back. 'You didn't know me five years ago, and you don't know me know. Not the real me. I was just a girl you wanted to sleep with. You didn't want anything else from me. Sex is easy for men like you. It's just a physical thing. Emotions don't come into it at all. I want more than that now. I want the physical and the emotional connection.'

He continued to look at her with his dark, smouldering eyes. 'Are you going to tell your fiancé about that little physical connection we had just now?'

'Let's just forget about it, OK?' Lexi said, hot in the face, even hotter on the inside where the pulse of longing still hummed like a tuning fork struck too hard. 'As far as I'm concerned, it didn't happen.'

Sam thrust his hands deep in his trouser pockets in case he reached for her again. He was sorely tempted. It would be so easy to haul her back against him and force her to admit the need he could see playing out on her features. He could see the battle she was having with herself. He was having it too. Was it because she was now off-limits that this need was so overpowering? He hadn't felt like this with other partners. Each time he had moved on without a backward glance when the relationship had folded. After a couple of months he hadn't even been able to recall their names. But something about Lexi drew him like a bee to a pollen-laden blossom. He ached for her. A bone-deep ache that was as strong as it had ever been. How long was she going to deny what was still between them? Or was this just a game to her, a way of paying him back for leaving without giving her notice

'Are you happy, Lexi?' he asked.

Her blue eyes met his, wariness, uncertainty shining there. 'What do you mean?'

'With this Matthew guy,' he said. 'Are you sure he's the right one for you?'

A defensive glitter came into her eyes. 'Of course he's the right one for me,' she said. 'I wouldn't be marrying him if he wasn't.'

'The way you responded to me just then made me think—'

'I don't want to hear this,' she said, swinging away in irritation.

'You can't just ignore what happened,' he said. 'You can't just push it under the carpet.'

'It meant nothing!' she said. 'I just got a little carried away. We both did.'

'Lexi—'

'Stop it, Sam,' she said with a warning glare. 'Just stop it, will you? I want to forget about it. It was a stupid mistake. You're right. It should never have happened.'

Sam strode over to her, right in front of her, so close he could smell her perfume again. So close he could have touched her. So close he could feel her sweet vanilla-scented breath wafting on his face. 'How can you even *think* of marrying that guy when just minutes ago I could have had you up against that wall?' he asked.

Her hand came up in a flash, connecting with his cheek in a hard slap that cracked through the air like a stockwhip.

Sam held himself very still, his eyes locked on hers. The air pulsated with the combined force of their anger. It was a thundercloud of frustration, a hurricane of hatred and longing, a lethal mix that could explode at any moment. He felt the tension in his body. The wires of his restraint were stretched to the limit.

He had never wanted anyone more in his life.

'Feel better now, do we?' he asked.

Her throat rose and fell over a tight swallow but her eyes still flashed at him with glittering heat. 'You insulted me,' she said. 'You as good as called me a slut.'

'I want you, Lexi,' he said in a low, husky tone. 'And you want me. Deny it if you must but it's not going to go away.'

'It has already gone away,' she said, swallowing again.

'You want me,' he said again. 'Go on, admit it.'

'I will do no such thing!' she said, struggling to put some distance between their bodies. 'You just want me because you can't have me.'

'Oh, I can have you,' he drawled. 'Make no mistake about that, sweetheart. Engaged or not, I can have you and we both know it.'

She pushed away from him, glowering at him with venomous hatred as she wrenched open the door. 'You're wrong, Sam,' she said. 'You're so wrong.'

'Let's see about that, shall we?' he asked.

Lexi closed the door on his mocking smile, running, stumbling down the corridor as if the very devil himself was at her heels.

CHAPTER SIX

EVIE was coming back into the hospital as Lexi was leaving it. 'Hey, what's the rush?' Evie asked. 'You look like you're running from a fire.'

Lexi worked hard to get her flustered features under some semblance of control. 'I have a lot to get done,' she said. 'Things to do, people to see, you know.'

'Have you been to see Bella?' Evie asked.

'Um…no,' Lexi said, averting her gaze. 'I got distracted with…with, er, something else.'

Evie cocked her head. 'What's that on your face?'

'What's what?' Lexi asked, putting a hand up to her hot cheek.

Evie peered closer. 'It looks like some kind of rash…' She straightened and gave Lexi a narrow-eyed look. 'Beard rash. Where the heck would you get beard rash from when your fiancé is several thousand kilometres away, working in a remote Nigerian village?'

'Evie, don't,' Lexi said, releasing an impatient breath. 'I'm really not in the mood for this.'

'It's Sam Bailey, isn't it?' Evie said, frowning.

'Don't be ridiculous.'

'I saw you talking to him the other night at the pub. You were by yourselves for ages, looking all cosy in the corner. What's going on?'

Lexi threw her older sister a look. 'You're a fine one to talk,' she said. 'Everyone was talking about you and Finn that night. Finn was looking at you as if he wanted to strip you naked right then and there. Have you got something going on with him?'

Evie pulled her chin back in disgust. 'Are you crazy? I hate Finn's guts. You know that. He's the most arrogant, bull-headed man I've ever met. He probably left the pub with one of the barmaids. It wouldn't be the first time. That's the sort of jerk he is. Anyway, stop changing the subject. What's going on with you and Sam Bailey?'

'Nothing,' Lexi snapped irritably. 'Why does everyone assume there's something going on just because we were once involved? There's absolutely *nothing* going on. How many times do I have to say it?'

Evie looked at her for a lengthy moment. 'You *are* in love with Matthew, aren't you?' she asked.

'Of course I love him,' Lexi said. And she meant it. She really did. Matthew Brentwood was one of the nicest men she'd ever met. He treated her with respect; he made her feel important and special. It wasn't his fault she didn't enjoy being intimate with him. He hadn't done anything wrong. In fact, he had been incredibly patient with her. She hated herself for disappointing him. So many other men would have ended the relationship but, no, he had insisted it would get better once they were married. She felt safe and secure knowing he would always be there for her in spite of her shortcomings. She felt a treasured part of his loving family. His parents and two sisters had welcomed her with open arms. Her relationship with Matthew would never be a hair-raising, white-knuckle roller-coaster ride; it was more like a safe, gentle cruise on a peaceful lake.

It was what she wanted.

'Loving someone isn't the same as being in love,' Evie said. 'Sometimes a relationship can feel right but be totally wrong.'

'There's nothing wrong with my relationship with Matthew,' Lexi said. 'I just wish people would mind their own business.'

'Sor-ry,' Evie said. 'No need to be so prickly.'

'I'm sorry,' Lexi said, her shoulders going down. 'I'm just dealing with some stuff right now.'

Evie frowned. 'What stuff?'

Lexi gave her sister a direct look. 'Did you know Dad had threatened to end Sam's career five years ago?'

Evie blew out a whooshing breath. 'I thought you might stumble across that sooner or later. I was hoping you wouldn't find out.'

'You knew about it and didn't *tell* me?' Lexi asked.

'I didn't find out about it until the other night at the pub,' Evie said. 'Finn thought it highly amusing to think of Dad trying to suck up to Sam. I asked him what the hell he meant and he told me he'd always suspected Dad had had something to do with Sam leaving. I had no idea he had pulled that sort of stunt. When we heard Sam had left, we all assumed he'd got some sort of scholarship to study overseas. Looking back now, I think Dad encouraged everyone to think that. He wouldn't have wanted anyone accusing him of blackmail.'

'No,' Lexi said bitterly. 'Instead, he made me think Sam had left because he couldn't care less about me. How could he do that? How could he act so despicably and think it wouldn't have consequences?'

'You can't change anything now, Lexi,' Evie said. 'You were so young back then. You wouldn't have stayed with Sam in the long term. Surely you realise that?'

'How do you *know* that?' Lexi asked with a furious glare. 'How can you be so sure of what I would or wouldn't have done?'

Evie frowned again. 'No need to bite my head off, Lexi.'

'I'm tired of everyone interfering,' Lexi said, clenching her hands into tight balls of tension. 'I'm so angry with Dad. I'm angry at Sam. But most of all I'm furiously angry at myself.'

'I don't see why,' Evie said reasonably. 'You thought you were in love and got caught up in the fantasy of it. It's what kids do.'

'I was nineteen, not nine,' Lexi said. 'I was old enough to know my own mind. I should have fought for what I wanted. Why was I so weak? Why didn't I stand up for myself?'

'Lexi…' Evie's tone softened. 'Just let it go, OK? You're going to make yourself miserable in the long run. You can't live your life looking back over your shoulder all the time. You're happy and settled now. Don't go stirring up a hornet's nest just for the heck of it.'

'You don't understand,' Lexi said, fighting tears. 'Dad ruined my life. He's ruined everything.'

'I know it's hard for you to finally realise Dad isn't perfect,' Evie said. 'You've had him on a pedestal for such a long time. And while I don't agree with his methods, I think his motives probably came from the right place. He was worried about you wrecking your life. Sam was so much older and he was battle-scarred. Dad could probably see that and just did what he could to protect you.'

'I wish he'd left me to sort my own life out,' Lexi said bitterly. 'Why did he have to play God?'

'Tread carefully, Lexi,' Evie cautioned. 'You've got enough on your plate with organising the ball as well as your wedding without looking for more drama from home. You know what Dad's like. He can be an absolute bastard if you get on the wrong side of him. I should know. I've done it enough times.'

'I don't care,' Lexi said with a steely look of determination. 'I'm going to have it out with him. I don't care if he gets upset and rants and raves. I want him to face what he's done. He's coming back tonight from his weekend away. I can't just ignore this. I can't let him get away with it. It's my life, my happiness we're talking about here.'

Evie let out a sigh. 'You won't get him to apologise, Lexi. You do know that, don't you?'

Lexi set her mouth into an intractable line. 'I want him to realise you can't use people like chess pieces on a board. You just can't do that.'

'Good luck with it, hon,' Evie said. She paused before she added, 'Oh, and maybe you should try a little concealer on that rash before you go home.'

Sam walked back to his office with the taste of Lexi still fresh on his tongue and the skin of his cheek still stinging from her slap. He knew he had probably deserved it. He had goaded her. He couldn't seem to stop himself from needling her. He had wanted a rise out of her. He had wanted her all stirred up and fiery. It made his blood thrum when she looked at him with those flashing sparks in her big blue eyes and her beautiful breasts heaving in anger.

He *had* wanted to kiss her. No point denying it. He

had wanted to from the first day he'd run into her in the car park. She kept waving that flashy engagement ring under his nose but the way she'd kissed him back just now made him wonder if she was as in tune physically with her fiancé as she was with him.

And that was another thing there was no point denying, even though she seemed stubbornly determined to do so. Their physical chemistry was as strong and overpowering as ever.

He was going to have to watch his step. Having an illicit affair with Lexi now wouldn't be a great career move, not with her engaged to one of the hospital's biggest supporters. But, oh, how he wanted her! It was a constant ache in his flesh. He had only to think of her and he was swelling with need.

He was still having trouble processing the news of her virginity. How had he not noticed that? It made him feel uneasy that he had rushed her into bed without considering the implications. They had mostly practised safe sex. Mostly. He had only once…OK, maybe it had been twice…failed to use a condom in his haste to have her in the shower. His stomach clenched when he thought of how much he had demanded of her back then. She had met those demands with unbridled enthusiasm but it still made him feel he had exploited her. There was so much about Lexi he hadn't known back then. But now he suspected her sassy, smart-mouthed comebacks were a shield she hid behind when she was feeling threatened. She played the nose-in-the-air socialite role so well. The way she looked down her cute little nose at him, calling him country boy as if he still had hay between his teeth. Hell, it only made him want her more!

Maybe he was being overly cautious about the career risk. Maybe a short get-it-out-of-his-system affair would clear the air between them. After it was over—and he knew it would be over within a month at the most because he never played for keeps—he could move on with his life and she could go and marry her millionaire. Of course he knew it was wrong; of course if he were the fiancé and she was having an affair with someone else he wouldn't stand for it; of course it was madness. Sheer madness. But right now he wanted her too much to get tied up in moral knots over it.

Susanne was behind the reception desk when Sam came back in. 'There's an organ retrieval scheduled at Sydney Met at six this evening,' she said. 'The patient's family have decided to withdraw life support. He's a twenty-seven-year-old motorcycle victim who sustained severe head injuries three weeks ago. His kidneys are going to Perth, his heart to Melbourne and his lungs here.'

'Whose blood or tissues match have we got?' Sam asked.

'Mr Baker with the chronic obstructive airways disease,' Susanne said. 'He's been on the priority list the longest.'

'Right,' Sam said. 'You'd better call him and let him know. And organise theatre space. Things are going to get busy around here.'

Lexi was in the main lounge room at the family mansion in Mosman when her father finally walked in. She had been pacing the floor for the last hour, anger roiling inside her like a turbulent tide.

'Hello, beautiful,' Richard Lockheart said as he sauntered in. 'How was your weekend?'

Lexi folded her arms and shot him a glare. 'I've had better.'

Richard moved to the drinks cabinet and poured himself a Scotch. He lifted the lid on the ice bucket to find it was empty. 'Be a darling and get your poor old father some ice, will you?'

'I think you're perfectly capable of getting your own ice,' she said through stiff lips.

Richard smiled indulgently as he looked at her, his dark brown eyes crinkling up at the corners. 'What's up, baby girl? That time of the month?'

Lexi suddenly realised how little she liked her father. Sure, she loved him, but she didn't much like him. Why had it taken her this long to see through his easy charm to the ruthlessly ambitious man beneath? If people got in the way of his plans he removed them. If people displeased him he made sure they lived to regret it.

She had always blamed her mother for deserting the family, but now she wondered if what Bella had said was right. Perhaps her father had had more to do with her mother leaving than anything else. She had heard rumours of his womanising behind her mother's back, but as a little girl she hadn't wanted to think of her father as anything other than blameless. It was a cruel shock to realise how she had been duped. How silly she had been to invest so much emotion and dedication in a parent who had callously used her for his own gain. Her whole life, both childhood and young adulthood, had been nothing but a house of cards that was now tumbling down around her feet.

'I found out about how you blackmailed Sam Bailey five years ago,' she said. 'How could you do that? How could you play with people's lives in such a heartless way?'

Richard's brown eyes hardened. 'You don't know what you're talking about, Lexi.'

'I *do* know what I'm talking about,' she said. 'You issued an ultimatum to Sam. He had no choice but to leave. He could have lost his career, but did you care? No. All you wanted was to get him out of the way so you could keep me under your thumb. You didn't even have the guts to tell me he was being appointed here. I had to find out by myself. How do you think I felt?'

'You're in charge of fundraising,' he said. 'You have nothing to do with the hiring and firing of staff. Anyway, I'd assumed you'd forgotten all about him by now.'

Lexi clenched her hands so tightly her nails dug into her palms. 'Like you do with all of your lovers?' she asked. 'Just how many were there while you were married to Mum? Four? Five? Ten? Or have you *forgotten*?'

Her father's mouth tightened and he put his glass down with a loud thwack on the bar. 'What is all this nonsense, Lexi?' he asked. 'I don't expect to come home after a hard day at the office to this sort of behaviour.'

'You don't know what a hard day's work is,' she tossed back. 'You spend most of your time at boozy business lunches and resort weekends paid for by other people. Grandad did all the hard work. You just sit back and enjoy the benefits. You pay other people to do the dirty work for you, like bring up your children, for instance. You don't even take time out of your busy social schedule to visit Bella in hospital.'

Richard's face was almost puce in colour. 'I will not have you speak to me like this in my own house.'

'You told lies about me to Sam,' Lexi said, her anger rolling in her like a cannonball on a steep slope, and she couldn't have held it back if she tried. 'You told him I was only sleeping with him as part of some sort of teenage rebellion. How could you have done that?'

Richard thumped his hand down on the nearest surface so hard it made the pictures on the wall behind shake. 'You were too young to know your own mind. I did what I had to do to protect you.'

Lexi felt like screaming. The hurt inside her was like a bottle of soda that had been shaken and was fit to explode. 'You had no right to interfere with my life,' she said. 'Not then and certainly not now.'

Richard gave her a disgusted look. 'I suppose he wants you back in his bed,' he said. 'Is that what this is about? You'd be a fool to jeopardise your engagement to Matthew. Sam Bailey will only use you to get where he wants to go. Don't ever forget that, Lexi. He's a boy from the bush who made good. A society bride like you would be the icing on the cake.'

'You have no idea how much damage you've done,' she said, too angry for tears.

'The only damage you should be worrying about right now is raising sufficient funds for the hospital,' Richard said with a sneer. 'Carrying on like a lovesick teenager while you're supposed to be concentrating on the ball is going to feed into people's doubts that you're not the right person for the job. I had to work hard to convince the board to agree to have you as Head of Events. If you stuff this up now, you'll not only be made a laughing stock but you'll make me look a fool as well.'

'I hardly think you need any help from me in making yourself look a fool,' she said. 'You do a pretty fine job of it all by yourself.'

Realising confrontation wasn't working, Richard put on the charm again. 'Now, now, baby girl,' he said. 'Aren't you being a little bit melodramatic? Forget about

Sam Bailey. He's nothing to you now. You're happy with Matthew. He's perfect for you. You don't want to upset him and his family when they've been so supportive of the hospital, do you?'

Lexi glared at him. 'Why is everything always about money with you?'

'Money is a universal language, Lexi,' Richard said. 'It opens lots of doors and it shuts some others.'

Lexi turned and walked out of the room with her heart feeling as if someone had reached inside her chest and ripped it out. There were doors she could never open again. They were shut tight against her. She had been locked out of her own life by walking through the doors her father had opened for her.

But the most important door of them all she had slammed shut all by herself.

CHAPTER SEVEN

'WHAT do you mean, the venue's been cancelled?' Lexi looked at her assistant Jane in horror a few days later. 'The ball is in two weeks' time!'

Jane grimaced. 'I know,' she said. 'The manager wants to speak to you personally to apologise. He said there was a fire in the kitchen that got out of control last night. There's extensive water damage from the fire hoses. They're doing what they can to redecorate but they've had to cancel all bookings for the next month. Shall I get him on the line for you?'

Lexi nodded and took the call in her small office. It was as bad if not worse than Jane had described. After talking to the manager it was clear that the ball could not go ahead as planned. The kitchen was out of action, for one thing, and the ballroom was the worst hit in terms of water damage.

What a disaster!

Lexi felt as if everything she had worked so hard for had been ripped out from under her. She had put so much of herself into this job. She had invested a great deal emotionally in order to get her life back on track. Her father's cruel taunt came back to haunt her. It wasn't just her own lurking doubts about her ability to make a worthwhile contribution to society; it seemed everyone else felt the same. Everyone saw her as a shallow party girl with no substance. They didn't know half of what she had sacrificed to protect Bella. They didn't know how desperately she wanted to succeed. Bella's future—her life, everything—depended on Lexi getting the funds for the new equipment.

She *had* to prove them wrong. She had to show everyone, including herself, that she was up to the task no matter what last-minute hurdles were thrown at her.

She had to *think*.

She had to think past the thick fog of panic in her head and find a solution. What solution? All the tickets had been sold. The silent auction items were organised and confirmed. Everyone was looking forward to the big night of wining, dining and dancing and now it was not going to go ahead, not unless she could find another venue that could house that number of people at short notice. She spent an hour on the phone in the vain hope of finding a suitable venue but nothing was available. It was wedding season after all.

She pushed back her chair and went back to where Jane was sorting the silent auction placards.

'Any luck?' Jane asked hopefully.

Lexi shook her head in despair. 'Unless someone cancels their wedding at the last minute, I'm totally stuffed. Everyone's going to think it's my fault.'

'I'm sure no one will think that,' Jane consoled her.

Lexi gave her a grim look. 'Won't they?' She paced the floor in agitation. 'I can hear them now: "Lexi Lockheart only got the job because of her father and look at what a rubbish job she did of it."' She stopped pacing to grasp her head between her hands. 'Grr! I can't believe this is happening to me on top of everything else.'

'It's certainly a difficult time for you with Bella in hospital and your wedding so close,' Jane said in empathy.

Lexi stopped pacing and looked at Jane. 'That's it!' she said.

'What's it?' Jane asked, looking shocked. 'You're not thinking of cancelling *your* wedding, are you?'

'The hospital,' Lexi said excitedly. 'We'll have the ball here.'

Jane gaped at her. *'Here?'*

'Yes,' Lexi said, tapping her lips as she thought it through. 'The forecourt is big enough for a marquee. The patients can even be a part of it that way, those that aren't too ill, of course. We can get the caterers to do extra nibbles and desserts for all the patients on the wards. It'll be brilliant!'

'It sounds great but what will the CEO think?' Jane asked.

Lexi snatched up her purse and phone. 'I'll go and speak to him now. Wish me luck.'

'Good luck!' Jane called as Lexi dashed out of the door.

Sam looked up at the clock on the wall. 'Time of death: four-forty-six p.m.,' he said in a flat tone.

'You did your best, Sam,' the anaesthetist said over the body of Ken Baker. 'He'd been on the waiting list too long. He would've died anyway. He went into this knowing there was only the slimmest chance of success.'

Sam stripped off his gloves and threw them in the bin, his expression grim. 'I'll go and speak to the family,' he said, his stomach already in tight knots at the thought.

Losing patients was part of the job. Every surgeon knew it. Sam knew it but he still hated it. He hated the feeling of failure. Even when the odds were stacked against him he went into every operation intent on proving everyone wrong. And he had done it—numerous times. He had won some of the most unwinnable of battles. His professional reputation had been built on his successes. He had lengthened people's lives, given them back to their families, given them back their potential.

But this time he had failed.

And now he had to face the family and still act as if he was in control when he felt anything but. The clinically composed veneer he wore was so thin at times he wondered why relatives didn't see through it.

The family was gathered in one of the relatives' rooms outside the theatre suites. Gloria Baker stood as soon as Sam came in. There was a son and a daughter with her, both teenagers about fourteen and sixteen. The son reminded Sam of himself at the same age: tall and awkward, both physically and socially. 'I have some very bad news for you,' Sam said gently. 'We did everything we could but he wasn't strong enough to survive the surgery. I'm very sorry.'

Gloria Baker's face crumpled. 'Oh, no…'

Megan, the daughter, wept in her mother's arms but the son, Damien, just sat there, expressionless and mute. Sam knew what that felt like. The inability to publicly express the devastation you felt inside. He could imagine what Damien was going through. How he would have to step up to the plate and support his mother and sister. Be the man of the house now his father had died. He would appear to cope outwardly and everyone would marvel at how brave he was being. Sam had done the very same thing but inside he had felt as if a part of him had been lost for ever.

'I'm very sorry for your loss,' Sam said again.

'Can we see him?' Megan asked.

'Of course,' Sam said. 'I'll organise it for you. Take all the time you need.'

Gloria wiped at her eyes. 'Thank you for being so kind,' she said. 'Ken knew he might not make it. He's been sick for so long. I just wish you had been here earlier to help him.'

'I wish that too,' Sam said.

'You can come through now,' one of the scrub nurses said to the family.

Sam stood to one side as the Baker family walked into Theatre to say their final goodbyes. There were some days when he really hated his job. He hated the pain he witnessed, he hated the ravage of disease he couldn't fix, he hated the blood loss he couldn't control, he hated the long hours of tricky, delicate and intricate surgery that ended with a flat line on the heart monitor.

He let out a sigh and turned for the theatre change room.

He couldn't wait for this day to be over.

After a prolonged and difficult meeting with the hospital CEO Lexi had finally been given the go-ahead to restage the ball in the forecourt of the hospital. Her head was full of ideas for how the marquee would look. She still had a heap of things to do but she had already organised the layout and decorations. The caterers were booked and she had selected the menu. A wine supplier had donated several cases of wine and champagne and the hospital florist had offered her services for the table arrangements. Lexi had even sent out emails to all ticket holders on the change of venue and was now in the process of pinning flyers to all the staff notice-boards throughout the hospital. After that horrible panic when she'd first received the news it felt good to be back in control of things.

The lift opened on the doctors' room floor and Lexi stepped out with her bundle of flyers. She ran smack bang into Sam's broad chest and the sheaf of notices went flying. The air was knocked out of her lungs and all she could manage was a breathless 'Oops!'

Sam narrowed his eyes at her. 'Don't you ever look where you're going?' he snapped.

Lexi gave him an arch look. 'I thought you always used the stairs?'

His jaw clenched like a steel trap as he bent to re-trieve the flyers. Lexi watched as his gaze ran over the announcement printed there. 'What's this?' he asked, swinging his nail-hard gaze to hers.

'It's a flyer about the ball,' she said, angling her body haughtily. 'There's been a change of plan.'

His dark brows met above his eyes in a frown. 'You're having the ball here? At the hospital?'

Lexi bent down to pick up the rest of the scattered bundle. 'Yes,' she said, tugging at one of the flyers be-neath his large foot. She looked up at him. 'Do you mind?'

He stepped off it and she straightened, making a point of smoothing the flyer out as if it was a precious parchment he had deliberately soiled with his footprint.

'What happened to the other venue?' Sam asked.

'A fire in the kitchen,' Lexi said. 'The firemen went a bit overboard with the water. The place is a mess.'

Sam was still frowning. 'But surely this isn't the

right place to have a function like that. Where are you going to house all the guests? The boardroom only fits twenty. That's going to put a whole new spin on dancing cheek to cheek. It'll be more like cheek to jowl.'

'I've organised a marquee,' she said with a toss of her head. 'It's all on the flyer if you'd take the time to read it.'

'Have you thought this through properly?' he asked. 'You're going to have people all over the place, some of them heavily inebriated. What about security? What about the disruption to the patients? This isn't a hotel. People are here because they're sick, some of them desperately so.'

Lexi rolled her eyes impatiently. 'I've already been through all this with the CEO. He's given me the all-clear.'

'A busy public hospital is not a party venue,' Sam said. 'It's a ridiculous idea. What were you thinking?'

Lexi was furious. She had only just managed to get the CEO on side. If Sam went up to him and expressed his concerns, the decision might very well be revoked. Her heart started to hammer in panic. She had to make this work. There was no other option. Her reputation was riding on this. She *had* to pull it off. 'Why are you being so obstructive about this?' she asked. 'Is it because I'm the one planning it? Is that it?'

'That has nothing to do with it,' he said with a brooding frown. 'I just don't think you've thought it through properly.'

Lexi glowered at him. 'Have *you* got a better idea, country boy? What about we throw a few hay bales around the local park and have a sausage sizzle and a few kegs of beer? Would you be more comfortable with that? Maybe we could even bring in some sheep and some cows for authenticity, or what about a pig or two? I bet that would make you feel right at home.'

Sam took her by the elbow and marched her out of the way of the interested glances coming their way. 'Will you keep your voice down, for heaven's sake?' he snarled.

She tugged at his hold but his fingers tightened. 'Get your hand off me,' she said. 'I'll call Security. I'll scream. I'll tell everyone you're harassing me. I'll… Hey, where are you taking me?'

Sam opened a storeroom door and dragged her in behind him, closing the door firmly once they were both inside. 'You want to pick a fight with me, young lady, then you do it in private, not out there where patients and their relatives can hear.'

'I suppose you think since you've got me all alone you can kiss me again.' She threw him a blistering glare. 'You just try it and see what happens.'

Sam gave her a taunting smile as he stepped closer. 'I can hardly wait.'

Her eyes rounded and she backed up against the storage cabinet, making it rattle slightly. 'Don't you dare!'

'What are you afraid of, Lexi?' he asked, picking up a strand of her hair and looping it around his fingers. 'That you might kiss me back and enjoy every wicked moment of it?'

He saw her slim throat rise and fall over a swallow and the way she sent the tip of her tongue out over her lips, a quick nervous dart that deposited a fine layer of glistening moisture on their soft pillowy surface. 'I'd rather die,' she said with a hoist of her chin and a flash of her bluer-than-blue eyes.

Sam knew he was not in the right mood to be rational. He knew he should have walked away from her and gone home and wrestled his demons to the ground the way he normally did. Take it out on the ocean where no one could see or hear. But being with Lexi even for a few stolen moments was what he wanted more than anything right now. He threaded his fingers through her hair, which felt like silk, fragrant silk that fell in a skein way past her shoulders. The blood was surging through his body, making him thick and heavy with want. She would feel it if he brought her any closer. Her feet had already bumped against his, her slim thighs just a hair's breadth away. 'Have you told your fiancé about us yet?' he asked.

Her eyes darkened like a thundercloud. 'No, why should I?' she said. 'There is no us. It's all in your head. You're imagining it. I don't even like you. I hate you, in fact. I can't think of a person I hate more. You're despicable, that's what you are. You think you can play games with people. You think you can make them do things they don't want to do. You want to make trouble. You want to mess up my life just when I've finally got it all…'

Sam brought his lips to the shell of her ear, trailing his tongue over the fragrant scent of her skin. 'Am I imagining this?' he asked.

He felt the expansion of her chest against his at her sharp intake of breath, her breasts brushing against him enticingly. 'Stop it,' she said in a whisper-soft voice but she didn't move away.

'And this?' he asked, stroking his tongue over the fullness of her bottom lip.

He felt her lips quiver as she snatched in another uneven breath. 'You shouldn't be doing this,' she said, her voice almost inaudible now. 'I shouldn't be doing this…'

'But you want to, don't you, Lexi?' he said, touching her mouth with his in a teasing brush of lips against lips. 'You want to so badly it's like a drug you know you shouldn't be craving but you can't control your need for it. It consumes you. It keeps you awake at night. Sometimes it's all you can think about during the day.' He teased her lips again, a little more pressure, lingering there a little bit longer until her breath mingled intimately with his. 'That's what it's like, isn't it, Lexi?'

Her eyelids came down, the long mascara-coated lashes screening the ocean-blue of her eyes. 'It's wrong…'

Sam cupped the nape of her neck. He felt her melt against him, like soft caramel under the heat of a flame. Her body meshed against his: her breasts to his chest; her slim hips to his achingly tight pelvis; her feminine mound brushing against the head of his erection, making him crazy with desire.

The sound of a mobile ringing from within the depths of Lexi's bag hanging off her shoulder fractured the moment.

'Are you going to get that?' Sam asked after several jarring peels of the ringtone.

She stepped away from him and fumbled in her bag to answer the phone. She looked at the screen before she answered, her cheeks going a deep shade of pink. 'Matthew…I…I was just going to call you.' She turned her back to Sam and continued, 'I miss you too… Yes… not long now…'

Sam let out a rough curse under his breath and, wrenching open the door stalked out, clipping it shut behind him.

Lexi checked both ways in the corridor before she left the storeroom. She patted her hair into place and walked briskly towards the medical ward to deliver the rest of the flyers as well as call in on Bella. She hoped Sam had already completed his rounds because she didn't want to run into him again, certainly not while she was still feeling so flustered. She had been so close to throwing herself into his arms. It had been a force so strong she had no idea what would have happened if Matthew hadn't called at that point.

Matthew.

Every time she thought of him the guilt was like a gnawing toothache. It just wouldn't go away. She would have to tell him about Sam, but how? How did you say to your loving and faithful fiancé that you were confused about your feelings for an ex? Their wedding was only a matter of weeks away. The dress was made. She had another fitting tomorrow. The invitations had long gone out and most of the RSVPs had been returned. Some people had even dropped in gifts, horrendously expensive ones too. How was she supposed to tell anyone, Matthew especially, that she was getting cold feet?

Lexi pulled herself back into line with a good mental shake. All brides got nervous before their big day. It was normal to have doubts. It was a big decision to get married. It was a huge commitment to promise to share your life with someone, to be faithful to them…

Her stomach flip-flopped as she thought of Sam's aroused body against her, and his mouth with its hot, sexy breath blending erotically with hers. She suppressed a forbidden shiver of delight when she thought about his tongue blazing a trail of fire over her sensitive skin. Her body was still aching from the hunger he had stirred in her. Would it always be this way? How was she going to navigate her way through her career and marriage to Matthew with Sam in the way?

She would be strong, that's how, she decided.

She would garner her self-control.

She would be *determined*.

Bella was thankfully alone when Lexi entered the room. She was receiving oxygen through a nasal prongs tube and resting with her eyes closed, but she opened them as soon as she heard Lexi's footsteps.

'Hi, Lexi,' she said. 'I was wondering if you'd forgotten about me.'

'Sorry, Bells,' Lexi said. 'I've been run off my feet with the charity-ball arrangements. I suppose you heard what happened?'

'Yes, one of the nurses told me,' Bella said.

'It's all under control now…sort of,' Lexi said. She tidied up some fallen rose petals on the bedside chest of drawers. 'Is there anything I can get you? Do you want a proper coffee from the café? More magazines?'

Bella shook her head. 'No, I'm waiting for Mr Bailey to come in. I was in the shower when he came past this morning. He's been busy in Theatre most of the day. His first transplant case, or so one of the nurses said. Have you run into him lately?'

Lexi felt the heat rush to her cheeks and turned back to the flowers, willing some more petals to fall so she could keep her gaze averted. 'Not recently,' she lied.

The skin prickled along her arms as she heard the sound of voices out in the corridor. Sam was speaking to one of the nurses, ordering some bloods and scans for another patient. Lexi would recognise that deep, mellifluous voice anywhere.

'Are you OK, Lexi?' Bella asked.

Lexi painted a bright smile on her face as she turned around with the vase of flowers in her hands. 'I'm going to change the water on these flowers,' she said.

Bella frowned. 'But one of the volunteer ladies already did it this morning.'

'It won't hurt to do it again,' Lexi said. 'I might even get you some new ones from the hospital florist. These are just about past it.' She dashed out of the room and without even giving the nurses' station a glance slipped into the utilities room further down the corridor.

'Your oxygen levels have improved a bit, Bella,' Sam said as he read through her chart. 'The infection seems to have more or less cleared. I'd like you to stay in over the weekend just to make sure things have settled. If everything's fine you can go home on Monday, but you must take things easy. We'll have you on permanent standby in case a donor comes up. Has the transplant co-ordinator talked to you about the routine?'

Bella nodded. 'I have to have a mobile phone with me at all times in case there's a match, and a bag packed for the hospital.'

'Good.' Sam clipped the chart back on the end of the bed. 'Who will be looking after you at home?'

'Um…Lexi mostly,' she said.

Sam felt a frown tug at his forehead. 'You don't have a nurse to come in or a regular physiotherapist?'

'Yes, but Lexi's the one who takes me to all my appointments and helps me get dressed if I'm too breathless.'

Sam thought of Lexi juggling the demands of her job as well as the substantial care of her frail sister. It was another reminder to him of how she hid behind the shallow socialite facade when it suited her. But did she ever get noticed for the personal sacrifices she made? How could she if it drew attention to how much Bella relied on her? It would make Bella feel like an encumbrance, and he suspected that was something Lexi would want to avoid, given no one knew how long Bella would be with them. 'I'll have a word with the nurse about a follow-up appointment in my rooms,' he said. 'I'd like to keep a close eye on things just to be sure that infection doesn't come back.'

'Thank you, Mr Bailey,' Bella said shyly.

Sam gave her a brief smile and left to write up the last of his notes in the nurses' station. On his way out of the ward he ran into Evie, who was presumably on her way to visit Bella.

'Sam, can I have a quick word?' she asked.

'Sure,' he said. 'How about in here?' He gestured to a small waiting area that was currently empty.

'It's about my sister,' Evie began as soon as they were alone.

'I'm discharging her on Monday,' Sam said.

'Not that sister,' Evie said with a direct look. 'I meant Lexi.'

Sam drew in a measured breath. 'I see.'

'Actually, I don't think you do see,' Evie said, shooting him a look. 'Lexi's in a good place right now. She's getting married in a matter of weeks. She doesn't need the complication of an ex turning up and distracting her.'

Sam raised an eyebrow. 'Distracting her?'

Evie narrowed her gaze at him. 'I think you know what I mean.'

'Lexi's an adult,' he said. 'She's entitled to do what she wants.'

Evie's hazel eyes were brittle as they stared into his. 'She doesn't know what she wants,' she said. 'That's half the problem.'

'Then she should be left to decide without the influence of others,' Sam said coolly.

'You don't understand,' she said. 'Lexi had a really rough time after you left. I was very worried about her. I'm sure she didn't tell me even half of what was going on. She didn't tell anyone.'

Sam felt something in his stomach turn over suddenly. 'What do you mean?'

Evie pulled at her bottom lip with her teeth before she answered. 'She was so…different after you left. She was flat, depressed even. She closed off from everybody. It was like a wall was around her. No one could get to her and she wouldn't allow anyone in. It's only been since she's been involved with Matthew that she's started to blossom again.'

'I'm not sure what this has to do with me,' Sam said.

Evie glared at him. 'It has *everything* to do with you. People are starting to talk about you both. They think something's going on between you two. Something serious.'

'Perhaps you've misheard the gossip,' he said. 'The rumours that are circulating are about you and Finn, not me and Lexi.'

A rosy flush stained Evie's cheeks. 'That's complete and utter rubbish!'

Sam cocked his eyebrow again. 'Is it?'

Evie folded her arms across her body, just like her baby sister did when she felt threatened, Sam noted. 'I saw Lexi's face the other day,' she said accusingly. 'She had beard rash.'

Sam kept his face blank. 'So?'

'So?' Evie fumed. 'You have no right to kiss her! She's engaged to another man.'

'I wouldn't kiss any woman who wasn't an active participant,' he said with deadly calm.

Evie's eyes flared with anger. 'So you're saying she actively encouraged you? That's an outright lie! She's not a slut, far from it. In fact, I suspect you were her first lover. Did you know that at the time? I bet that's why you targeted her. Quite a notch on your belt, wasn't it? The youngest Lockheart sister. What a trophy to flash around.'

Sam tightened his mouth. 'I think you should concentrate on your own life and let your sister get on with hers.'

'You're not good for her, Sam,' Evie said. 'You unsettle her. She deserves to be happy. She deserves someone who'll love her, not use her as a stepping stone to get where he wants to go.'

'Is that what you think this is about?' Sam asked, frowning.

'What else could it be?' she asked. 'You don't love her, do you? If you loved her you wouldn't have let anyone stop you from seeing her. You would've fought for her no matter what it cost you personally or professionally.'

Sam gritted his teeth until his jaw ached. 'I don't love anyone like that,' he said.

Evie gave him a pitying look. 'Then maybe you should learn.' And with that she was gone.

CHAPTER EIGHT

For the last couple of weeks Lexi had more or less managed to avoid any lengthy contact with her father. She had worked late and then gone to the gym in the evenings, barely exchanging more than a few desultory words with him before she went to bed at night or left for work in the morning. But on the weekend before the ball she knew it would be harder to keep out of his way unless she had a plan to keep away from the family mansion for most of the time.

She had a dress fitting in the city at ten and rather than drive and struggle with finding somewhere to park she decided to catch a ferry across the harbour. It was one of those perfect Sydney spring days: warm and sunny, with a light breeze with a smell of summer to it. The harbour was dotted with yachts making the most of the wonderful weekend weather. Lexi wondered if Sam was out there somewhere, carving through the sparkling water, but she didn't see any vessel called *Whispering Waves*, even though she looked long and hard.

After the fitting Lexi did a bit of shopping, more than a bit, she thought a little ruefully as she juggled the bags of lingerie, clothes, shoes and make-up in both hands as she made her way back to Circular Quay for the ferry late in the afternoon. Rather than go straight home she wandered for a while along the Neutral Bay marina, looking at the million-dollar yachts moored there. There were a couple of yachties about doing maintenance, the smell of fresh paint in the air. The distinctive clanging sound of the rigging knocking against the masts in the breeze made her think of how wonderful it would be to just hop on a boat and sail away into the sunset, away from all of life's complexities. She wondered if that was what Sam did to relax after complicated surgery. She could picture him standing at the helm, his strong, tanned arms hauling sails and spinnakers up and down, enjoying the challenge of conquering the powerful and sometimes unpredictable conditions.

At the far end of the marina Lexi saw a white yacht with dark blue lines painted on the sides and in simple cursive the name *Whispering Waves*. There was no sign of anyone about so she walked closer. It was a beautiful vessel, not top-end luxury but close to it. It was at least forty feet long and well maintained, the paintwork looked fresh and the decks were varnished a rich jarrah red.

Lexi checked if anyone was watching before she climbed aboard, her shopping making the task a little more difficult for her, but somehow she managed to get on deck in one piece with all her shopping still safe. She had a quick look around; rationalising that it was her duty as Head of Events to ensure the yacht was suitable for a party of eight for lunch.

To her surprise the door to below deck was unlocked. She had a little battle with her conscience as she thought about having a quick peek around. It was trespassing, she knew that. But then she knew Sam. That kind of made a difference, didn't it? Anyway, she'd only take a minute to two. He would never even know she had been on board.

She strained her ears for any sound below, and once she was certain all was clear, she went down the steps to look inside. It was so much more spacious than she had imagined. There was a kitchen with all the latest appliances off the lounge and dining area. There was plenty of storage along the sides of the living area and a bar with a drinks fridge set in next to a sound system. There was a bathroom and toilet complete with shower and vanity. She opened another door and found the master bedroom with its own en suite. The bed was made up with white linen with a black trim, and black and white patterned scatter cushions were placed neatly in front of the large soft pillows.

Lexi was about to test the bed when she heard a footfall on the deck above. Her heart gave a little flutter as she considered her options.

Come out or hide.

How was she going to explain being in his bedroom? Why, oh, why hadn't she thought about the possibility of him returning? He had probably only stepped off the yacht for a few minutes. It was going to take quite some talking to get herself out of this sticky situation. She could just imagine the conclusions he would jump to. There was only one thing to do…

She chose to hide.

There was a row of tall cupboards on one side of the master bedroom. The first one she opened was filled with drawers that weren't big enough to hide her things so she quickly opened the next one. She stuffed her shopping bags below some of Sam's wet-weather gear, closing the door as softly as she could. Her heart was still galloping as she opened another closet. It had more hanging space and was just big enough for her to squeeze in amongst Sam's casual shirts. But while it was an excellent hiding place, she decided against closing the door completely as the lock was a one-way affair. While she wouldn't go as far as describing herself as claustrophobic, the thought of spending the next hour or two—or longer—locked inside a dark cupboard didn't hold much appeal, so instead she hooked the tip of her index finger around the edge to keep the door ajar.

Lexi heard Sam move about above deck. She pictured him doing maintenance like the other men she'd seen. Scrubbing the decks or fixing the stay ropes or some such thing. He probably wouldn't stay long. It was coming on for six p.m. He'd probably leave in a half an hour, tops. Maybe even fifteen minutes. Ten if there was someone watching over her.

Sam frowned as he released the mooring ropes. Did he really have it so bad that he could smell Lexi's perfume wherever he went? He breathed in again, deeper this time. No, he was imagining it. All he could smell was the briny ocean, which was exactly what he needed right now. This was where he could forget about yesterday's failure. He had the rest of the weekend to be alone out on the harbour, to sail, to fish, to think, to find that inner calm he badly needed right now.

He started the engine and motored out of the marina, giving a wave to one of the young lads who'd helped him rig up a new sail the other day.

He had just enough time before sundown to get to his favourite hideaway. He could already taste that first refreshing sip of beer.

OK. Lexi tried to talk herself out of panic when she felt the yacht moving away from the marina. He was probably just taking it out for a test run. That's what yacht owners did sometimes. They didn't always go out for the whole weekend. He would come back and she could slip away without him noticing. It'd be a piece of cake. He would never know he'd had a stowaway on board.

After a while she lost track of time. How far was he going for pity's sake? New Zealand? The Cook Islands? She was hungry, so hungry her stomach was making noises not unlike the growl of the yacht's engine.

Finally, after what seemed like hours, the movement stopped. There was the mechanical sound of an anchor being released and then silence all but for the gentle slip-slap of water and the mewling cry of a seagull passing overhead.

Lexi's finger was aching from being curled around the cupboard door for so long. Her need for the bathroom had long overtaken her need for food. She would have crossed her legs if there had been room.

Sam's footsteps sounded again, closer this time. Lexi held her breath, her heart beating so hard and fast it was like a roaring in her ears.

She heard the sound of clothes being removed, and then—heaven help her bladder—the sound of the shower running. After the longest three minutes of her life she heard Sam towel himself dry and then open the cupboard with the drawers inside.

Beads of perspiration were trickling between Lexi's breasts. Her breathing was now so ragged she felt like her lungs were going to collapse. She looked down at the sliver of light coming through the gap where her finger was keeping the door ajar. She very carefully and very slowly brought her finger out of sight, holding her breath as she closed the cupboard with a soft click. She fought against the panic of being locked in a confined space.

It was dark.

Very, very dark.

Another cupboard opened further along the wall and she heard the rustle of fabric and then a slide of a zipper. Lexi knew what was next. He had just put on his jeans, now he would come looking for a shirt. There was no point in cowering in the dark in the hope he wouldn't see her. Of course he would see her. She would have to brazen it out and think of a very good excuse, like in about two seconds flat, for why she was in his shirt cupboard.

Sam opened the cupboard door and reared back in shock, a swear word slipping out before he could stop it. 'What the freaking hell are you doing?' he asked.

Lexi stepped out of the cupboard with a yellow shirt in one hand and a blue one in the other. 'I'm thinking the blue,' she said, holding it up against his shoulder, her head tilted on one side musingly. 'It goes better with your eyes. Yellow is so not your colour. It washes you out. Makes you look anaemic.'

Sam was still trying to get his heart rate under control. He really wondered for a moment if he was suffering a hallucination. But, no, it was Lexi in the flesh all right, every gorgeous inch of her, on his boat, alone with him. A hint of devilry made his mouth kick up at the corners. She was alone with him for the rest of the weekend. 'I hope you've packed a toothbrush because I'm not turning back to take you home,' he said.

'You have to take me home,' she said dropping the shirts, her sassy facade slipping. 'You have to turn back right now. Right this instant. I had no idea you were planning to sail to Tahiti or wherever it is you've taken me.'

Sam gave a soft chuckle. 'Tahiti sounds nice,' he said. 'I've never been there—have you?'

Lexi pushed past him to the en suite. She turned and glared at him before she went in. 'Do you mind giving me a little privacy?'

He folded his arms across his naked chest, jeans-clad legs slightly apart. 'Don't mind me,' he said. 'I've heard it all before.'

She narrowed her eyes to paper-thin slits. 'I hate you, do you realise that? I positively loathe you.'

'Probably a good thing considering you're engaged to someone else and we're stuck on this boat together until tomorrow evening at sundown,' he said.

Lexi's eyes went wide in horror. 'You're *kidnapping* me?'

'I'm not asking for a ransom so, no, I'm not kidnapping you,' he said. 'You invited yourself on board so you'll have to obey the captain. That's me, if you haven't already figured it out.'

Lexi flung herself into the en suite and snapped the lock into place. She wanted to drum her fists on the door and scream like a banshee. If anyone found out she was on Sam's yacht for the weekend her life would be over. She would never live it down. The gossip would be unbearable.

No one needs to find out.

The traitorous thought slipped into her mind like a curl of smoke under a door. She had her mobile phone with her. She could text her sisters to say she was away for the weekend with a friend. She didn't have to say which friend. She didn't have to say it was her worst enemy. Hopefully they wouldn't put two and two together. Evie and Bella both knew she was trying to keep her distance from their father. They would assume she was staying out of town or something to avoid him.

Lexi came out of the en suite to find Sam had gone on deck. She made her way up to the bridge where he was standing looking towards the west, where the sun was sinking. The sky was a rich palette of red and ochre and gold. A flock of fruit bats flew past on their way to feed on the native trees and shrubs of the bushland on the shore about fifty metres away. It was a pictur-esque spot and the tranquillity after the hectic pace of the city earlier was not lost on Lexi. She breathed in deep, salty breaths and the scent of eucalypts that had spent all day being warmed by the sun.

Sam turned to look at her. 'Would you like a drink?' he asked.

Lexi folded her arms crossly. 'I suppose you always keep champagne on ice in case you get lucky.'

His eyes smouldered as they held hers. 'Always.'

Lexi glared at him defensively. 'I was doing an in-spection. I happened to be in the area and saw your boat so I decided to have a look around.'

'Did it pass muster?' he asked with a teasing glint, 'or do you think the closet is too small?'

She tightened her mouth. 'You could definitely do with some more hanging space.'

He bent to pick up a loose rope, coiling it expertly in his hands as he continued to look at her. 'I think we both know you weren't really doing an inspection,' he said. 'You must have known I was about. The boat wasn't locked up. You were having a little snoop and then you heard me come back on board so you went into hiding.'

She threw him a petulant look. 'I wasn't *hiding*.'

He elevated one dark eyebrow. 'What were you doing?' he asked. 'Colour co-ordinating my shirts?'

Lexi brushed some hair back off her too-hot face. 'It was a knee-jerk reaction,' she said. 'I didn't know who was coming. It might have been a robber or a vandal or…or something…'

'Or a kidnapper.' A lazy smile played around the corners of his mouth.

Lexi bit her lip. 'Did you mean it when you said you won't take me back home until tomorrow evening?'

He stepped over a guy rope and came to stand closer to her. 'This is the first free weekend I've had in months,' he said. 'I wanted to spend it out on the water. Commune with nature. Relax, chill, unwind.'

'I'm sure you'd much rather be alone so if you just set me off somewhere I'll catch a cab back,' Lexi said.

Sam laughed. 'You see any cabs along this part of the coast?' he asked.

Lexi looked at the coastal reserve that fringed the shore for miles along the headland, and frowned. She swung her gaze back to Sam's amused one. 'You have no right to keep me here against my will. I bet you're doing this on purpose to ruin my reputation. That's what this is about, isn't it?'

'No,' he said, taking her by the upper arms and bringing her flush against his rock-hard chest. 'This is what it's about.' And then he covered her mouth with the blazing fire of his.

It was an earth-moving kiss. Lexi felt her legs weaken like overcooked spaghetti as his mouth crushed hers in a deeply passionate assault on her senses. His tongue was a sensual sword that divided her lips to receive him. There was no denying him access. She had no willpower. No self-control. No determination. All

she had was red-hot need. So hot it was burning from
the soles of her feet, running up her legs, racing up her
spine like a flame following a pathway of spilt gaso-
line. His tongue tangled with hers, teasing it into a sexy
dance, taming it with the commanding thrust of his. She
whimpered against his lips, her need for him so consuming she was almost sobbing with it. Her feminine
folds were heavy with longing, the walls of her womanhood moist with the heat of hungry, rapacious desire.

Sam's grizzled jaw grazed the soft skin around her
mouth as he shifted position. He cupped her face with
his hands, his tongue snaking around hers in an erotic
tangle that sent a rush of heat over her skin.

'I want you so badly,' he said against her swollen
lips. 'I've never wanted anyone more than I want you
right now.'

Lexi could feel the potent power of his erection
against her belly. She could feel her body responding
to his just as it had in the past. There was no need for
words even if she could have found her voice. She let her
body communicate all the pent-up longing she felt. She
pushed herself against him, her breasts tight and sensitive, and her feminine mound contracting with a pulse
of longing so strong she felt her legs sway beneath her.

Sam's hands gripped her hips, holding her against
him, the friction of his arousal a torment to her senses.
She welcomed the heat of him, rubbing against him
shamelessly to assuage the ache that consumed her.

He slipped a warm hand beneath her top, pushing
her bra aside to tease her nipple with the broad pad of
his thumb. It was exquisite torture to feel him reclaim
her flesh with the blistering heat of his touch. She gave
a soft cry as he replaced his thumb with his mouth, his

tongue swirling and stroking before he sucked on her with just the right amount of pressure.

She threw back her head in wanton abandon, arching her spine to give him greater access to her breasts. He moved from one breast to the other and back again, ramping up her desire until it was an all-consuming wave that threatened to sweep her away completely.

Lexi placed her hands on his chest, her mouth teasing his with little kittenish bites. Right now she was not the Lexi who was engaged to Matthew Brentwood. She had turned into a wild tigress of a woman eager to mate with her alpha male. Her body was Sam's and Sam's alone. It responded to his with a fervour that was unmatched by anything else in her experience.

Sam's mouth took control of the kiss, one of his hands in the small of her back while the other worked on removing the rest of her clothes. Lexi stepped away from the soft pile of her garments, her mouth still locked on the fire of his. She felt the warm brush of his fingers against the hot wet heart of her. Her flesh was so responsive she knew it was too late to call an end to this madness. She felt the overwhelming pull of release deep within her body, all the nerves singing along the tight wires of her muscles as every sensation gathered to that one intimate point. One more stroke of his fingers and she plunged into the abyss, her body shaking with the tremors that rolled through her like the waves against the shore.

Sam held her as she came back from paradise but she could see his body was in urgent need of its own release.

'Condom,' he groaned against her mouth. 'I need to get a condom.'

Lexi was momentarily jolted out of the sensory spell.

She suddenly felt the enormity of what she was doing. Sex was not just about physical needs being satisfied, or at least it wasn't for her. Her hands stalled in their exploration of his chest, her gaze lowered, her teeth sinking into her lip.

Sam lifted her chin to lock her gaze with his. 'You're not comfortable with taking this any further?' he asked. 'We don't have to. I understand. I really do.'

Lexi looked into the darkness of his desire-lit eyes and felt herself drowning. 'It's been such a long time,' she said. 'I'm not sure I can satisfy you the way I did before…'

He brushed her mouth with his, softly. 'Tell me to stop and I'll stop,' he said.

She cupped his face with her hands, her eyes dropping to his mouth. 'I don't want you to stop,' she said, surprised at how much she meant it.

He carried her below deck to his bedroom, placing her gently on the mattress. He looked down at her as she covered herself with her hands, as if she was embarrassed at being naked in front of him. 'You still OK with this?' he asked.

'Don't mind me,' she said. 'I'm just having a fat day.'

Sam smiled. That was what he loved about Lexi, the way she said the opposite of what he was expecting. He reached for a condom and applied it before joining her on the bed. He anchored his weight on his forearms, careful not to crush her. He couldn't help thinking of the first time he had made love to her. It had been rough and fast, over within seconds for both of them. He had hurt her. She had reluctantly admitted that. It tormented him to think he had done that to her. He should have prepared her young body with gentle handling, making sure her tender flesh could accommodate him. He would make up for it this time. He would worship her body the way he should have done the first time.

He started by kissing her mouth in a soft caress that gradually deepened. Her tongue met his and danced with it in a rhythm that was as old as time, a sacred rhythm that spoke of human connection at its most elemental.

Something shifted in his chest as he felt her arms come up around his neck, her fingers delving into his hair as her soft mouth responded to the gentle pressure of his. It was like a slip of a gear, a stumble of the heart that he hadn't been expecting.

She grew impatient beneath him, lifting her slim hips, searching for him. Sam worked hard to control his urge to fill her. He had never had a problem with anyone else. Control came easily to him, but not with Lexi. He felt the magnetic pull of her core. He smelt the feminine fragrance of her, the sexy salt and musk that stirred his senses into overload.

He went back to her breasts with his mouth, teasing her with his lips and tongue until she whimpered and clawed at him. He continued down her body, dipping his tongue in the shallow cave of her belly button before going to her feminine folds. She was wet and swollen, like a precious hothouse flower, fragrant and heady, luscious and exotic.

He teased her apart with his tongue, taking his time, delighting in the cries she tried to suppress, relishing the way her back lifted off the bed as she convulsed.

Sam watched as her breasts rose and fell as she came back down to earth, her blue eyes looking almost shocked at how she had responded. He kissed her inner thigh and worked his way back up her body, taking his time, making sure she was ready for him to possess her.

'Please…' Her voice was a thready sound, an edge of desperation in it. 'Oh, Sam, *please*…'

Sam positioned himself, intending to string out the pleasure a little longer, but Lexi clearly had other ideas. She lifted her hips and he suddenly had nowhere to go but inside her. He surged in with a deep groan of pleasure as her tight body gripped him. He felt the ripples of her flesh, the intimate grasp of her massaging him until he was hovering on the precipitous edge of his control. He increased his pace, delighting in her slippery warmth as she wrapped her legs around his hips. Her supple body thrilled him, the way she had no inhibitions, the way she was so generous with her touch and caresses. Her mouth was soft but demanding, her tongue teasing and playful as it tangoed with his. He was getting closer and closer to the point of no return. It was a force building within him that was so powerful he could feel it roaring through his veins like a bullet train.

He pulled back from the brink to caress her with his fingers, to make sure she was with him when he finally fell. She gasped out loud as he played with her. He knew her body like he knew his own. He knew exactly what pressure and pace she liked, what she needed in order to be fulfilled. He felt the moment when she lost control; he felt the tight spasm of her body around him, milking him of his essence. He lost himself in her, falling, falling, falling into that blessed whirlpool of absolute, ultimate pleasure.

Sam held her close in the aftermath. He listened to the sound of her breathing slowly coming back to normal. For a moment it was easy to forget why he shouldn't have been lying with her breasts crushed against his chest and her legs still hooked around his hips.

'Oh, God,' she said.

Sam propped himself up on his elbows to look at her. 'Was that an "Oh God, I just had amazing sex" or an "Oh God, what have I done?"'

Her teeth pulled at her lip in that engaging way of hers. 'Both…'

He brushed the damp hair off her face with one of his hands. 'It was always going to happen, Lexi,' he said. 'I think we both knew that in the car park that day.'

She rolled out from under him and got off the bed. Her hair was all mussed up and her lips swollen from kissing. She took one of his shirts out of the closet and slipped it over her nakedness. His shirt was too big for her but Sam thought it looked far sexier on her than any lacy negligee.

He dealt with the condom before he went to where she was standing, grasping the edges of his shirt together to cover her body. He touched her on the cheek with one of his fingers. 'Hey,' he said. 'You don't have to hide yourself from me, Lexi. I know everything there is to know about your body.'

She gave him an agonised look. 'You don't…not really…'

He frowned as he looked at her. 'What do you mean?'

'Sam, I feel…I feel so guilty…'

He tipped up her chin with the same finger. 'It was just as much my fault as yours,' he said. 'I should've turned around once I found you on board and then none of this would've happened.'

She pulled his hand down from her face, stepping away from him, her arms wrapping tightly across her body again. 'I'm not talking about just now,' she said.

Sam frowned as he brought her back to face him with his hands on the tops of her shoulders. 'What *are* you talking about?' he asked.

He saw her throat go up and down and her eyes watered up, glistening with tears that threatened to fall any second. She bit her lip again, but still it trembled. Her whole body began to shake as if gripped by a fever.

'Sweetheart, what's wrong?' he asked, holding her steady with his hands on her upper arms.

She looked into his eyes for a long moment. 'Sam...I had a termination,' she said in a broken whisper. 'I had an abortion.'

He looked at her in a dumb silence. It took at least thirty seconds for him to process her words.

An abortion.

Which meant she had been pregnant at some point.

He said the first thing that came into his head. 'Was it mine?'

She turned away as if he had struck her. 'So that's the most important thing for you to establish, is it?' she asked.

Sam was having trouble keeping a lid on his emotions. Lexi had been pregnant. She had been carrying *his* child. He had never envisaged himself as a father. It had always been in the too-hard, too-emotionally-challenging basket. And yet for a brief time, a few weeks, he had been a father, or at least a potential one. 'I'm sorry,' he said. 'That was unforgiveable of me. I wasn't thinking. Of course it was mine.'

'I didn't know what to do,' she said, still not looking at him. 'I was so frightened and alone. I went to your flat but you'd gone. I didn't know who to turn to.'

Sam thought of how it must have been for her, so young, so inexperienced and yet pretending to be so street smart. Her father wouldn't have been much use, or her mother. What else could she have done?

And yet…

He had almost been a father.

He thought of how it would be to have a son or daughter, a combination of their genes. What would their child have been like? His mind raced with images of a platinum-blonde little girl or a light brown haired little boy. Little arms and legs, fingers and toes, soft wispy hair…

'I'm sorry,' he said bringing himself back to the moment with an effort. 'I know it's not enough but I'm truly sorry you had to go through that.'

She looked at him then, her gaze accusatory, incisive. 'You're angry,' she said. 'You think I did the wrong thing. Go on, say it. I can handle it. You think I did the wrong thing.'

Sam felt ambushed by emotion. He wasn't used to dealing with this bombardment of feeling. 'What do you expect me to say?' he asked. 'Congratulations on your abortion? For God's sake, Lexi, I might act all cool and controlled most of the time but you've just laid a whammy on me so you're going have to allow me a minute or two to process it.'

Her eyes were glistening with tears as she glared at him. 'Do you think it was easy to make that decision? I *agonised* over it. I cried and cried for what might have been, for what I wanted. But in the end I felt I had no choice but to do what I did. Do I think I did the right thing? Yes. Do I think I did the wrong thing? Yes. It was both the right and the wrong thing. Sometimes the hardest decisions in life are.'

'The decision to terminate a pregnancy is never an easy one,' Sam said. 'I don't believe any woman goes into it lightly. Even when it's clearly the right decision even on medical grounds it can take years if not a life-time to resolve the guilt surrounding it. But if it's any comfort, I think you did the right thing, Lexi. You were far too young for that sort of responsibility. And, quite frankly, I'm not sure I would've been much help even if you had been able to tell me. I would've supported you, of course, but it would have been hard for both of us at that point in our lives.'

She let out a wobbly sigh. 'I'm so sorry…'

Sam stepped up to her and cupped her face. 'Don't be,' he said firmly. 'It's in the past. Let it stay there. You can't change it.'

'I'm glad I told you,' she said on another sigh. 'It's been so hard keeping it to myself for all this time.'

Sam frowned. 'You haven't told your fiancé?'

Her cheeks grew pink and her eyes moved away from his. 'I've wanted to…so often, but the time has never seemed right.'

'Lexi,' he said. 'You're marrying this guy in a mat-ter of weeks. You need to tell him everything.'

She flashed him a glare over her shoulder. 'Like what happened here just now?' she said. 'You think I should tell him I had ex sex because I was feeling a bit lonely?'

Sam clenched his jaw. 'Is that what you think?' he asked. 'You were feeling a bit lonely so you jumped into bed with me? Lexi, you know that's not what hap-pened. We had sex because we can't keep our hands off each other. It has nothing to do with loneliness, yours or mine.'

She turned away, her body hunched as if she wanted to curl up and hide. 'I can't imagine you'd ever be lonely,' she said. 'You probably have heaps of women flocking after you wherever you go.'

'I've had relationships,' Sam said. 'Nothing serious and nothing lasting. I guess I'm not built that way.'

She turned and looked at him. 'So you're not thinking of marrying and having a family someday?'

Sam shook his head. 'Not my scene, I'm afraid. With a fifty per cent divorce rate I don't like my chances of getting it right. I don't want to screw up someone else's life as well as my own.'

'But your parents were happy, weren't they?' she asked.

Sam thought of his father and mother and how his mother's chronic illness had had such an impact on their relationship. How his father had limped along for the last twenty years, half alive, isolated with grief and guilt. 'Yes, but their relationship was one of those once-in-a-lifetime ones,' he said. 'Not everyone can achieve that. It's not realistic to expect there's someone out there who will meet all of your physical and emotional needs. And speaking of physical needs, is that your stomach I can hear growling with hunger?'

She put her hand over her stomach. 'You can hear that?'

'No, but I'm starving and I figured you might be too after all that exercise.'

Her face coloured up again. 'Why does being here with you feel so right but wrong as well?' she asked in soft voice.

Sam brushed her cheek with his finger. 'I think what you said a minute ago is very true. Sometimes some of life's hardest decisions are both right and wrong at the same time. Let's just say this is right for now and leave it at that.'

CHAPTER NINE

LEXI had a shower while Sam made dinner. She tried not to think about the moral implications of spending the rest of the weekend with him on his boat. It was as if she had stepped into a parallel universe, one where she and Sam were able to be together, enjoying each other's company, taking things as they came rather than planning too far ahead.

She looked at her engagement ring and felt like she was looking at someone else's hand. She grappled with her conscience before she tugged the diamond off. She had to use some soap to remove it. Was that a sign of some sort? she wondered. She looked at the pale circle of skin where the ring had hidden her flesh from the sun. She knew she would have to talk to Matthew. But she wasn't prepared to do it via email or over the phone. She needed to see him face to face to explain…

To explain what exactly? That she was in love with another man?

Lexi let out a sigh as she reached for a towel. There was only one man she could ever love and that was Sam. She loved him with her heart. She loved him with her mind. She loved him with her body. She felt like her life was incomplete without him in it. Being without him was like only wearing one shoe. Her life felt out of balance. The love she felt for him was the love his parents had felt for each other. A love Sam didn't feel for her. He had made that pretty clear. His relationships were 'nothing serious and nothing lasting'. That included her. What he was offering her was casual and temporary, a weekend of sensual delight, but then what? He would go back to his life and she would go back to hers.

Maybe she wouldn't have to tell Matthew. Maybe she could just let this weekend be her attempt at closure and leave it at that. She would move on with her life, get married and have babies and build a future with a man who loved her, instead of pining after a man who didn't and never would.

Lexi dressed in one of the new outfits she'd bought that day: a white halter-neck top and slim-fitting taupe pants. She bundled her damp hair up in a knot on top of her head, sprayed her wrists with the perfume she carried in her bag, and applied a light layer of lip gloss before joining Sam in the kitchen dining area.

'That smells delicious,' she said, sniffing the air appreciatively.

Sam turned from the pot he was stirring and handed her a glass of wine he had poured. 'Here you go,' he said. 'Dinner won't be long.'

Lexi took the wine and angled her head to see what he was cooking. 'What are you making?' she asked.

'Mediterranean fish casserole,' he said. 'One of my colleagues in the States is married to a chef. She took me on as a project and taught me to cook a little more than the meat-and-three-veg routine I'd grown up with.'

'You obviously enjoy it,' she said.

'Yes, I find it relaxing,' he said, putting the wooden spoon on the counter. 'What about you? Do you cook or leave it to the servants?'

Lexi slipped back into socialite mode. 'Of course,' she said airily. 'Why do something so menial when you can pay someone else to do it and clean up afterwards too?'

'What if you run out of money one day?' he asked.

'As if that's going to happen,' she said. 'I'm marrying a rich man, remember?'

Lexi watched as he turned back to stirring the pot, the line of his back and shoulders now tense. She wished now she hadn't goaded him. The atmosphere had changed to one of enmity and stiffness when before he had been so tender with her over the termination. 'Can I help with anything?' she asked.

'It's cool,' he said. 'I've got it all under control.' He turned and leaned back against the counter to look at her, his eyes running over her in appraisal. 'You look particularly beautiful,' he said. 'That wasn't what you were wearing before.'

'Lucky I did some shopping today,' Lexi said. 'Otherwise I would've had to go naked.'

His eyes smouldered darkly. 'Suits me.'

'I bought just about everything else but I didn't buy a toothbrush,' she said. 'I don't suppose you happen to have a spare?'

'I always keep a supply of basic necessities on board.'

Lexi gave him a cynical look. 'In case you get lucky.'

His mouth tilted in a sexy smile. 'I guess you could say today's been my lucky day.'

Lexi frowned and averted her gaze. 'Sam…'

One of his hands came down on her bare shoulder, the other touching her beneath her chin and forcing her gaze back to his. His eyes were dark and serious. 'If you really want to go back, I'll take you back,' he said.

Lexi didn't want to go back. She didn't ever want to

go back. She wanted to stay on his boat with him for ever without the intrusion of other people telling her what she should and shouldn't do. 'No,' she said in a whisper-soft voice. 'I don't want to go back just yet.'

He brushed her forehead with a kiss before he stepped away to go back to his cooking. 'Good, because I've had a hell of a week and I really need to clear my head.'

Lexi watched as he went back to the simmering pot. He was frowning as he stirred the casserole, the set to his mouth almost grim. 'You want to talk about it?' she asked.

One of his shoulders went up and down. 'It's OK. I deal with this stuff all the time—patients dying on the table because they're too sick to survive the surgery. It's part of the job. You win some. You lose some. But I hate losing. I never get used to it.'

Lexi put her glass down and moved to stand behind him. She wrapped her arms around his waist and pressed her cheek to the hard wall of his back. 'I'm sorry,' she said softly. 'It must be so hard for you. No one thinks of how the surgeon feels. Everyone feels sorry for the patient and the relatives, but what about the surgeon who has to try to sleep at night haunted by all those people he wasn't able to save in time? It must be absolute agony for you.'

He turned in the loop of her arms and brushed a wisp of hair off her forehead with a gentle finger. 'We're supposed to get hardened by it during our training,' he said. 'I'm usually good at keeping my emotions separate. I have to, otherwise it can cloud my judgement. But I lost a patient yesterday. I guess that's why I bawled you out about the change of venue for the ball. I was in a foul mood. I'd just left a family to say goodbye to their husband and father in Theatre. He died during the procedure.'

Lexi looked up at him in distress. 'Oh, Sam, and I was such a cow to you.'

He gave her a rueful smile. 'I probably deserved it. I seem to always be baiting you. I guess I like getting a rise out of you. You're so adorable when you're spitting chips at me.'

Lexi gave him a sheepish look. 'I didn't mean it about the hay bales and farm animals…especially the pigs. That was a bit low.'

He grinned at her and walked her back against the table with his thighs against hers. 'Yes, you did, you little minx,' he growled playfully.

Lexi shivered as his lips found her neck, nipping at the skin in little bites that sent electric shocks throughout her body. He finally came to her mouth, sealing it with a kiss that made every nerve tingle with delight.

'I thought we were going to have dinner,' she said somewhat breathlessly.

'Later,' he said.

Lexi closed her eyes as she gave herself up to his kiss. It was tender and searching, as if he was looking for the young innocent girl she had been, as if he was trying to redress the past by retracing his steps, doing things differently this time. She kissed him back with equal tenderness, enjoying the new-found intimacy that was so much more than two grappling bodies intent on sensual pleasure but more of a meeting of two spirits who found something special and priceless only with each other.

Sam finally eased his mouth off hers and brushed her hair back from her forehead, giving her a bemused smile. 'You constantly surprise me, Lexi Lockheart, do you know that?'

Lexi gave him a shy smile in return. 'Oh, I'm full of surprises, that's for sure.'

He reached for her ring hand, looking down at it before he met her eyes. 'Where's your engagement ring?' he asked.

Lexi couldn't read his masked expression. 'I…I took it off.'

'I don't suppose you tossed it overboard.'

She pulled her hand out of his and stepped away from him. 'Is that what you'd like me to do?' she asked.

He looked at her for a long moment. 'What *are* you going to do?'

Lexi bit her lip. 'I'm not sure…'

'Seems pretty simple and straightforward to me,' Sam said.

'Oh, really?' she said.

'Yeah,' he said. 'You shouldn't be marrying a man who doesn't satisfy you.'

Lexi put her hands on her hips. 'How do you know he doesn't satisfy me?'

He gave a shrug of one shoulder as if he didn't care either way. 'I figure if you were getting what you need from him, you wouldn't be here with me.'

'Maybe I need more than he can give me,' she said. 'You said it yourself. It's hard to find someone who meets all of your physical and emotional needs.'

'Do you love him?' Sam asked.

Lexi let out a snort of derision. 'Who are you to ask me about love?' she said. 'You don't love anything but your career.'

'Do you love him?' He repeated the question, more forcefully this time, which put her back up.

'Of course I love him!' She almost shouted the words.

'And yet you've told him nothing about what happened between us five years ago.'

Lexi glared at him. 'It's in the past. It should stay there.'

'I beg to differ, sweetheart,' he said. 'What's happened over the last couple of hours suggests it's not staying in the past. It's spilling into the here and now and at some point you're going to have to deal with it. You have to tell him.'

She gave him a cutting look. 'What do you want me to say to him? Do you want me to tell him you seduced me when I was barely out of school?'

His brows clamped together in a brooding frown. 'Don't go pulling that card on me, young lady,' he growled. 'You lied to me about your age. I wouldn't have touched you if you hadn't thrown yourself at me like a ten-dollar whore.'

Lexi raised her hand but he intercepted it midair, his fingers so tight, so cruelly tight she felt tears smart in her eyes. 'Let go of me, you bastard!'

'Stop it,' he said in a gritty, deadly calm voice. 'Get control of yourself.'

Lexi flew at him in a rage so intense she even frightened herself. She wanted to hurt him. She wanted him to have physical scars similar to the deep, painful emotional ones she had carried for so long. She fought him, tooth and nail, kicking at him, screaming words of abuse she had never used on anyone before.

But it was all in vain because he was too strong, too determined, too in control.

He held her until the fight went out of her. She went limp in his arms, her energy gone as if someone had pulled out the power source from her body.

She started to cry. Not soft little sobs but great big hulking ones that ripped at her chest like a pair of metallic claws. Tears rolled down her face but she could do nothing to stop them as Sam was still holding her in an iron grip.

But finally he relaxed his hold and the fingers that had bitten into her flesh began to stroke and soothe her instead. 'Hey,' he said softly.

'Don't you "hey" me,' she said, but not with any venom. She was way past that.

Sam drew her close against his body, his arms wrapping around her, his body moving from side to side in a soothing rocking motion, similar to one a loving mother did to a distressed child, not that Lexi had much memory of that experience, but she missed it all the same. 'Shh,' he said gently. 'No more tears, OK? I'm sorry. I didn't mean it. You didn't throw yourself at me.'

Lexi nestled against his strength and solid warmth. 'I did,' she mumbled against his chest. 'I acted like a tart. I'm so ashamed of myself. I don't know what came over me.'

She felt his hand stroke the back of her head, holding it close to his body. 'I could've walked away,' he said. 'I should've walked away.'

Lexi lifted her head off his chest to look at him. 'Why didn't you?'

His eyes were dark and warm, like melted chocolate. 'The same reason I didn't turn this boat around when I found you in my cupboard,' he said. 'I wanted you.'

Lexi felt her heart slip sideways in her chest. He wanted her, but for how long? Should she ask him? Would he put a time line on it? Or should she just take what was on offer and leave everything else to fate? 'I need to freshen up,' she said, lowering her gaze in case he saw the longing in hers.

He gave her a pat on the bottom. 'Take your time,' he said. 'I can hold dinner.'

The night sky was amazing as they sat out on the deck after they had eaten. Sam glanced at Lexi, looking as beautiful as ever though she was wearing one of his warm fleece jackets that swamped her slim frame. The wind had picked up, bringing with it a chill that was a reminder that the long lazy days of summer were still a few weeks away.

So too was Lexi's wedding, he thought with a clench of his gut. She may have taken her ring off but she seemed just as determined as ever to go ahead with the marriage.

He wasn't sure how he was going to deal with that day in November. It wasn't as if he would be invited. He wouldn't accept if he was. What he couldn't understand was why she would still want to marry someone who clearly wasn't meeting her needs.

He hated to think of her marrying for money. It didn't fit well with the Lexi he knew now. The Lexi who put her sister's health and happiness above any of her own needs or desires, the Lexi who worked so tirelessly for the benefit of the hospital charity.

But, then, people married for a host of different reasons: companionship; security; common goals...*children.*

Sam thought back to when he had seen himself following in the footsteps of his father and grandfather and great-grandfather before him. Being a husband, then becoming a father, raising a family, providing for them. In the days before his mother had become so des-

perately ill he had thought about building a life with
someone, having a brood of kids. It had seemed the normal thing to do. But then his mother had got sick and
he had watched as his father had struggled to juggle
everything: the farm and finances; Sam's needs; and
those of his mother. It had broken his father, made him
half the man he had been. His strong, tall, capable father had seemed to diminish and age right in front of
Sam's eyes. It had terrified Sam to think that might one
day happen to him.

Lexi was looking up at the sky. 'I think I can see a
satellite,' she said.

'Where?' Sam said, joining her on the cushioned seat
at the stern.

She pointed to a moving light in the black velvet of
the night sky. 'Can you see it? It's moving from left to
right. It's just passing the Saucepan.'

'Got it,' he said, breathing in her fragrance. 'I
really missed seeing the southern sky when I was in
the States.'

She turned her face towards him. 'What did you miss
the most?' she asked.

He put an arm around her shoulders and pulled her
closer. 'Lots of things,' he said. 'The smell of the dust
when the rain first falls in the bush, the sound of kooka-
burras at dawn and sunset, the sound of rain falling on
a tin roof back at home.'

She traced each of his eyebrows with a fingertip.
'Have you ever thought of working in the bush?' she
asked.

He captured her finger and pressed a soft kiss to
the end of it. 'Yes, of course, but I'm so highly trained
now I'm of more use in the city. It's ironic really as
the only reason I became a transplant surgeon was to

help people like my mother who couldn't access services in time.'

'Why did you become a heart-lung transplant surgeon?' she asked. 'I thought you were planning on specialising in renal surgery?'

'I had a great mentor in the States,' he said. 'He encouraged me to choose the heart-lung route. He thought my skills were more appropriate for heart-lung transplants. It's more challenging surgery. You need nerves of steel. You need to be able to maintain control under impossible circumstances. You have to be able to switch off your feelings and concentrate on the mechanics of the operation. Not everyone can do it.'

'What if there was a fund to help country people?' she asked.

'There isn't one,' Sam said. 'Bush people mortgage their homes and sell off all their assets to access what city folk take for granted. The expenses are crippling. It's not the medical bills so much but the travel and accommodation. Patients can spend months going back and forth over long distances. It's not within most people's budgets to do that.'

'What if I raised some money for a fund for exactly that purpose?' Lexi asked.

Sam brushed her soft mouth with his thumb. 'Haven't you got enough on your plate already with raising funds for the unit?'

'I can do both,' she said. 'I've already been thinking about raising the funds to buy a house for relatives to stay in, similar to what the children's hospital has. Instead of a fast-food chain funding it, we can do it with charitable donations.'

Sam stroked a finger down the curve of her cheek. 'If

you weren't working for the hospital as Head of Events, what else would you be doing?' he asked.

She lowered her gaze, her fingers toying with the collar of his open-necked shirt. 'I'm not sure…'

'You must have some idea,' he said. 'What did you want to be when you were a little girl?'

A faraway look came into her eyes as she looked past his left shoulder. 'I wanted to be a ballerina,' she said. 'I wanted to dance on the world's stage. I used to practise in front of my mother's cheval mirror. I dreamed of wearing a sparkling tutu. I dreamed of dancing at a Royal performance. I pretended I was Cinderella…' Her voice trailed away and her shoulders dropped.

'So what happened?'

She let out a sigh and went back to playing with the buttons on his shirt. 'My feet got sore.'

Sam lifted her chin. 'If that was the case there would be no ballerinas in the world.'

She looked at him with sad blue eyes. 'I couldn't do that to Bella,' she said. 'She used to look at me so wistfully when I got taken to my ballet class by our nanny. She would sit on the sidelines and watch with those sad grey eyes of hers. She didn't do it intentionally. She's not like that. But I felt so guilty. I had to stop. I had to stop a lot of things I loved… It's kind of been the story of my life.'

Sam had heard similar stories throughout his professional life but none had touched him more than Lexi's. She had given up so much to protect her sister. Did anyone realise how much she had sacrificed?

Her father?

Her mother?

Her older sister Evie?

Even Sam hadn't properly understood until now.

There was probably a litany of things she had sacrificed in her effort to protect Bella from feeling inadequate. 'You're a very sweet person, Lexi,' he said. 'But why do you always hide behind that I-don't-give-a-damn-what-you-think facade?'

'Because sometimes it's easier to pretend I don't care,' she said. 'I've got used to putting my feelings to one side.' She gave him a little twisted smile. 'Maybe I'm like you in that regard. I can switch off my feelings when it suits me.'

Sam felt like he had just been hoisted with his own petard. 'It's not always as easy as I make it look,' he said, frowning at her.

'What are you saying, Sam?' she asked with an arch of a slim brow. 'That you sometimes feel more than you let on?'

He held her ocean-blue gaze, determined to outstare her. 'I can't give you what you want,' he said. 'I'm not the right person for you. I've never been the right person.'

She got up and moved a few feet away, finally turning to stand and look at him from the mast, her expression cool and distant. 'Are you the right person for anyone?' she asked.

Sam looked out over the crinkled sea gilded by the silvery moon that had come up. 'When my mother died my father never really got over the loss. I know for a fact he blames himself. They didn't have the money to send her to the city for help. For the last twenty years he's lived like a hermit. I don't think he's ever looked at another woman. Can you imagine that? Twenty years he's lived like a monk because he can't bear the thought of replacing my mother.'

'He must have loved her very much,' Lexi said softly.

Sam let out a hissing breath. 'That's exactly my point,' he said. 'He loved her too much. She wouldn't have wanted him to waste his life like that. She would've wanted him to move on, to find someone else to build a future with, maybe even have another child or two, someone who could take on the farm since I had other plans.'

'Maybe there is no one else who can take your mother's place,' Lexi said. 'Maybe your father has always known that in his heart. Maybe he's perfectly happy living with his memories of their time together.'

Sam frowned at her darkly. 'He should've moved on by now.'

'Why should he?' she asked. 'Is it so hard for you to realise that his love for your mother was enough to satisfy him for a lifetime?'

'I can't imagine loving someone like that,' he said almost savagely. 'It's not what I want for myself.'

'I feel sorry for you, Sam,' Lexi said. 'You've closed yourself off in case you get hurt. But life is all about being hurt. It's not something we can control. There's no switch we can turn off to stop us feeling the pain of losing someone, of loving someone so much we don't feel we can go on without them. We grieve because we love. We might as well be dead if we didn't feel something. It's what makes us all human.'

Sam looked at her standing there, the angles and contours of her beautiful face cast in an ethereal glow by the moonlight. She looked like a mermaid that had come up from the depths of the sea. Her long hair had worked itself loose from the knot she had restrained it in earlier. It was lying about her shoulders and down her back in a silky tangle that his fingers itched to run through. 'Do you love your fiancé like that?' he asked, hating himself for asking it, hating himself even more for wanting to know.

Her eyes moved away from his. She stood stiffly, her gaze on the dark endless sea that moved like a ripple of silk under the caress of the light late-night breeze. 'What I feel for Matthew is nothing to do with you,' she said.

'So you're still going to marry him.'

'Is that a question or a statement?' she asked as she turned and met his gaze, hers diamond-sharp.

'Which would you answer with the truth?' he asked.

She turned away from him to look back to the wrinkled black blanket of the ocean. 'I don't have to tell you anything,' she said. 'I'm just here for now. That's what you want, isn't it? Something casual and temporary. No strings. No feelings. Just a physical connection you could get with anybody.'

'Not just anybody,' he said, coming up behind her to cup her upper arms with his hands. 'It doesn't feel quite like this with anyone else.'

Lexi closed her eyes as she felt his body brush against hers from behind. His mouth was already at her ear lobe, his teeth tugging at her in playful little bites that sent arrows of delight down her spine. He lifted her hair off the nape of her neck and kissed her there in soft movements of his lips against her super-sensitive skin. She shivered in delight, her whole body alert to the proud jut of his erection pressing against her bottom. She leaned back into him, her head lolling to one side as he worked his magical mouth on her neck.

Did he mean it?

Was *she* the only one who made him feel like this?

Lexi didn't know for sure but when she turned in his embrace and offered her mouth to his, she knew with absolute certainty that she would treasure every moment of this weekend with him, for she suspected these memories would be all she would have of him once it was over.

The rest of the time out on the water with Sam was like a fantasy come to life. Sleeping in Sam's arms at night to the gentle rocking of the yacht was like a dream come true. Waking to his caresses, to the hot urgency of his mouth and hands and surging male body had made her soar to the heights of human pleasure.

Watching the sun come up together made her feel close to Sam in a way she had not felt before. She had never seen him in such a relaxed and playful mood. It was as if he was determined to make this short time together as pleasurable for her as possible. There was no further mention of the past or her engagement. It was a no-go area they had seemed to reach by tacit agreement. Lexi was relieved for she knew she had some hard thinking to do in the days ahead, but for now she was content to treasure every precious second with him.

When the wind came up Sam taught her how to sail, showing her how to go about by ducking under the boom and reeling in the ropes. It was an exhilarating experience and one she knew she would never forget. They had a picnic on an isolated beach that Lexi hadn't even known existed. They swam, but not for long as the water hadn't yet warmed up enough to be comfortable, but Lexi soon grew warm again when Sam enveloped her in his arms and made love to her on the sand.

But eventually the weekend drew to a close. It had to.

Sam's relaxed mood seemed to dissipate the closer they got to the marina on Sunday afternoon. His features took on a cast of stone and when he smiled at something she said it didn't reach his eyes.

Lexi watched as he steered the yacht back into its mooring position. Once it was secured and locked up he helped her step onto the marina walkway and carried her bags of shopping for her. They got to the end of the walkway and an awkward silence fell.

'I'll give you a lift home,' Sam said, not looking at her.

'No… Thanks anyway but I'd better make my own way back,' Lexi said.

Another painful silence passed.

'I guess I'll see you at the hospital,' Sam said, his expression still inscrutable.

'Guess so,' Lexi said, forcing brightness into her tone. 'And the ball. I can't believe it's next weekend. Have you got a mask to wear?'

'I'm working on it.'

Lexi shifted her weight from foot to foot. 'I had a great time,' she said, looking up at him. 'Thanks for… for everything…'

'Pleasure.'

Well, there had certainly been plenty of that, Lexi thought. Her body was still tingling inside and out.

She started to walk away but Sam suddenly snagged one of her wrists and turned her back to face him. She looked into his unfathomable dark brown eyes and felt her heart trip. 'I want to see you again,' he said, the words low and deep as if they had been sourced from somewhere deep inside him.

Lexi moistened her suddenly dry lips. 'Sam… This is not exactly easy for me…'

A flinty look came into his eyes. 'What's not easy?'

he asked. 'Hasn't the last day and a half proved any-thing to you?'

Lexi drew in an uneven breath, hope flickering in-side her chest like a tiny candle flame in a stiff breeze. 'I'm not quite sure what it is you're offering…'

'You know damn well what I'm offering,' he said. 'I'm offering you the most passionate, pleasurable ex-perience of your life.'

'An affair.' It wasn't a question or a statement but an expression of heart-wrenching disappointment. Pain hurtled through her like a cannonball, knocking over all her hopes and dreams like ninepins. He didn't want her for ever. He never had. But in spite of the roaring passion that existed between them it still worried her to think he only wanted her now because someone else had already staked a claim.

'I've always been clear on what I can and can't give you, Lexi,' he said. 'I haven't made any false promises to you and I'm not going to make them to you now.'

'I know,' she said on a sigh that prickled her chest. 'I know…'

He brushed her cheek with the back of his bent knuckles, his eyes gentle and warm as they meshed with hers. 'If ever you need a hideaway I'll keep that cupboard empty just for you,' he said.

Lexi gave him a bittersweet smile. 'You do that, country boy.' And then she picked up her bags and left to make her way home.

CHAPTER TEN

Finn Kennedy was just about to go home before his throbbing headache turned into a migraine when he got a call from Evie in A and E. He had been having trouble with his arm all day. He had dropped a coffee cup in the doctors' room but thankfully no one had seen it. The pain behind his eyeballs was like dressmaking pins stabbing at him as he tried to concentrate on what Evie was saying.

'We've got a post-op patient of yours in,' she said. 'A Mr Ian Reid with a swelling in his groin. You did a heart-valve op on him eight days ago. He's in pain and the swelling's getting bigger. I think you need to see him.'

Finn rubbed at his aching temple for a moment. The last thing he wanted to do was head into Theatre feeling the way he did just now. What if his arm let him down at a crucial moment? Dropping a coffee cup was one thing, severing an artery was another. 'I'll be down to see him in a few minutes,' he said. 'I have a patient in ICU I have to check on first.'

'We're pretty busy down here,' Evie said. 'The ambos have rung ahead about a stabbing coming in any minute.'

Finn ground his teeth. 'I said I'd be down there, Evie. Just give me five minutes, OK?'

The phone slammed down in his ear.

Finn walked into the cubicle where Ian Reid was propped up in bed, having just finished a sandwich and a cup of tea. A young nurse, Kate Henderson, was just about to clear the tray away.

'Would you like another drink, Mr Reid?' Kate asked.

Finn glared at the nurse as he indicated for her to leave the cubicle to speak to him away from the patient. 'How could you be so stupid as to have fed this patient?' he roared. 'What the hell are you thinking? He's come in with an obvious hematoma over his femoral puncture site, he's obviously still bleeding, he obviously needs emergency surgery, and you're serving him high tea, for God's sake!'

Kate blushed to the roots of her hair and her chin started to wobble uncontrollably. 'But he was hungry, Dr Kennedy. I didn't know he was going to Theatre.'

'Didn't Dr Lockheart inform you of his condition?' Finn asked, frowning furiously.

'Um…she mentioned to make him comfortable until you arrived,' Kate said.

'Comfortable?' Finn said with a sneer. 'Well, he's not going to be very comfortable if he vomits when he's anesthetised, aspirates and ends up on a ventilator in Intensive Care, is he?'

'But I didn't know he needed Theatre…'

'Well, you damn well should have checked,' Finn said. 'Anyone with any sense and experience could tell he was in dire straits and would've taken the initiative to fast him. What are they teaching you lot at university?'

Kate started to cry, her shoulders shaking as she stood with her head bowed before him.

'Oh, for pity's sake,' Finn said. 'Stop acting like a child and get an orderly down here and have them get this patient up to Theatre before any more harm is done. He'll have to have a crash induction and we'll just have to hope to hell nothing goes wrong before we get this bleeding under control.'

Kate scurried off, still brushing at her eyes as she went.

Evie frowned and followed Finn into the office, closing the door for privacy. 'What was that all about?' she asked.

Finn began writing up his patient notes and didn't even acknowledge her with a look. 'What was what all about?' he asked.

Evie ground her teeth as she took in his devil-may-care demeanour. 'You had no right to speak to that young nurse like that,' she said. 'This is only her second day in the department. She's still finding her feet.'

Finn scrawled his signature on the foot of the page before he cut his hard, ice-blue gaze to hers. 'She can find her feet somewhere else,' he said. 'I haven't got time to babysit silly little schoolgirls.'

'That's hardly fair, Finn, you know how hard it is for the new graduates these days,' Evie said. 'They don't have a lot of on-the-ground experience when they come to us.'

Finn gave her a hard look. 'Then you should be watching for slip-ups like this. It's my name that will be dragged through the courts on a malpractice suit if something goes wrong. What the hell are you doing down here? Running a bloody crèche?'

Evie flattened her mouth in annoyance. 'You really get off on intimidating everyone, don't you?' she asked.

He eyeballed her for so long the air almost started to pulse with tension. 'You want to pick a fight, princess?' he asked. 'Just keep going the way you are.'

She stood her ground, even though her stomach gave a funny little wobble as his ice-pick gaze pinned hers. 'Why do you do it, Finn? Why are you so determined to alienate everyone?'

His eyes were like stone as they held hers, his jaw just as unmalleable. 'I'm not here to win a popularity contest.'

'Maybe not,' she said. 'But it doesn't mean you can't demonstrate a bit of emotional intelligence from time to time, especially with younger members of staff. You're meant to be a role model. Monkey see, monkey do, re-member?'

'Leave it, Evie,' he said, tossing the file on the desk with an impatient flick of his hand, his forehead criss-crossed with a brooding frown.

'No, I will not leave it, Finn,' she said. 'You can't come into my department and throw your weight around, or at least not on my watch.'

His lip curled upwards in a smirk as he stepped to-wards her. 'Your watch?' he asked. 'Since when have you been appointed Department Head?'

Evie was the only thing between him and the door and she was determined not to move until she had said her piece. But it was hard work staring him down when he was so big and so threatening and so very close. She could feel the heat coming off his body. She could smell his scent: one part aftershave and three parts potent, hard-working male. She could feel herself responding to his nearness. She could feel her skin prickling as he sent his gaze on an indolent perusal of her body. Those Antarctic, unreachable, unreadable eyes seemed to be slowly but surely stripping her of every stitch of clothing, leaving spot fires burning in their wake. 'I might not be a head of department but I'm responsible for the staff who work with me,' she said, trying to keep her voice steady. 'It's about being a team. We're meant to be working together, not against one another.'

Finn's hooded gaze burned into hers. 'You want to get out of my way, princess?'

Evie felt a warning shiver scurry down her spine like a small furry animal but she still didn't budge. A perverse desire to get under his skin kept egging her on. 'What are you going to do, Finn?' she asked. 'Throw me over your shoulder, caveman style?'

His eyes gleamed menacingly and she felt his warm breath skate over her uptilted face. 'Now, that sounds like a plan,' he said, planting a hand either side of her head, trapping her within the cage of his strong arms.

Evie sucked in a quick little breath that felt like it had tiny rose thorns attached as he moved just that little bit closer. His hard, muscular chest brushed against the swell of her breasts and his belt buckle poked her in the belly, an erotic hint of what would happen if she allowed him any nearer. Her body flared with heat at his disturbing proximity, her skin tingling with awareness, her scalp prickling all over. His eyes were a deep and dangerous blue sea of male desire as they held hers. Her heart started to flap at the wall of her chest like a shredded truck tyre against bitumen. And her mouth went totally dry as his loomed inexorably closer...

A rumble of voices in the background suddenly lifted Finn's head. 'Might want to open that door, Evie,' he drawled mockingly as he stepped back from her. 'Your *team* might be wondering what's keeping you from doing your job.'

Evie moved aside to let him pass, her heart still flip-flopping against her ribcage as she sent him a contentious glare. 'Go to hell, Finn.'

He flicked her cheek with a lazy finger on the way past. 'Been there, done that and thrown away the T-shirt long, long ago,' he said, and then he left.

'What's been eating at Finn Kennedy lately?' Julie, one of the nurses on duty, asked Evie a little while later as they were clearing up a cubicle after a patient had been transferred to ICU. 'He's been wandering around like a bear with a sore head.'

Evie peeled off her gloves and tossed them in the bin. 'I have no idea,' she said. 'He's always been a law unto himself.'

A head popped through the curtains from the next cubicle. It was one of the other nurses who had worked with Finn earlier. 'That's because he *has* got a sore head,' she said. 'I saw him pop a couple of paracetamol before he left. Mind you, who wouldn't get a headache working here? Patients are lined up three deep in the waiting room and there are no beds.'

Evie frowned. 'Finn had a headache?'

The nurse nodded. 'He saw me looking at him while he was getting the painkillers and said he was fighting a migraine.'

Evie let out a breath and sank her teeth into her bottom lip. 'He should have said something…'

Julie gave a snort as she bundled up the linen in her arms. 'Yeah, right, that sounds like something Finn Kennedy would do.'

Evie took off her stethoscope and ran the rubber tubing through her fingers. Finn had seemed particularly snarly this evening. And she had gone at him all guns blazing. If he was struggling with a migraine it was no wonder he had lost his temper with the junior nurse. And he'd had to take Mr Reid to Theatre. It would have been a nightmare for him if he hadn't been feeling well.

She glanced at her watch. Her shift was nearly over. It was late but not too late to deliver an apology in person.

Finn's penthouse apartment light was on. Evie had checked before she had knocked on the door but it seemed a decade or two before he answered.

The door swung open and he scowled down at her. 'What do you want?'

'How's your headache?' she asked.

His frown deepened. 'What headache?'

'The headache that made you act like an absolute boor in A and E earlier this evening,' she said.

His hand fell away from the door and tunnelled through his hair. 'It's fine,' he said in a gruff tone. 'I've taken something for it. It's almost gone.'

Evie sidled past him in the doorway.

'What are you doing?' he asked, shooting her a glare.

'I've come to apologise.'

'For what?'

'For laying into you the way I did,' she said. 'I didn't realise you were ill.'

His brows snapped together. 'I'm not ill.'

'You have a headache.'

'So?'

'Doesn't that qualify as being ill?'

'Not if it doesn't interfere with my work,' he said.

'But it does interfere with your work,' she argued. 'The way you spoke to that poor girl was—'

He opened the door and jerked his head for her to leave. 'Don't let me keep you.'

Evie ignored the open door. 'Have you had migraines before?' she asked.

'Go home, Evie,' he said grimly. 'I don't need a diagnosis. I had a tension headache. I get them occasionally. Everyone does. Now leave.'

'There have been a number of times at work when I've seen you struggling with your co-ordination,' she said. 'I've seen you drop things. And that facial stitching you abandoned that time? It was like you couldn't get your fingers to work. Now you're having migraines. Have you thought of having some scans done to rule out anything sinister?'

Finn let out an impatient curse. 'I haven't got a brain tumour,' he said. 'I haven't got anything. Now get out of here before I lose my temper.'

Evie moved even further into his apartment, trailing her fingers over the leather sofa as she walked by to look out of the bank of windows overlooking the harbour. She affected an air of calm she was nowhere near feeling. Finn was intimidating at the best of times, but in this mood he was lethal. He reminded her of an alpha wolf who had taken himself away to lick his wounds without the cynosure of critical eyes. The thing she had to establish was if the wound he was hiding was self-inflicted. That was the one question she dreaded asking but ask it she must.

'What the hell do you think you're doing?' Finn asked.

Evie turned and looked at him, taking a deep breath

before she asked, 'Is it alcohol? Have you got a hang-over?'

His expression became thunderous. 'What are you implying?' he asked.

Evie rolled her lips together for a moment. 'You know what people are like, Finn,' she said. 'They talk, gossip, spread rumours.'

'Then they can bloody well talk,' he said. 'I don't drink on the job. Never have, never will.'

'I want to believe you but—'

'I don't give a rat's backside if you believe me or not,' he shot back. 'Now, I'm going to say this one more time. Leave.'

Evie folded her arms and eyeballed him. 'Aren't you going to offer me a cup of coffee or something?'

His face was a blank canvas. 'No.'

'You don't give a damn about anyone, do you?' she asked.

'Not particularly.'

'I'm trying to understand you,' she said, her voice rising in frustration. 'But you're so damned obstruc-tive. Why can't you at least meet me halfway?'

Finn shut the door with a definitive click; the gun-shot sound of it making Evie flinch. She drew in an uneven breath as he sauntered over to where she was standing, his long legs eating up the distance in a mat-ter of strides.

His features were harsh as he looked down at her, his cold, unfathomable eyes nailing hers. 'What is it you really want, Evie?' he asked. 'A cosy chat over coffee or a quick tumble in the sack to let off some steam?'

Evie felt her face flash with heat. 'You think I came here to sleep with you?' she asked.

'Yeah, that's what I think.' His eyes flicked to her

mouth before coming back to mesh with hers, challenging her, provoking her, *arousing* her.

She straightened her spine and sent him a withering look. 'Strange as it may seem, Finn, I don't want to dive headfirst into your bed,' she said. 'Call me picky but I don't care for where you've been just lately.'

He gave her a devilish smile as he stepped into her body space. She tried to move away but the sofa was in the way. He captured some strands of her hair and looped them around his fingertip, a disturbingly intimate tether that sent her heart into an erratic rhythm. 'Liar,' he said. 'We both know why you're here, princess. You want me to finish what I started back in the office.'

Evie ran her tongue out over the chalk-dry surface of her lips. 'Y-you're totally wrong,' she said in a husky whisper that didn't really help her denial one little bit. 'I just wanted to check that you were all right. I was concerned about you.'

He fisted some of her hair in his hands; the tugging should have been painful but instead it was intensely erotic against her scalp. His eyes dipped to her mouth, lingering there for a heart-stopping moment before he came back to her gaze. 'Keep your concern for someone who wants it,' he said. 'I have no need or desire to be taken care of and certainly not by you.'

'Why must you block anyone getting close to you?' Evie asked.

His fist tightened on her hair, making her toes curl inside her shoes. His eyes blazed with heat as they bored into hers. 'I'm not blocking you now, princess,' he drawled. 'You can get as close to me as you want. I won't stop you.'

Evie snatched in a prickly breath. 'I'm not talking about physical closeness.'

He bent his head to her neck, his lips nibbling on her skin in a teasing caress that sent a shiver down the length of her spine. 'It's the only type of closeness I want,' he said. 'And you want it too, don't you, Evie, hmm?'

Evie wished she could deny it but her legs were already folding beneath her as his tongue moved across her lower jaw, making every nerve spring to attention. She tilted her head to one side to give him better access, her eyes closing as ripples of pleasure flowed through her body. He got closer and closer to her mouth without actually touching her lips. It was a torturous assault on her senses. She felt her lips buzzing with need as he advanced and retreated, again and again and again, until with a little whimper of desperation she finally took matters into her own hands and pressed her mouth to his.

Fireworks went off in her body as he took control of the kiss. His lips moved against hers with bruising pressure, his tongue not asking for entry but taking it in one savage thrust that lifted every hair on her head, including the ones he still had fisted in his hand.

He turned her in one deft movement and began walking her backwards to the nearest wall, his muscled thighs moving against hers in a commanding and totally provocative manner. She felt the surge of his erection against her belly as her back hit the wall, the rock-hard length of him pulsing with the drumbeats of raw, primal, male need. Her body was aflame, her feminine core already seeping with the dew of her longing. It was a raging fever in her blood, a full-throttle rush of sexual need on a scale she had never felt before. She felt wanton and wild with his mouth crushing hers. She gave another whimper as his mouth ground against hers with savage intent, his tongue demanding hers submit to his. She fought him every step of the way for supremacy. She used her teeth, small nippy bites and harder ones, but he refused to allow her control.

'Damn you,' he growled against her mouth as he tugged at her top to uncover her breasts. 'Damn you to hell.'

'Damn you right back,' she said as she held her arms up over her head so he could remove her top with a reckless abandon she suspected she might regret later when common sense returned.

He kicked the top away with his foot as his mouth ground against hers, his hands roughly caressing her breasts through the lace of her bra. It was exhilarating to feel his warm hands on her but she wanted more. She wanted to feel him skin on skin. She wanted no barriers between them.

Evie put her hands behind her back to unhook her bra, letting it drop to the floor at her feet. Finn murmured with approval and left her mouth to suck savagely on her right breast. She gasped out loud at the impact of his hot mouth on her puckered flesh. He swirled his tongue round her nipple, his teeth nipping at her, tugging, pulling and teasing in a cycle of pleasure and pain that had her totally at his mercy. His mouth was ruthless, hot and insistent, determined and dangerous as it toyed with her sensitive flesh.

She didn't waste time on his shirt; instead her hands went straight to the waistband of his trousers, fumbling over the fastening in her desperate haste to feel him under her fingertips. He was so hard it made her insides quiver in a combination of anticipation and trepidation.

She could feel the pulsing heart of him pressing against the restraint of the fabric of his underwear as she undid his zipper.

A hot burst enflamed her insides as she finally uncovered him. The arrantly male jut of his body was smooth as satin but as hard as steel. Her hand moved up and down his length, slowly at first, exploring him, delighting in how aroused he was.

He gave a guttural groan and wrenched her hand away, pushing her almost roughly back against the wall as he lifted her skirt, his fingers pushing aside her knickers to slip with devastating thoroughness into the hot, wet heart of her.

Evie arched up in aching need to feel more, to have more of him, to have all of him. She could feel the tension building inside her, the dizzying rush of her blood, the emptying of her brain but for the fiery sensations coursing through her.

His mouth came back to hers in a hard kiss that had an undertow of desperation in it. His tongue duelled with hers in an erotic mimic of how he wanted to possess her. Her body thrilled at the sensual promise, the inner walls of her core pulsing with the need to feel him moving inside her. Every nerve in her body was screaming for more. For more of his touch, for more of his branding kisses, for the release she wanted more than her next breath.

He made another rough male sound deep in his throat as she moved urgently against him. He hoisted one of her legs around his waist, positioning himself before driving so deeply into her silky warmth her head banged against the wall.

Her gasp was swallowed by his mouth as it plundered hers. The friction of his body within hers sent shockwaves of delight through her. She felt pleasure in every part of her from her curling toes to her prickling scalp where one of his hands had locked onto her hair to anchor himself.

It was a rough coupling, a desperate, urgent mating that bordered on animalistic. He thrust deeper and deeper, and harder and harder, his breath a hot gust near her ear as he laboured over her.

Evie felt the first faint flutters of orgasm, the tiny ripples that rolled through her, gathering speed with each pounding movement of his body within hers. She felt her body chase the delicious feeling, all her intimate muscles tensing for the freefall into ecstasy.

Suddenly it consumed her.

It picked her up like a giant wave and thrashed her about before spitting her out the other side, spent and limbless.

She was so sensitised she felt every pulsing moment of Finn's release. She felt the way his body tensed all over before that final explosive plunge into his own paradise. Her inner core felt each and every aftershock and her mouth accepted each and every earthy gasp from his.

Evie felt him slump against her, his head buried against her neck, his breathing ragged and uneven. Her hands slipped under the loose tails of his shirt, her fingertips memorising every knob of his vertebrae. He flinched as she touched him between his shoulder blades so she backed off. But then she felt the puckered flesh of the scar he had sustained during combat and her fingers stalled…

As if he sensed her hesitation he pulled back from her, his expression shuttered as he refastened his trousers. 'You should have gone home when I told you to,' he said.

'I don't like being told what to do,' she said. 'You should know that by now.'

'Here,' he said, tossing her bra and top at her. 'Get dressed.'

Her heart sank. But what had she expected? Evie considered defying him but decided against it. Somehow having a discussion with her topless and him fully clothed didn't really appeal. Once she was decent she turned and searched his features. Was he really so cold he could push her out the door as if nothing had happened between them just now? It might have been rough sex. It might have been rushed and raw and performed with most of their clothes still on, but it had been the best sex she'd ever had. For a brief moment she had felt a connection with him that had superseded the mere physical. She had felt his vulnerability in their passionate embrace, the way he had lost himself in her body as if she was the only one who could reach inside him and soothe and comfort the dark bleakness of his soul.

'Let me see it,' she said softly. 'Let me see your scar.'

He scowled at her menacingly. 'I'm not a freak show, Evie. You got what you came for, now get the hell out of here.'

Evie dug her heels in. Any reaction from him was better than no reaction. Red-hot anger was better than chilly indifference. 'You got that when your brother was killed, didn't you?' she asked. 'You were almost killed as well.'

His jaw clicked as he ground his teeth. 'Get out.'

'You feel guilty that he died instead of you,' she went on. 'That's why you punish yourself by working such crazy hours. You close yourself off from everyone because you don't believe you deserve to be happy because you lived and he didn't.'

She saw his hands clench into fists and a vein bulge in his neck. His eyes were blue chips of ice, hard and unyielding, distant, closed off, angry. 'Get out before I throw you out,' he ground out.

Evie raised her chin. 'I think you care about people way more than you let on,' she said. 'Take me, for instance.'

His lip curled mockingly. 'I just did.'

A dagger pierced her heart but she went on regardless. 'You hate yourself for needing anyone. You keep everything and everyone on a clinical basis. We just had amazing sex and yet you just trivialised it as if it meant nothing. You cheapened it as if I was just another girl you picked up at a bar. But I'm not just another one-night stand. I'm someone who cares about you. Don't ask me why but I do.'

He gave her a flinty look. 'Are you done?'

Evie let out a breath. 'You don't believe me, do you? You don't believe anyone can care about you. Why do you believe that? Why do you think you're so unworthy of love?'

'Love?' He spat the word out as if it was acid. 'Is that how you have to justify what we just did? You're using the wrong four-letter word, princess. What we just did was have a good old fashioned—'

Evie closed her eyes as if that would stop her hearing the coarse word, but of course it didn't. She opened them again to see him looking at her with that same mocking expression. She felt hurt beyond description. She was nothing to him other than a sexual outlet, one of many he had used. Their intimacy hadn't touched him at all. She had imagined it. Her overwhelming attraction to him had distorted her judgement. She felt used, cheap, like a piece of trash he no longer had any use for. 'You really are a piece of work, aren't you, Finn?' she said with an embittered look.

He leaned indolently against the sofa, his eyes running over her lasciviously, smoulderingly. 'You ever feel that itch again, princess, just knock on my door and I'll gladly be of service,' he said.

She turned for the door, wrenching it open before she threw him a glittering look over her shoulder. 'Don't hold your breath,' she said, slamming the door behind her.

Finn pushed himself away from the sofa, cursing. He had just broken his own code with Evie. Evie, of all people! He should have known she wasn't the type of woman to play by his rules. It would never be just sex with Evie Lockheart. She pushed against his boundaries in a hundred different ways with her concerned looks and soft voice and those velvet hands touching him as if he was the most fascinating specimen of manhood. For a moment there he had lost himself in her.

Totally lost himself.

Felt things that he had no right to be feeling.

He didn't do feelings.

He didn't do emotional connection.

He didn't want to feel anything for her. And he certainly didn't want her feeling anything for him. But the sex had been mind-blowing, even if it had lacked finesse. All he had wanted to do was bury himself in her and forget about everything except the way his body felt gripped tightly by hers.

And it had felt incredible.

She had met him physically in a way he had not expected. Her body had been so responsive to his. He had felt every silky ripple of her skin, every tight spasm of her orgasm, every breathless gasp of her breath into his mouth as he'd driven them both into oblivion.

It had been much more than a meeting of bodies in the primal act of mating. He had felt the stirrings of a much deeper bonding that had terrified him. Evie had revealed her vulnerable side, citing feelings for him he had never asked for, never sought, and secretly dreaded.

He had a feeling she could see inside him, the *real* inside—the inside where the ragged edges of his soul barely held him together any more. His emotional centre had been bludgeoned in childhood and then obliterated completely the day Isaac had died.

He was dead inside, dead emotionally. But Evie with her soft hazel eyes kept stroking at the cold heart of him with her looks of concern and her questions about his health. It was as if she was determined to perform cardiac massage on his lifeless soul.

Allowing someone, *anyone*, into the locked and bolted heart of him was unthinkable. He never wanted to feel anything for anyone again. He didn't want anyone to feel anything for him either because he was sure he would only let them down just as he had his brother.

He was used to being alone.

It was the only place where he truly felt safe.

CHAPTER ELEVEN

'You won't believe the juicy piece of gossip I heard on the weekend,' Lexi's assistant Jane said as soon as Lexi came in on Monday morning.

Lexi kept her expression blank but her heart gave a little stumble of panic. 'Oh?' she said offhandedly as she leafed through some donation slips.

'Your sister and Finn Kennedy had a blazing row in A and E,' Jane said. 'They tore strips off each other.'

'So?' Lexi said, privately releasing a sigh of relief the gossip hadn't been about her and Sam. 'It's not the first time they've locked heads and it probably won't be the last.'

'Yes, but that's not all,' Jane said. 'Finn had her backed up against the door in the office and it looked like he was about to kiss her. It was only because one of the staff came past that he didn't.'

'I still don't think that means they're an item,' Lexi said.

Jane leaned forward conspiratorially. 'Not only that. Evie went to his apartment later that night. One of the nurses who lives in the same block saw her.'

Lexi put the donation slips down and gave Jane a look of reproach. 'That doesn't mean anything. She might've gone there to talk about a patient or something, or maybe she went there to try and smooth things over.'

'Can't have worked 'cause they're still at logger-heads,' Jane said. 'Everyone's talking about it. Mind you, I can see what she sees in him. He's seriously gorgeous with that sexy stubble and that haven't-slept-properly-in-weeks look. What woman wouldn't want to jump into bed with him?'

Lexi had her own complicated love life to deal with without getting embroiled in her sister's, but when she happened to run into Evie in one of the staffroom bathrooms a couple of days later it was obvious Evie had something on her mind.

'Lexi, I want a word with you,' Evie said, blocking the main door with her body so no one could disturb them.

'Sure,' Lexi said. 'What's up?'

Evie narrowed her eyes at her. 'What the hell are you up to with Sam Bailey?'

Lexi felt her chest freeze in mid-inhalation. 'I'm not sure what you mean.'

'You don't?' Evie said with a raised brow. 'Well, how about I spell it out for you? I was on late shift last night with an intern who happened to be working on his father's boat at the weekend. He said he saw you getting on Sam's boat on Saturday afternoon. He also said he saw you leaving it the following evening.'

Lexi chewed at the inside of her bottom lip. 'I know it looks bad…'

'Bad?' Evie's tone was incredulous. 'Do you realise what'll happen if this does the rounds of the hospital? You're putting everything in jeopardy. Your engagement, your work for the transplant unit, not to mention Sam's reputation. Do you realise that?'

'What about you?' Lexi said, going on the defensive. 'Everyone is talking about you going to Finn's apartment late at night. Do you want to tell me what time you left or is that no one's business but your own?'

Evie's mouth flattened. 'At least I'm not supposed to be marrying another man next month. You can't have it both ways, Lexi. You have to make up your mind. Matthew doesn't deserve this.'

'I know, I know, but I'm so confused,' Lexi said, fighting tears. 'I can't get a call through to him to even talk to him. What am I supposed to do? Send him an email or a text and tell him I'm in love with someone else?'

Evie's shoulders dropped as she let out a sigh. 'God, I didn't realise things were that bad,' she said. 'You really love him…Sam, I mean?'

Lexi nodded miserably.

'And what does Sam feel?' Evie asked. 'Does he love you?'

'No…' Lexi's chin wobbled. 'He's never loved me.'

Evie let out another sigh and reached for Lexi, hugging her tightly. 'Then you've got yourself one hell of a problem, hon,' she said.

'Tell me about it,' Lexi said, and burst into tears.

The night of the ball finally arrived. The marquee at the front of the hospital looked spectacular. Starched white linen tablecloths adorned each table set with gleaming silverware and crystal glasses. Black and gold satin ribbons festooned the chairs and crystal candelabra centrepieces gave each table an old-world charm.

The press had arrived to document the event, cameras flashing everywhere just like at a Hollywood premier as the guests walked up the red carpet accompanied by the beautiful music of a string quartet.

The men were dressed in black tie suits, the women

in gorgeous evening gowns, and almost everyone had entered into the spirit of the occasion by donning a mask.

Lexi was wearing a backless silver satin gown, nipped in at the waist and floating to the floor in a small but elegant train. She had chosen a Venetian mask, which covered most of her face, and her hair she'd had professionally styled in a glamorous pile on top of her head.

Evie had arrived and had spoken briefly to Lexi but she seemed to be doing her best to avoid Finn, who looked particularly dashing in a mask that only revealed his piercing ice-blue eyes.

Lexi knew the exact moment when Sam arrived. The fine hairs on the back of her neck lifted and she swung her eyes to the entrance of the marquee where she found him looking straight at her. The slow burn of his gaze made her feel as if he was seeing right through her evening gown to the tiny strip of lace that was her only item of underwear.

He looked magnificent in a black tuxedo, and the black highwayman's mask he was wearing gave him a devilishly sexy look that made a hot flood of desire rush over the floor of her stomach and flow tantalisingly between her thighs.

He looked away to respond to another guest who had spoken to him, and Lexi took a much-needed sip of her champagne to settle her nerves.

Other guests came in and drinks and canapés were served. Some masks had to be removed for guests to eat and drink, but they were still a great ice-breaker and everyone seemed to be having fun as they perused the silent-auction items set up along one wall of the marquee.

The evening progressed with a fork-food buffet dinner, which Lexi had specifically organised so people could mingle rather than be stuck at one table. The dancing had already started and the music was up-beat and got even the most determined wallflowers up on their feet. Lexi could see Sam dancing with Suzy Carpenter, one of the nurses with a reputation for sleeping around. Lexi wondered if Sam would be one of Suzy's conquests by the time the night was over. It certainly looked like that was Suzy's goal if the way she was draping herself all over him was any indication, Lexi thought, turning away in disgust.

Lexi had so far been too busy seeing that everything ran smoothly to get on the dance floor herself, but then she heard the band strike up the opening bars of the song that had been her first dance with Sam on the night they had met five years ago. A rush of emotion filled her, and she quickly walked out of the marquee, not sure she could bear seeing Sam dance their song with someone else.

She was standing looking at the view of the harbour when she felt someone come up behind her. 'They're playing our song,' Sam said, his broad shoulder brushing hers.

Lexi turned and looked up at him. 'You remembered?'

He held out his arms for her to step into them with a crooked smile on his face. 'How could I forget?'

She stepped into his arms and sighed as her body came up against his. She laid her head on his chest and moved with him as the slow romantic ballad took her back in time. 'I've missed you,' Lexi said. 'I can't stop thinking about the weekend, how wonderful it was.'

Sam rested his chin on the top of her head as the song changed to a poignant minor key. 'I've missed you too,' he said, his legs moving in time with hers.

They danced through another number, a slow waltz

that made Lexi feel like she was floating on air instead of dancing with her feet firmly on the ground. It always felt like that in Sam's arms. Her worries and cares slipped to the back of her mind when his arms held her close against him. She felt protected and safe, his arms like a shield to keep the world and all its disappointments away from her. He might not love her the way she wanted to be loved but she was sure he felt something for her, something more than just transient lust. But would it be enough to sustain a relationship between them? And for how long? A week or two? A month? Three months?

And what was she going to do about Matthew? He had promised to match the funds she raised this evening. How could she tell him she no longer wanted to marry him? How could she reach him before she went any further with Sam?

Lexi felt Sam's lips moving against her hair. 'What are you doing after this is over?' he asked. 'Do you want to come and spend the night with me on my yacht? Tomorrow we could go out on the water. Just the two of us. No interruptions.'

Lexi looked up into his handsome face. 'Sam...'

A frown settled between his brows. 'You haven't told your fiancé yet, have you?'

She lowered her gaze, staring at the bow tie at his neck rather than meet his gaze. 'I have responsibilities, Sam. I've made a commitment to the hospital and I can't just walk away. It's not that simple. People are relying on me.'

Sam's features darkened with cynicism. 'It's about the money, isn't it?' he said. 'You'd do anything for Brentwood's money, wouldn't you? You'd even sell your soul.'

Lexi stepped back and hugged her upper arms against the light chill in the air. 'Sam, you're asking too much and giving too little,' she said. 'You want me to give up my life for you but what are you promising in return?'

His eyes glittered darkly. 'Isn't what we have together enough for now?' he asked.

Lexi opened her mouth to answer when she heard the sound of footsteps and two male voices approaching.

One was her father's.

'I think she went out there,' Richard said. 'She's probably gone off to the kitchen to sort something out with the caterers. She won't be far away. Do you want me to call her on her mobile? I'm pretty sure she has it switched on.'

The other voice was her fiancé's.

'No,' Matthew Brentwood said, anticipation and excitement evident in his voice. 'Don't do that. She has no idea I'm here. She walked past me three times already and didn't recognise me. I want it to be a surprise when I finally take off my mask.'

Lexi looked at Sam in wide-eyed panic. *Matthew was here?* Her heart threatened to beat its way out of her chest. She couldn't breathe. She felt trapped. Claustrophobic. Her stomach was churning. She wasn't prepared. She needed more time. She needed to get her emotions in check.

Sam gave her a look that cut her to ribbons. 'Thank you for the dance,' he said. 'I hope you enjoy the rest of your evening.' And without another word he strode away, not back into the marquee where all the laughter and music and frivolity was happening but into the anonymous darkness of the night.

CHAPTER TWELVE

IT TOOK Lexi over a week to find the courage to tell Matthew their engagement was over. It was the worst feeling in the world to have broken someone's heart, and not just Matthew's heart but his parents' and sisters' too.

After she had said spoken to Matthew she stood outside the Brentwoods' lovely family home, the house she had come to think of as her second home, and knew she would never be back.

It would have been easier if Matthew had been angry at her, furious with her for betraying him. But instead he had just been sad, utterly and indescribably sad. His grey-blue eyes had looked stricken as she had told him she couldn't marry him. He hadn't shouted. He hadn't hurled abuse at her. He hadn't even withdrawn his offer of matching the amount of money she had raised for the transplant unit. He had honoured his promise, which made the breaking of hers that much harder for her to do without feeling appallingly guilty, even though she knew deep in her heart she was doing the right thing.

As soon as Lexi's father found out he told her to pack her bags and leave. He ranted and raved, shouting and swearing, thumping his fists on the table, reminding Lexi of a child having a tantrum because he couldn't have his own way. Unable to bear it any longer, she packed a few things before she made her way to Sam's apartment.

She rang the doorbell but there was no answer. A sickening feeling of déjà vu assailed her. Surely he hadn't left without telling her? But of course not, she reassured herself. He was working at the hospital. He had a two-year contract with an option for five. He was probably on call or something.

Sam wasn't at the hospital either, Susanne, his practice manager, informed her. 'He had a heart-lung transplant this morning,' she said. 'He did his rounds straight after he saw a few patients in the rooms. You might find him down at the marina. He's probably gone out for a quick sail. He should be just about back by now.'

'Thanks, Susanne.' Lexi turned to leave.

'Oh, and, Lexi?' Susanne said.

Lexi turned at the door. 'Yes?'

'I'm sorry to hear about your engagement,' Susanne said. 'I heard about it from one of the staff.'

'Thank you,' Lexi said. 'But I think it's for the best.'

It was almost sundown by the time Lexi got to the marina. Her heart sank when she couldn't see Sam's boat anywhere in sight. Then in the distance she could see his yacht motoring back to the marina. She drank in the sight of him. She hadn't seen him since the night of the ball. He looked so gorgeous standing at the helm of his boat, steering it into its mooring place.

She stood with her bags at her feet, waiting for him, her heart beating hard and fast in excitement and longing.

He looked up and saw her, a frown carving into his forehead when his gaze went to the bags at her feet. Once the boat was tied up securely he jumped down on the marina to face her. 'What are you doing here, Lexi?' he asked, still frowning formidably.

Lexi's stomach did a queasy little turnover. 'I've come to tell you I've called off my engagement,' she said.

'I already heard about that in the doctors' room this morning,' he said, as if it was the most insignificant news, like the current price of milk or bread.

Lexi licked her dry lips. 'I would've liked you to have been the first to know but my father took it upon himself to tell everyone what a disappointment for a daughter I've become because I cancelled my wedding within a couple of weeks of the ceremony.'

'It's your life, not his,' he said, his face set like marble.

Lexi let out a rattling breath. 'Sam? Is everything all right?'

His eyes were blank. 'Sure? Why wouldn't it be?'

She bit her lip. 'I just thought you'd be more…more excited about me ending things with Matthew. I thought you'd be thrilled we can be together now. I'm free, Sam. It can be just you and me. We can be together all the time.'

Sam glanced at her bags before returning his gaze to hers. 'I offered you an affair, not a place to stay,' he said. 'Nothing serious and nothing long term, remember?'

Lexi looked at his mouth speaking those cruel, heartbreaking words and wondered if she had misheard him. She moistened her lips again. 'Sam, I love you. Surely you know that by now? I love you and I want to be with you.'

His jaw was tight, his eyes hard and impenetrable. 'I don't love you, Lexi. I've never loved you. I'm happy to enjoy an affair with you but that's it. Take or leave it.'

Inside Lexi's chest she felt her heart had broken off in a thousand sharp-edged pieces, each one scoring at her lungs every time she took a breath. 'You can't mean that, Sam,' she said, tears building up in her eyes. 'I've given up everything for you. I can't imagine life without you. How can you do this to me?'

Sam's expression was still locked down. 'I haven't done anything to you, Lexi. You've done it to yourself.'

'You asked me to end my engagement!' She didn't care that her voice was shrill.

'I didn't ask you to do any such thing,' he said in a steely voice. 'I just asked you how you could possibly think of marrying a man who didn't satisfy you. You were marrying him for all the wrong reasons. I did not at any point offer to take his place at the altar.'

Lexi swallowed her anguish with an effort. Pride was the only thing she had left and she clung to it with the desperation a drowning person did a life raft. She would have to walk away. She would have to rebuild her life. She would have to learn to be happy without Sam, the only man she had ever loved, the only man she *could* ever love. There would be no happy ending. No marriage and making babies together. It had all been a fantasy that she had mistaken for the real thing. *Again.* Yet again she had been duped by her own foolish, romantic dreams. 'I hope you find what you're looking for, Sam,' she said in a cold, hard voice. 'And then when you find it, I hope it gets snatched away from you and you never get it back.' And then she picked up her bags and walked back up the marina, out of his life for good.

Sam watched her walk away, the words to call her back lodged in the middle of his throat where a choking knot had formed. Seeing Lexi on the wharf with her bags packed, ready to move into his life, had made him panic. But, then, ever since he had heard she had called off her engagement he had felt conflicted. He had felt the same gut-wrenching agitation the night of the ball when he'd heard the sound of her fiancé's voice.

Up until that point Sam had assumed Matthew Brentwood was one of those rich, shallow guys who had plucked the prettiest girl from his social set and got engaged to her because it was the thing to do. But hearing Matthew's excitement at seeing Lexi again had hit Sam in the gut like a wildly flung bowling ball.

The man loved her, *really* loved her.

Sam needed time to think, to process what it meant now Lexi was free. He felt uncomfortable with the prospect of being forever labelled as the man who had come between her and her fiancé, especially when he wasn't sure he could offer her more than a resumption of their affair. He *wanted* to offer more but he didn't know if he was capable of opening up that part of him that had closed down so long ago.

Lexi deserved better than another casual fling with him. She deserved to be loved totally and completely, but he wasn't sure he was ready to make that sort of emotional commitment, or at least not yet.

Sam threw himself into work over the next couple of weeks but even after the most gruelling days he still hadn't been able to sleep at night. He thought about Lexi all the time. He hadn't seen her at the hospital. He had heard via one of the nurses that she had taken some leave. The days seemed so long and pointless without the anticipation of running into her in one of the corridors or on the ward. He hadn't realised how much he had looked forward to those offchance meetings, those little verbal stoushes that had made his blood bubble with sexual excitement in his veins.

Even being out on his boat wasn't the same any more. He could still smell the fragrance of her perfume. It had seemed to permeate the very woodwork of its every surface, torturing him with a thousand little reminders of her: the way she had squealed as she had jumped into the cold water of the ocean; the way her naked body had been wrapped around his on the hot sand as he'd possessed her; the way her soft mouth had pleasured him; the way she had stroked and caressed every inch of his body until he had thought of nothing but the incredible release he felt with her. Even his shirts smelled like her. Wearing them was like wrapping himself in her.

He wanted to rewind the clock, to go back to the marina and do it all differently. But every time he called her phone it went straight to the answering service. And each time he hadn't said anything. Not a word. Hell, it was so pathetic. He had been as tongue-tied as any shy young teenager asking a girl on a first date.

Sam drove up to visit his father on the weekend to distract himself from the habit he'd developed lately of incessantly checking his phone for texts or missed calls. He was acting like some of the teenagers he saw around town, their phones never out of their hands, their fingers constantly texting or scrolling.

Jack Bailey enveloped him in a bear hug as soon as he arrived. 'I hope you don't mind, Sam, but I've invited a young lady to join us for dinner,' he said.

'Come on, Dad,' Sam said with an edge of irritation. 'You know I hate it when you try and hook me up with women. I can find my own dates.' *And lose them, not once but twice.* Would Lexi ever forgive him for that?

he wondered. Probably not. No wonder she wasn't taking his calls.

'This one's not for you, son,' Jack said grinning. 'Jean's my date.'

Sam stared at his father with his mouth open. 'You've got a *date*?'

Jack beamed. 'It's only taken me twenty years to put myself out there but she's great, Sam. She reminds me of your mother. I guess that's why I fell in love with her.'

Sam was still gobsmacked. 'You're in love?'

'Yep, and I'm getting married,' Jack said.

'Married?'

Jack nodded happily but then his expression turned sombre. 'I grieved too long for your mum,' he said. 'I guess I felt so guilty about her dying because I couldn't afford the health cover. But life is short, Sam. You of all people know that. No one knows how long we have on this earth. We each of us have to grab at what happiness we can before it's too late. Your mother would've wanted me to be happy. She would want you to be happy too.'

Sam rubbed one of his hands over his face. 'Yeah, well, I'd like to be happy but you won't believe the mess I've made of things…'

His father listened as Sam told him what had happened. 'Sounds bad, son, especially when she won't even take your calls. What are going to do?'

'What are you doing for the next couple of days?' Sam asked. 'Do you fancy some time out on the boat?'

'Sure,' Jack said with a twinkle in his eyes. 'Are we going fishing?'

'Yeah,' Sam said with a slowly spreading smile. 'You could say that.'

* * *

Lexi was walking along the beach at Noosa on the Sunshine Coast of Queensland when she saw him. At first she thought she had imagined it, conjuring him up out of a bad case of wishful thinking. But the closer he came the faster her heart began to beat until it was even louder than the sound of the waves crashing against the shore.

She wanted to turn and walk back the other way. That's what her head was telling her to do but for some reason her feet weren't co-operating. They were stuck in the soft sand as if it had suddenly turned into concrete.

'Lexi,' Sam said, coming to stand in front of her.

She gave him a brittle look. 'I don't have anything to say to you.'

'Maybe not, but I have something to say to you.'

She rolled her eyes and started walking away. 'I can just imagine what it is,' she said, her bare feet making squeaking noises on the pristine sand. 'You want me to have a sordid little affair with you until you find someone else who interests you more.'

'No,' Sam said. 'That's not what I want to say. Anyway, no one interests me more than you do.'

'Sure, and I believe you,' Lexi said, throwing him a fulminating look over her shoulder.

Sam looked at her flushed features. Her long blond hair was blowing across her face and she kept flicking it back with angry movements of her hands. She looked like a mermaid. His very own gorgeous sea nymph. How could he have ever imagined his life without her in it? 'Don't you want to hear what I've come all this way to say?' he asked.

She frowned at him furiously. 'You think I would

agree to have a relationship with you after the way you treated me?'

'You took me by surprise, turning up at the marina like that,' he said. 'I wasn't prepared. I needed more time to think things over.'

'*I* took you by surprise?' she flashed back. 'I thought you were going to welcome me with open arms and instead you sent me away as if I was nothing to you but an annoying little tramp.'

'I know,' Sam said. 'It was unforgiveable.'

'You've got *that* right, country boy,' she said, stomping away again.

Sam had to trot to keep up. He caught one of her arms and turned her round to face him. 'Lexi—'

'If you don't let me go this instant I'll scream for the lifeguard,' she said. 'I'll say you're attacking me. I'll tell him you're a stalker. I'll tell him you've been calling me about a hundred times and never saying anything, not a single word. I'll tell him…I'll tell him you broke my heart and I'll probably never ever be happy again…' She choked back a little sob.

Sam looked at her with melting eyes. 'Lexi, darling,' he said, holding her close so she couldn't run away again. 'You know how hopeless I am with words. I can only manage one or two when I'm feeling under pressure. I just clam up. But there are three words I wanted to say to your face. I love you.'

'No, you don't.' Her eyes flashed at him. 'I bet you're just saying that to get me back into your bed.'

Sam lifted her chin, a soft smile playing about his mouth. 'I knew you probably wouldn't believe me so that's why I have a back-up plan.'

Lexi wrinkled her forehead. 'A…a what?'

Sam turned her so she was facing the ocean. There

was a yacht out behind the small breakers. Lexi could just make out the name on the side—*Whispering Waves*. 'You sailed all the way up here?' she asked, looking back at him.

'Yeah,' he said. 'What do you say to a few days out there all by ourselves? You, me and the wind.'

Lexi pulled out of his hold. 'I think I'll pass,' she said stiffly, and continued walking.

'Darling, will you just give me a couple of minutes of your time?' he said. 'I have to get back to my yacht before my dad sails it into a reef or something.'

Lexi stopped and looked at him. 'Your dad's out there?'

'Yeah,' he said. 'One of us had to man the boat. I could hardly send him along the beach to ask you to marry me.'

She looked at him with her head at a wary angle. 'What did you say?'

Sam smiled at her. 'Will you marry me, Lexi?'

Lexi's eyes started to tear up. 'You want to marry me?' she asked in a choked-up voice

'Sure do,' he said. 'And I want everyone to know.' He turned her to face the sea. 'See?'

Lexi looked at the mainsail of Sam's yacht as the wind filled it, revealing the words in large blue letters: *Will you marry me, Lexi?*

'So what do you say, darling?' Sam asked. 'Will you be my wife and the mother of my babies? I don't care how many we have. I just know I want to have them with you.'

Lexi blinked back tears, her throat so tight with emotion she could barely speak. 'Yes,' she said, throwing herself into his arms. 'Yes!'

Sam swung her around, holding her tightly against

his body. 'Thank heaven,' he said. 'You had me worried there for a moment.'

Lexi slipped down his body to look up at him. 'What changed your mind? I thought you never wanted to get married? I thought you didn't believe you could love someone enough to spend your whole life with them.'

He cupped her face in his hands. 'I watched my father grieve for my mother for twenty years. I swore I would never love someone that much. But what I've realised is you can never love someone too much.' He pressed a gentle kiss to her mouth. 'You've taught me that, Lexi. Life is about loving with your whole being, not just part of yourself. And I want to spend the rest of my life loving you like that—totally, completely, absolutely.'

Lexi smiled as she looked into his soft dark brown eyes. 'How long do you think your father can handle that boat without you?' she asked.

'Not very long,' Sam said. 'Why?'

She looped her arms around his neck. 'Because I have something to see to first, that's why.'

'Oh?' he said. 'What's that?'

'This,' she said and pressed her mouth to his.

* * * * *

WEST WING TO MATERNITY WING!

BY
SCARLET WILSON

First published in Great Britain 2012
by Mills & Boon, an imprint of Harlequin (UK) Limited.
Harlequin (UK) Limited, Eton House, 18-24 Paradise Road,
Richmond, Surrey TW9 1SR

© Scarlet Wilson 2012

ISBN: 978 0 263 89170 6

Harlequin (UK) policy is to use papers that are natural, renewable
and recyclable products and made from wood grown in sustainable
forests. The logging and manufacturing process conform to the
legal environmental regulations of the country of origin.

Printed and bound in Spain
by Blackprint CPI, Barcelona

Dear Reader

This is my second story in the fictional setting of Pelican Cove based around the White House medical staff.

Picking a setting for a story is always difficult. When I started to write these stories I could see Pelican Cove very clearly in my head. A small town, sort of based on *Murder She Wrote*'s Cabot Cove, but set on the Californian coast. I also found a picture of a beautiful studio flat in San Francisco and used that as the setting for Lincoln's apartment. I almost wish I could have stayed there myself!

Part of this story is about a young woman who has had breast cancer. I took this part of the book very seriously, and spoke to a number of women who have beaten this disease. I hope I've captured realistically everything that they told me. The most poignant part for me is the scene in front of the mirror with Amy and Lincoln. I just hope I've done it justice.

I love to hear from readers, so please come and visit me at: www.scarlet-wilson.com

Many thanks

Scarlet

This book is dedicated to my aunt—Margaret Wilson.
Not everyone is as lucky as I am to have such a
fabulous auntie. One who offers unfailing support to
her three nieces and many great-nieces and nephews.
And brings us wonderful holiday stories of
'exploding' strawberries and cream!

And to my editor, Sally Williamson,
thank you for bringing me into the Mills and Boon
family and looking after me so well.
It's been a pleasure working with you.

And to women the world over who've suffered
from breast cancer. This one is for you.

PROLOGUE

LINCOLN ADAMS stuck his fingers into the collar around his neck and pulled—hard. The collar was at least an inch too small for him. It didn't matter that the whole ensemble was Italian made from the finest materials. The suit trousers were an inch too short and the waist was an uncomfortably snug fit. He kept his arms firmly by his sides, his hands clenched in his lap, because if he leaned forward onto the table in front of him, the jacket would stretch across his back, restricting his movements. It was bad enough having to borrow someone else's clothes, but when they were a size too small... The sooner he was out of here the better.

The White House press secretary swept across the room in a flurry of eye-catching blue silk with a tailored black jacket on top. Every pore of her skin emanated professionalism and efficiency, and she knew how to work a crowd. This was all her fault.

He gave a forced smile at David Fairgreaves, who sat down next to him. The old man didn't look in the least fazed by the pandemonium surrounding him. In fact, he looked as if he might actually be enjoying it. Was he mad? Then again, for an international-award-winning doctor, this would be all in a day's work.

Diane Green stood behind the podium next to him.

Almost instantaneously the cameras started snapping around them and the noise level increased frenetically. She raised her hand and the press pack heeded. She had the information they'd all been waiting for.

'Thank you for joining us here today at Pelican Cove for our happy announcement. You will all be aware that President Taylor and his wife, Jennifer, were expecting their first baby on seventeenth October. However, today, on the twenty-third of August, Charles and Jennifer Taylor are delighted to announce the arrival of…' she paused for effect '…the First Daughter, Esther Rose Taylor, weighing four pounds ten ounces.'

The room around her erupted, questions being shouted from every angle. 'Isn't the baby too early?'

'What was the First Lady doing in Pelican Cove?'

'Where is her own obstetrician, Dr Blair?'

'Was the President here?'

'Where did the name come from?'

But Diane Green was the epitome of calm. Continuing with her carefully prepared statement, she lifted her hand again until the room was silent. 'Esther Rose Taylor was born at thirty-two weeks gestation. The First Lady had been ordered to rest in the last few weeks of her pregnancy and had come to Pelican Cove to do exactly that. She was accompanied by her obstetrician, Dr Blair, who unfortunately had a myocardial infarction in the last few days. As a result of that the First Lady was looked after by…' Diane Green gestured towards the seats to her right '…Dr David Fairgreaves, one of the foremost leading obstetricians in America, and Dr Lincoln Adams, one of our finest neonatologists.' She gave a little nod towards the reporters. 'I am pleased to report that the President was here for the arrival of his daughter and she is named after Jennifer

Taylor's beloved and much-missed grandmother. Any
questions regarding the health of the First Lady and the
First Daughter—' a genuine smile swept across Diane
Green's lips, as if she was still to get used to saying that
'—can be answered by our two highly qualified doctors here.'

Once again the room erupted and Lincoln Adams
took a deep breath as this time the barrage of questions
was directed at him. *Let me out of here!*

Amy Carson sat on the cold, clinical hospital bed, usually occupied by a patient, her hands fixed firmly on her
swollen stomach. The plaster was falling off the ceiling
above her and the wall hadn't seen a coat of paint in—
How long? What did the patients who usually ended
up in this room think? The role reversal of staff member to potential patient wasn't lost on her. Everything
about this place was bland. Did she really want to end
up delivering her baby in a place like this?

She gulped. How had she ended up here? The door
opened and the nurse appeared again, wheeling the trolley that held the foetal monitor and sphygmomanometer. Amy felt herself tense. She knew it was going to
be the same again—borderline.

She loved her colleagues here, but none of them had
the specialist skills and expertise that this baby would
need. More than that—nowhere in the surrounding area
had facilities to deal with a premature baby. Everything
about this made her uncomfortable. If only Lincoln
would answer his phone...

Movement on the television in the corner of the room
caught her eye. She leaned forward. 'Can you turn that
up, please, Lynn?'

Her colleague nodded and automatically twisted the

knob on the antiquated television set. 'Delighted to announce the arrival of...'

Amy listened to the announcement. Another baby
born too early. But probably the most famous baby in
the world. A baby that would have the most prestigious,
experienced medical care that money could buy.

No! Surely not? Amy's chin dropped to her chest.
Lincoln Adams. *Her Lincoln Adams* was shifting uncomfortably on the screen in front of her. He tugged
at his shirt and answered question after question about
the baby's condition. His voice was rich, smooth. If she
couldn't see his image on the television in front of her,
she'd imagine he was the calmest man in the world. But
he wasn't. And she could tell he hated every moment
of this.

Delivering the President's baby. Wow. So that's
where he'd been.

Her heart constricted in her chest. Six years and he
still had the same effect on her—even in her current
state. She watched as he took a question from a blonde
journalist, dazzling her with his twinkling blue eyes
and easy smile. He was still a flirt. It was so ingrained
in him that he didn't even realise he was doing it. One
smile from Linc and the journalist, covering the biggest story of her life, was a babbling mess.

She pointed at the screen as the nurse, Lynn, resumed
her checks. 'I know him.'

Lynn's eyes darted over to the screen, taking in the
hunk currently filling the screen. Amy bristled. She
could almost hear her thoughts.

Lynn gave a small smile. 'Well, you're a lucky lady,
then. I imagine he's one of the best neonatologists in
the world if he's looking after the President's baby.'

'He is. I tried to get hold of him yesterday but he

didn't answer the text I sent him. I guess he was busy.' The message "*I need your help*" had been direct and to the point without revealing anything. Her voice was quiet, thoughtful. Her hands rubbing up and down her stomach. 'How is it?' she asked as Lynn unwound the blood-pressure cuff. She knew the answer before Lynn spoke but her head was currently in another place. There was only one person in the world she trusted right now to take care of her baby.

Lynn frowned. 'Actually, it's a little higher. I'm sorry, Amy, but as a fellow professional I'm not going to beat around the bush. With your other symptoms, it's definitely looking like borderline pre-eclampsia. The good thing is we've caught it early. It's time to see your obstetrician. And from one colleague to another, I definitely think it's time to stop work.'

Amy nodded her head, tears prickling at the sides of her eyes as she swallowed the lump in her throat. 'I can't let anything happen to this baby,' she whispered. 'He's my only chance.'

Lynn wrapped her hand around Amy's. 'I know that.' She hesitated, glancing towards the television. 'Maybe it's time to ask a friend for help?' Lynn's eyes fixed on the television screen. 'If I knew my baby was going to come early I'd want the finest neonatologist in the world to be at the delivery.' Her voice was firm and strong. 'Wouldn't you?'

Her phone beeped and she reached into her pocket. Two words. Anything. Any time.

Their eyes met. Amy bit her lip and took a deep breath, the shine of unshed tears visible in her eyes. 'Exactly how far away is Pelican Cove?'

CHAPTER ONE

LINCOLN burst through the doors to the adjoining office and wrenched the scarlet tie from his throat. The force popped the button on his shirt and sent it flying across the floor.

David Fairgreaves strolled in behind him and lifted one grey eyebrow. He took off his suit jacket, hanging it on the chair behind him. 'Problem, Lincoln?' He looked vaguely amused, another irritation to add to Lincoln's list.

Lincoln stalked over to a nearby shelf and pulled down a pair of green scrubs—he wasn't wearing this damn too-tight suit a second longer.

Washington's finest shirt lay in a crumpled heap at his feet as he pulled the scrub top over his head and turned to face David. 'How can they ask questions like that?'

David gave a little shrug of his shoulders, picked up an apple from the nearby table and crunched into it, putting his feet up on the desk. 'They're animals.'

Lincoln shook his head. 'How can you stand it? How can you sit there and smile at those idiots?'

'You've got to give it some perspective. I've just looked after the First Lady. It's news that they'll report all around the world. And they'll all be looking for their own spin—their own edge to make them stand out from the pack. Truth be known—I really don't care what any of them think. The only thing I care about is my patient.'

Lincoln stared at him. David was the only reason he'd come here in the first place. The chance to work with the man who'd been the first to retrieve stem cells was too good an opportunity to miss. The irony of it was—he looked like a bumbling old fool but was probably the most forward-thinking clinician Lincoln had ever met.

David caught him with his sharp gaze. 'What's with you anyway? You've been like a bear with a sore head all afternoon.'

Linc sighed. The man missed nothing. 'I got a strange text message last night from someone I haven't seen in years—at least, I think that's who it was from. I've texted back but I can't seem to get a signal right now, so I don't know if she's replied.' He held his cellphone up near the window and turned in various directions. Still no signal.

David gave him a knowing look. 'I take it this was a female someone?'

Linc nodded and smiled. 'Let's just say it was an unexpected blast from the past.'

'A good one?'

'She certainly wasn't that easy to forget so I hope so. But with everything that's happened in the last two days I've just not had a minute.' He ran his fingers through his dark brown hair. 'I can't remember the last time I actually slept.'

David nodded. 'Having the head of White House Security turn up at your door at three in the morning and tell you to pack up to deliver the President's baby would flatten most men.' He frowned. 'Your text. Was it from a real friend? Or a fair-weather friend? I've experienced lots of those—people who the minute you appear in the media have apparently been your "best friend" or "closest colleague" for years—even though they don't know when your birthday is or what car you drive. Fame does funny things to folks—you need to be careful, Lincoln. This is a whole new ball game for you.'

Lincoln looked thoughtful. He gestured towards the door. 'Well, that was my first official television appearance, so she can't have known anything about it. She sounded—I don't know—in trouble.'

'Just what every man loves—a damsel in distress.' David flashed him a smile. 'Come on, Lincoln, let's go and look after our girls.' He tossed his apple core into a trash can on the other side of the room.

'I told you to stop calling me that. It's Linc. My friends call me Linc.'

David looked aghast. 'Linc? Certainly not. You, my friend, are named after the finest President we've ever had and you should wear that name with pride.' He put his hand on the doorhandle as a frown puckered his forehead. 'Just don't tell Charlie Taylor I said that.'

Lincoln laughed. 'I may well use that as blackmail material.'

Amy glanced at her watch as the cab seemed to meander up the coastal road. The traffic was almost at a standstill and she watched as only a few vehicles got through the cordon in front of them. The rest were directed to turn and head back down the hill. Her stomach churned. This had to be the worst idea she'd ever had.

A uniformed officer approached the cab and rapped

sharply on the window. He glanced in the back seat towards Amy. 'Where are you headed?'

The taxi driver gestured behind him. 'Got a pregnant lady to drop at the hospital.'

The cop gave a little start. He looked like a man who had heard every line in the book today but he leaned forward a little to get a better look. He obviously hadn't heard this one yet. 'Can you step out the car please, ma'am?'

Amy fumbled for the doorhandle and stepped out into the warm sea air. She pulled some money from her purse and handed it to the driver. 'Thanks very much.'

The cop ran his eyes up and down the length of her body. It was almost as if he was checking she actually *was* pregnant. Her white tunic and expanding trousers flapped in the wind, exposing every part of her body, including the currently out-turned umbilicus. She pressed her hands self-consciously over her stomach.

'Your name, ma'am?'

'Excuse me?'

'You have to give me your name—and the name of the doctor you have an appointment to see.'

Amy hesitated. 'I don't exactly have an appointment, but I'm here to see Dr Lincoln Adams.'

The cop looked down at the list in his hand and stared at her. 'This isn't exactly the time for social calls.' His eyes narrowed suspiciously, 'Dr Adams, he's a neonatologist, isn't he?' He nodded towards her stomach. 'What do you want to see him for? You haven't had your baby yet—shouldn't you be seeing an obstetrician?'

Amy sighed. The sun in Mendocino Valley was strong. She could feel it beating down on the pale skin at the parting in her red hair. A parting she usually always kept covered—too bad she'd forgotten her sunhat.

She swallowed nervously. Trust her to get the cop who was smarter than the average bear.

She fumbled around her bag, looking for the bottle of water she had been drinking in the cab. Two hours in a cab with no air-conditioning with the heat so strong you could practically see it rising from the ground. Four hours in a train beforehand that had been packed with tourists. This trip had been a nightmare. There was no way she wasn't getting to see Lincoln.

She pulled her tunic from her sweating back. At least the sea winds around her were giving some relief.

'Ma'am?'

The cop was getting annoyed. She could sense that good cop had retreated and bad cop was hovering near the door.

'Here.' She pulled out a battered envelope from her bag containing her medical notes. 'Give these to Lincoln Adams, he'll see me.'

The cop rolled his eyes. 'Dr Adams is currently looking after the First Daughter. He won't see you or anyone else.' He pointed in the direction of a cluster of reporters as he handed the notes back to her. 'Nice try, though.'

Amy felt a wave of panic wash over her as her baby gave a few anxious kicks. This heat was really starting to get to her. What if Lincoln wouldn't see her? What if he refused to look after her baby when it was born? What if didn't even *remember* her?

The blood rushed to her cheeks. Surely he hadn't forgotten her? How could he possibly forget those six months spent on the Amazon aid boat? She couldn't forget a single minute. The hours they hadn't spent working, they'd spent in his bed—and neither of them had been sleeping.

Trouble was, even though she remembered every

minute of their time together, did he? She'd heard
sneaky rumours that Lincoln had had a long line of female friends on his Amazon trips. Was it possible she
had been just another pretty face to him? Had she just
been a summer-long fling?

Six months with the most gorgeous man on earth.
A man who hadn't cared about appearances. He hadn't
been looking for a designer-clothed, styled woman,
piled with make-up. Which was just as well since her
luggage had gone astray at Iquitos airport in Peru and
hadn't arrived until two weeks later. She'd spent the first
two weeks with her hair pulled back in her solitary hair
bobble, wearing pale blue or green surgical scrubs and
paper knickers. Just as well her breasts hadn't been big
enough to really need the support of a bra.

She looked downwards. Things had certainly
changed in the last six years. In more ways than one.
Her extended stomach was definitely evidence of that.

Her hands went back to guarding her stomach. Her
precious bundle. Her one and only chance of motherhood. Was it so wrong to want the best man in the land
to look after her baby? More than that, someone she
trusted. Someone she'd seen battle the odds to help a
baby survive. Someone who refused to take no for an
answer.

She wanted that. She wanted that for her baby—
her son. Lincoln was the best neonatologist she'd ever
worked with. If anyone could help her with an early
delivery, it was him.

Her eyes drifted upwards. The cop was dealing with
someone else now and looking more and more agitated
by the minute. The sun was obviously getting to him
too.

She looked around her. Security was everywhere.

And no wonder. If reports were to be believed, the President, the First Lady and the First Daughter were currently in the hospital at the top of the hill. So how was she going to get in there?

Amy took a deep breath. 'Officer, officer!'

The cop scowled at her and walked back along the cordon. 'You again. What do you want?'

'You never let me finish,' she panted as she pushed her stomach out as far as she could. 'Lincoln Adams—he's my husband. So you have to let me in to see him.'

Where had that come from?

Amy was starting to feel light-headed. She really needed a seat. Oh, boy. She was definitely going to be caught out now. The cop squinted at her, 'You do know I'll radio up and check, don't you?' It was almost as if he could read her panicking mind and was giving her a last-minute opportunity to give up the madness, admit that she'd lied and retreat—never to be seen again.

But Amy was determined. She would see Lincoln, no matter what. She would get him to look after her son, no matter what. She drew herself up to her whole five feet five inches and stared him straight in the eye. 'Can you tell Dr Adams that his wife, Amy Carson, is here?'

'Different names, huh?' The cop eyed her suspiciously as he lifted his shoulder to speak into the radio attached to the front of his protective vest.

Amy's hands rested on the steel grating in front of her. Her eyes drifted across the nearby ocean. It was beautiful here. But the Californian heat seemed to be suffocating her. She could feel the sun beating down, making her itchy and scratchy. In fact, her whole body felt itchy. She pulled her smock top away from her body in an attempt to get some air circulating.

She blinked. A wave of nausea swept over her. Her head was beginning to spin. Suddenly watching the boats bobbing up and down in the cove didn't seem like such a good idea. The momentum of the waves was making her feel worse, her legs turning to jelly, and little patches of black had appeared at the edge of her vision...

'Ma'am! Ma'am, are you okay? Quick! Someone get me an ambulance!'

'Dr Adams!'

The voice cut across the emergency department like a siren. Lincoln spluttered his coffee all down the front of his scrubs and onto his open white coat. He glanced at the cup of lukewarm coffee. His first since yesterday and he wasn't going to get to drink it. He tossed the cup in the trash and turned towards the voice.

James Turner. Head of the President's security detail. Not again. This man was beginning to haunt his dreams—both at night and during the day.

But something was wrong. He had someone—a woman—in his arms. Linc strode towards him as James Turner unceremoniously dumped the woman on top of a gurney behind one of the sets of curtains. Beads of sweat dripped down his forehead and nose. Linc wondered if he'd managed to change out of his obligatory black suit at all since he'd arrived in Pelican Cove.

'I think I found something belonging to you, Dr Adams.'

'To me? I don't think so.' Lincoln shook his head and moved over to the gurney.

'Really?' James Turner raised an eyebrow. 'You mean you don't recognise your own wife?'

'My what?'

'I knew it. Another scam artist. It's ridiculous the lengths some of these reporters will go to. Don't worry, I'll get rid of her.'

Linc moved nearer the woman on the gurney. Her head and body were turned away from him but from the back the curly red hair looked like someone else's. Someone he'd known five years ago. Only then she'd spent most of the time with it tied up in a ponytail, not spread across her shoulders and back, like it was now.

He leaned closer, then started. Yip. That definitely was a very pregnant abdomen. At least six months. His eyes flickered to her face. Pale skin, flawless, almost translucent, with a faint sprinkling of freckles across her nose. And she was out cold. And James Turner was trying to pull her upwards, obviously thinking she was faking.

'Stop!'

This time his voice was every bit as loud as James's had been.

The cold, hard stare he was getting used to met him again.

'Get your hands off her.' Lincoln walked around to the other side of the gurney. He had to be sure. He had to be sure his eyes were not deceiving him.

No. They weren't. This was Amy Carson. This was *his* Amy Carson. The one he'd spent six hot, sweaty months with on the Amazon aid boat. Spending the days looking after a range of newborn ailments and spending the nights lost in the sea of her red hair. And he could absolutely authenticate it was her natural colour. This was definitely Amy Carson. The same one that had asked for help only forty-eight hours ago.

A very pregnant Amy Carson.

'What happened?' he asked James, as he spotted the

crumpled envelope at the top of her bag. No one usually carried an envelope that size—not unless they were carrying their hospital notes.

'I got radioed from the checkpoint. She was apparently making a scene, saying she had to see you. The cop on duty had her sussed the moment he saw her. The paparazzi have been trying every angle to get up here. Never thought they would resort to this, though. It's really taking it a bit too far. She collapsed down at the checkpoint a few minutes ago.'

Lincoln stuck his head from behind the curtain. 'Nancy, I need some help in here. Can you get me a foetal monitor, please?' he shouted to one of the E.R. nurses. He turned back angrily to James, 'And you? Go and get David Fairgreaves and tell him I need him to see a patient.' He yanked the cardiac monitor leads and BP cuff from the wall. 'Not every person you meet is trying to get to the President, Mr Turner.' He touched the pale face lying on the gurney. 'She—' his voice lowered automatically '—was trying to get to me.'

He waited for James to depart and pulled the curtain tightly closed.

Amy Carson.

The girl he'd searched for. The only girl to ever get under his guard. He'd almost resigned himself to the fact he wasn't going to see her again. But here she was, in the flesh, right before his eyes again. Except her flesh had expanded considerably, creating a nice neat bump under her breasts. Nothing like how she'd looked the last night he'd seen her as she'd danced about their cabin in her underwear, laughing and teasing him. This time she wasn't laughing at all, she was out cold. And she'd been looking for him. What on earth was going on?

Nancy came in, clutching the Doppler scanner, and

grabbed a nearby patient gown. She pushed Lincoln aside as he struggled with Amy's long white smock top. 'Here, let me,' she said, as she deftly manoeuvred the top out of place, replacing it with a Velcro-fastened green gown. Her hand slid underneath the gown as she attached the leads from the cardiac monitor and pressed the button to switch the machine on. Lincoln fixed the cuff on Amy's arm and watched for a few seconds as it inflated. Without saying a word, he already knew what it would say.

Nancy pulled a white plastic patient clothing bag from the locker and folded Amy's white smock. Her eyes fell on the patient notes, still in their battered envelope, currently lying at the bottom of the bed. 'Have you read those yet?'

'No. I haven't had a chance. Why?'

'Do you know her?'

He hesitated. But Nancy was as sharp as a tack. 'Do you want me to get someone else to see her?'

Linc shook his head. 'I asked James Turner to go find David Fairgreaves for me.' He waved his hand over Amy's stomach. 'I'm not an obstetrician.'

Nancy picked up the notes beside the bed and started to write down her heart rate and BP. 'I need a name, Linc.'

Lincoln picked up the Doppler scanner and put a little gel on Amy's stomach. He pulled her maternity trousers down slightly, adjusting them to reach the area that he needed to. He slid the transducer across her abdomen and after a few seconds he heard it. There. Thump, thump, thump. Like a little butterfly beating its wings. The baby's heartbeat. Whatever had happened to Amy, her baby was safe. A smile broke out across his face.

'Linc, I need a name—for the admission notes?'

'It's Amy. Amy Carson.'

'Do you know her date of birth?'

He blinked. 'August 14.'

Then he realised something. He picked up the buff-coloured folder from the bottom of the gurney. 'You could have got all that from the notes she brought with her.'

Nancy smiled. 'Yes, I could have. But the fact you know it makes it all the more interesting why this young lady ran the gauntlet today to see you. Pelican Cove just got a whole lot more interesting. Something you want to tell me, Dr Adams?' Her eyes were fixed expectantly on Amy's stomach—as if Lincoln had a closely guarded secret to tell. She leaned over and stuck the tympanic thermometer in Amy's ear.

He shook his head firmly and let out an almost forced laugh. 'You can't possibly think…'

Nancy rolled her eyes. 'I never said a word.' She picked up the notes. 'I'll go and get Ms Carson logged into the system…' her eyes swept over the nearby locker '…and bring her some water. I think she'll need it. This girl's overheated. I wonder how long she was standing out in the sun.'

Lincoln watched as she swept out of the cubicle. His eyes drifted back to the monitor.

Amy's heart rate was slow and steady but her BP…? It was way too high. He glanced at the chart. Her temperature was above normal too. He pulled up a nearby chair and sat down next to her. The noise of the E.R. seemed to fade away.

It was the first time he'd seen her in six years. His Amazonian fling. One of the best things that had ever happened to him. Six months of hard work and great sex. She'd left to go back to the US for a holiday but had told him she would be coming back in a few weeks to rejoin the boat. Next thing he knew, two weeks had passed and she'd quit. With no reason. And no forwarding address.

So what had happened to her? What had she been doing for the last six years? And why had she texted him two days ago, asking for help? Was it about this? About being pregnant?

Because this was last thing he'd been expecting.

Over the last few years he'd tried to push Amy completely from his mind. And if thoughts of her ever did creep in, they certainly didn't look like this! He'd always imagined he might meet her again on another aid boat or working in a different hospital. He certainly hadn't expected her to seek him out as a patient. And it made him almost resentful. A sensation he hadn't expected.

He reached out and touched her skin again. She was hot. She hadn't had a chance to cool back down in the air-conditioned E.R. One of her red curls was stuck to her forehead and his fingers swept across her skin to pull it back.

She murmured. Or groaned. He wasn't sure which. His hand cupped her cheek for a second. Just like he used to. And her head flinched. Moved closer. As if his hand and her cheek were a good fit. As if they were where they were supposed to be.

Something stirred inside him. And he shifted uncomfortably. They hadn't made each other any promises. He'd been surprised that she hadn't come back—had been surprised that she hadn't got in touch. She'd had his mobile number, scribbled on a bit of paper, but he hadn't had hers. She hadn't brought her phone to the Amazon with her, thinking it would never work there.

And she couldn't remember her number. But it hadn't mattered, because he'd thought he would be seeing her again in two weeks.

Only he hadn't. Not until now.

That was the trouble of having a reputation as a playboy—sooner or later you started believing your own press. Everyone had expected him just to take up with the next pretty nurse that crossed his path—so had he. But something had been wrong. That pale-skinned redhead hadn't been so easy to forget. Amy Carson had got under his skin.

Even two years later, when he'd found himself swept along into an engagement with an elegant brunette, something just hadn't felt right. The first whiff of wedding plans had made him run for the hills. And he hadn't stopped. Until now.

His eyes darted to her notes and he picked them up, flicking them between his fingers. He wasn't her obstetrician, he shouldn't really read them. But he had acted as an E.R. admitting doctor, so surely that meant he should find out about his patient's history?

But he couldn't. He couldn't do that. There was a boundary here. David Fairgreaves was much more qualified to look after her and he would be here in a matter of minutes. There were some ethical lines that he wasn't sure he wanted to cross.

He looked at her overstuffed black shoulder bag. Maybe he should look in there? Maybe she might have her mobile and there could be someone he could contact for her? Or what about a next of kin? She was pregnant, so there was probably a husband.

The thought stopped him dead. He stared at her left hand. It was bare. Did that mean there was no husband? So who was the baby's father?

He pulled the bag up onto his lap. For some reason it felt wrong. Awkward. To go searching through an almost stranger's bag. Years ago, as an attending doctor he would have had no qualms about this. Lots of patients came into the E.R. in an unconscious state and had their pockets or bags searched. This was something he'd done a hundred times before. So why didn't he want to do it now?

And then it happened. Her dark green eyes flickered open. And a smile spread across her face. 'Linc,' she whispered huskily, her lips dry and her throat obviously parched. 'Do you always search through your wife's handbag?'

CHAPTER TWO

HE STARTED. For a second he'd been lost in his own thoughts. He should have known better. That was what you always got from Amy. *Miss Unpredictable*. That was the nickname the staff on the aid boat had given her. She'd never said what you expected her to say. Maybe that was what made her so unforgettable.

Everything about her was the same. And yet, everything about her was different. She gave a little smile as she tried to sit up on the gurney and he moved swiftly to her side to help adjust the backrest and pillows, automatically pressing the button for the electronic BP monitor again. Her smile was disarming him. It reminded him of a hundred things that weren't appropriate for an E.R. It reminded him of a hundred things that probably weren't appropriate for a pregnant lady. He felt his breath leave his body—had he been holding it? And felt the tension leave his shoulder muscles. He could stop worrying. She was awake.

'So what's the problem, *Mrs Adams*?'

Amy's heart was fluttering in her chest and she didn't know if it was to do with her medical condition or from the effect of seeing Lincoln in the flesh again. Thank goodness she was currently lying down, because she was sure her legs had just turned to mush. Old blue eyes was back. All six feet, broad shoulders and dark curly hair of him. Hair you could just run your fingers through...

Her grin spread wider, then she laid her hand on his arm. 'I'm sorry about that, Linc. But it's like Fort Knox out there and I really needed to see you.' Her mind was spinning. Could he hear her heart beating frantically in her chest? Could he know the effect that he still had on her, six years on? She hadn't expected this. She'd expected to get in here and persuade him to look after her baby if she delivered early. Instead, she found herself being pulled into his deep blue eyes. Deeper and deeper.

'Amy, I'm happy to see you. Doubtless, I would have been happier if it was six years ago, but you didn't need to lie to get in here.'

She sat back against the pillows. 'Wow. You don't beat about the bush.'

'Neither do you apparently.' His eyes were resting on her abdomen but his voice had reverted back to teasing.

She took a deep breath. It didn't matter that something was currently doing flip-flops in her stomach. She needed to focus. To let him know how important he was to her right now. 'I did need to tell lies to get in here, Linc. It was really important that I see you and the cop had already told me to go away.'

'So you decided to faint?' He raised his eyebrow at her.

She gave a little laugh. 'Nah, the heat decided that for me.' Her eyes fixed on his and she hesitated a little. 'I did try to text you—but you weren't answering—and then I saw you on the television this morning and realised where you'd been.'

He pulled the chair back over and sat next to her

again. 'Yeah, I've been kind of busy. And I should warn you—I haven't slept in two days.'

She rolled her eyes. 'Oh, no! You're like a bear with sore head when you don't sleep. I pity the poor nursing staff working with you.'

A lazy smile crept across his face. 'You're the second person to say that to me today.'

She felt something wrench at her. It was so easy to fall back into their way of teasing each other. It was so easy to forget the most obvious reason she was here. Six years felt like nothing. It was almost as if the last time they'd spoken had been yesterday. She knew him so well. But who else knew the same things about him that she did?

She bit her lip. There was every chance that Lincoln was happily married. But she wasn't here looking for romance. She wasn't here because he was the best lover she'd ever had. This was even more personal than that. He had no idea how much life had changed for her in the last six years. She was only half the woman he used to know… She gave herself a shake. She was here to find someone she trusted to look after her baby. The most precious thing in the world to her.

He shook his head. 'Enough about me. Let's get back to the matter at hand.' His voice dipped. 'Why are you here, Amy? What do you want from me?'

The professional head was gone again. This time, the hundred questions that were spinning around his head in frustration came bubbling to the surface. He hadn't seen her in six years. She'd appeared out of the blue, pregnant and asking for him. What on earth was going on?

She touched her abdomen. 'I have signs of pre-eclampsia and this baby means more to me than anything in this world. If my baby is born prematurely I want him to have the best chance in the world.' She hesitated for a second, before looking into his eyes. 'And I knew the best chance for my baby would be you.'

Lincoln shook his head and his brow furrowed. He waved his arm. 'You must know a dozen doctors who could take care of your baby. Why me, Amy?'

Her answer was immediate and straight to the point and he could see tears glistening in her eyes. 'I might know a dozen doctors, Linc, but none of them are like you. You're the best. The best neonatologist I've ever known. You did things on that boat that TV movies are made out of—with virtually no equipment and only the most unskilled staff.' She gestured towards herself.

He shook his head. 'You're not unskilled, Amy. You're a damn fine nurse and you know it.'

'I'm a damn fine *theatre* nurse, Linc. I had no experience at all with neonates. I went there as a specialist nurse in eye theatre, and that was fine for all the cataract, squint and glaucoma surgeries. I even managed to struggle through with cleft-palate surgeries and emergency appendectomies. But I'd never really worked as a general, medical or paediatric nurse before—I'd never looked after pregnant women before. I was seriously out of my depth and you helped me—you know you did.'

Lincoln leaned over and took her hand again. 'But we were a team, Amy, we helped each other. Everyone was selected because of their individual skills and level of expertise. But at the end of the day we treated what came through the door.'

She shook her head. 'No one was as dedicated to those babies as you were, Linc. You were the one who would stay up half the night, watching over them.' His brow furrowed. 'Why was that, Linc? I asked before, but you wouldn't tell me.'

He shrugged his shoulders and she could see him searching for the words. His eyes looked darker than normal, heavier from fatigue. He sat down next to her. 'My sister had a premature baby around twenty years ago. There weren't any facilities near where we stayed and her daughter—my niece—died.'

Amy took a sharp breath and rested her hand on his shoulder.

He gave a rueful smile. 'My sister was ten years older than me at the time. I watched my little niece struggle for breath, turn blue and die. Our family didn't really talk about it after that. It was too painful. I hadn't really been interested in school before then. I was just coasting along. But everything changed after that. I knew if I wanted to be a doctor to help babies like my niece, I had to knuckle down and get the grades—so I did. Medicine for neonates has come a long way in the last twenty years. If my niece had been born now, she would have survived.'

'You never said anything. Why didn't you tell me this on the boat?'

Lincoln met her with a pointed stare. 'Some things are easier not to talk about—don't you think?'

The heavy air hung between them. Amy held her breath, waiting to see if he would say anything else.

'Dr Adams?'

A nurse appeared at the curtains, with David standing behind her. 'They need you in NICU.'

NICU. The neonatal intensive care unit. A place that normally didn't exist in Pelican Cove—there had never been a need for it. A place that currently held the First Daughter. In the last two days more personnel and sup-

plies had been transferred down from San Francisco
Children's Hospital than he'd thought possible. Didn't
there have to be more than one baby for it to be termed
an NICU? He pushed the thoughts from his mind.

'What can I do for you folks?' David strode through
the curtains with his normal joie de vivre. Lincoln's
eyes met his and he lifted the battered envelope from
the bottom of the gurney and handed it to him. 'I need
you to see a friend of mine, please, David.'

David's face changed, his eyes taking in the patient
on the bed. The pregnant patient on the bed. He pulled
the notes from the envelope, glancing to see which hospital they had come from, then gave Lincoln an inquisi-
tive stare.

'My patient now, Dr Adams.' David's manner was
brisk and to the point. 'I'll let you know if I need you.'
His tone was almost dismissive. Whilst at times he gave
the impression of being a bumbling fool, as a clinician
he was second to none. And Lincoln knew it—it was
why he'd asked for David's help. Amy couldn't be in
safer hands. But there was no mistaking who would be
in charge here.

Linc took a deep breath and stepped away from the
gurney. 'I'll be back,' he muttered, his eyes not meeting hers, and he stepped through the curtains.

David's hand caught his shoulder. 'Dr Adams?'

The professional title. He must be annoyed. 'Yes?'

'Just remember your first and *only* priority is the First
Daughter. Don't let other things get in the way. Don't
get distracted.'

'You think I am?' The words came out automatically,
snappier than he expected.

David's voice was quiet. The voice of years of learning and experience, both academically and human. 'I

think you could be. Let me handle this.' He turned and ducked behind the curtains, pulling them tightly shut behind him.

Linc walked the few hundred yards along the corridor. Pelican Cove was a small community hospital, not a sprawling metropolis with new technology sprouting from every corner. That was why, when the First Lady had gone into labour here, he'd had to transfer staff and equipment from San Francisco Children's Hospital to ensure the safe delivery of the thirty-two-weeker.

As usual, the black-suited security detail was at the door—it was getting to the point they just blended into the background. He pushed open the door to the newly kitted-out NICU. The heat encompassed him immediately, the temperature warmer in here to compensate for the early arrival's rapid heat loss.

He walked over to the incubator. Two of his best nurses were on duty.

'What's up?'

For a premature baby, the First Daughter had an air of determination about her, obviously a chip off the old block. She'd come out screaming, breathing on her own and continued to do so.

He glanced at the nearby monitor. Her O2 levels were good and there was no nasal flaring.

'She's not feeding well. In fact, we can't get her to latch on at all.'

Lincoln frowned. A common complaint in premature babies who hadn't yet learned how to suck. 'What about kangaroo care?'

Ruth, the nurse, nodded and stared down at her charge, 'The only reason Esther is back in here is because Jennifer Taylor is currently sleeping. She's exhausted. Up until now it's been skin-to-skin contact the whole time. Six hours since delivery and we've not managed to get her to feed yet.' She leaned over the incubator. 'And little missy is getting cranky.'

Lincoln scrubbed his hands at the nearby sink. He'd already examined Esther just after delivery, but there was no harm in rechecking. He pulled on some sterile gloves and slid his hands into the incubator. He ran his hand around and inside her mouth, ensuring her palate was correctly formed. Checked her skin tone, colour and fontanel for clinical signs of dehydration. Sounded her chest to check her heart and lungs and gently probing her small abdomen. Once he was finished he stripped off his gloves, washed and dried his hands again and checked her charts.

'Okay, there are no immediate problems, except her blood glucose has dropped slightly since delivery. Once Jennifer Taylor wakes up, can you give me a shout and I'll go and have a chat with her? I'm really reluctant to start any kind of supplementary or tube-feeding. At thirty-two weeks I think she's more than capable of breastfeeding and I don't want to do anything that will jeopardise that. We might have to suggest that Jennifer expresses some milk in the meantime to try and get some fluid into her.'

Ruth gave a nod. 'I'm sure she'll be awake shortly. I'll give you a shout.'

Lincoln entered some notes in the electronic record and went back outside, glancing at his watch. Half an hour. Would David Fairgreaves be finished with Amy yet?

He walked over to the nurses' station, glancing around him before picking up Amy's notes. They were thicker than he would have expected for a healthy woman her age and he started to flick through them to read over her obstetric care. If he was going to look after her baby he needed to know what he was dealing with. *IVF pregnancy.* The words caught his attention instantly.

Why had Amy needed IVF? His fingers went backwards through the notes—away from the area of his expertise—and froze at the long clinical letter near the end. His eyes scanned it quickly, his breath catching in his throat. The diagnosis was in bold type at the head of the letter. Breast cancer. Amy had breast cancer.

No. She was too young. She didn't smoke, rarely drank alcohol, and lived a relatively healthy lifestyle. How on earth could she be a candidate for breast cancer? It seemed unreal. Even though the words and clinical evidence were there in front of him. He couldn't believe it. It was almost as if he were reading about someone else.

His eyes raked the letter for a date. And his brain did rapid calculations. He felt himself sag into a nearby chair.

Six years ago. Her diagnosis had been made six years ago when she'd left the Amazon boat. Had she known she was sick? Why on earth hadn't she told him?

His hands skipped over her treatment plans, test results—some good, some bad. He turned to the inside cover of the notes, searching for her next of kin.

Nothing. No one listed. He'd known that her mother and father had died a few years before she'd joined the boat. She'd gone through all this herself?

Something twisted in his gut. Surprise. Anger. Hurt.

She hadn't told him—and he was hurt. Six months he'd spent with her. They might not have confessed undying love to each other, but surely she'd known he would have supported her? Wasn't that what friends did?

After all, that was why she was here now. She needed help—or her baby did. She obviously felt she could ask him for help now, so why not then?

He could feel the tension in his neck and jaw. Irrational anger built inside him. His fingers brushed the notes again. He had to push this stuff aside. He had to deal with her in a professional capacity.

He edged back along the corridor, approaching the curtains quietly. Two seconds later he heard a peal of laughter.

Not girly. Not tinkling. Deep, hearty, genuine laughter. David had obviously turned on his natural charm again. The man could have people eating out of his hand within two minutes of meeting them. Something about the ease and instant familiarity between the two of them bothered him. Made him want to march into the cubicle and stand between them. How crazy was that?

Linc cleared his throat loudly and edged his way between the curtains. 'How's things?'

David turned to face him, his head flicking back towards her. 'Amy? Are you happy for Dr Adams to know about your condition?'

Amy blinked. They obviously hadn't had that part of the conversation yet. 'Actually, Dr Fairgreaves, Lincoln's the reason I'm here. If this baby is coming early, I'm hoping that Lincoln will look after him for me.'

Lincoln cast his eyes over the monitor again, noting her rising blood pressure. 'And is it, David? Is this baby coming early?' Did he really want to have two premature babies in a community hospital not designed for the task?

David's face remained static, expressionless to the

underlying current of tension between the two of them. He nodded briefly and handed the notes to Lincoln.

'Ms Adams in twenty-eight weeks pregnant. For the last few days Amy has shown some mild signs of pre-eclampsia. A slight rise in blood pressure, a trace of protein in her urine and some oedema. However, on today's examination things appear to have progressed.'

He pressed a finger lightly into the swollen skin around Amy's ankle, leaving a little dimple in the pale flesh that remained there once he removed the pressure.

'Pitting oedema is now evident, her BP, both systolic and diastolic, has gone up by another 10mmg and the amount of protein in her urine has increased.' He gave Amy a wry smile. 'I'm giving Ms Adams the benefit of the doubt that she didn't have the easiest job getting here today and that could account for the rise in blood pressure. She also assures me that, as of yesterday, she is now officially on maternity leave from her full-time job.' His eyes went carefully from one to the other.

'For the next twenty-four hours I've agreed with Ms Adams that she requires some careful monitoring. We're going to monitor her blood pressure, her fluid intake and output and do a twenty-four-hour urine collection. So...' he looked directly at Lincoln '...your services aren't required in the immediate future but...' he gave a little nod to Amy '...I'm not ruling it out.'

David took a measured breath, his cool grey eyes resting on Lincoln. 'I'm sure you realise the importance of ensuring Ms Adams has a calm environment. I trust there will be no problems?'

Linc shifted uncomfortably. So David definitely had heard the earlier exchange. And even though his words were phrased as a question, this was a direct instruction.

Linc fixed a smile on his face. 'Absolutely, Dr

Fairgreaves. Thanks very much for agreeing to monitor Amy.'

His point made, David's face relaxed and he gave a nonchalant shrug of his shoulders. 'Hey, what else am I doing?' Then he slid out between the curtains.

The silence screamed in Lincoln's ears. She was watching him again, waiting to see what he would say. His hand automatically ran through his dishevelled hair—what he wouldn't give for a shower and a comfortable bed right now. What he really needed was twelve hours' solid sleep, with some serious blackout blinds. But the way his brain was currently spinning, there was no chance of that.

He pulled the chair over again and sagged down into it. 'Okay, Amy. Let's get to it. What's going on here? Where do you normally stay? And what did David mean about maternity leave? Where do you normally work?'

She crossed her hands in her lap. 'Wow, an interrogation. Or is it an interview? Is this how you talk to all your potential patients, Dr Adams? Do I have to pass muster before you'll take my son on as your patient?'

He shook his head. Sleep deprivation was making him ratty. It didn't matter what he'd read in her notes. He wasn't going to make this easy for her. She was going to have to tell him herself. 'This is how I talk to the girl who walked away six years ago without a backward glance, and then turns up when she sees me on television.'

Amy felt her bottom lip tremble. This wasn't going well. She could see he was tired. She knew he would be under extra stress looking after the First Daughter, but perfect timing was the one thing she didn't have here. And she needed the assurance of Lincoln's help now.

'That's not fair and you know it.'

He shook his head in frustration. His voice was quiet but even. 'I know.'

She switched into professional mode. 'Okay, Dr Adams. I normally live in Santa Maria in Butte County—around four hours from here. I work in one of the free clinics there. And my maternity leave started...' she glanced at her watch '...officially around twelve hours ago.'

Her notes were still in his hands. But he wasn't looking at them. It looked as though he hadn't read them. It would be so much easier if he did, then at least he might understand why she'd left.

'Why me, Amy, and why now?'

A loud burr came from the monitor beside her and the electronic blood-pressure cuff started to inflate again. Amy winced as the cuff over-inflated on her arm. Linc watched with alarm as the reading on the monitor climbed higher and higher. One-eighty...one-ninety...two hundred. *Please don't let her blood pressure be that high.*

Amy's voice cut through his thoughts. 'There are a lot of kids currently alive in the Amazon because of you, Linc, and you know it. Kids who would have died if you hadn't been on that boat.'

She saw him bite his bottom lip. Linc was a team player, not a glory hunter. She knew how uncomfortable he'd been in that press interview. He must have said the words 'I have a fantastic team' at least five times. She knew he wouldn't be interested in the chat-show interviews or celebrity magazine spreads that would materialise in the near future.

A black-suited figure crossed the gap in the curtains. She waved her arm. 'Look at all this, Linc. When the First Lady went into premature labour, who did they call? You. They must have been able to get almost any doctor in the world, but they chose you to look after the First Daughter. The first presidential baby in nearly fifty years. What does that tell you?'

'It tells me I was in the wrong place at the wrong time, Amy, nothing else.' He shook his head, 'You make it sound grander that it actually was. Abby Tyler was the admitting physician here in Pelican Cove. She works with me at San Francisco Children's Hospital. They asked her for a neonatologist and she recommended me.'

Amy waved her arms, 'And you're telling me that the whole secret-service brigade out there didn't check your credentials? To make sure that only the absolute best of the best was looking after the President's baby? I seriously doubt that. Hell, the other doctor is an award-winner.'

He smiled at her. 'You'll find it hard to believe, but that was sheer coincidence. David Fairgreaves has a boat moored in Pelican Cove, the man is an old sea dog. Whenever he's here, Abby has an arrangement to call him for any obstetric emergencies. He apparently likes to keep his hand in.'

Amy folded her hands across her chest. 'Oh, come on. You're telling me the secret service didn't check on him too? Especially that old stony-faced one. Does he ever smile?'

Linc laughed at her description of James Turner, the head of the presidential security detail, the original man-in-black. 'I think I've only seen him smile once in the last three days—and that's when he told Luke Storm, one of the other docs, that he couldn't leave. Somehow I think his job must drain all sense of humour from his body. He spends his life looking over his shoulder for potential threats to the Presidential family.'

The blood-pressure cuff stopped abruptly. The hiss of air seeping out from it. Linc glanced at the screen again—150/96. A bit higher than before, but not yet dangerous. Still worth keeping an eye on. His eyes fell to his watch. There were a million things he wanted to say right now. A million things he wanted to know. Six years to catch up on. But David had been right. He had other duties—other priorities—that he couldn't get distracted from.

'I'm sorry, Amy, but I seriously need some shut-eye and I've a neonate to deal with who doesn't want to feed.'

Her eyes fell to the notes, still clutched in his hands. She couldn't hide the slight tremor in her voice. 'Will you read my notes and tell me if you'll agree to be my baby's doctor?' Her hands were back at her stomach, protectively rubbing her extended abdomen.

The notes. She knew exactly what he would read in there. But for some reason he didn't want to give her an easy way out. Why couldn't she just find the words to tell him? She had no idea he'd already read them. And he was beginning to feel too tired to care.

'In the interests of professionalism I'll read your notes, not now—later—but I want to hear everything—straight from the horse's mouth, so to speak. There's nothing in these notes that you won't be able to tell me yourself. I'll come back later. We'll talk then—and I'll decide if I can be your baby's doctor or not. I can't do it if there's going to be a conflict of interest for me, and…' his eyes rolled towards the outside corridor as he gave her a crooked little grin '…your timing could have been better.'

Amy watched as he exited through the curtains, her throat tight.

She needed him. She needed him to be there for her baby—and for her. He was the best in the world. No one else would do. She couldn't lose this baby.

It had all seemed so simple in her head. As soon as she'd known she was at risk of pre-eclampsia, she'd known she had to find Linc. She'd seen him bring neonates that should have died back to life. And that was normal for him.

The long line of mothers who'd queued up on the banks of the Amazon to show them their healthy, growing children—children he had saved in previous years—was testament to that.

There had been no doubt in her mind. This was all about her baby. All about the little boy currently growing in her stomach.

So why was she feeling like a teenager with a school-girl crush? She hadn't thought about Lincoln for the last five years.

No. That wasn't strictly true. He'd crept into her dreams on a few occasions—all of them X-rated. But dreams you couldn't control. Truth be told, she hadn't let herself think about playboy Linc for the last five years. Too much potential for heartache. She'd had to concentrate all her energy on beating the cancer.

And now she was only here because she needed him for her son. Really.

When she'd had her detailed scan she almost hadn't asked what sex her baby was. But at the last moment she'd changed her mind. She'd wanted to prepare for her son or daughter. She'd wanted to pick his pram, his bedclothes and the paper for his nursery wall. She'd even picked his name. Zachary. Zachary John Carson.

She whispered the name as her hands ran over her stomach. 'Stay inside just a little longer, Zachary. I need you to be as healthy as can be when you come out. Momma needs to know that you're going to do just fine.' A tear slid down her cheek and the anger started to rise in her chest.

Why should the First Lady's baby be any more important than hers? And why did she, after everything she'd been through, have to develop a condition that could threaten her baby?

But this was it. Cancer had crept through her body tissues and the chemotherapy had ravaged them. She'd lost her ability to have a baby naturally and this embryo was her last chance. Her only chance.

So how come she couldn't just focus on her baby?

From the first second she'd opened her eyes and seen Lincoln again, her heart had gone into overdrive. There were so many things about him she'd forgotten. His intense gaze. His lazy smile. His flirting. The way he could comfort her with the touch of his hand and the stroke of his finger.

And the camouflage he kept around himself.

She'd seen how he jumped from being really comfortable around her one minute, like it had only been a few days since they'd seen each other, since they'd slept together and been wrapped in each other's arms, to shifting into the professional role, the possibility of being her baby's doctor and all the lines that blurred in between.

But she wasn't asking him to be *her* doctor, so surely that simplified things?

So why did her heart keep beating rapidly in her chest every time he was next to her? Why did her hairs stand on end when he touched her and make her feel as if an electrical charge had run up her arm?

Amy squeezed her eyes shut tightly. She couldn't allow herself to feel like this. Lincoln wasn't interested in her. She was a six years past girlfriend who'd had a mastectomy and was carrying a child that wasn't his. Why would he even give her a second glance?

He was only being kind. He was only being a friend. He couldn't possibly want anything else from her, could he?

This was Lincoln Adams. And yesterday this gorgeous blue-eyed, brown-haired doc had been announced on television as looking after the First Daughter. He was world news. Women would be throwing themselves at his feet.

She had to concentrate on the most important thing right now—a safe delivery and outcome for her baby. She'd come here to find Lincoln Adams because he was the best doctor to care for her baby. Nothing else. No matter how he currently made her feel.

CHAPTER THREE

'Linc? Linc?'

The voice was quiet, softly spoken, but the hand pressing down on his shoulder was firm, stirring him from the first hour's sleep he'd had in two days.

'What...what is it?' His hands automatically went to his sleep-filled eyes and he rubbed hard. He looked around him. He'd sat down for just a minute in the NICU, waiting for the First Lady to awaken and try to feed her baby again, but the heat from the unit had enveloped him and before he'd known it...

Val, one of his nurses, was standing next to him smiling. 'Wake up, sleeping beauty, you're needed.'

'Is Jennifer Taylor awake?'

Val nodded. 'She's been awake for the last half-hour. Both Ruth and I have tried to assist her with breastfeeding, but the truth is we just can't get this baby to latch on.' She glanced down at her watch. 'And if we're going to follow the protocols we normally use at San Fran then we're at our time limit for getting some fluids into this baby. You're going to have to come and talk to her.'

Linc gave a nod, stood up and tried to flatten his rumpled scrubs. He walked over to the nearby sink and splashed some cold water on his face and hands.

Neonates could be hard work. Esther, who had been

born at thirty-two weeks, hadn't yet developed her natural mechanism to suck and feed. It was a common complaint in premature babies and one he was used to dealing with. The last thing in the world he wanted to do was to put a tube into the baby's stomach and feed it artificially. The First Lady wanted to breastfeed and he would make sure that he and his staff did everything they could to make that happen.

He pulled some paper towels from the nearby dispenser and dried his face.

'Have you had any success expressing some breast milk?'

Val nodded. 'Ruth's in there with her now—we knew that would be the next step.'

Lincoln took a deep breath and pushed open the door into the adjoining room. Charles Taylor, the President of the United States, was perched on the edge of the bed one arm wrapped around his wife's shoulders, the other cradling daughter Esther. By neonatal standards Esther was a healthy weight at just under five pounds. Would Amy's baby be so lucky? Where had that come from? Lincoln felt a little shudder drift down his spine. He had a job to do. He couldn't allow himself to be distracted.

Jennifer's brow was furrowed, her eyes fixed on the pump that the nurse Ruth was using to help her express some milk from her breasts. She looked exasperated as the smallest trickle of creamy breast milk started to collect in the receptacle.

'What's wrong with me?' she gasped. 'Is that it? No wonder my baby can't feed.'

Lincoln crossed the room in a few steps and sat down at the bottom of the bed. This was no time for pomp and ceremony. The last thing he wanted was for Jennifer to think she was failing at feeding her child.

'Give it a few minutes, Jennifer. Ruth is an expert at this and it takes a bit of time for your milk to come in. Remember, Esther is a tiny baby and she won't need a huge amount to start with.' He pointed at the small amount already collected. 'That is called colostrum. And it's like gold dust for babies. It contains antibodies and is rich in protein and carbohydrates—exactly what your baby needs.'

The tears were already starting to form in Jennifer's eyes. 'But she won't feed. I can't get her to take anything.'

Lincoln nodded. 'And that's entirely normal for a thirty-two-weeker. Her natural instincts to suck and feed haven't kicked in yet. Sometimes it can take a few weeks. In the meantime, we have to look at how to get some fluids into her. The last thing we want is for your baby to dehydrate.'

Jennifer sagged back against the pillows behind her. The effect of the relaxation had an immediate impact on the flow from her breasts. 'Look, there's some more. Once we have a few more mils we'll start to look at an alternative method for getting some breast milk into Esther. Any extra milk we can refrigerate or freeze.'

'But I want to breastfeed. I told everyone I want to breastfeed.'

Lincoln could see the stress on Jennifer's face. He reached out and automatically touched her hand. 'And you will. In the meantime, in order to keep your daughter from screaming the house down, we'll give her your breast milk another way.'

'How?'

'There's two possibilities and it all depends on the

baby. We can try cup feeding or finger feeding. What we definitely won't do is put your breast milk into a bottle.'

'I've never heard of these. How on earth can a baby drink from a cup?' She turned to face her husband. 'Have you ever heard of these?'

Charles lifted his eyes from his daughter, still caught in the rosy glow of new parenthood, smitten with his daughter's face. 'Nope, you've got me. Never heard of them.'

Lincoln smiled. 'The word *cup* might not be strictly true. We don't use a regular cup—we use a medicine cup and, to be honest, this type of feeding isn't anything new, it's been around for a long time. We place the edge of the cup at the baby's mouth and bring the liquid up to baby's lower lip, so she can lap it up—a bit like a pussycat. It can get a little messy.' He smiled at Charlie, who still had his suit on. 'We can you give something to change into.' He nodded at Val, who had just detached the breast pump. 'One of us will take some time and teach you how to do it. It can take a little bit of practice to get it right. It does mean, though, that you can both help with Esther's feeding.'

Charlie gave a broad smile. There was no mistaking the joy in his eyes as he looked at his daughter. 'Whatever she needs,' he murmured.

Lincoln watched Jennifer's face. She looked a little easier. 'This is only a temporary measure to help get some fluids into Esther. We'll still try putting Esther to the breast and encouraging her to latch on.'

'Wouldn't it just be easier to put a tube down?'

'In theory it might be. But if we feed Esther by tube and she has the sensation of feeling full, she won't have any motivation to suck. That's what we really need to work on. Feeding by tube would be the last resort and I don't think we'll need to do that.'

Jennifer nodded slowly. 'So how do you know if she's getting enough?'

'We'll monitor her diapers and check the tone and elasticity of her skin.' His eyes caught sight of Val, transferring some of the breast milk into one of the medicine cups. He stretched his hands out towards Charlie. 'Do you mind if I take her for a minute? We want to be sure and have her wrapped up securely before we start—little hands can make a terrible mess when we're cup feeding.' He smiled at the President's suit. 'Wanna play doctor for the day and change into a set of scrubs?'

Charlie nodded. 'Come with me,' Ruth, the other nurse, said as she headed towards the door. 'I'm sure we can find something for you.'

Lincoln tried hard to focus on the task at hand. Getting the First Daughter to feed should be his first and only priority. So why were his thoughts filled with pale skin and red, curly hair?

The buzz from the monitor and the tightening cuff on her arm woke Amy from her daze. Damn cuff. How was anyone supposed to sleep with this stupid thing going off every thirty minutes? No wonder her blood pressure was rising—she couldn't get any peace and quiet.

A smile crossed her face. Things were different from a patient perspective. She'd never really given much thought before to the electronic monitoring devices that she used as a nurse. Cardiac monitors that beeped incessantly, IV fluid pumps that alarmed when they needed changing and syringe drivers that required hourly monitoring. It was no wonder patients complained.

She turned her head and glanced at the screen beside her. Damn! Her blood pressure hadn't gone down
at all. The curtains surrounding her had been pulled
tightly and lights around her had been dimmed. What
time was it? Was it night-time? It must be—she'd just
been about to slip into another X-rated, Lincoln-filled
dream. Definitely not suitable for a hospital stay.

She swung her legs from the trolley and reached for
her bag. Somewhere in the depths of this giant tote bag
should be her watch—she'd slipped it off earlier when
her wrist had felt uncomfortable. She rummaged around
inside the bag—lipstick, phone, receipts, purse, um-
brella, spare undies, fold-up flat shoes, pens, pens and
more pens. Ten minutes later she gave up. She pulled the
cuff from her arm, the ripping Velcro echoing around
the quiet emergency department. Where had everyone
gone?

As her bare feet hit the cold linoleum floor her head
swam a little. How long had it been since she'd eaten?
Judging from how her stomach felt, it must have been
hours. A little gust of cold air struck her back. Blast!
She still had on her hospital gown. It fastened down
her back and currently felt like fresh-air fortnight back
there; thank goodness she had respectable undies on.
She grasped the back of her gown in her hands and
stuck her head out between the curtains, glancing one
way, then the other, out into the eerie silence, before
heading towards the nurses' station. It was deserted and
according to the white board on the wall she was the
only patient currently in the E.R. No wonder it was so
quiet around here.

Then the thought struck her. Of course there were
no other patients—the President and the First Family

were in this hospital. She'd only got in here by default. Fainting at the police cordon could do that for you.

A packet of half-eaten cookies sat on the desk. She looked around again. Still no people. Well, if someone wanted to leave an open packet of cookies unguarded they could take the consequences. She flopped down into one of the nearby chairs and grabbed a cookie, oblivious to the crumbs falling down the front of her hospital gown, and closed her eyes. Bliss.

'Do you always steal the staff food?'

Amy's eyes shot open and she spluttered, which turned into a cough as part of a cookie lodged in her throat.

Lincoln looked amused as he went around behind her and gave her two hard slaps on the back.

She coughed the piece of cookie back up, catching it in her hand before depositing it in the trash can. She held her hands up. 'Guilty.'

She looked around the darkened corridors. 'Where did you spring from? I never even heard you. This place is like a scene from a bad slasher movie.'

Lincoln laughed, looking at the deserted corridors. He pointed to a door down the hallway. 'I came from the staffroom, where the current E.R. staff are watching reruns of the baby announcement. Don't think they've ever had it so quiet. And you...' he pointed at her '...are apparently resting peacefully with a still-border-line blood pressure and signs of pre-eclampsia.'

Amy rolled her eyes. She lifted her leg and stuck it on the nearby chair, prodding around her ankle and then further up her shin. 'I think the oedema is getting worse.'

Lincoln bent his head towards her leg under the

dimmed lights. He was so close she could feel his breath on her skin. He ran his hand up and down her leg.

Wow! A physical examination wasn't supposed to feel like that. It wasn't supposed to make your skin prickle and your blood heat. Thank goodness she'd shaved her legs, or the hairs would currently be standing on end!

But what about him? How was he feeling right now? Did he know the effect he was having on her? Lincoln had always had a wicked sense of humour—was he teasing her? Knowing that her insides had currently turned to mush?

'Any oedema around your abdomen?'

His voice broke through her thoughts. So much for illicit daydreams. She bit her lip and shrugged her shoulders. 'To be honest, I didn't really look when I woke up. I was too busy in the hunt for food.'

'Do you want me to get you something to eat?'

'Can you? This place looks as if it's closed down for the night.'

'Aha.' He put a finger to his lips. 'I might only have been here for two days but I prioritised. I made sure I'm best friends with the canteen staff. What do you want?'

Pictures of barbecue chicken breasts, fresh green salads and French fries swam in front of her eyes. Closely followed by images of scrambled eggs and sausages. It was amazing the weird cravings that pregnancy gave you—even in the middle of the night. She sighed. 'To be honest, Linc, I'll take whatever I can get.'

He stretched out his hand towards her in the dim light. She hesitated, just for a second. Was this a doctor-patient thing? No. It wasn't. David Fairgreaves was her doctor. Linc was her friend. Her good friend. A friend she was going to have to persuade to take care of her baby.

She reached up towards his hand. 'You're going to have to heave, Linc, I don't think I can get out this chair.'

He enclosed her hand with both of his and gave her a gentle tug from the low-seated chair. The momentum caught her unawares and she took a few steps forward, her hands coming automatically upwards and resting on his hard chest.

And she stopped.

Both hands were resting on his firm muscle, his face just a few inches from hers. In the dim light she could see his dark-blue-rimmed eyes pulling her in. See his perfect skin, with a light stubble on his chin. Before she knew it, her fingers had moved upwards and touched his shadowed jaw. *This was how her dream started.* A smile broke across his face, his hand moved across her back and she felt two fingers resting lightly at the base of her spine, between the gap in her patient gown. Would he kiss her?

When was the last time she'd felt like this? When was the last time she'd wanted a man to kiss her? To feel his touch on her skin? Her lips tingled, aching to feel his pressing against them. Her tongue ran along them, desperate to give them some moisture and invite him in.

'I don't know if I'm dressed appropriately for the staff canteen,' she whispered.

He looked downwards. His eyes following the gentle swell on one side of her breast. Her breath caught in her throat. Would he look to the other side? Would his face register disgust or displeasure?

Neither. His eyes stayed fixed on one side. As if there

was nothing wrong. As if the gap on the other side was the most natural thing in the world. Something lurched inside her and she almost jerked in recognition of what it was. Acceptance. This was her. This was her body shape now. And there was no need to feel ashamed or embarrassed. Her skin flushed. For the first time in a long time she felt like a woman again. His lips brushed against her ear, his voice husky. 'From where I'm standing, you look just fine.'

I'm dreaming. This isn't really happening. I'm still lying on that hospital gurney, waiting for the BP cuff to go off again.

Light spilled across them. The door from the staffroom opened. A person still facing inside and laughing at the jokes stood with their foot jammed in the door, sending bright white light spilling down the corridor towards them.

Lincoln stepped backwards. For a second he looked like the proverbial deer caught in the headlights, before he regained his composure and cleared his throat.

'The canteen,' he said. 'I was going to take you to the canteen.' It was almost as if he was saying the words out loud to remind himself what he was supposed to be doing.

His hands fell back to his waist and he gave her a nod in the other direction. 'The canteen's this way, Goldilocks. Let's see what we can get you to eat.'

He took a few long strides ahead of her, making short work of the corridor and pushing open the swing door at the other end and holding it open for her.

'I think Goldilocks was a blonde, not a redhead,' she murmured as she followed him, still grasping self-consciously at her gown.

'But look how much trouble she got into for the

search for food,' he replied promptly, sending another smile across her face. The easy banter between them was returning as quickly as it had left. Linc was obviously relaxing again. And she was glad. That was when she liked him best.

They stepped into the canteen, which was bathed in the usual bright hospital lights. Amy squirmed, looking around at the deserted tables and chairs. 'Are you sure we can get something to eat?'

Lincoln nodded, smiling at her again as though his moment of discomfort had passed. 'Sure we can. They've got to feed the nightshift, remember?' He ducked behind the counter and into the kitchen beyond. Amy could hear the happy chattering inside and looked at the empty canteen around her. Even this was strange. She was used to sitting in hospital canteens in her uniform, not in a patient gown. On past occasions when she'd had her surgery and treatments she'd never even made it down to the hospital canteens. At that point food had been the last thing on her mind. A few minutes later Lincoln came out, clutching a tray with a teapot and cups.

'Food will be out in a minute,' he said as he set the tray down on the nearest table. Amy gave him a smile. 'I didn't know you were a tea drinker.' She lifted the cups from the tray.

He wrinkled his forehead. 'Generally I'm not. But I didn't want to come out here with a double-shot coffee when you probably aren't drinking it right now.'

His eyes rested on her extended abdomen and she nodded knowingly. 'It's been a slow, hard fight to stop the addiction to the double shots we used to drink.'

His face broke into that easy grin again. The grin he'd given her when it had just been the two of them, standing in the dim E.R. He lifted the lid of the teapot and gave the water a little stir.

The door clanged open behind them and a little grey-haired lady appeared with a plate in either hand. The delicious aroma of food swept around them and Amy's stomach responded by rumbling loudly.

'Oh, wow!' she said as the plate was set before her. 'Thank you so much.' She beamed. The steam was rising from the freshly made pancakes on the plate, with a pile of sausages and scrambled eggs on the side. 'You must have read my mind,' she said accusingly at Lincoln. 'I was dreaming about these earlier.' *Better than telling him what else she'd dreamed about.* She picked up the pepper pot and sprinkled pepper over her scrambled eggs. 'I am so-o-o hungry.'

He sat for a few seconds, watching her. The way her hair fell over her eyes, one delicious auburn curl just begging to be tucked behind her ear. Sitting like this, her extended abdomen was tucked under the table. For a few seconds he could actually forget she was pregnant. Forget she was here, looking for his help because she was afraid she was about to have a premature baby. He could forget the questions spinning in his head about the pregnancy, the conception, the father. All the things he wanted to ask her about. Right now, the clock was spinning backwards in his head. Back to those six precious months when she'd been *his* Amy. Back when they'd been in the first flush of heat and passion. When they hadn't been able to keep their hands off each other. When stifling hot long days had turned into even hotter and longer nights.

The pale green colour of the hospital gown reminded him of the scrubs they'd worn on the boat. A colour that seemed to reflect the darker green of her eyes, drawing his attention to them from the first second he'd seen her.

Damn! He could kick himself. Was there something else he could have done to find her? Why hadn't he insisted on getting her phone number?

The last six years could have been entirely different.

She leaned back in her chair with a contented and relaxed look on her face, her extended abdomen becoming visible again and jolting him back to the here and now. 'Oh, wow, Linc. I don't know who made those pancakes but we should wrap her up, steal her and take her home with us.'

Her eyes flew open and she sat bolt upright. Had she just said that out loud? Oh, no! 'I didn't mean… I mean I wasn't suggesting…' She couldn't find the words, her brain was scrambled at her ridiculous faux pas. Fatigue and irritability had definitely got the better of her. It didn't help that Linc was sitting staring at her with his fork poised frozen just outside his mouth. But he didn't look shocked. He didn't look upset. He looked…amused.

'Relax, Amy,' he said in a teasing tone. 'Don't get wound up. I know what you meant and we certainly don't want your blood pressure getting any higher.' The gleam in his eyes spoke a thousand words that he wasn't saying out loud.

And then he couldn't stay silent any longer. The frustration from earlier in the day came bubbling to the surface and he wanted to hear the words coming from her lips—not read them in her medical records. 'Why didn't you come back? You left for a two-week holiday and never came back. What happened?'

The question jolted her back to reality. No pleasant-

ries. No niceties. What had happened to playboy, sexy
Linc? This was right at the heart of the matter.

And she'd known at some point he'd ask her. And
she'd practised what she would say in her head. Words
that she'd rehearsed a hundred times in the cab on the
way here. Words that just seemed to stick in her throat.

'Well?' He was still staring at her. With those big
dark blue eyes. She'd seen eyes like that on a model ad-
vertising aftershave once. Everyone had commented on
them. But that guy's eyes weren't a patch on Linc's. That
guy didn't have a dark blue rim encircling his bright
blue iris. Something that pulled you right in and didn't
let go. Her hand ran down his arm and her fingers intertwined with his. She needed to do this. She needed
something familiar. Something to give her strength right
now. It didn't matter if he had a wife outside. They were
friends. Or they *had* been friends. And right now she
needed her friend's support.

She needed to make him understand why she hadn't
come back to the boat. And she already knew how he'd
respond—he'd want to know why she hadn't told him at
the time. But those were all questions she could field.
She needed his skills right now, and his expertise for
her baby.

'I was sick, Linc. I couldn't come back.' The words
were faint, almost whispered, and his head jerked upwards from its focus on their intertwined fingers.

This was where he could make it easy on her and
tell her he'd read her notes. But he didn't want to, he
wanted to hear her say the words. 'What do you mean,
you were sick?'

She shook her head, a watery sheen across her eyes.
She gave his hand a little squeeze. Why did she have to
tell him here? In this hospital canteen in the middle of

the night? Why couldn't they be sitting somewhere in private, looking out over that wonderful cove?

She took a deep breath. 'I had breast cancer.' There, she'd said it. The words that no one liked to say out loud. The words that people normally whispered around about her.

His face didn't change. And she almost wished she hadn't told him. But she had to. She had to make him understand why this baby was so important to her. Why this baby was her only chance.

Then he did it. The one thing he used to do all the time. He rubbed his thumb lightly along the palm of her hand. The softest of touches. The most delicate of touches. Like he'd used to do when they'd had a stressful day on the boat. When there had been too many patients and not enough staff. When they hadn't been able to treat everyone they'd wanted to. When patients had got really sick, and some had even died.

His face was serious now. And in amongst all this madness—the press pack outside, the security staff everywhere, him looking after the First Daughter—she knew she had made the right decision. Linc was one of the good guys. He would help her. She could feel it.

He cleared his throat. 'Why didn't you tell me?'

She sighed. 'How could I tell you that, Linc? I went home for a holiday. I had the first proper shower in months and felt a lump under my breast. And I'd no idea how long it had been there. Two days later I had a fine-needle biopsy that told me I had cancer.' Her finger reached up and twiddled one of her long red strands of hair, her other hand still intertwined with his. 'I'd only known you six months. You were on a boat on the Amazon, thousands of miles away. How could I phone and tell you I had cancer and needed treatment?' She flung her arms in the air in an act of exasperation. 'Let's face it, Linc, I was your yearly summer fling.'

He winced at the harshness of her words. So she *had* heard about his reputation. He'd always hoped no one had mentioned that fact that each year he'd had an affair with a colleague on the boat. He wanted to shout out, *Of course you should have told me!* But he understood the futility of the answer. Amy was right. They had only known each other a few months. And life on the Amazon was all-consuming—you lived in each other's pockets and had very little time off. Everything was about the work and the people. Lots of medics had relationships on the Amazon boats, but when they got back to normal life the relationships tended to fall apart as they found they had nothing in common any more. What would he have done if she'd told him? Left the boat? Gone to find her? Would she even have wanted him there?

His anger from earlier felt misplaced. If the shoe had been on the other foot and he was one who had been sick, would he have told Amy?

He wasn't sure and he hated to admit that. Would he really have wanted to put that responsibility onto her? He would have hated it if she'd felt obliged to help him out of an innate sense of duty, especially when he didn't know how she felt about him.

His lips tightened and he gave her hand another squeeze. 'So what happened, Amy?' Although he couldn't help it, his eyes went automatically to her breasts. The professional in him knew better than that. But the personal element kept distracting him. He'd had his hands all over those beautiful breasts. And as for the pink rosy nipples…

He saw her shift uncomfortably, her hands rising to her chest. 'I had a mastectomy on one side.' The words were simple, but they masked how they made her feel. What would Linc think of her body shape now if he could see it? The two of them had danced naked around his little cabin and the memories of that now could make her cry. She could never do that now. Never feel that confident in her body.

'Really?' Now he couldn't avert his eyes because, if she'd had a mastectomy, it wasn't apparent. And he'd only flicked over the treatment plan—he hadn't read it in detail. 'Did you have a reconstruction?'

Her hands self-consciously stayed where they were. And under them she could feel the long-term results of her disease—full, soft breast on one side and a gap on the other side, currently filled with a pale pink silicone breast enhancer. 'I meant to but, no, not yet,' she murmured.

His brow crinkled. 'So what stopped you?' She was a beautiful young woman. It seemed strange she hadn't completed her treatment and moved on to the next part of her life. Most young women he'd ever met, and it was only a few, who'd had breast cancer had had some kind of reconstruction done at a later date.

Amy ran her hands over her baby bulge. 'I haven't really had time to get around to it. But it's in my plans.'

Lincoln's eyes fell again to her stomach. His brain was working overtime, trying to remember dates. If she'd had a cancer diagnosis just after leaving the boat, then undergone surgery and treatment, could she have had five years cancer-free before falling pregnant?

No. It didn't add up. According to his calculations she just fell short. Lots of physicians were wary about the effect pregnancy hormones could have on cancer cells. Was it really wise for her to be pregnant? What age was Amy? Thirty-two? She could have waited another year before doing this. Had someone pushed her into it?

He remembered the empty next-of-kin box in her notes and tried to pull his professional head back into place. 'Do you have a husband? A boyfriend I can call for you?'

She shook her head. 'It's just me, Linc.'

The enormity of the words hit him. She was alone. And while one part of his heart wanted to suddenly break into song, he immediately felt angry. Who had left a woman like this, alone and pregnant, after she'd already been through breast cancer?

He stood up, his voice rising in pitch, 'What do you mean, you're alone? Where's the baby's father? Why isn't he here with you?'

'It's just me,' she repeated, the words almost whispered. Most days she was fine with this. Most days she was confident and sure of herself. Confident in her abilities to be a single parent and to stay on top of her previous diagnosis. But sometimes, just sometimes, particularly when someone made a comment around her, she realised the enormity of the task in front of her. If this baby was born prematurely then she might have to deal with a whole host of complications. How would she feel then? Would she still feel confident in her abilities?

Then there was Linc, standing in front of her and right now looking like her knight in shining armour. But what if he refused to help? What if, over the last six years, he'd met someone, fallen in love and now had a whole host of other responsibilities that meant he wouldn't be comfortable helping her?

She raised her eyes to meet his. 'What about you, Linc? Are you on your own, or are you playing happy families somewhere with a wife and a houseful of kids? Is there a real Mrs Adams?'

She held her breath. Why was this answer so important?

Linc looked momentarily thrown by the question. A flickering parade of a variety of short-term lovers passed in the blink of an eye, ending with an image of an irate brunette. He hesitated then answered, 'No. There's no Mrs Adams. It's just me.'

Amy could almost feel the relief flush over her body. Then curiosity got the better of her. 'So what happened? Did the playboy never meet his match? Haven't you met Miss Right?'

The words hung in the air. She saw a flash of something in his eyes—was it annoyance? Linc looked uncomfortable, as if he didn't know how to answer that question.

'I thought I had. I was engaged a few years ago to girl called Polly, a pharmaceutical rep. We even had the wedding planned. But in the end it just didn't feel right. So I had to end it.' He gave a rueful smile. 'And it wasn't pretty.'

Amy sat back in her chair. 'What happened?' She was fighting the horrible sensation that was creeping across her skin. Lincoln had been engaged. It made her feel sick.

'I called it off just after we'd paid the deposit for the reception, the photographer and the cake. I came home to find my apartment cleared out and samples of wedding cake smeared into my suits.'

Amy's eyes widened. 'Wow. I guess you weren't popular, then. The playboy struck out.'

He paused, stopping his mouth from saying the first words that came into his brain.

Amy Carson had shaken him to the core. He'd been a fool, with a playboy reputation that he hadn't ever meant to earn. It had only been when she'd never come back that he'd realised how special she'd been.

She was joking, he could tell by her tone, but the playboy jibe had cut deeper than he liked, leaving him feeling distinctly ill at ease. It was too late at night for conversations like these. He looked at the half-eaten plate of food in front of her. 'Do you want anything else?'

She shook her head and rubbed her hands across her stomach. 'I don't think I've got room for any more. Junior takes up more space in here than you think.'

'Junior?' He raised his eyebrow at her. 'That's what you're calling your baby?'

She shrugged her shoulders. 'Well, I know I'm having a boy and I have picked a name, but I want to wait until he's here before I share it. So for the moment he's Junior.'

Lincoln's brow furrowed. 'I'm kind of surprised you found out what you were having. I would have taken you for a surprise kind of girl. We used to call you Miss Unpredictable on the boat.'

'You did?' Her eyes widened. She'd never heard the nickname before and, what's worse, it suited her—or at least it used to. She couldn't afford to be unpredictable any more. Amy's lips tightened. 'I wanted to plan ahead. Decorate the room for the baby coming, pick him some clothes, buy a stroller.' She stared off into the distance. 'I always thought I'd want it to be a surprise too, but when the time came I had to have a few detailed scans and because I work in a hospital where they do maternity care I'm used to looking at scans—it was kind of hard to hide the obvious.'

Lincoln's brow furrowed. 'Why did you need detailed scans? Did they suspect a problem?' He hadn't seen anything in her notes that would have made him think there was something wrong with the baby.

Amy lifted her eyes to meet his and for the first time tonight he noticed how heavy they were. She was exhausted. She leaned her chin on her hands. 'No. No problem. It's just that the clinic where I had my IVF wanted to keep a close eye on me. My embryos had been frozen for five years and then there was a problem…'

'What problem?'

She sighed. 'I had been planning on using the embryos but I was going to wait until I was five years clear of disease and I'd had my reconstruction surgery.'

'So what happened?'

'The storage facilities were compromised.' She lifted her hands. 'We live on the San Andreas fault. Earthquakes are an occupational hazard.'

'An earthquake? Surely any IVF storage facility made plans for that?'

'Even the best plans can be compromised. The DEWAR tank containing my embryos developed a slow liquid nitrogen leak. Some of my embryos perished in the thawing process but I was lucky. A few good-quality embryos survived and I had to make a decision quickly about what I wanted to do.'

He gestured towards her stomach. 'So you went ahead with implantation before you were ready?'

'I had to, Lincoln. This was my only chance to have a child of my own.' She leaned back in her chair again. Was it the conversation making her uncomfortable or was it something else? That was the third time she'd shifted position in as many minutes. She shrugged her shoulders, 'I'm not really that different from lots of other people who find themselves pregnant before they'd planned to be.'

He shook his head, 'But you are different, Amy. You've got a completely different set of circumstances. You had a disease that threatened your life. This baby didn't materialise out of thin air—or as the result of failed contraception.'

'I know that, Linc.' Her eyes clouded over. 'You can't possibly understand.' Her voice lowered. 'You can't possibly know how it feels to have the world whipped out from under your feet. One minute you think you have your whole life to plan a family, to choose when you have it and with whom. Then the next minute you're asked hard questions and you've got about two minutes to make up your mind—because they have to schedule surgery for you and a whole plan of chemotherapy. And in the meantime the clock is ticking because every second you delay could be the second that means your cancer grows and spreads somewhere it shouldn't. The second that could be the difference between life and death for you.'

Lincoln drew in a deep breath. She was tired, he knew she was tired. It was two o'clock in the morning and she was sitting in a strange place, with symptoms that could affect her baby, and with someone she hadn't seen in six years. So why did it feel as if someone had just fastened a thick fist around his heart and squeezed tightly? Why did the heart-wrenching words she'd just said make him feel as if his stomach had just turned inside out?

She fixed her green eyes on his. 'This was it for me, Linc. This was my only chance to have a baby of my own—and even then there was no guarantee that the embryo would take. But I had to try. I couldn't give up that one chance just because the timing wasn't perfect.'

'And the father?' It was a loaded question, and the one he was most interested in.

She gave a rueful smile. 'I didn't have a significant other when I was diagnosed with breast cancer and I was advised to freeze embryos instead of eggs. So I used a sperm donor. What else could I do?'

A sperm donor. An anonymous man who would never know he was the father of Amy's baby. Did that make him feel better or worse?

The words were echoing in his head. *She didn't have a significant other when she was diagnosed.* But she could have. She could have had him.

He looked down. The plate of pancakes and scrambled eggs that had seemed so appetising ten minutes ago now seemed to turn his stomach. The last time he'd felt like this he'd been out on the town with his friends and had had no idea how or when he'd got home.

Amy shivered. The hairs on her arms were standing on end. How stupid of him. He was sitting here in theatre scrubs and a white coat and all she had on was a hospital gown. He was an idiot. He pushed his chair back. 'Come on,' he said as he walked around the table and put his arm around her shoulders. 'You're cold. It's time I tucked you into that extremely comfortable hospital gurney and let you get some rest again.'

She rolled her eyes and nodded as she stood up next to him, her small frame fitting perfectly under his arm.

Then something struck him. Amy was wrong. He did know how it felt to have the world whipped out from under your feet.

It had happened to him six years before when she'd gone on holiday and had never come back.

CHAPTER FOUR

LINCOLN glanced at his watch as he strode down the darkened corridor. Twenty-four hours later and he still hadn't left this place. Sleep was apparently for the faint-hearted. At least that's what Val, the nurse practitioner, had told him when she wakened him at 2:00 a.m. to come and help with baby Esther.

Jennifer Taylor was really struggling with breast-feeding. Esther, on the other hand, had taken to cup feeding like a duck to water. She was already sleeping for two-hour stretches, but still showed no interest in latching onto her tear-filled mother.

Lincoln knew that the next few days were crucial in helping establish the feeding and that mother-baby bond. There was also the small issue of the world's press. They had developed a persistent interest in how the premature First Baby was being fed. There was no way he was going to say that even though the First Lady had attempted to breastfeed, it had so far been unsuccessful. What kind of message was that to send? And more importantly how would that make Jennifer feel? If people knew that the First Lady had chosen to breastfeed her baby, it could encourage other expectant mothers to do the same. This was a chance to try and influence other people to give their baby the best start in life.

Then there was the matter of Amy. And how he felt about her being here.

In one way, he was relieved he'd finally seen her again. But circumstances for both him and her weren't great. Had she really just come looking for him again to be her baby's doctor? Or could there be something else?

There was no getting away from the fact she was pregnant, had pre-eclampsia, and in all likelihood would deliver this baby early. But deep down Lincoln really wanted to believe there was more to this. More than just the fact he was a good doctor.

He stopped at the door to the side-room and pushed it gently open. 3:00 a.m. and Amy was sleeping soundly on her side with the arm with the blood-pressure cuff attached lying above the covers. The soft hum of the cuff starting to inflate began and Amy started.

'Damn cuff,' she muttered under her breath.

Lincoln smiled and sat down on the chair next to her bed. She was definitely a restless sleeper. Her brow furrowed and her nose twitched as she lay against the pillows, her long red curls spilling over the covers.

He almost felt guilty watching her like this. But he hadn't had much of a chance to talk to her today and she'd been moved from the E.R. to one of the ward side-rooms for monitoring.

Her eyelids flickered open as the cuff tightened on her arm. 'Linc?' she whispered, peering at him through sleep-filled eyes.

He leaned forward and touched her arm. 'Hi, Amy.'

She didn't move, didn't seem surprised to see him. Instead, she seemed to snuggle even closer into the pillows, as if she was sinking into a dreamlike state. 'Hi, yourself,' she murmured as a smile danced across her lips. 'Did you bring food?'

He blinked and held up his empty hands remorsefully.

'No, sorry.' His eyes flickered around the room to the empty bed table and locker. Amy didn't know anyone here. She wouldn't have had any visitors today. No one to bring her grapes or magazines or the occasional bar of chocolate. Why hadn't he thought ahead? 'Do you want me to go and get you something?'

She grimaced as the cuff reached its tightest point, shifting onto her back. 'No, it's fine really. Just wishful thinking perhaps.'

He smiled and leaned forward. 'Wishful thinking about what?'

She ran her tongue along her bottom lip and shrugged her shoulders. 'That when the hero finally appears he usually brings the sleeping princess some gifts. I was kinda hoping for cookies.'

'So now I'm the hero?'

'You were in my dream…' Her voice trailed off, as if she hadn't really thought about what she was saying. Her eyes fixed on his, which were fixed on the monitor at her side. The thoughts of a medic were written all over his face. So much for dreaming.

'David started me on some anti-hypertensives today.'

He pulled his eyes from the monitor screen—conscious of the fact she'd been watching him. 'And how do you feel?'

He knew better than to rely on readings from instruments when a patient could tell you exactly what you needed to know.

Amy gave a sigh of relief as the cuff released then

propped herself up in the bed. She pushed her hair out of her eyes, tucking it behind her ears.

Lincoln fisted his hands, resisting the urge to do it for her.

'Crabbit.'

'What?' That got his attention. *Miss Unpredictable*.

She gave him a wicked smile. 'Crabbit—that's how I feel. I could cheerfully take that blood-pressure monitor and lob it out the nearest window.'

He gave a rueful smile. 'It is kind of noisy.'

'It's not the noise—it's the discomfort. Every time I think I'm about to fall asleep the damn thing goes off again.' She narrowed her eyes. 'I thought hospitals were supposed to be places of rest, Dr Adams?'

'No chance,' he muttered, sagging back in the armchair, his legs and arms flopping in exhaustion.

She raised her eyebrow. 'No rest for the wicked?'

He shook his head. 'I don't know about the wicked but there's definitely no rest for me. I keep snatching a few hours here and there, but I feel as if I'm walking about this place in a trance.'

Amy nodded slowly. It was always like this for a doctor on call. As soon as their head rested on the pillow, their pager would go off again. By the end of their shift they looked like death warmed over.

Although still one of the best-looking men she'd ever laid eyes on, Lincoln looked tired. Bags hung under his eyes, and the little lines surrounding them seemed deeper—more ingrained.

She was angry with herself. Had she forgotten the amount of responsibility he had right now? He must be stressed up to his eyeballs, and her presence here couldn't be helping.

She felt a surge in her chest. Her heartbeat started to

quicken. Lincoln was looking tired and vulnerable, but sexy as hell. He was watching her through half-shut lids and it was sending tingling sensations along her skin. Why had she come to find him? Was this only about safeguarding her baby? Or was this about something else?

In the whole six years since she'd left the boat she'd never met anyone else like him. No one else had had the same effect on her that he'd had. And it wasn't just the sexual attraction. It was the friendship, the conversation and the flirting. And she'd missed it. She'd missed it all.

There was no one else about. It was just the two of them. Maybe for five minutes she could forget about things. She could forget that she'd had breast cancer. She could forget about the problems with her pregnancy. She could just be Amy. And he could just be Linc.

She pulled the cuff from her arm.

Lincoln watched as she lifted the covers and slid her legs to the side of the bed, turning to face him. Long, slim, white legs with only the tiniest bit of oedema around her ankles. And red-painted toenails with tiny silver stars.

He'd forgotten about that. He'd forgotten that she loved nail art and although, as a nurse, she couldn't have it on her fingernails, he'd never seen her toenails without it.

'Nice stars,' he murmured, his eyes fixated on her toes. She slid forward to the edge of the bed, the loose T-shirt she was wearing hitching up around her hips and sliding down one of her shoulders. The movement gave him the tiniest glimpse of bright pink panties. The lights in the room were dimmed—to let her sleep whilst still being observed by the nursing staff. Her tangled red hair was loose around her shoulders, creating a perfect frame for her white skin and dark green eyes. Something had changed. Something was different.

His breath hitched in his throat. It was how she was looking at him. Her gaze was intent and he heard her take a deep breath and let the air out slowly through her pink lips. For the first time since he'd met her two days ago she didn't seem afraid. She didn't seem worried. She seemed strong and self-confident.

Her hand reached over and took his. 'So, Lincoln…' Her voice was low, husky. 'If you're so tired, what are you doing here in the middle of the night, visiting me?'

He heard the words, but was too captivated by the picture in front of him to answer. A smile appeared on her lips and she turned his hand over in hers, running her fingertips lightly across his knuckles then across his palm. Did she know what she was doing?

She moved his hand towards her body and rested it firmly on her hip. Yes, she knew exactly what she was doing. Amy lifted her hands to his head, running her fingers through his tousled hair. He let out a groan, his other hand automatically lifting to cradle her other hip. He closed his eyes as her fingers trailed over the top of his head and down towards his neck.

The sensations igniting within him were spurred by memories of the past. Six years he'd waited for this. Six years he'd waited to have her in his arms again. He ignored the tiny red flags in his brain. The ones that tried to make him think rationally. Right now he didn't care about professional boundaries. Amy wasn't his patient—and never would be. Her touch was like a drug. His sleep-deprived brain was addicted. His head and neck were on fire underneath her fingertips and he wanted more, he wanted to be closer.

It was instinct. Pure instinct. He heard her feet touch the floor in front of him and he pulled her towards him, lifting his head as she bent hers to meet his.

There was nothing unsure or unconfident about this kiss. Her lips met his, full and plump, kissing him as if her life depended on it. His lips parted as her tongue entered his mouth and he pulled her closer. He ignored the extended abdomen and pushed his hands up the length of her back and into her tangled hair.

Ringlets. Little spirals. That's what he felt. On a lazy day he would have lain next to her in the bed, pushing his fingers gently into her hair, teasing the curls. Tonight he just wanted to touch her hair. Mess it up. Feel it between his fingers again. Remember everything about what it felt like to touch.

And her skin. He wanted to feel her soft, smooth skin. His hand fell to her bare shoulder, running along the curve of her neck, across her delicate bones and back again to the base of her neck, where his fingers danced lightly across her skin again. She gasped, her legs wobbling, her lips releasing from his and her eyes catching his in the dim light. 'Oh, Linc,' she groaned, 'you *know* what that does to me.'

And he was there. Caught in this moment. Mesmerised by the woman before him. His hands curved around her back, sliding under her T-shirt, his fingertips dancing up and down her spine like butterfly wings. His lips touched her ear, his voice deep with desire. 'I remember *exactly* what this does for you.'

Amy tipped her head back, revealing the pale skin on her neck as he bent his head towards her. This was just like the dream she'd had. This was exactly what Lincoln had been doing to her. Only this time it wasn't in her imagination. It was real. She could feel him. She could smell him. She could *taste* him.

And nothing tasted as good as this.

Well, maybe almost nothing.

Her hands dipped lower. He was still wearing the hospital-issue scrubs. The lightest, flimsiest material in the world. She could feel him pressing against her. But it wasn't enough. She wanted to touch him.

Her hands slid beneath the thin material, to what she imagined was his trademark white jersey boxers underneath. A surge of pleasure swept through her as she felt his back stiffen and his breath catch as she touched him. Running her fingers up and down his length. When had the last time been she'd felt this much in control? When had the last time been she'd had any sort of sexual encounter? Had even thought of sex?

This was exactly how she remembered it. Every pleasurable second.

His hands swept around from her back towards her breasts. Towards her *breast*. And she stopped. Her heart beat furiously against her chest. Panic overtook her.

She'd been so busy thinking about other things, she'd forgotten about this. She'd forgotten about the fact she was no longer a whole woman. Her hands jerked back from where she'd been holding him. Back to her breasts. Back to her *breast*.

Lincoln froze, feeling her instant stiffening and her pull away from him. What was wrong? He didn't want this to stop. He didn't want this to stop at all.

'Amy?'

He lifted his head from her neck and pulled back, watching her in the dim light. She looked stricken and her cheeks were tinged with pink. She was embarrassed? Why on earth would she be…?

Then it hit him like a blow to the head as he realised how her hands were positioned. He lifted his finger to her pale cheek and stroked it gently as a slow, silent tear slipped down it.

He moved forward, this time to sit alongside her at the edge of the bed and put his arm around her shoulders. She was trembling.

'I'm sorry,' he whispered, 'I didn't think. I just acted on instinct.' He pulled her closer and dropped a kiss on her head as she rested it against his shoulder. 'But you should know, Amy, that it doesn't matter to me.'

He could hear her breathing, ragged and uneven. So he held her closer, wrapping both arms around her. His mind was whirling. Was this his fault? Had he taken advantage of her?

No. He didn't think so. She'd seemed sure. Confident about what she was doing.

Her hand reached over and squeezed his. 'I wasn't thinking either. I haven't been close to anyone since I had my surgery. I didn't know what to expect.'

Linc stepped in front of her, cupping her face with his hands. 'I wasn't trying to make you uncomfortable. I would never do that to you.'

She nodded. 'I know that, Linc, it's just that…I'm not comfortable with it yet. I don't feel right. I don't feel normal.' The tears were flowing freely down her cheeks now. She looked down her uneven frame. 'This just doesn't feel like me.'

Her voice was shaking as she struggled to get the words out. 'And now with everything else…'

He brushed one of the tears from her cheek. 'I know this is hard. But you're still Amy. You're still little Miss Unpredictable that I met six years ago on the Amazon.' He pointed a finger to the centre of her chest. 'I don't need to tell you this, but it's what's in here that counts—not what's outside. Look how many kids we worked with on the boat who had facial abnormalities, what did we tell them?'

She collapsed back against the bed, her head in her hands as the sobs racked her body. 'But that's just it, Linc, I feel like such a fraud. I said all those words to those kids. But now that it's me, I don't believe them, I don't believe them in here.' She prodded at her heart. 'I don't want to be like this. I want to have my body back. The one I'm comfortable in. I had my surgery planned—I even had a date set. Then this...' she pointed at her stomach '...other stuff happened and everything else had to go on hold.'

'Have you ever spoken to someone about this?' Linc's professional head was pulling into focus. This sounded like someone who hadn't really come to terms with what had happened yet.

And he was used to this. Used to dealing with patients and their families. Used to seeing women who had healthy pregnancies then, for unknown reasons, went into premature labour and often had to deal with very sick babies with a whole range of complications. The counsellor attached to his NICU in San Francisco was one of the most essential members of staff. His unit couldn't function without her.

He walked over to the bathroom and grabbed some toilet tissue, handing it to Amy and sitting back down on the bed beside her. 'I'm sure there is someone who you will be able to talk to about this.'

Amy pushed herself up on the bed and blew her nose. 'I've tried, Linc. I went to a local group. It was all women who had breast cancer. But I just didn't fit in. There were some really strong personalities—some women were really against any type of reconstructive surgery. They thought you should embrace the fact you'd had a mastectomy and beaten the disease.' She shook her head. 'But that just wasn't me. It wasn't how I felt about things.'

Linc touched her arm. 'But there has to be more than one group. Maybe you could try another one, with different personalities?'

Her hands settled over her stomach and she raised her red-rimmed eyes to meet his. 'It's more than that. When you touched me...' Her voice faded out.

'What? When I touched you, what?' He didn't want to push, but right now it was clear that Amy needed to talk.

She buried her head in her hands again. 'It didn't feel right. When you used to touch me, I loved the feel of your hands on my breasts. This time your hands came round and I expected what I used to feel. Except this time I felt nothing. It was like a big blank. I wasn't ready for that.'

Lincoln bit his lip. 'Amy, the part of you that's missing is important. You had a huge amount of nerve endings and fibres that just aren't there any more. So it will feel different when someone touches you.'

She lifted her hand and pressed it against her absent breast. 'But I didn't know it would feel like *this*.'

Linc lifted his hand. A loose curl was dangling in front of her face and he brushed it aside, tucking it behind her ear. He gave her a little smile. 'Maybe it's time to relearn things. Maybe you just have to take it slow.'

Amy's hands fell to her extended abdomen. 'I just feel as if there's so much going on right now.' Her hands stroked up and down her bump. 'I don't know if I can do all this at once. I'm so worried about the baby. My blood pressure isn't getting any better and I'm worried about an early delivery. David said he would review me again in the morning, but I can already tell that the symptoms aren't getting any better.'

Lincoln tucked his arm back around her shoulders. 'Don't focus on the bad, focus on the good. Your symptoms haven't got any worse, that's what's most important here.'

She nodded and leaned her head against his shoulder again. 'I know that, but I still can't help worrying.' She reached over and placed her palm on his chest. 'And it doesn't help that the best neonatologist in the world still hasn't told me if he'll look after my baby.'

Lincoln threaded his fingers through hers. 'Amy, of course I'll look after your baby. That was never in any doubt.'

'Promise?'

'Promise.' He stood up, straightening his scrubs and bent forward, lifting the covers and sweeping her legs back up onto the bed. He glanced at his watch. 'Now, Ms Carson, you should be getting some rest.' He picked up the discarded blood-pressure cuff and fastened it back onto her arm. He raised one eyebrow at her. 'Keep it on—doctor's orders. And I'll come back and see you in the morning while David is here.'

Then, just when it seemed he'd reverted back to doctor mode, he stopped and looked at her. She could see the dark blue rims around his eyes. He was watching her. And it seemed as if there were a million things going on his brain, a million things still unsaid. 'Just tell me what you want from me.'

She opened her mouth. She couldn't say what she wanted to. She couldn't say that she wished she could turn back the clock six years and pick up the phone to call him. She said the easiest thing that came to mind. 'I need you to be my friend right now, Linc.' The air deflated from her lungs. This was so *not* what she wanted to say. But anything else right now just seemed too hard.

His lips turned upwards, but the smile was almost… disappointed. The heat and passion that had been in his eyes earlier had vanished. Now his eyes seemed cool, resigned to their fate. He lifted his hand and his finger stroked the side of her cheek. 'Night-night, Amy.'

She turned on her side and snuggled under the covers. 'Night-night, Linc.'

He headed towards the door, pulling it gently shut behind him before taking a few strides down the corridor.

He stopped for a second and leaned against the concrete wall. The coolness spread through his thin scrubs to his heated skin. What was he doing? No—what had he just *done*? His brain was spinning. Should he have professional boundaries with Amy if he was going to take care of her baby?

Did that mean he should step away from her completely? Let some other doctor take care her and her imminent arrival?

He banged his head on the wall. Maybe that would knock some sense into him. Ever since he'd set eyes on her again, she had been all he could think about. Every time he was in the same room as her he just wanted to touch her.

Now he'd just agreed to look after her baby.

But how could he have said no? How could anyone in his position have said no?

Right now Amy needed him. But not in the way he wanted. She wanted to be friends. Friends? Could he do that?

The blood was still coursing through his veins from her earlier touches. The cool concrete wall was doing nothing to soothe the heat emanating from his skin.

He glanced at his watch again. The one thing that Lincoln really needed right now was a good night's sleep. A chance to clear his head and sort out his thoughts. He glanced back towards the dim light filtering out from under her door. But what were the chances of that?

Amy huddled under the covers as the damn cuff started to inflate again. Her body couldn't stop trembling.

She'd kissed him. She'd kissed Linc again. And it had been every bit as wonderful as she'd imagined it to be.

She'd touched him. She'd felt the strong muscular planes of his body under her fingertips.

The tears started to fall again on her already damp pillow. And he'd touched her. And said it didn't matter to him. He hadn't run screaming from the room because she'd had a mastectomy. He hadn't cared that she wasn't a whole woman any more. He didn't even seem to care that she was carrying an anonymous donor's baby.

But did he mean any of it? Because he might have touched her—brushed against her almost—but he hadn't *seen* her.

Lincoln had always been a gentleman. He'd always been a man with a good heart. Was he taking pity on her because of her current predicament?

Or could he really look at her as a real woman?

Amy pulled the covers up around her head. Maybe if she didn't think about this stuff right now it would go away. Maybe this was all just a bad dream and she would wake up in the morning, six years in the past, in her own apartment, ready to return from her holiday to the Amazon aid boat and her hot new doctor friend.

If only…

Lincoln had told her to focus on the good things. Not to think about the bad. She started to count them off in her head. So far, all her cancer check-ups had been clear. In a few months' time she'd reach the golden 'five years cancer-free'. She was being looked after by one of the best obstetricians in the country. There. Two already. This wasn't so difficult.

The finest neonatologist she knew had agreed to look after her baby. She'd just had the most erotic kiss she'd experienced in six years. She'd just felt like a woman again for the first time in six years.

Her mind drifted. Dark tousled hair. Electric blue eyes with a dark blue rim. Broad shoulders and firm, hard pecs.

Amy groaned and pulled the pillow over her head.

Linc. All about Linc. This clearly wasn't working.

'Dr Adams, a word, please.'

Lincoln glanced over his shoulder and heaved a huge sigh. James Turner was standing behind him with his arms folded tightly across his chest. He was quite possibly the last person Linc wanted to see right now. His temper was short and his nerves frayed. Not to mention there wasn't a single thought in his head that currently made sense.

'What word do you want, Mr Turner? How about "busy", "hungry" or "tired"? I'll let you pick.' He closed the notes he was writing in and stood up, sliding them back into the filing cabinet.

James's face remained fixed. 'She has to go.'

Lincoln turned to face him. 'Who has to go?' It was

late, his brain was buzzing and he had about ten other things to do right now.

'Your friend Amy Carson. She fainted and now she's better. It's time for her to go home.'

'Really?' Lincoln raised his eyebrow as he tried to control his temper at the sheer cheek of the man. 'And what makes you think that's your decision?'

'I'm in charge of the security for the First Lady. Everything around here is my decision. And I don't make compromises.'

Lincoln stepped forward until he was only inches from James's face. 'I don't like what you're inferring.'

'I don't care.'

'Well, in that case show me your medical degree, *Mr* Turner. Because unless you've got one, I think you'll find this is a medical decision—not a security decision.'

James scowled at him and shook his head. 'Don't make this into something it's not, Dr Adams. This isn't a medical decision, this is personal. Your lady friend turned up here to see you and blagged her way in. She shouldn't be here and she's compromising the safety of the First Lady and the First Daughter, so she has to go.'

Lincoln felt a red mist start to descend over his eyes. He jerked open the door of the filing cabinet and pulled Amy's notes back out. He didn't need to flick through them—by this point he knew them off by heart. 'Let's see. Ms Carson has protein in her urine, her blood pressure is above normal and pitting oedema is evident in her legs and abdomen. She is showing classic signs of pre-eclampsia.' He slammed the notes shut. 'She is at risk. Her baby is at risk. She didn't blag her way in here, Mr Turner, she's been admitted to this hospital because she's sick.'

'She can't be sick here, it's a security risk.'

'Don't be so ridiculous. Is there a pecking order here? Did I imagine it or did the doctors here tell me that you pulled up outside with the First Lady in labour, with no warning, no prior planning? Did you get turned away? Is the First Lady's baby more important than Ms Carson's? Is that the way things have become in the US?'

James pulled a stick of gum from his pocket and popped it in his mouth. 'So transfer her.'

'What?'

'Transfer her somewhere else. They can look after her.'

The man was inhumane. Linc wondered if he was actually a machine. James was immune to anger—he obviously enraged everyone he came into contact with. It was time for a new angle. Lincoln took a deep breath and leaned against the filing cabinet. 'Fine. But if she goes, I go. I've agreed to be her neonatologist. I need to be there when she delivers. And to be frank, I don't care where that is. Make the arrangements, Mr Turner, let me know when we leave.' He turned away and started walking down the corridor. He got six strides before he heard the voice behind him.

'You can't be serious.'

Linc turned back towards the incredulous voice. James had followed him along the corridor. 'You're going to walk away from the First Lady? It's the best publicity you'll ever get,' he sneered.

Linc smiled. 'And if you've done your homework, Mr Turner, you'll know that I'm the doctor that doesn't like publicity and doesn't want it.' He tilted his chin. 'So what's it to be, Mr Turner? Because I'm too tired to fight with you about it. Do you want to arrange the transfer or not?'

James hesitated for a second. Lincoln could see a tiny muscle twitching under his eye. He was furious and Lincoln couldn't have cared less.

He let out a sigh. 'Okay, she can stay.'

'Finally, something we agree on.' And before he could answer Lincoln walked into the on-call room and slammed the door.

CHAPTER FIVE

DAVID stood at the bottom of the bed, his forehead puckered with a frown. 'Can you recheck her blood pressure manually, please?' He nodded to one of the nearby nurses.

He scribbled something in the notes before giving Amy a little smile. 'I'm a bit of a traditionalist.' He gestured towards the monitor. 'Some studies have shown that automated methods can underestimate systolic blood pressure, so I like it double-checked with a mercury sphygmomanometer. Trouble is, in the world of technology they can be hard to find these days.

He glanced back at Amy. 'Yesterday's blood results were fine, but I want to see what today's are like.' He lifted the bed covers and examined her legs and ankles, before unhooking the stethoscope from around his neck. 'Can I take a listen to your chest, please?'

Amy nodded and leaned forward as he lifted her T-shirt, placing his cool stethoscope on her skin. 'Take a deep breath, please.'

Amy breathed in and out slowly as the stethoscope moved from under her breast to her back.

The nurse appeared back at the door with a manual sphygmomanometer in her hand. She took a few seconds to wind it around Amy's arm before inflating the cuff then placing the stethoscope inside her elbow. A few seconds passed before she released the valve and turned to David. 'Same as the machine. One hundred and fifty over one hundred.'

David gave a sigh and stood back.

Lincoln appeared at the door. 'Knock, knock.' He walked into the room, 'How are things, David?

'Your friend Ms Carson is proving quite an enigma.' He pointed at her chart. 'Her blood pressure is still borderline despite her being started on anti-hypertensives yesterday. There's still some protein in her urine. But her lungs are clear and her peripheral oedema seems to be improving.'

He turned back to Amy. 'Any other symptoms?'

She shook her head.

'Then we have a problem.'

'What?' Lincoln's head shot upwards. 'What do you mean, there's a problem?' He moved over to the side of the bed next to Amy.

David gave a little smile. 'In normal circumstances, at this stage, I would probably ask Amy to rest at home and come into the hospital every day to be monitored.'

Lincoln's brow wrinkled. 'I don't understand. What's the problem?'

David gave his shoulders a little shrug. 'It's my understanding that Amy doesn't stay around here. I can't exactly send her home and ask her to come in every day for monitoring if she lives four hours away.'

Amy nodded her head in relief. Thank goodness. For a second there her heart had been in her mouth—she'd wondered what David was about to say.

'But isn't it best she stays here if she's at risk of pre-eclampsia?' Lincoln looked agitated.

David shook his head. 'Not at this stage. Her symp-

toms aren't severe. Her blood pressure is still borderline and we've started her on some treatment.' He gave
Amy a serious look. 'However, you still require careful
assessment, daily blood and urine tests, and blood pressure monitoring. We also need to keep a close eye on
you to ensure you don't develop any other symptoms.'

Amy gave him a smile. 'So what do you suggest, Dr
Fairgreaves?'

'I suggest I give you a little more freedom.'

Amy's smile broadened. 'That sounds good.'

David gave a final glance at his chart. 'For the moment I'm going to recommend your blood pressure is
monitored four-hourly. I'm still recommending rest for
you. But I don't think a gentle walk outside in the fresh
air will cause you any problems.' He gave Lincoln a
little nod. 'Providing, of course, you have some super-
vision.'

Lincoln nodded his head in agreement. 'I think I can
manage that.'

'I thought you might.' David touched Amy's shoulder. 'I'll come back and review things later once your
blood test results are available. In the meantime, enjoy
the sunshine.'

David turned and walked out the door, leaving
Lincoln and Amy staring at each other.

'I don't know if I'm happy about this.'

'What's wrong, Linc, scared to take a girl to lunch?'

Linc folded his arms across his chest. 'You make
that sound like a challenge.'

'It was. I know you won't be able to resist. You were
always a sucker for a challenge.'

His eyes went over to the nearest window. In the last
seventy-two hours all he'd seen of Pelican Cove had
been the inside of this hospital. White walls and pale

grey floors. The thought of getting out into the sunshine and down onto the nearby beach definitely appealed. Fresh air and the smell of the ocean, just like back home at Fisherman's Wharf. He couldn't think of anything better. Amy looked as if she could do with a change of scenery too. Being hospitalised was enough to send anyone crazy. He gave her a wink. 'I have a baby to check on. I'll be back for you in an hour.'

Lincoln picked up baby Esther from the crib in NICU. She opened her pale blue eyes and scowled at him, her tongue automatically coming out and lapping. He sat down in the nearby chair and picked up her chart. 'Hungry again, little lady? How about trying to latch onto your mom?'

Val appeared at his side. 'She's still being a little madam. We're trying to get her to latch on every time she's due a feed. But she's still not managing.'

Lincoln ran his fingers over the thick dark hair on her head, checking her fontanel, laughing as her tongue came out again. 'Let's take you to Momma and see how you do.'

He went into the room next door where Jennifer was lying on her bed, staring out the window. She sat up as soon as Lincoln came in carrying her daughter.

'Hi, Dr Adams. Is my girl looking for food again?' Jennifer swung her legs out of the bed and moved over into the nursing chair, settling a pillow on her lap and holding her arms out to take Esther. She arranged Esther comfortably and lowered her nursing bra to reveal her dark nipple, and spent the next few minutes trying to get Esther to latch on. Lincoln moved over to her side. 'Would you like to try another position?'

Jennifer rolled her eyes. 'What do you suggest? I've

tried the cradle hold, the cross cradle hold, the foot-ball hold and the side-lying position. If you've got any others, feel free to tell me.'

Lincoln put his hand on her shoulder in reassurance. 'I know this is hard, Jennifer, but just persevere. Every time she's due to feed, put her to the breast and eventually her sucking reflex will kick in. Look at the way she's extending her tongue. She's doing really well with the cup feeding and she's almost regained her birth weight. She's only lost a few ounces—that's really good for a premature baby.'

He watched as Esther wrinkled her nose and started to wail in frustration, one little arm escaping from her blanket and pushing upwards. 'Here,' he said, taking her from Jennifer and wrapping her firmly in the pale pink blanket again. 'Let's try again for a few more minutes and if it doesn't work, I'll go and get you some of the milk you expressed earlier.'

Jennifer nodded and sat patiently while Lincoln tried to help her latch baby Esther onto her breast. After a few false starts Esther eventually tipped her head backwards and enclosed her mouth around her mother's nipple, but only for a few seconds.

Jennifer gave an exasperated sigh. 'No one tells you it's going to be this hard.'

Lincoln nodded. 'It is hard.' His eyes had a know-ing glint in them. 'And although I've had no personal experience, from what I hear, when it does work noth-ing can compare.' He fixed her with one of his dazzling grins.

Jennifer shook her head. 'You're an incorrigible flirt, you do know that, don't you?'

Lincoln rolled his eyes. 'Me?' He pointed at his chest in mock horror. 'Never.'

She sighed. 'You are. There should be a licence against men like you. You're all big blue eyes and movie-star smiles. The nurses around here are practically falling on their feet around you. How many nurses' numbers have you got in your phone?'

Lincoln had the good grace to look embarrassed. 'None. Well—none from Pelican Cove,' he added. 'Anyway, Val and Ruth don't give me a second glance.'

She laughed. 'That's because they know you. They've obviously developed an immunity to you. It's all those other poor souls that haven't met you before I feel sorry for.'

She looked at him carefully. 'You don't even know you're doing it, do you?'

Lincoln gave a shrug and picked up one of her apples from the nearby fruit bowl, taking a big bite through the green skin. 'I don't know what you're talking about.'

He gave her a few seconds to think, as he looked around the room. Presents for the baby had been arriving from all around the world.

'Looks like you're going to need a room just for the presents soon.'

Jennifer looked embarrassed. 'Yes, I know. They've come from everywhere. There's no way in the world I'll be able to use all of this. If I'd been in Washington, one of my aides would have taken a note of them all, so we can send thank-you notes.' She bit her bottom lip. 'But I had a bit of temper tantrum and insisted all the aides leave. And I haven't had time to even look at most of them. I'm sure I can find a good home for some of these things.' She picked up the nearest parcel, with beautifully knitted matinee jackets in white and pink. 'What about the NICU? You work in there, Lincoln, could they use some of these?'

He gave her a smile. 'I'm sure we could. San Francisco has lots of families that need some support. Our unit often has to do fundraising so all donations are gratefully received.'

Jennifer eyes swept over the room. 'I've no idea what kind of thing would be best for your unit. Do you want to give me a list?' She pointed towards the door, where the latest pile of parcels had just been delivered. 'And I'm terrified in amongst all this stuff there's going to be a present from my Great-Auntie Bertie that I'll miss, or something from my third cousin twice removed.'

Lincoln laid a gentle hand on her arm. 'Maybe it's time to relent and tell James Turner you want one of your aides back. These presents look like a full-time job.'

Jennifer frowned. 'They do, don't they.' She bent her head as she adjusted her daughter in her arms. 'And to be honest, I want to spend my time concentrating on Esther.'

'That's the way it should be.'

Jennifer looked up again. 'If there's anything you want to take in the meantime—I mean, if there's any-thing you think the people in Pelican Cove might need—just take it.' She waved her arm, 'It's not like I'll miss it.'

Lincoln gave a wry grin. 'Actually, there is some-thing, but it's not what you think.'

Jennifer raised her eyebrow in interest. 'Really? Now, that sounds fascinating. What is it?'

Lincoln bent over and picked up a battered sunhat from beside the bed. 'Can I borrow this? I'm taking a friend for lunch and I think she might be a little unpre-pared. A sunhat would be perfect.'

A knowing smile spread over Jennifer's face. 'Would that sunhat be for a pregnant pale-skinned redhead?'

Lincoln started. 'How on earth…?'

She tapped the side of her nose. 'I'm the First Lady, Linc. I know everything.' She laughed. 'Actually, does she need some maternity clothes? I've got a whole wardrobe full that I won't need. Help yourself.' She pointed to the wardrobe in the corner of the room.

Lincoln wrinkled his nose. He hadn't even thought about clothes. And truth be told, Amy probably needed more than a sunhat. Would she be offended if he took her some of the First Lady's maternity clothes? No. He didn't think so.

He gave a little nod. 'Actually, that might just be perfect. Now, let's see if we can get Esther latched on again.'

Amy was sitting on the edge of her bed, wearing the same white smock top and maternity jeans she'd had on three days ago when she'd been admitted. Her eyes widened in shock as Lincoln burst through the door, having changed into jeans and a T-shirt, his arms jammed with clothes, which he dumped on the bed next to her.

'What on earth…?'

'Sorry I'm a bit late,' he said breathlessly. 'I was checking on the First Baby and Jennifer asked if you'd like some of her maternity clothes. She says she won't be needing them any time soon. I hope you don't mind—I said yes on your behalf. I wasn't sure if you'd brought any more clothes with you.' Lincoln held his breath. Had he just committed a huge female faux pas?

Amy turned and looked at the pile of clothes next to her, fingering the expensive fabrics of the designer clothes. 'Wow!' she whispered, as she took in the

wide range of styles and colours. Her dark green eyes
turned to Lincoln, who breathed a huge sigh of relief.
She wasn't angry. Instead, she looked like a child in a
sweetie shop. 'She said I could have all these?'

Lincoln nodded and shrugged his shoulders. 'She
wanted someone else to have the use of them. She
thought you were probably the same size as she is.'

Amy nodded and picked up a summer dress em-
broidered with tiny flowers. She held it up next to her.
'What do you think Linc?'

'Will it go with this?' He held up the battered summer hat. 'This is what I originally asked for—thought
you might need it out there.' He pointed out the window at the blistering sunshine. 'Looks like we're in for
a scorcher.'

Amy was rummaging through the clothes on the bed
and pulled out a pale green bolero cardigan to match the
summer dress. 'Perfect!' she exclaimed, before heading
off to the bathroom. 'Just give me a few minutes until
I get changed.'

'Take all the time you need,' murmured Lincoln at
her retreating back. This was the Amy he knew. Happy
and bubbling with excitement. When had the last time
been he'd seen her like that?

A vision from the night before flashed in front of his
eyes. Images of a beautiful redhead with seduction in
her eyes. And he quickly shook it off. This was Amy
Carson—friend. Not Amy Carson—former lover. He
had to keep things amicable between them. More importantly, he had to keep his mind from wandering.

Amy pushed open the bathroom door, a broad smile
across her face. 'Well, Linc, what do you think? Do I
look like First Lady material to you?' She swished her

flouncy dress, which came to just above her knees, from side to side.

Lincoln tried to stop his mouth from falling open. Pretty as a picture. The words danced around his mind. The dress fitted perfectly, with the cardigan over her shoulders to stop her fair skin from burning and her curly red hair framing her face. His eyes fell automatically to her legs. There was only the slightest amount of oedema around her ankles. A non-medic wouldn't even notice and that was a good sign. He tossed her the sunhat. 'Here you go, don't want you getting scorched out there in the sun.'

She laughed and stuck the hat on her head. 'Have you got any food?'

'Have I got any food?' Linc let out a hearty laugh, 'Amy, when have you *ever* known me to go anywhere without food?' He pointed to the door, where a small picnic basket sat on the floor, with a picnic blanket tucked under the handle.

'Where on earth did you get that from?'

'The kitchen staff. They love me. No, no, you don't.' He whipped the basket back up as she attempted to open the cover and peer inside. 'You don't get to look until we are sitting comfortably on the beach. *Then* you get to look.'

'If you're going to make me wait it had better be good, mister.' She folded her arms across her chest. 'How far away is the beach anyway?'

Lincoln picked up another bag he'd left at the doorway. 'Apparently about two minutes down a path at the side of the hospital. Or we can take the path at the other side and head down to the harbour. Neither is too far and you should be fine, so take your pick.'

'The beach. Definitely the beach. I can't remember

the last time I smelled the ocean.' She wrinkled her nose. 'I don't think I could take the smell from the fishing boats today.'

Linc gave her a smile and extended his arm towards her. 'Then let's go.'

Nope. She wasn't imagining it. There were definitely tingles shooting up and down her arm. Her hand was tightly enclosed in his as he led her down the stone path towards the beach. It wasn't particularly steep, or treacherous, but there was something nice about holding hands. Something familiar and yet intimate at the same time.

The beach already had a number of families set up for the day, with chairs and blankets spread out across the sand, and numerous little kids running around covered in white sunscreen, carting buckets filled with sea water across the sand. Linc pulled the blanket from the under the handle of the hamper and spread it on the sand. 'Is here okay with you?' he asked.

Amy nodded and settled down on the blanket. She slipped off her sandals and buried her toes in the sand. Bliss.

She shaded her eyes from the glare of the sun, already beating down on her pale legs. Thank God she'd thought to pack some factor fifty. It was a gorgeous day, but she didn't want to end up frying in the sun. Her fingers caught the fine cotton material of her dress—the First Lady's dress—and a little smile appeared on her face. The pale green material, dotted with tiny pink, blue and cream flowers, was gorgeous, the style perfect for her extended abdomen. She couldn't have picked a more perfect dress if she'd tried.

With the hat firmly on her head and the cardigan protecting her shoulders, she leaned back on her hands and looked out over the ocean waves. Pelican Cove was apparently renowned for its surfing and today was no exception. There were numerous surfers out on the waves, their brightly coloured boards and shorts making them easy to pick out against the deep blue ocean.

Surfing. Another thing on the list of things she'd never tried. Maybe, once her baby was here, she would give it a go.

Lincoln pulled food from the basket and began setting it out on the blanket—chunky brown bread sandwiches, a pile of fruit and some sodas. He glanced around about them, acknowledging a few smiles and waves from people he recognised. People from the hospital at the beach with their families.

He'd only been here a few days and already people were recognising him. Was Pelican Cove really that small? Or was it just that friendly?

He watched as one of the nurses walked past, hand in hand with a chubby toddler. She gave him a small smile and joined her husband on a nearby blanket. Was that what they looked like? His head flicked from side to side. Did the other people on the beach assume that they were a family? He, Amy and the bump. Lincoln swallowed the lump currently fixed in his throat. That's what they must look like—walking down the coastal path hand in hand, like a husband and wife with a baby on the way. Lincoln felt uncomfortable.

What did he want people to think? Amy had already told people that she was his wife. No one had questioned her different surname. Did they know she'd been lying? Or were they just being polite, and not asking any questions? Even Val and Ruth, the two NICU nurses he'd brought with him from San Francisco's Children's

Hospital—two nurses who had known him for the last five years—hadn't asked him about his *wife*. They knew he wasn't married. So why hadn't they asked any questions?

His eyes were drawn back to Amy. There was a smile on her face as she stared towards the ocean. Jennifer Taylor had been right about them being the same size. The outfit fitted perfectly, complementing her skin tone, even down to the wide-brimmed floppy hat.

The same question kept turning over and over in his mind. Why was Amy here? Was this just about her baby? Or had something else motivated her to come? Sure, he might be a good neonatologist, he might even be a great neonatologist, but there must have been someone else she worked with that she could have trusted— trusted with the life of her baby. Was it really just him? And was it really just his skills and expertise? Or was it something else, something deeper that had brought her here? And why, right now, was his stomach clenched in the hope that it was?

He blinked. Amy hadn't moved, her eyes still fixed on the horizon. 'What are you looking at?'

She smiled and turned towards him, leaning back on one of her elbows. 'The surfers. Something on my list.'

'Your list? What's that?'

She gave a little sigh. 'When I was sick I made myself a list of things I'd like to try once I was well again. It kind of helped me get through the bad days—the days when the chemo made me sick to my stomach and I thought I'd never get out of bed again.'

Lincoln felt a chill running down his spine. The thought she'd been *that* sick, *that* unwell really unnerved him. Why hadn't someone been there for her? Why hadn't *he* been there for her?

He forced a smile onto his face. 'So, surfing's on the list?' She nodded. 'What else?'

Amy leaned over and picked up one of the sandwiches he'd unpacked. She nibbled at a corner of it. 'There are lots of things. Lots of places I want to visit. Lots of things I want to experience that I haven't tried before.' Her hands ran over her stomach and her eyes met his. 'But there's one thing on the list that I've already got.'

He nodded. It was obvious that would be on the list. She'd had to undergo a cycle of fertility drugs to stimulate her ovaries before undergoing chemo so it kind of went without saying that having kids would be on the 'want to' list.

'Anything else I can help you with?'

She raised her eyebrow at him. 'You want to help with what's on the list?' She looked a little unsure.

Lincoln nodded. 'Why not?' Was it guilt that was making him say that? Guilt, because he hadn't been there for her when she'd been sick—even though she hadn't asked?

Amy shifted uncomfortably. 'I've never actually shown anyone my list,' she murmured.

Lincoln sat backwards. 'You actually have it—a list—written down?'

She nodded slowly, looking slightly amused. 'That's what a list is, Linc.'

This time as she watched him his smile reached his eyes, right up to the corners. Not like a few minutes ago. His eyes were twinkling. 'I thought we were talking hypothetical, I didn't realise you'd actually written it down.'

Amy bent forward and rummaged around her bag, unzipping a pocket inside and pulling out a piece of red paper, which she carefully unfolded and placed in the middle of the blanket. Lincoln leaned forward, intrigued. 'Silver pen?' He raised his eyebrows at her. 'Red and silver...' he nodded towards her feet '...just like your toes.'

Amy looked surprised and wriggled her toes in the sand. 'I hadn't even thought of that, and I was planning on changing my toes.' She wiggled them again. 'I like the stars but thought maybe midnight blue with gold stars this time.' She gave a little smile. 'More dramatic.' She waved her hand at the list. 'That's why I picked the red paper and silver pen, I wanted it to look bold, strong and powerful. Make me feel confident that I would be here to complete it.' Her voice had faded away and she was staring out at the ocean again.

Almost on instinct Lincoln reached out his hand and intertwined his fingers with hers. It was comfort, that was all. He was comforting a friend, showing support. So why did he feel the need to tell himself that inside his head?

He looked down at the paper again and gave her fingers a squeeze. 'I think I would have to be a billionaire to help you with some of the things on this list.'

Amy looked embarrassed, pink tingeing her cheeks. 'Not all of them.' She leaned her head over next to his. 'Some of these were just wishful thinking.'

He quirked one eyebrow. 'That would be the two-carat diamond ring and the trip to Monte Carlo?'

She nodded. 'Exactly.' And took another bite of her sandwich. 'The others are much more reasonable.'

He looked at the neat, deliberate writing in front of him. Small script, carefully written.

1. Do whatever it takes to have a family.
2. Buy a gorgeous two-carat diamond ring.

3. Go on a trip to Monte Carlo and take a photograph outside the Hotel de Paris.

4. Learn to surf.

5. Learn to salsa.

6. Go to a *Star Trek* convention.

7. Travel on the cable cars in San Francisco.

8. Go back on the Amazon Aid Boat.

9. Join one of the social networking sites and find old friends.

10. Learn how to crochet and crochet a baby blanket.

A higgledy-piggledy, jumbled-up list. No priorities, just everything down there on paper.

The list looked a little well worn—rough around the edges—as if she'd pulled it from her bag on many occasions to read it. The red paper was still bright and the silver ink still glistened in the sun. It should be a happy, sunny list.

But it terrified him. Because for him it was evidence that at some point Amy had actually thought she was going to *die*. She'd actually put pen to paper and written a list of things she still wanted to do. She may have said the list was to make her feel better, but Linc was no fool. People didn't just write these lists to plan ahead—they wrote these lists as things to do before they *died*. And the thought made him feel physically sick. The sun was shining in the sky above him but the hairs on his arms were standing on end—as if he'd just walked through a chilly morgue.

He tried to push his thoughts away. He couldn't think about this. It was making him question everything about himself and his relationship with Amy. They'd been skirting around things. Playing at being friends—when they both knew there was a huge potential for more.

Did he want to have a relationship with Amy? Was it sensible? What if this pregnancy made her cancer come back? How would he feel then? And what about Amy's baby? Sure, he'd considered all the clinical aspects of a premature baby, but he hadn't considered the emotional aspects. The emotional aspects of having a relationship with a woman who had another man's baby. At least he had the satisfaction of knowing that the sperm donor would never appear. But that was little consolation if something happened to Amy. Would he be prepared to take on another man's child? Could he even consider bringing a baby up himself—one he had no genetic relationship with—if something happened to Amy?

Lincoln gave himself a shake. The sun was getting to him. He tried to focus on the list again and found his heart beating furiously in his chest. He looked at the items again. It couldn't be a coincidence—the boat and finding old friends. She'd produced a list when she'd been at her lowest ebb and two of the references on it could be about him.

Okay, so the list didn't say 'Find Lincoln Adams'. But why would she want to go back to the Amazon aid boat? And why would she decide to look up old friends? Was it really all just some strange coincidence, or was he making a mountain out of a molehill?

He cleared his throat, readying himself to ask the obvious question. 'So how many of these have you actually done?'

Amy gave up on the sandwich and picked one of peaches he'd unpacked from the picnic basket, taking a big bite and letting the juice trickle down her chin. 'From the list?' He nodded. She was licking the juice from her fingers now. 'Just two.' Her voice sounded bright and breezy, as if she were discussing the latest episode of her favourite TV drama, instead of the 'try before you die' list.

He gave a little laugh. 'You're joking, right? Two? In five years?'

A wicked smile stole across her face. 'Let's just say I had a bit of a slow start,' she teased. Her hands rubbed her bump. 'And, anyway, this is a pretty big one. It's taken up a lot of my time.'

Lincoln leaned backwards. 'Okay, I'll give you that.' He watched as she discarded the half-eaten peach, wrapping it in a napkin and pulling out a lemon cupcake. 'Do you finish anything you eat these days?'

Amy peeled the case from the cupcake, tapping her stomach again. 'Not much room in here these days. I tend to eat little and often at the moment. I only really finish anything if it's the middle of the night—for some reason I'm always starving then.'

'So what was number two?'

'What?' Amy was lost in the land of lemon cupcake.

'You said you'd done two things on your list. Number one is obvious so what's number two?'

Amy waved her hand. 'Oh, that was easy. I made myself a page on one of those social networking sites so I could track down some old friends.'

And with that wave of her hand Lincoln felt his insides plummet. She'd done the social networking, she'd tracked down 'old friends' and he obviously wasn't among them.

He shifted uncomfortably on the sand. 'Which one did you use?'

She named the most popular one around, one where he had a page posted.

He bit his bottom lip. 'So did you track down your old friends?'

Amy picked up a can of soda. 'Yeah, loads of them. All my old classmates from high school, old nursing friends from college, and people from some of the towns we stayed in as a kid—we moved about a lot.'

Lincoln asked the next question with a sinking feeling. 'So how many friends have you got, then?'

'Eight hundred and forty-two.' Eight hundred and forty-two. As if it were the easiest thing in the world. Pushing his paltry twenty-six 'friends' into oblivion. Amy changed position on the blanket. Moving up on to her knees and digging deep in the basket, she lifted her eyes, giving him an innocent smile. 'You know I reconnected with loads of people from the Amazon aid boat—Lily Carter, John Rhodes, Frank Kelly, Gene Hunt, Milly Johnson…' She finally found what she was looking for, a bunch of green grapes, and pulled them out from the basket. 'You know—you should join.'

For the first time in years Lincoln could feel the flush of colour in his cheeks. 'I've got a page,' he murmured.

'You have?' Her eyes were that bright, sparkly way again. 'You should send me a friend request, then—I'll accept.' A definite twinkle had appeared in her eye. She was teasing him again.

He rolled over on the blanket, groaning and putting his head in his hands. 'Okay, spill. How come you never sent me a friend request? You seem to have sent…' he waved his arms in front of him, out toward the ocean '…everyone else in the world one but me.'

Amy lay down next to him, resting her head in her hands, her hat flopping over her eyes. She was so close the length of her body was touching his, her bare legs next to his, the brim of her hat almost touching his head. She looked out toward the ocean, back at the surfers, and gave a little sigh.

'It just didn't feel right.'

His face was shadowed under her hat, his blue eyes even darker than normal. 'What do you mean, *it didn't feel right*?'

She looked downwards, towards the sand that was now trickling through her fingers. 'Some people knew that I'd been sick. They might have asked me how I was doing. I didn't want you to read it online.'

Lincoln opened his mouth and then stopped. It was time to use his head, not blurt out the first thing that came to mind. He pushed the thoughts of why she hadn't sent a private message to one side—along with the quip about whether it was more appropriate for her to turn up unannounced as his pregnant wife.

'I tried to find you, you know.' His fingers delved in the sand next to hers, pulling tiny pieces of a million years ago and rubbing them between his finger and thumb.

Her hand had stopped in mid-air. Her face turned to his. 'You did?' She looked shocked—surprised—as if it was the last thing she'd expected. Her green eyes were fixed on his, as if she was holding her breath, waiting for his response.

He moved his fingers from the sand and brushed them off, putting his hand over hers. 'Of course I did.' He was looking directly at her. Something he hadn't done much in the last few days. Last time he'd looked at her like this had been when they'd kissed.

His finger touched her cheek. 'I'd just had the best six months of my life—professionally and personally—and then poof!' He blew into his fingers. 'The best thing disappeared.'

Amy could hear thudding in her ears. Was that the sound of her heart beating? Had he really just said that?

She felt a tingling sensation across her skin. Wasn't this what she'd really wanted to hear but he'd never said? She couldn't stop staring into those eyes. Those dark blue rims were really fascinating up close. Her throat felt dry, closed up, and she swallowed nervously. 'You never said anything,' she whispered. 'I thought I was just your summer fling.'

'I think six months qualifies as a little more than a summer fling.' He blinked, breaking off his gaze and staring back down at the sand. 'And, anyway, what was there to say?' His voice sounded rueful. 'I met a gorgeous girl and spent six fantastic months in bed with her, then she disappeared.' He never lifted his head, just kept staring at the sand, his hand scooping up big piles that he let run through his fingers again.

'I contacted a few people and tried to get your number, called Human Resources—who said that you'd quit. No one else on the boat seemed to have contact details for you. So that was it.'

So that was it. It sounded so final.

'You should have told me, Amy. You should have told me you were sick.' The sand was trickling through his fingers again. 'I don't think I can forgive the fact you didn't tell me.'

The words spun around in her head. After all this time, and all her explanations, he was still angry with her. The tiny spark that had been ignited inside her was dying. Being described as someone he'd 'spent six fantastic months in bed with' didn't fill her with inspiration. It made her feel like a sex object. Not a living, breathing human soul.

Not someone who he'd connected with. And definitely not someone he might have loved.

CHAPTER SIX

LINCOLN laid baby Esther on the scales again. Four pounds twelve ounces. A slight increase on her birth weight and she was finally feeding well. He gave Jennifer a little smile. 'Well, I think I can officially give the First Daughter a clean bill of health. There's really no reason to keep her here any longer.'

'I can go home?' The relief in Jennifer's eyes was apparent. Her husband, Charlie, had had to leave again two days ago and she was anxious to be with him.

Lincoln gave a nod.

'Do you have a preferred paediatrician in Washington? I'd like to handover to him or her before you go home.'

Jennifer gave a little nod. 'David Fairgreaves recommended someone to me—Linda Hylton. Have you heard of her?'

Lincoln nodded. 'We were paediatric residents together. She's great and she'll look after you. I know her number so I'll give her a call this afternoon.' He rolled his eyes at the black-suited figure visible through the glass in the door. 'I'll speak to your security detail. If you go home tomorrow, I'd expect you to see Linda in the next few days.' His nose wrinkled. 'I don't suppose you're going to be able to attend a regular appointment.'

He shook his head, 'Obviously not. Once I've spoken to Linda, I'll give James Turner her information and let him sort the appointment details out. Are you happy with that?'

Jennifer gave a watery smile. 'I'll just be happy to get home,' she whispered, then looked up again. 'Wait a minute—is Linda Hylton one of your love victims? Should I be careful what I say about you?'

Lincoln rolled his eyes. 'I don't know where you get these crazy ideas. I don't go out with *every* woman I meet.'

Jennifer folded her arms. 'So what was wrong with Linda Hylton?'

Lincoln smiled. 'Okay, you got me. She was dating one of my friends. Satisfied?'

Jennifer nodded her head, stifling her laugh.

'What about some help with your breastfeeding? Do you want me to arrange some support for you?'

Jennifer breathed a sigh of relief. 'Thankfully that's the one thing that I arranged a few months ago. I've got a friend who's a specialist NICU nurse in Washington—she's taking a leave of absence from her work for a few weeks and she's going to be around.'

Lincoln sat in the chair next to her, scribbling a few notes in the chart. 'Let me try and sort out the logistics of this.' He glanced around her jam-packed room, where even more presents seemed to have materialised. 'You just worry about how you're going to fit all this stuff into Air Force One.'

Jennifer shook her head. 'Now, now, Lincoln. It's only Air Force One if the President is on board—I thought everyone knew that. It's just an ordinary plane without him.'

Lincoln shook his head. 'I wouldn't let you fly with a

neonate this young on an *ordinary* plane, Jennifer. But I'll do a final check on Esther before you go. Everything looks fine, so I don't imagine there will be any problems.'

Jennifer paused. 'Just out of interest, Linc. What does your "friend" make of your flirting?'

He stopped. The question had thrown him. He shrugged, shuffling the notes in his lap. 'Funnily enough, she's not interested in this hot body, she's only interested in my clinical skills.'

Something about saying those words made his stomach clench. He'd said them in jest but the irony wasn't lost on him. Amy had been clear about why she was here. For his skills as a neonatologist.

He went to stand up but Jennifer reached over and touched his arm. 'Did she like the maternity clothes?'

'Yes…yes, she did. Thank you. And you were right. They fitted perfectly.'

Jennifer gave a little nod, a little smile appearing on her face. 'I thought they might.' She waved her arms around the room. 'And your friend—does she need anything else? Anything for her baby?'

He shook his head. 'She's picked out most things and paid for them already. She just needs to pick them up.'

Then it struck him. Pick them up. From where? Suddenly it all seemed so ridiculous to him. How on earth was she going to be able to pick up her baby things?

He'd seen the baby catalogues stuffed in her bag and she'd showed him the items that she'd chosen. A white wooden baby crib and chest of drawers, a bright red pram and stroller, a zebra-print baby seat and a polished wooden high chair.

All apparently paid for and waiting in a store in Santa

Maria, Butte County. Four hours away from where he stayed in San Francisco and even further from Pelican Cove.

'Thanks for all your help, Lincoln...' The First Lady was talking to him but his mind had drifted off. He was just about to discharge baby Esther, which meant that he, and his whole entourage of staff and equipment, should pack up and leave. Leave to go back to NICU at San Francisco Children's Hospital. Something that deep down he knew they all wanted to do.

But that would mean leaving Amy with no facilities for her baby. No staff and no equipment for a premature delivery. Her blood pressure was still borderline, with no particular response to the anti-hypertensives. She should be reviewed on a daily basis. Who would do that if they all left?

'So I was wondering if you would mind?'

'Mind? Mind what?' Lincoln snapped out of his thoughts with the distinct impression he'd just missed something important.

Jennifer laughed, the amused expression on her face unhidden. 'You haven't listened to a single word I said—have you?'

Lincoln felt embarrassed.

'You're too busy thinking about a beautiful redhead, I imagine.'

'What? No? Of course not.' He was babbling and he knew it.

'Oh, don't make excuses, Linc, you've done everything you can for me...' she bent her head and kissed her baby on the forehead '...and Esther.' She waved her hand in the air. 'So go and see your lady friend.'

Lincoln's lips formed a tight smile and he left the room, stopping in the middle of the corridor. What on earth was he going to do? He'd promised to look after Amy's baby—how could he do that in San Francisco?

He strode quickly down the corridor. Right now he needed someone to talk to. Someone who could give him some advice. But all his friends were in San Francisco, and the only other people he knew well were Val and Ruth. He couldn't discuss Amy with them, it just wasn't his style.

He walked out the front doors of the hospital into the Californian sunshine. It was another gorgeous day. Just like the one a few days ago when he'd taken Amy for the picnic on the beach.

The day that had left an awkward and uncomfortable silence between them. He'd obviously said something to offend her—but, for the life of him, he couldn't think what it was. She seemed almost…disappointed in him.

Lincoln walked over to one of the benches outside the hospital doors and sat down. He took a long, slow breath, in and out. He had to take some time to think about this—think about what to do.

If he discharged baby Esther tomorrow, he would have to tell Amy that it was time for his staff and equipment to leave Pelican Cove. So why did his stomach churn at the mere thought of that?

He stared out over the ocean, watching the crashing waves. It was time to stop skirting around the edges. It was time to face up to the facts. How did 'playboy Linc' really feel about Amy?

He could remember how much he'd missed her when she'd left the boat. But then he'd thought it was only a holiday and she'd be back before he knew it. Except she hadn't been.

When she'd gone on holiday it had hit him how much he missed her. He'd lain awake in his cabin at night, listening to the sounds of the Amazon rain forest, his thoughts filled with her, stealing his sleep away from him. He'd watched the calendar hanging in the galley, counting the days until she came back.

Except she hadn't.

And the feelings that had descended on him when she hadn't returned had been a first for him. He had been frustrated beyond belief by the fact that no one had been able to tell him where she was, or why she hadn't returned. Most of the other staff had just shrugged their shoulders and said it happened often—people went home to their nice, clean homes and calm lives, and decided not to return to the damp, humid conditions of the Amazon.

Everyone just seemed to accept it and carry on with their lives—whilst Lincoln had felt as if he was losing his mind.

So he'd pushed it all away. Put his mind on the job at hand, the fate of a thousand people living on the banks of the Amazon and coming for medical care and treatment. Then, six months later, his new position in the States at San Francisco's Children's Hospital and the chance to be part of a world-class team had arisen.

But he couldn't shake her from her his mind. He couldn't replace her in his thoughts with the next nurse that came along—the next woman who showed interest in him. Even his potential bride didn't push her from his thoughts. Poor Polly didn't deserve the cold way he had treated her, but in the end he just couldn't stop the visions of the long red curly hair and dark green eyes.

Even months later, in another world, another city, he would see a turn of a head, a flash in the corner of his eye and the feeling of his heart in his mouth when he'd thought he'd glimpsed her again, only to have it plummet seconds later at the realisation it wasn't her. It wasn't Amy.

And then, a few days ago, he'd seen her again and all those feelings came rushing back. His skin on fire, his heart pounding in his chest, and the sick feeling in his stomach when he realised she was unwell, and then again when he realised she was pregnant.

The horror when she told him she'd been ill. Breast cancer. Even now, the mere thought of it made him angry. Those tiny malicious cells growing around her body, filling her with disease. Filling her with fear for her future. Then the horror of her treatment—treatment that some people maintained was worse than the disease. How on earth had she managed that on her own?

He shook his head. How would he have coped if it had been him? Could he have been so brave? So sure? So steadfast? So determined? Then the list—the list she'd written to get her through. To give her focus and a way ahead.

Another sensation surrounded him and he sank his head into his hands. Because this feeling made him feel sick to the pit of his stomach. Guilt.

Guilt about the relief he'd felt when she'd revealed that there was no one in her life. No husband. No father for the baby.

Was that wrong of him? Was it wrong of him to feel that way? Was it wrong that those words had given him a small sliver of hope?

And what about the baby? If Amy's condition didn't improve, her baby could arrive in a matter of a few weeks, or even days. Would that change the way he felt about her? He was a playboy, no matter how much he detested the word. He'd never given children a second thought—well, not children of his own.

His stomach was churning. Any day now he was going to have to pack up and leave. But what would happen to Amy then?

She could stay here in Pelican Cove. David would continue to be her obstetrician. But there was no neonatologist if she had an early delivery. It was routine procedure that any woman at risk in Pelican Cove would be transferred to San Francisco. His home. Chances were, he would have ended up being her neonatologist by default if she'd turned up there.

This was so complicated. Should he offer her help? Support? What would he do if this was just another female friend? If this wasn't Amy—a woman who messed with his mind just by being there?

The most sensible solution was to invite her to stay with him in San Francisco and let her continue her obstetric care there until the baby arrived. That's what he would do for anyone else. Anyone he considered a friend.

The thoughts jumbled around in his head. But was that really sensible? She could deliver in two days or two weeks. How would it feel to have Amy in his apartment—under his roof?

Lincoln closed his eyes and took a deep breath. He was helping a friend. And maybe, just maybe, if he kept repeating that, he might actually believe it.

Lincoln stood at the nurses' station and looked over Amy's chart quickly. David had reviewed her again this morning, taken more blood samples and adjusted her blood-pressure meds.

The handwritten script in the case notes was precise. David felt she was teetering at the edge. She was still clearly at risk of her pre-eclampsia developing into the full blown disease. He wanted her treated with caution and monitored daily.

Lincoln understood. And strangely it filled him with confidence that he'd made the right decision and was about to take the right steps.

He leaned over to the nearest computer and checked his e-mail account. Because he was away from his normal hospital, all his e-mails were currently being diverted to his personal account. 'What the…?' He leaned in closer to his account. Three thousand e-mails. He squinted at the screen. A voice behind him laughed, leaning over his shoulders.

'Wow,' she said, 'that's a *lot* of friend requests.'

Lincoln shook his head, 'I don't get it,' he mumbled, the thoughts of his paltry list of twenty-six friends the day before bewildering him. 'Who on earth are all these people?' His eyes ran up and down the names on the list. 'I don't even recognise any of them.'

The nurse behind him patted him on the shoulder. 'That's what happens when you appear on the TV as the President's doctor, handsome.' She gave a little laugh as she walked away.

Lincoln sat for a few seconds. Instant fame. He hadn't even given it much thought. One television appearance and suddenly half the world wanted to be his 'friend'.

A small hand positioned itself on the box on the counter next to him. 'Lincoln, we didn't know you cared.'

His hands shot out and grabbed the cake box and carton of coffee on the counter. 'I don't.' He gave the nurse a smile. 'Hands off. These are my bargaining tools and I think I'm going to need them.'

She shook her head. 'Just don't let her throw them off the wall—those cupcakes are too good to waste.'

Amy's door was slightly ajar and he could see her lying in the darkened room. Her blinds were drawn to block out the glaring sun and she lay on her side on the bed, her eyes closed, wearing a pale blue smock and drawstring linen trousers.

'Knock, knock.'

Her eyelids flickered open, a smile starting on her face before her brain switched into gear and she remembered she was angry with him.

She pushed herself up the bed. 'Hi, Lincoln, what do you want?'

He put his gifts on the bedside table, pushing it up towards her until it sat just before her extended abdomen.

Amy took a deep breath. Coffee. That was definitely coffee she could smell. She lifted the lid on the cup and inhaled. Even better, it was a caramel latte. She'd seriously thought about killing someone for one of these the other day.

She pulled the pink ribbon on the cake box, tugging it clear and lifting the lid on the box. Cupcakes. Strawberry, chocolate and lemon. And all of them had her name written on them. Literally.

Her taste buds started watering. Lincoln knew her well. The best way to her heart was through her stomach. What was he up to?

She picked up a pink cupcake, peeled the paper case and took a bite. 'Mmm. I know that there is probably an ulterior motive to these…' she raised her hand '…but I don't want you to tell me what it is until I've finished eating. I *don't* want you to spoil this.' She eyed the cup. 'I thought you weren't letting me drink coffee?'

'It's a special occasion.'

She took a sip of the caramel latte. Perfect. Her taste buds exploded. Oh, how she'd missed this. Her eyes swept over the box of cakes. Could she eat another before he started speaking? Probably. They were tiny—two bites and they were gone. Her fingers hovered over a chocolate cupcake, the next in the box.

She lifted her eyes to look at him. Lincoln was sitting in the chair next to her bed, waiting patiently for her to finish. But he didn't look ill at ease or nervous. No, he looked cool, calm and confident. In short, he didn't look like a man who thought he'd have to bribe his way into the room. He looked like a man who'd already made whatever decision had to be made. And it made her feel distinctly uncomfortable.

She set down the chocolate cupcake, praying whatever he said wasn't about to ruin her appetite. 'What do you want, Linc?'

He nodded slowly, his eyes fixing on hers. 'We need to talk, Amy.'

She bit her lip. Where was this going to go? 'What about?'

He sat a little straighter. 'Baby Esther is ready to go home—to go back to the White House. She's ready for discharge, and once I finish her paperwork, the plans will be in place.'

Amy nodded. What did this have to do with her?

Lincoln's face was serious. 'Once she's ready to go, *I* have to go. *We* have to go.'

The penny dropped. Like a huge boulder throwing itself off the edge of a cliff. 'Oh.'

She should have known this was coming. At first, it hadn't even occurred to her—the fact that Lincoln wouldn't be staying here. She'd been so caught up in getting to where he was and making him agree to look after her baby that she'd had tunnel vision. But after a few days stuck as an inpatient in Pelican Cove she'd started to worry. The First Lady wasn't likely to stay here for long. What would happen then? The truth was, she'd more or less expected to have her baby in a matter of days. But Junior seemed to be making his own plans.

'So, it's time to make a decision.' Amy felt as if she could throw up. Once baby Esther left, there was no reason for any of the staff or facilities that had been spirited into Pelican Cove to stay. What about her? What about her baby? And why did Lincoln look so calm?

'I need to pack up all the NICU equipment and arrange for my staff to return to San Francisco.'

Duh. She'd just realised that.

'I need to return to San Francisco, as I've got duties and commitments there...'

She nodded dumbly. Of course he did.

'So I thought it best to make some arrangements for you and the baby.' He picked up her chart. She hadn't even noticed him bringing it into the room. *Arrangements*. Did he know how clinical that sounded?

'David still has some concerns about your condition. You're coming up on twenty-nine weeks, but your blood pressure is still borderline—even with the anti-hypertensives—and you're still showing protein in your urine.'

His hand brushed against hers, his voice softening, becoming less businesslike and more friendlike. 'Chances are, this baby is still going to come early. You came to Pelican Cove because you wanted me to be the one to look after your baby. Is that still what you want, Amy?'

She nodded. Words escaped her right now. Her mind was too full of jumbled thoughts to say anything coherent. Where was this going?

Lincoln nodded and gave her a little smile. 'In that case, I think I might have found a solution for us, then.'

'Solution?' The word gave her hope. Because, right now, she needed some.

'You can come back to San Francisco with me.' There. He'd said it. The words that had been coiled up inside his chest since he'd came to the conclusion a few hours ago. In his head, that made perfect sense.

Right now he was leaving out the way he felt drawn to her room in the hospital, day or night, for no good reason. She was like a magnet to him and he was instantly drawn.

And in his head that was perfect. She'd disappeared out of his life before and he'd no intention of letting it happen again. But this time he'd be more careful. Amy had searched him out. She'd come to find him. She wanted his skills and expertise—and she could have them. And maybe it could give him some time to work out how he felt about her.

It took him a few seconds to realise she hadn't spoken. She seemed frozen to the spot, or to the bed. Her mouth was hanging open, and her hands had the slightest tremor.

Time to fill in the blanks. Time to persuade her it was most reasonable and viable option for her.

'I know you've been looked after in Santa Maria— but you came here because you didn't have a physician there you could trust. And the most important thing is that you have someone you trust looking after your baby.

'David will be staying in Pelican Cove. He could continue to treat you, if that's what you prefer. But even he is worried about an early delivery. The normal protocol in Pelican Cove is that someone in your condition would be transferred to San Francisco Children and Maternity Hospital—where we have excellent facilities for neonates.' He let her take in the words, rationalise it in her brain.

'I can arrange for one of the obstetricians there to take over your care. There are two I would absolutely trust with my life. I wouldn't recommend them to you otherwise.' He ran his fingers through his tousled hair, a sign of his nerves. Was this going well?

'We could arrange to get there tomorrow. I'll get one of the obstetricians to review you immediately and decide on how to proceed. If there's any emergency, I'll be close by and available to be at the delivery.'

His words hung in the air. There. He'd said them. And whilst he knew every word he'd said was true, there was still that tiny little bit of him that knew there was an element of emotional blackmail in there. He was using her fear for her child to get her exactly where he wanted her.

He didn't like the word *manipulate*. It seemed like something from a bad-guy movie. Something that the villain did. But he'd never said he was perfect. He'd never said he didn't have flaws. He was just a man. Trying to get his girl.

Amy's hands were resting on the bedside table—probably to control a tremor. She thought of her empty apartment in Santa Maria, with the baby's things still flat-packed into boxes. She didn't have any family any more, but she had good friends there who were happy to help out and support her. She was lucky that she had regular hours at the clinic that meant she could plan her childcare hours in advance. So why did it feel as if all the plans she had made were crumbling around her?

'But where would I stay? I don't know anyone in San Francisco?' It looked as if it was just one of a million thoughts that were currently scurrying around in her brain.

'That's easy. You'll stay with me.'

Amy choked, then coughed and spluttered, her face turning redder and redder by the second. Lincoln jumped to his feet and leapt behind her, thumping his hand on her back until she stopped then grabbing a glass of water from the nearby locker and handing it to her. 'Here, take this.'

She took a little sip, taking in deep frantic breaths, trying to fill her lungs with the air that seemed to have been sucked from them when he'd said those words.

She blew the air out slowly through thick pursed lips, then turned to face him. 'How on earth can I come and stay with you, Lincoln? You haven't seen me in six years. You don't owe me anything. Yes, I want you to deliver my baby but I don't expect anything else from you, and I certainly don't expect *this*.'

Her voice was slow and steady, but he could see the panic in her eyes. She was frantic, swimming in an ocean where she was out her depth and being pulled out with the current. Seemed she was as scared of the scenario as he was.

'Amy, the fact is you can stay anywhere you want to. But if you are going to come to San Francisco, it makes sense that you stay with a friend. There's no point in running up a hotel bill—you could deliver tomorrow, or in six weeks' time. And in your current condition it makes even more sense if that friend has some medical expertise.' The words were plain. Sensible, and he knew it. They sounded rational and reasonable.

They didn't tell her that his heart was suddenly thudding against his chest and his stomach was turning inside out at the thought of her not agreeing to this.

'I'd like to think that as soon as we get to San Francisco one of my colleagues will assess you. They might even want to admit you. But if, like Pelican Cove, they want to see you on a daily basis, it makes sense that you stay with me. I live five minutes away from the hospital in a two-bedroom apartment. I've got a housekeeper that comes in twice a week, so you won't feel obliged to do anything. Just relax with your feet up and wait for this baby to arrive.'

She was still silent. It looked as if she were trying to formulate words in her brain. Was she looking for an easy way to let him down? To tell him she couldn't possibly stay with him? He couldn't hear that.

It was time to play his trump card.

He kept his voice strong and confident. He wanted her to feel assured, safe. He also wanted to play to her fun side. 'Look at it this way, Amy, you'll get to do another thing on your list.'

'My list?' Her eyes were blank, as if the list was the last thing on her mind.

Lincoln nodded and touched her hand. 'I didn't mention where I stay, did I? I've got an apartment in Fisherman's Wharf in San Francisco. It's actually just where the cable cars turn to start their journey again. You'll have number seven on your list at your fingertips.'

Even as he said the words he questioned his wisdom. Doing something on her list was never going to be the deciding factor for her. But right now desperate times called for desperate measures. And he'd use whatever it took.

She looked a bit dazed, shocked.

'Amy?'

Her voice had the slightest tremor. 'It's a lot to think about.' She stood up and pushed the bedside table away, walking over to the window and looking out over Pelican Cove. Her hands were placed protectively over her stomach, as if she were cradling her baby inside.

Inside her brain was in turmoil. Why hadn't she planned ahead? Why hadn't she foreseen this? The safety of her baby was always going to be paramount, but what about the safety of her soul?

The last few days had brought a huge surge of emotions to the fore. Maybe they were pregnancy related? But right now every time she was in a room with Lincoln she couldn't think of anything else.

The thought of running up a hotel bill made her blood run cold. Her maternity salary was comfortable enough to cover her rent and outgoings, but not unexpected outgoings like these.

Stay in his apartment? He must be out of his mind! She had visions in her head of two lions stalking around their prey. That's what it would feel like. How could she possibly be relaxed around Lincoln when every second she would be waiting to see if he would touch her, look at her, take her in his arms and…

'I don't think it would work.' The words were out before she had a chance to think about them.

'Why?' Lincoln looked confused. He walked towards her and put his arms on either side of her shoulders. His face seemed so open, so honest. With no concerns, no worries. He really didn't know. He really didn't realise what he did to her.

But, then, how could he, if she'd never told him?

'I... I...' Her throat was dry, her tongue sticking to the top of her mouth.

'It's the perfect solution—surely you can see that?' Then he did it. He gave her that killer smile. The one that used to unnerve her from across the room and make her knees buckle. The smile that sent a thousand feather-like touches skittering across her skin. And something inside her heart lurched.

Hope. The feeling she'd felt when she'd seen him on television and had known she'd be able to find him and ask for help.

The sensations that had engulfed her when she'd first set eyes on him after six long years.

The heat and warmth that had swept through her body when he'd touched her, when he'd kissed her.

The look in his eyes on the beach when he'd told her that he'd searched for her and it had sent loose a thousand butterflies, beating their wings inside her chest.

Hope.

A sensation she only recognised now. The same sensation she'd steeled inside herself when she'd written the list.

He reached up, catching a curl of hair that had fallen in front of her eye, tucking it behind her ear. He was looking at her with those dark-rimmed eyes. She was mesmerised. And she wanted more.

Maybe this was the way to get it.

'You're right,' she breathed. 'It makes perfect sense. When do we leave?'

CHAPTER SEVEN

AMY looked out of the apartment window, across the rippling San Francisco bay to Alcatraz. What a view. It was strange how a piece of rock could seem so foreboding and enigmatic, rising up from the grey waves. Even from this distance she could see the ferry pulling in again, no doubt unloading its cargo of tourists all anxious to capture the moment on camera.

Everywhere she looked there were tourists. The iconic Powell-Hyde cable car turntable at Fisherman's Wharf was practically under her nose, with a constant stream of people lining up to get their photo snapped next to it. She looked back over her shoulder, into the spacious wooden-floored apartment. This really was a prime piece of real estate and she shuddered to think how much it had cost.

Amy glanced at her watch for the third time in ten minutes. 'Resting' wasn't easy for a girl who was used to being on her feet in a busy ward for twelve hours a day. Three long days she'd been looking out of this window into the wonderful world of bustling San Francisco beneath her. Currently just out of her reach.

Daily hospital monitoring and strict bed rest. It almost sounded like a prison sentence. The irony of the view of Alcatraz wasn't lost on her.

Her blood pressure hadn't improved, her urine still had protein in it, but thankfully her oedema was under control and she hadn't developed any other symptoms. It hadn't stopped her newest obstetrician, Cassidy Yates—a statuesque blonde who watched Lincoln out of the corner of her eye—from referring to the local protocols and administering some steroids to help develop the baby's lungs in case of early delivery. For the past three days Amy had travelled with him into work and he'd dropped her at the day unit for monitoring and assessment.

Twenty-nine weeks and three days. Right now her extended abdomen felt like a ticking time bomb. Then there was being *here*. In Lincoln's apartment, surrounded all day by little pieces of him.

The good thing was…he'd been the perfect gent. Welcoming, considerate and ever attentive. The frustrating thing was…he'd been the perfect gent. And it was driving her crazy.

Amy sighed and flopped down into the nearby red leather armchair, pushing until the seat tilted backwards and the leg rest sprang out. There was nothing to do—Lincoln had said he would take care of dinner, so all she could do right now was wait.

The trouble with waiting was that it left too much time to think. Too much time to look out at the busy life below and wonder when you could be part of it again. She felt a sharp kick under her ribs and drew a deep breath. She pulled up her smock top to reveal her baby bump.

She watched the squirms under her skin—if this were a movie, any minute now a twelve-armed alien would burst from her stomach. Baby Zachary had obviously decided to have a party in there, and he was certainly beginning to object to the reducing space. Her hands hovered just above her belly, wondering where the next punch would appear. It really was amazing to think that she would hold him in her arms soon. What would he look like? Would he have red hair and pale skin like her? Or the physical characteristics of his sperm donor father?

She could remember the details on the resume. Sperm Donor 867. Dark hair, green eyes (best to choose someone with the same eye colour you had), over six feet tall, college education. But did any of that really matter? Would genetics really decide the sum of her baby? Was it all nature or was it nurture?

She lifted her hands to her head, gently massaging her temples. Her head was starting to throb slightly, nothing to worry about—not enough to search the cupboards for paracetamol, just enough to annoy her thought processes.

What would her son's interests be? Her sperm donor had been a jock—no doubt about that. Every sport known to man had been on his list of interests. What did she know about football? But he'd also been academic, and had specialised in education.

So would her son be like his father or more like her? Reckless at times, occasionally unpredictable? In future years would she have to sit up at night, worrying about what time he would come in?

Zachary squirmed again under her skin, as if sensing her breath was currently caught in her chest. Why did she feel so panicked? She'd started this process six years ago—more than enough time to think about the end product. She'd spent the last two weeks worrying about premature birth and safe delivery. So why now was she panicking about hair colour and little-boy interests?

'That's some sight.'

Amy let out a shriek, pulling down her smock top and leaping up from the chair. Lincoln stood leaning against the doorframe, his arms folded across his chest, a smile of amusement on his face.

'Lincoln! I didn't hear you.' She could feel the colour rushing into her face. 'Where did you spring from?'

He crossed the room in a couple of steps, his hands resting lightly on the tops of her arms. 'Where I always spring from—work. Sorry, didn't mean to scare you.'

'You didn't… Well, you did, but I think that I… I mean…'

'You're babbling.' His voice was calm, but there was a distinct twinkle in his eye that even she could notice in the dimming light.

She looked around her. When had it got so dark? 'What time is it?'

'Just after seven. Sorry I'm a bit late, we had an emergency in NICU.'

She gave a quiet nod—she could hardly object, conscious of the fact that in a few days' or weeks' time her baby could be the emergency in NICU.

'I guess I lost track of time,' she murmured looking back out over the bustling city. Last time she'd looked outside it had been late afternoon. Had she drifted off to sleep? Her stomach growled loudly, reminding her of why she'd been waiting for Linc. 'Did you bring dinner?'

'Ahh…about that…' His forehead puckered in a frown.

This time it was her turn to smile. 'You forgot—didn't you?'

'Not exactly.' He extended his arm towards her, trying to push aside the delicious thoughts of the scene he'd just witnessed, his brain swiftly improvising. 'I decided to take you out to dinner. You must be going crazy, stuck in my apartment.'

Amy pressed her palms against the window. 'I don't know if crazy is the right word, but I definitely feel as if I'm missing out on something. I've dreamed about exploring San Francisco for years, and now that I'm here I feel as if it's just outside my reach.' She turned to face him and flattened her back against his picture window. 'I want to ride on the cable cars—I don't want to watch them turn underneath me. I want to do the boat trip to Alcatraz and stand in the cells and feel the atmosphere of the place. I want to go down to Pier 39 and have my picture taken next to the Fisherman's Wharf sign. I want to go and explore Chinatown. I want to eat there, see the colours and smell all the wonderful food. I want to spend the day wandering around Fisherman's Wharf wondering what type of ice cream I want to eat next. I want to sit in some of the quayside restaurants and eat all the fish on the menu.'

Lincoln raised his eyebrow at her, folding his arms across his chest. 'You have been going crazy in here, haven't you? Why didn't you say something sooner?'

She sighed. 'You've been busy, Linc. The last thing you need to do is try and entertain an uninvited house guest.'

He shook his head. 'Why do you keep saying stuff like that?'

'Stuff like what?'

His brow was puckered again. '*Uninvited* house guest.' He looked annoyed. 'You're not uninvited. I invited you.' He swung his arms wide, 'This is my home. I wanted you here.'

Amy licked her lips, as if she was preparing to say something. Her eyes were fixed on his again. And he could sense something. Something bubbling just underneath the surface, getting ready to erupt. The hairs stood up at the back of his neck, making him feel distinctly uncomfortable. All of sudden he felt as the though the walls of his spacious apartment were starting to close in around him.

'Come on.' He extended his arm towards her, anxious to break the tension between them. 'You can pick wherever you like. Let's eat.'

The street was packed. The early evening tourists were crammed onto the sidewalks, reading menus and deciding what restaurant to eat in. Lincoln weaved seamlessly through the crowd and pushed open a heavy wooden door, holding it open until Amy was safely inside.

She blinked furiously, her eyes struggling to adjust to the gloomy interior, but Lincoln took her hand again and eased her through the dimly lit restaurant, pulling her into a wooden seated booth.

'I thought I was getting to pick?'

He rolled his eyes. 'If we'd waited for you to pick, we'd still be standing on the sidewalk at midnight, peering at menus.'

He handed her a plastic-coated menu. 'What do you want to eat?'

Amy looked around her. The gaudily decorated interior of fake wooden barrels and ship's wheels draped with Hawaiian garlands left her speechless. To say nothing of the life-size pirate standing the corner of the room.

'This looks like a bit of a tourist trap,' she mumbled,

her eyes running over the menu in the hope it could re-
deem itself to her.

Lincoln leaned back in the booth, 'That's the beauty
of this place,' he said, a smile plastered across his face.
'It looks dark and seedy. But it hides San Francisco's
best-kept secret. My mate Johnny is the chef and he
makes the best food in the world.' He leaned across the
booth towards her. 'So what do you fancy?'

The English terminology made her blink, as did the
double meaning. What she 'fancied' wasn't on the menu
in front of her. But right now she couldn't even contem-
plate what she 'fancied'. Not while she currently felt like
a beached whale.

Her tongue ran nervously along her lips, her eyes
fixed on the plastic menu—because looking upwards
would mean staring into those deep blue eyes and she
couldn't face that right now. Junior gave another kick
and she winced.

Lincoln's hand shot across the table and caught hers.
'Are you okay? Is something wrong?'

Yes, yes, something was wrong. Her brain couldn't
focus. Her rational thoughts had left the building. She
wanted to blurt out everything that was currently spinning around in her head. She wanted to tell him that
she wished she'd called him six years ago when she'd
got the cancer diagnosis. She wanted to tell him that
she wished the baby she was currently carrying in her
belly was his, instead of donor 867's. She wanted to tell
him that she wished she'd had her surgery and her body
looked normal again so she could finally stand and look
at her naked reflection in the mirror again. She wanted
to tell him that her back ached, her feet were sore and
her headache was really starting to annoy her—but he'd
just taken her out and the last thing she wanted to do

right now was head back to the apartment. Because there it would just be the two of them. Alone.

Suddenly the grubby-looking restaurant didn't seem so bad. At least there were other people around.

A man appeared and slapped Lincoln on the shoulder. 'Who's the lovely lady, Linc? And why haven't you introduced me?'

Lincoln smiled. He seemed relaxed and easy in here and the tension that had been between them seemed to have left his tightened shoulders. He held his hand out towards Amy. 'This, Johnny, is my good friend Amy Carson. She's never sampled the delights of your cooking, so I hope you're going to impress her—otherwise she'll bend my ear all night for bringing her to such a dive.' He gave her a little wink across the table.

Johnny laughed. A deep, hearty laugh that seemed to come from all the way down at his toes. 'Impress? Me? Once I've fed this lady, she'll never look at you again, Linc.' He bent his head and picked up Amy's hand, kissing it with a flourish. 'So, beautiful, what can I get you?'

Amy looked back at Linc in panic. She hadn't even read the menu properly yet.

Lincoln pointed towards her. 'Why don't you decide for us, Johnny? Only be careful what you give my pregnant friend, we're hoping to avoid an early labour.'

Johnny's eyes turned to where Amy's extended abdomen was tucked neatly under the table in the darkened booth. He beamed. 'Congratulations, beautiful lady. I'm sure I can rustle something up that will delight your little bambino.'

He wandered back off to the kitchen and left the two of them sitting in the booth. Amy held her breath. Johnny was obviously a friend; would he assume the baby was Lincoln's? Or was her imagination just making wild leaps?

She could be a colleague from work, a neighbour, an old friend from school. There was no reason for Johnny to think anything else. So why was half of her hoping that he was?

Her stomach growled loudly. 'So what am I going to get to eat, Linc? With my current busy lifestyle, food is becoming a very important part of my day.'

Lincoln smiled at the lilt in her voice. This was the Amy he remembered. A bit cheeky, with a definite sarcastic edge. Not the nervous and uptight woman he'd spent the last few days with.

'I think I can safely say you'll get a feast fit for a king.'

'Or a queen?' The teasing tone was apparent.

'Ouch. Yes, or a queen.' He rested his head on his hands. 'What did Cassidy say today?'

Amy could feel the smile drop from her face. Why was it the mere mention of that woman's name automatically put her hackles up? Cassidy had only ever been pleasant and professional to Amy, but Amy could see the way Cassidy looked at Lincoln—even if he couldn't. His easy flirtatious manner was coming back to bite him on the...

'Nothing's changed. I've to go back tomorrow for more of the same.'

Lincoln leaned back and looked at her face. She looked vaguely irritated, as if she was annoyed. Surely, at this stage, no news was good news?

'So what's with the long face?'

Amy took a deep breath. This was where she should play the nice house guest. Happy, amenable and anxious to please.

Except these pregnancy hormones were driving her nuts. Her aching back was driving her nuts. Living under the same roof as Lincoln was driving her nuts. And seeing some gorgeous, statuesque blonde looking at Lincoln, *her Lincoln*, the way that woman did was driving her nuts.

She opened her mouth to speak just as Johnny reappeared and slid the biggest platter known to man onto their table. Grilled shrimp, Dungeness crab, scallops and crab cakes with rice and salad on the side. Then another plateful with grilled chicken, peppers, onion, a bowl of ratatouille and some garlic bread. Johnny folded his arms across his chest. 'Before you start, I know all of this is high in Omega 3 and can assure you it's all completely fresh and fully cooked. No tuna, no tilefish, no mackerel. All safe for a pregnant lady.' He shrugged his shoulders. 'But I also made you some chicken and garlic bread in case you were a little wary.'

Amy's face relaxed as the wonderful smell of freshly cooked fish wafted towards her. Her smile lit up her face. 'Johnny, how can a girl come to Fisherman's Wharf and not sample the Dungeness crab?'

She lifted her napkin from the table and spread it across her bump. 'Not the most glamorous, I know, but I'd hate to ruin these gorgeous clothes that you stole for me from the First Lady.'

Lincoln laughed as he pulled a plate towards him and started lifting some food from the platter. The maternity clothes had been a godsend. Today Amy was wearing a deep purple smock, which complemented her red hair and pale skin perfectly. In fact, every time he saw her she had a different outfit on. He had the distinct impression that the First Lady had known exactly the impact her 'cast-off' clothes would have. Brownie

points. Big time. 'I didn't steal them. She wanted you
to have them. And it's obvious you're making good use
of them—that's what she wanted.'

Amy lifted a fork to her mouth. 'So are you going to
tell me anything interesting about the First Lady?'

'And break patient confidentiality?' He'd raised one
eyebrow at her, in mock indignation, then bent over and
took a bite of his crab, shaking his head as he quickly
swallowed. 'Nope. I'm not going to tell you a thing.
Except she wanted you to use those clothes. Oh, and
that she called me an incorrigible flirt—how dare she?'

Amy laughed. 'Well, she got that right.'

'I do not flirt, I'm just a friendly person,' Lincoln
protested.

Amy rolled her eyes. 'Women fall at your feet everywhere, Linc.'

He paused for a second, as if lost in a thought,
'Mmm, not all women. It's only useful if it's the woman
you want.'

The air seemed to go silent around them. Amy bit
her lip. *What did that mean*? Did he mean her? Had
she fallen at his feet on the Amazon boat and he hadn't
wanted her to? Or was he talking about now, and how
she was trying to keep her distance? She had no idea
what was going on inside his head.

Amy took another bite of her shrimp, then broke the
garlic bread in half, handing it to him across the table.
A little twinge came across her back. Junior felt as if he
was turning around inside her right now. She crossed
then uncrossed her ankles, trying to find a more comfortable position.

'Everything okay?'

'That's twice you've asked in the last fifteen minutes.'

'And that's twice I've caught you looking at me as if you want to take a meat cleaver to my head.' Lincoln put his food back on the plate. 'So spill, Amy, what's eating you?'

'Nothing.'

Lincoln gave a sigh and lifted his glass of root beer, which had magically appeared at his side. 'So, if nothing's wrong, quit being snarky. I've had a crappy day at work and I just want to come home and relax.'

'Snarky? Is that even a word?' She couldn't help it. No matter how hard she tried, the words were practically a growl.

He lifted one eyebrow at her again. It was a habit of his that was really beginning to annoy her. No matter how chilled she tried to be.

'Amy, I'm only going to ask this once more. What's wrong?'

All of a sudden the gorgeous platter of food didn't seem so appetising. It looked as if it could catch in her throat and choke her to death. Worse, she could feel tears start to form in her eyes. Why was she about to cry? What the hell was wrong with her?

She gulped as one tear escaped and slid down her cheek and she fumbled for her napkin. 'Nothing's wrong. And everything's wrong. That's just it, Linc. I don't know what's wrong—I just know something is.'

Within seconds he'd reached across the table and captured her hands in his. She could feel the warmth from his hands creeping up her arms. Her hands felt cold, like blocks of ice. Truth be told, her whole body felt like that.

Another tear slid down her face and she pulled her hand away, brushing the paper napkin against her face. 'Damn pregnancy hormones,' she muttered.

'Don't, Amy. Don't do that. Don't blame this on the fact you're pregnant. We both know it's not that.' His voice cut through the dim light like a brilliant strobe, making her breath catch in her throat. He was looking directly at her, one hand now at the back of his head, pulling at his hair. His frustration was evident.

Silence. She didn't know what to say. She didn't know what she should say. She didn't know what she *could* say.

In her head it was easy. She was a princess in a pink satin dress, standing at the top of her tower, and he was Prince Charming on the white charger below. But she wasn't a child, and this wasn't a fairy-tale. This was real and in her head the princess wasn't pregnant with a sperm donor's baby and hadn't suffered from breast cancer and had a mastectomy. In her head the princess was the perfect healthy, whole, fertile partner that Prince Charming deserved.

Something she would never be.

'You do know she's got a crush on you—don't you?'

'What?' Lincoln looked confused at the change in subject. 'Who?'

'Cassidy Yates, that's who.'

Lincoln shook his head in bewilderment. 'No, she doesn't—that's ridiculous.'

Amy banged her hand on the table. 'Oh, yes, she does! I can see it every time she looks at you.'

Lincoln slammed down his glass, sloshing root beer all over the table. 'And why does it matter? Why does it matter if she does have a crush on me? Why does it matter to you?'

She could feel her lips trembling and her hands begin to shake. He was angry. She'd never seen Lincoln angry before.

And it knocked the wind clean out of her sails.

He pushed himself up. 'This isn't about Cassidy Yates. This could *never* be about Cassidy Yates. This is about you and me, Amy. Don't pretend it's anything else.'

She could see the fire in his eyes, the pent-up frustration so tangible she could almost reach out and touch it.

Something gripped around her heart, squeezing it tightly. Could she tell him that she loved him? Could she say that right now she couldn't bear to be in the same room as him because she ached for his touch? Could she tell him that she wished she could turn back the clock six years?

No. No, she couldn't. Because Lincoln didn't need half a woman. He needed a whole one. He didn't need a woman who was carrying someone else's baby—a woman who would never be able to have any more natural children. He needed someone else, he *deserved* someone else. Someone who could give him children of his own.

But being around him and knowing that hurt like hell.

She had to get of there.

'I can't do this, Linc.' She stood up and slid out from the booth. 'I can't do this right now.' Her shaky voice grew firm, determined. 'This isn't a good time.' Her hands rested on her belly. 'I need to concentrate on this. I need to concentrate on *him*. Nothing is more important than this baby. I can't let anything else confuse me.' Try as she may and no matter how steady her voice was, she couldn't meet his gaze. One look into those eyes right now and she could crumble.

Lincoln's voice was barely contained. 'So I "confuse"

you now? That's rubbish and you know it.' He came around and stood directly in front of her, his hands touching her shoulders. 'Tell me, Amy. Tell me how you feel.'

Her resolve started to shatter underneath her. Tears started to spill down her cheeks again. 'I don't know. I don't know how I feel. I don't know if any of these feelings are real, or if they're just a huge rush of hormones and nostalgia.' She flung her arms out in frustration, then raised her hands to her temples. She winced as her fingers touched the sides of her forehead. 'I can't sort anything out in my head right now. I can't think. I can't concentrate.' She shook her head furiously. 'I can't get rid of this damn headache!'

Her eyes finally met his. 'I didn't come here for me, Lincoln. I didn't come here for you. I came here...' she pressed her hands to her belly again '...for my son.'

Lincoln threw his hands up in frustration. He couldn't stand this any longer. He'd spent the last few days tiptoeing around her. Keeping his distance—even though it was killing him. Giving her space, giving her time.

'So this is all about the baby? Nothing else?'

'I can't let it be.'

The heavy silence pressed in on them as they stared at each other in the dimly lit room.

Lincoln wanted to storm out. He didn't need this. Six years of wishing you could see someone again, talk to them. And this was it.

Someone who pretended things weren't happening. Someone who tried to put a cap on their emotions. Someone who wouldn't face up to the facts between them. Someone who wouldn't even give him a chance. Enough was enough.

The headache was pounding in her ears. The breath

in her chest started to tighten. Zachary started kicking, as if he could feel it too. Her head was swimming and heat started to creep over her body. What was this?

Blackness crept into the edges of her eyes. She blinked twice. Had some lights just gone out? Then panic crept across her chest. Her legs starting to buckle underneath her. 'Lincoln…'

He looked upwards just as she crumpled to a heap on the floor—too late to save her from smacking her head on the thick wooden planks. *'Johnny!'*

He turned her on her left hand side, making sure her airway was clear and checking her pulse. *'Get me an ambulance!'* His hands fell to her abdomen, feeling the little life inside pushing against him.

He squeezed his eyes tightly shut as guilt engulfed him. This could be a dozen different things, but he knew right now which one it would be—eclampsia. The headache, she'd said she had a headache and he hadn't listened. She'd been checked that morning at the hospital, but this was new, this was a different complaint and one that could be a sign of eclampsia. One that should have made him take her straight back to hospital.

Instead he'd been too self-absorbed. Too worried about developing a relationship with her that would meet his own needs. Too worried that she wouldn't tell him how she felt. He'd been angry. Shouted at her, probably raised her blood pressure.

He'd promised to look after her baby. He'd promised her a safe delivery.

Her body started to twitch. The first signs of a seizure. What had he done? Lincoln watched as things started to slip through his fingers—like the grains of sand on the beach.

He lifted his head. *'Where the hell is that ambulance?'*

CHAPTER EIGHT

Lincoln shifted his position, his aching limbs objecting to the firm hard-backed chair. Was it possible his body was getting used to no sleep?

A little grunt came from under his chin. Baby Carson wriggled in the strip of cloth currently cocooning him against Lincoln's bare chest. It was almost as if the baby could hear the steadying beat of Lincoln's heart and was trying to get closer to it. He could feel the heat from his body wrap around the little figure, currently nestled under his shirt. He, better than anyone, knew that kangaroo care offered a huge range of benefits for pre-term babies—normalising temperature, heart and respiratory rate, decreasing stress, reducing risks of infection and promoting earlier discharge for premature babies. As a neonatologist he was a huge advocate for the technique. But he'd never actually done it himself. He'd never actually been the one sitting in the dead of night with a three-pound baby strapped to his chest. He swallowed the lump in his throat. He had to do this. He had to do this for Amy.

Cassidy Yates touched his shoulder. 'How you doing, Linc?' She sat down in the chair next to him, her blonde hair pulled backwards in a bun, her eyes lined and tired.

He moved forward to speak, but a little squeak from

the baby made him shift back to his original position. 'Is something wrong?' His voice was strained. *Please let Amy be okay.*

Cassidy shook her head. 'There's no change, Linc. She still hasn't woken up.' Cassidy gave a sigh. 'It's only been forty-eight hours.' A tight smile appeared on her face. 'She'll wake up today. I know she will.'

The words hung in the air between them. Both of them hoping they'd be true.

Lincoln brushed his hand against hers. 'This is my fault, Cassidy, not yours. I was the one who took her out to dinner. I was the one she got into a fight with. I didn't even realise she had any other symptoms.' He moved his hand back and ran it through his hair. 'If I'd been paying enough attention...'

'Stop it, Linc. I was her obstetrician. I should have admitted her.'

Lincoln shook his head. 'But why? You'd monitored her every day. There had been no change in her symptoms. What reason could you have for admitting her?'

Cassidy sighed. 'Good old-fashioned instinct. I knew this wasn't going to turn out well. I let Amy down.'

Lincoln looked at the little bundle under his chin. He reached up and stroked a gentle finger across the top of the baby's soft fontanel. The first few sprigs of dark hair were just starting to appear.

Cassidy leaned forward in her chair, staring at Linc with her weary eyes. 'I told her to phone me as soon as any other symptoms appeared. How long did she have that headache, Linc? Why didn't she phone me?'

Because of me. Guilt tightened across his chest. Cassidy hadn't slept in the last two days. She was worried sick. She felt guilty—as if she'd made a mistake. But she hadn't. *He had.*

Deep down he knew why Amy hadn't phoned. She hadn't been focusing on her symptoms. She'd been fixated on the fact that she thought something was happening between Lincoln and Cassidy. *She'd been jealous.* And it had affected her relationship with her obstetrician.

Lincoln cringed. He couldn't believe it had come to this.

Seeing Amy lying on the floor of the restaurant, seizing, had been the single most terrifying moment of his life. Never had a five-minute ambulance journey seemed so long.

And the E.R. events that had followed had felt like an out-of-body experience. For once, he hadn't been in control. He'd watched as they'd put her on monitors, inserted IVs and catheters, and stabilised her. Once the seizure had been under control, a quick confab with Cassidy and the anaesthetist had resulted in a rapid trip to Theatre and an emergency Caesarean section.

Two hours after he'd brought her in her son had been screaming in his gloved hands in the operating room.

And then he'd made the biggest decision of his life. Because that's when it hit him. Like a lightning bolt. He loved her.

And he couldn't be the baby's doctor. No matter what he'd promised Amy, he couldn't be the neonatologist her child needed.

He'd too much emotional investment in this. And it would ruin his objectivity.

Yes, he could stand on the sidelines and discuss clinical decisions with the surrounding physicians but he had to step back. He had to take himself out of the equation. Because he didn't feel like a doctor around Amy's son. He felt like a parent.

But the one thing Amy had asked him to do was be her son's doctor. And chances were she would never forgive him.

Cassidy stood up again. 'I'm going back to ICU. She's going to wake up today. I want to be there.' Her voice was steady and determined, but Lincoln didn't know if she was trying to convince him or herself.

His hands cradled the little baby next to his chest. In most cases kangaroo care was carried out by the mother. But in this case, while Amy was unavailable, it seemed the most natural thing for him to be doing.

But he'd had no idea it would feel like this. The feel of the tiny translucent skin against his, the feeling of the little body warming against his, had swamped him. All this time he'd only really thought about Amy. He hadn't really brought her son into the equation. And now he was here, front and centre, and for the first time in his life Lincoln hadn't been able to distance himself into professional mode. He hadn't been able to sit on the sidelines and watch. He'd had to make sure he was in the middle of it all. No one else was allowed to carry out care for the baby.

And it would be easy right now to pretend this was all about guilt, and that he felt he owed it to Amy to look after her little boy. If that was how he felt, he could have stayed in doctor mode, in clinical mode, and done the best job that he could. But it wasn't how he felt. He could see Amy in this baby. And all the feelings he felt for her, whether he'd vocalised them or not, seemed to be intensified into this tiny body. Who could have known it could feel like this?

He'd often heard parents talk about being swamped by their feelings. But he'd never experienced it. Not like this. And he couldn't even begin to explain it. He had no genetic connection to this child. He had no parental rights. Amy could wake up today and tell him she never wanted to see him again. And he knew all of that. But it didn't change how he felt.

He shifted the little feeding tube currently taped to the side of the baby's nose. Amy had wanted to breast-feed her baby, so they'd used some of the breast milk available in the NICU, but so far Junior hadn't responded to cup feeding or finger feeding and with a premature baby time was of the essence, so they'd had to resort to placing a small tube down into his stomach. So every few hours Lincoln got a small syringe and fed Amy's son tiny amounts of breast milk. Anything to help him.

'Okay, Junior, let's get you back inside your incubator for a while. I need to go and see your mommy.'

He glanced down at his rumpled clothes—the same shirt and jeans he'd been wearing when Amy had seized in the restaurant two days ago. He really needed to get changed.

Lincoln placed the baby carefully back inside the incubator, pulling a little blue hat over his head. He checked the chart hanging at the end of the crib. Baby Carson was actually doing quite well. His weight at three pounds eight ounces was good, and gave him a ninety-five per cent survival rate. The steroids had obviously done their job of maturing his lungs and he'd come out screaming and breathing on his own. There had only been a few incidences when he'd tried to feed that his oxygen saturation had dropped. And since he'd had the tube put down, there had been none.

The little guy had fighting spirit. Now, if only he had a name.

But Amy hadn't told him what she was going to name her son—she'd expected to be there to do that herself.

Lincoln felt the small hand wrap itself around his finger. *Please let her wake up soon.*

Amy felt weird. She was having a dream. But instead of a nice, pink, floaty dream, this was a strange, distant far-away dream. And her throat ached. Her mouth was dry and felt brittle and she couldn't even swallow. Her head was pounding and noises were disturbing her peaceful sleep. She couldn't concentrate. Maybe if she could just have a drink of water...

Her eyes felt heavy, crusted, and she struggled to pull her eyelids apart. White. That was all she could see. *What was that?*

She moved her hands. Something was hurting her wrist. Like a little pinch, a little squeeze. Her hands moved to her stomach, seeking the comfort of the rounded bump she'd spent the last few months embracing. The firmness was gone. In its place only soft sagging skin. Alarm bells started racing in her head. Something wasn't right. Where was she? What was happening?

She could feel something pressing on her face and she reached up to pull it aside. She started struggling to breathe, taking short, rapid breaths. A figure appeared in her line of vision. Blonde. Boobs. Was it Barbie?

The voice was talking, but she wasn't sure what it was saying. A strong, calm voice. 'Amy. Amy. Calm down. Everything's fine. It's Cassidy Yates. You're in hospital—in San Francisco Maternity. Here...let me put this mask back on your face for a few moments.' The figure moved around to the side. 'I'm going to raise your bed slightly, Amy.' There was a buzzing noise and Amy felt herself move upwards. The white view changed to a hospital scene.

A hospital scene she should be familiar with. A busy ICU. As a former theatre nurse she'd spent many hours transferring patients to and from Theatre to ICU and back again. But even the familiarity didn't help.

There was a sense that something was wrong. She didn't feel right. She felt…empty.

Then it struck her. Her brain shifted sharply into focus and a million panicked thoughts filling her mind. 'My baby? Where's my baby?' Although she felt as if she was shouting, her voice was quiet, barely a whisper.

Cassidy leaned forward, touching her hand and squeezing it tightly. 'Your son is fine, Amy. He's in NICU. Lincoln's with him—I don't think he's left his side in the last forty-eight hours.'

Amy blinked. This wasn't real. This couldn't be happening. What did she mean—the last forty-eight hours?

The confusion must have registered on her face. Cassidy kept hold of her hand. 'Amy, do you remember anything about what happened?'

Amy shook her head. Her mind was currently mush. She couldn't take in where she was, let alone anything else.

Cassidy bent closer, reaching up and moving some loose strands of hair from her face. Why was this woman being so nice to her? Something turned inside her stomach. *She didn't like this woman*, but she couldn't remember why.

Her eyes went downwards. There was an IV in her hand. That's what the strange feeling was at her wrist. The tape surrounding it was catching the little hairs on her wrist. Tiny pieces of the jigsaw puzzle started slotting into place in her brain. Cassidy was talking again. 'You had a seizure, Amy. Two days ago. Lincoln brought you in, we stabilised you, then we had to take you to Theatre and deliver your baby. You've been in here ever since.'

Amy clung to the one part that registered in her brain. 'Zachary. How is Zachary?'

Cassidy's face broke into a smile. 'Zachary? That's what you're calling your son? What a beautiful name.' She glanced over her shoulder. 'Lincoln will be so pleased to hear it. He's been calling him Junior these last two days.'

Amy tried to pull her dry lips together again. 'Lincoln's looking after my son?'

Something registered on Cassidy's face. A fleeting glance, as if she shouldn't say something. But she pressed her lips together. 'Yes…and no.' It took her a few seconds to decide what to say. 'He's not your son's doctor. But he's been acting as a…surrogate parent for the last two days. He hasn't left Zachary's side. He's been doing all the kangaroo care for your son.'

Images flooded into Amy's mind. Her brain was still befuddled. Lincoln with her baby. Holding her baby, feeding her baby. She knew Zach would have been in safe hands. But hadn't he promised to be her baby's doctor?

'I don't understand…'

Cassidy stood upright, the relief on her face obvious. 'Oh, good, he's here. I'll let him speak to you himself.' She gave a final squeeze to Amy's hand. 'I'll come back later—to talk with you about your treatment.'

She walked towards Lincoln and gave his shoulder a little squeeze on the way past.

Amy watched as the green-suited figure appeared

in the doorway. Her eyes were taking a little time to focus. Why was that?

Then she felt him engulf her in a hug, pulling her head and shoulders clear of the bed and into his chest. He held her so tightly she started to cough.

He released her quickly. 'Sorry. I'm just so pleased you've woken up. I've been so worried.' He clasped her hands, words tumbling from his mouth. 'The baby's doing well. He's breathing on his own—right from delivery—and he's a good weight for twenty-nine weeks: three pounds eight ounces. He's not feeding on his own yet, we've had to put a tube down, but I've made sure that he's getting breast milk. Oh, and you need to tell me his name, so I can put it in his records.'

Lincoln. It was definitely Lincoln. He was babbling. She didn't have any problem focusing up close. She could see his green theatre scrubs, his tousled dark hair and blue-rimmed, tired eyes. There was a definite shadow around his jaw—she'd felt it brush her cheek as he'd hugged her.

She blinked, focusing further—giving her brain time to make sense of it all in her head. She could see the deep lines etched into his forehead and filtering out from the corners of his eyes. Had they always been there? He looked exhausted.

She blinked. And in that instant there was something else. A fleeting picture of a darkened restaurant and a smell…a strong smell of fresh fish. The memory gave her a jolt, startling other little pieces of the jigsaw puzzle into place. An expression on Lincoln's face that she didn't recognise. He'd been angry with her. They'd been fighting.

That's why he looked like hell.

His fingers touched the inside of her palm. 'Amy, are you with me?' The anxiety was back.

She nodded, her dry tongue coming out and trying to lick her lips. He responded instantly, picking up a glass of iced water with a straw from her bedside table. Where had that come from?

He held the straw at her lips and she sucked deeply. 'Steady,' he said, pulling it away for a second then bringing it back to her again. He let her take some more sips. 'Better?'

She nodded and let out a sigh. 'Zachary. Zachary John Carson. That's my son's name.'

His eyes met hers and he nodded in recognition. 'It's a beautiful name.'

'I want to see him.' Now she'd found her voice again, it was steely and determined. A wave of emotions rode up inside her, like a crest of a wave. She'd missed the first two days of her son's life. She hadn't been the first person to hold him, to hear him cry or feed him. She'd missed so much already. 'I want to see him now.'

Lincoln hesitated. 'You've just woken up, Amy, I don't think you're stable enough to go to NICU. And I'm sorry, but I can't bring Zachary in here.' He waved his hand around the ICU. There were four other adult patients in the room. One was attached to a ventilator—that must have been the burring noise that she'd heard—and two others had assisted ventilation. 'There's too big a risk of exposure to infection.'

Amy knew he was being eminently sensible. But forty-eight hours' worth of post-birth hormones didn't care. 'I *need* to see my son.'

Something washed over Lincoln's face. Guilt. Why did he feel guilty? 'I know you do, Amy.' His hand was still pressed next to hers. 'Let me see what I can arrange. I promise you'll see your son soon.'

For a second she thought he was going to bend over and kiss her. But he hesitated midway across the bed, pulling back and heading out the door in his green scrubs.

And that's when the floodgates opened.

Two hours later she was ensconced in a side room. Lincoln pushed the neonate crib into the room and Amy's breath caught in her throat. Her son.

That tiny little scrap she could see through the plastic was hers. Her baby. Wrapped in a pale blue blanket with a tiny knitted cap on his head. Fists punching angrily in the air. And a tiny plastic tube coming from his nose and taped to the side of his cheek.

Her breast ached. She wanted to feed her baby. She wanted to feel his little body next to hers. She could feel her lips tremble as Lincoln lifted him out of the crib and handed him to her.

Zachary gave a little groan and snuggled towards her—a natural response. She felt transfixed. His little eyes were screwed up, his skin pale just like hers, a few tiny strands of dark hair on his head. The wrinkled forehead smoothed out and his eyes blinked open, staring upright straight into her eyes. Her heart gave a little flutter at the blue eyes, then she realised that all babies were born with blue eyes. His eye colour could change over the next year. The thought brought a little smile to her face.

The next year. She was going to spend all that time with her son. She might have missed the first few days but there was nothing to stop her now. A little warmth spread across her chest. She lifted her finger and stroked it down her son's button nose. He was all hers. Six years she'd waited for this moment, and now she finally had her child in her arms.

Lincoln shifted his feet beside her, obviously not wanting to interrupt her first few moments with her son. She blinked back the tears forming in her eyes. 'Thank you for looking after him,' she whispered.

He looked uncomfortable. He sat down in the chair next to her bed, bringing him level with her. 'I need to tell you something.'

'What?' She couldn't take her eyes from her son.

'I couldn't do what you wanted me to.'

Cassidy's words started to float around her brain again. This time, though, they started to register. Something about Lincoln not being her baby's doctor...

She found the little hospital band attached to his tiny wrist and rotated it. Baby Carson. Three pounds eight ounces. And his date of birth. Dr Lomax. Who was Dr Lomax?

A surge of anger struck her. Her cold stare fixed on Lincoln. 'What is it you want to tell me, Lincoln?'

She could see the pain on his face. This wasn't easy for him—but right now she didn't care. She'd asked him to do one thing for her. One thing. She'd travelled miles to find him, to find the best doctor to look after her son—and now this.

He ran his fingers through his hair the way he always did when he was nervous. 'I'm really sorry, Amy. This is all my fault. I should have kept a better eye on you—I shouldn't have taken you out to dinner. This would never have happened if I'd kept in the role I should have—as the doctor for your son.' He shook his head and lifted his eyes to meet hers. 'But I just couldn't.'

Amy took a breath. The air felt tight in her chest. 'What do you mean, this is all your fault? How is any of this your fault? Lincoln, you let me stay in your apartment—you drove me to hospital every day, how can you possibly think this is your fault?'

'Your headache. You told me you had a headache and I ignored the signs, something a doctor on his game would never have done. I could have got you to hospital sooner. I should have been paying attention.'

She shook her head. '*I* should have paid more attention. Not you. I'd had that headache all day, but I thought it was nothing. Cassidy warned me—she gave me a list of signs and symptoms to look out for, and told me to come straight back to hospital if I developed any of them. But it seemed so mild, so subtle. It didn't even start to bother me until later in the day. I honestly thought it was just a headache. I never thought it would lead to this.' She glanced down at the bundle in her arms. 'Do you honestly think I would have put my son at risk? The headache was so mild that I hadn't even thought about taking anything until we were out. Up until then it really felt like nothing.'

The lines in his forehead were deeper than normal. She was doing nothing to alleviate his guilt. What else did he want to tell her?

Lincoln leaned forward in the chair, resting his arms on the side of her bed. 'When I saw you seizing…it was the worst five minutes of my life. By the time we got here and stabilised you then made the decision to take you to Theatre, I knew I couldn't be Zach's doctor.'

'What do you mean, you couldn't be my son's doctor?' Her voice had a cold, hard edge to it. 'It was the one thing I asked you to do for me, Lincoln. It was the *only* thing I asked you to do for me.'

'I know, I know.' The anguish in his voice was apparent, and she knew he was struggling to find the words.

'Who is Dr Lomax, Lincoln?'

'He's my colleague. My friend—someone I would trust with my child's life. As soon as I held Zach in my arms in Theatre, I knew I had to get someone else to do the job. I couldn't think straight. I couldn't think like a doctor while I was looking at him. I couldn't be the professional that I needed to be. I couldn't step back and see the wider picture. All I could see was the woman I loved lying on the operating table and her twenty-nine-week-old son in my hands. I knew I had to get someone else to do the job.'

His words hung in the air.

He loved her. He'd said it. Words that she'd been waiting to hear. So why wasn't she jumping for joy? Why wasn't she shouting it from the rooftops?

He was looking at her, waiting for her to respond. She tried to sort out her brain. She wanted to tell him that she loved him too. But something was stopping her. Something was pressing down on her chest, willing her not to say those words.

She kept her eyes on her baby. She didn't want to look at those dark-rimmed blue eyes. She didn't want them to pull her in and say something she would later regret.

Her son was staring up at her. Could he see her yet? Could he see the anguish on her face? How well could a twenty-nine-weeker see?

'Cassidy said that you'd looked after him, that you'd done kangaroo care. That you hadn't left his side for forty-eight hours.'

'I couldn't be his doctor, Amy, but that doesn't mean I don't care—it means I care too much. I didn't want anyone else to do his care. I wanted to be by his side. I wanted to watch over him. I wanted to feed him.'

A single tear slid down her face. It was just as she'd feared. He was professing not only his love for her but for Zach too. This should be what happy endings were about. But she still couldn't lift her head to meet his gaze.

Her feelings for him were so strong. Since the first time she'd seen him again, all her thoughts and memories of him had increased tenfold. He was everything she could ever want.

But what did that make her to him?

She didn't want to be his charity case. His poor ex with a baby he felt sorry for. He was feeling guilty right now. Guilt that he was confusing with love. He didn't love her. She wasn't the whole, healthy woman she'd been before.

She was damaged goods. Her body would never be the same again, even if she had the reconstruction surgery.

And Zach was it for her. She would never be able to have more natural kids. Her eggs were gone. Finished. And Lincoln…he was just starting out. He should have a whole brood of children of his own. And a happy, healthy wife who could give them to him.

She didn't want him to settle. She didn't want him to settle for her and Zachary. Even though it could make her happier than she'd thought possible, she wanted him to have the chance at life that she'd missed out on.

He stood up and moved to the side of the bed, sliding his arm around her shoulders and bending over to look down at Zach. 'Do you feel well enough to try the kangaroo care for a little while? Do you think you could manage him strapped next to your chest?'

She nodded. She couldn't speak right now. Words were just too difficult. He'd just stood up, not waiting for a response from her. He seemed to accept that she couldn't say the 'I love you' words back. What did that mean?

'Do you need some analgesia for your section wound before we start?'

She shook her head. The Caesarean section wound wasn't nearly as painful as she'd imagined. Maybe being unconscious for the first forty-eight hours had helped. The nurse had given her a couple of painkillers when she'd woken up and she felt fine.

Lincoln rummaged around in her locker. 'Let's find you something else to wear. That hospital gown won't do.'

He was right. The traditional hospital gown, with its Velcro fastenings at the back, wouldn't suit. He pulled out a pair of loose yellow jersey pyjamas, with buttons down the front. 'What about these?'

Amy nodded her head. Her tiny son was still in her arms. A nurse came into the room and between her and Lincoln they helped Amy freshen up and then secure her son next to her.

The next few hours passed swiftly. Amy tried to get her tiny son to latch onto her breast, and when that failed, she managed to express some of her milk to feed to him via the tiny tube down his nose. The nurse rechecked her vital signs and reduced some of her IV infusions.

Cassidy came and checked on her twice. She talked her through the events and her subsequent care, warning her that women could still have seizures after delivery and that she would need to be observed for the next few days.

And Lincoln floated in and out of her room all day, taking Zachary back to the nursery for a spell then bringing him back to her later.

It was almost as if the words hadn't been spoken—or never been heard. Life was beginning to tick along as normal. Why did that make her feel so empty inside?

Lincoln wheeled the cot back along the corridor to NICU. Zachary was doing well and seemed a little brighter since his mother had woken up. Although he hadn't managed to latch on today, there was every chance that he'd start breastfeeding soon and then his tube could be removed.

So why did life feel at a standstill?

For Lincoln, the instant feeling of relief when Amy had woken up had now been replaced by a feeling of worthlessness. She didn't blame him for her deterioration, she hadn't even been too angry when he'd told her he couldn't be Zachary's doctor. In fact, she'd hardly said *anything*, even after his heart had been in his throat and he'd said those words. The *I love you* words.

And there had been nothing—no response. It was almost as if he hadn't spoken.

Lincoln looked at the little baby lying in the crib beneath him. Zachary Carson. Every day he grew more attached. Every day he noticed something else about the little guy. Something new.

But what if this was a recipe for disaster? Amy had never said anything to make him think she was looking for anything else from him.

He still couldn't get to the bottom of what Amy wanted and it frustrated him beyond belief. She'd come here saying she wanted his skills and expertise as a doctor. But from the moment they'd set eyes on each other again, the tension in the air had been palpable.

He loved it that she was unpredictable. He loved it that she flirted with him. He loved it that they still seemed to fit together like pieces in a jigsaw puzzle.

But Amy was different too. Illness had changed her. A high-risk pregnancy had changed her. She wasn't as confident as she used to be. Sure, he knew that her body had changed, but something else had changed deep inside her. Was it her feelings of self-worth? He just couldn't put his finger on it. He couldn't really understand. And it was making him tiptoe around about her, something he'd never had to do before.

Then there was the guilt. Guilt that she'd come to him for help and he'd let her down. He'd let his guard down. He didn't want to be Amy's son's doctor.

One of the NICU nurses walked past and gave him a little smile. Carrie. Blonde. Cute. Nice butt. The old Lincoln would have chased her out the door. The old Lincoln would have had her number in his phone in two minutes flat.

Lincoln moved into autopilot. He lifted Zachary from the crib, strapped him to his chest and nestled him under his shirt.

He had absolutely no doubt about where he wanted to be. The effect of seeing Amy again after six years had been like a punch to the face. No woman had made him feel the way she did. He hadn't recognised love because he'd never felt it before. He didn't know what to say to her, when to back off, or when to move closer.

This was a steep learning curve.

But he'd never been one to shirk a challenge—and this was one thing he was determined to master.

CHAPTER NINE

AMY swallowed nervously as she climbed the steps towards the apartment. Her arms couldn't hide the slight tremor in them as she carried her precious bundle upstairs to the place she was currently calling 'home'.

This was nothing like she'd imagined. Zachary was six weeks old—he shouldn't even have been born yet. But his feeding and weight gain had been sufficient for him to be discharged from San Francisco's Children's Hospital. His skin had lost that translucent look and his little body had finally managed to store a tiny amount of fat and fill out a little.

His wide blue eyes had obviously started to focus and she could see him studying her face at times and reacting to her expressions. And at five pounds he was even big enough to wear some of the premature baby clothes she'd carefully folded in a drawer in Lincoln's apartment.

But all of this still unsettled her. She was in San Francisco—this wasn't home to her—but it could be. The longer she stayed here, the more she loved this city, from its quirky visitors and attractions to its deep-rooted history and traditions. She loved looking over to the Golden Gate Bridge, she loved the bustling people around Pier 39. She loved the rattle of the cable cars.

And most of all she loved the staff attached to San Francisco's Children and Maternity Hospital. Unlike most hospitals, she'd yet to meet a member of staff who hadn't been warm and friendly, who hadn't made her feel at home. She was sure that being a good friend of one the consultants helped. But it was also a place she could see a future in, a place where she would be happy to go to work. So why the strange feeling in her stomach?

Lincoln had arranged for Zachary's baby items to be delivered to San Francisco from Santa Maria. Literally overnight the white wooden baby crib and chest of drawers had appeared in her bedroom in Lincoln's apartment. The zebra-print baby seat was currently sitting next to the sofa in the living room. And the red pram was parked at the bottom of the stairs. All awaiting the arrival of baby Zachary.

She thought that she would have loved this moment. To finally bring her son home from hospital was a huge step. She should be singing from the rooftops. She should be telling the whole world that Zach was well enough to come home. But she wasn't. She couldn't.

She was nervous. She felt sick. Her stomach was churning. Was this new-mother nerves? Or something else?

The patient, easily accessible staff in the NICU were no longer by her side. The emergency monitors and equipment were no longer ready to be pulled over at a moment's notice. All the little queries or insecurities she'd had in the last few weeks couldn't be answered by another person in the room. Or could they?

Because Lincoln was here with her. Lincoln hadn't left her side. Or Zachary's.

He'd done everything he could to help her. He'd bent

over backwards to be accommodating. And as much as she was grateful, it was going to make it so much harder to say goodbye...

Because right now she knew that was what she had to do.

Lincoln slid his key into the lock in the door and pushed the buttons to turn off the alarm. He held the door wide for her. She gave a little smile and carried Zachary into the apartment, walking over to one of the huge windows. 'What do you think, Zach? Do you like this place?'

Because she certainly did. So why did she feel as if she had to leave? Why, when the man of her dreams was offering her love, did she feel as if she had to retreat to the distant hills? Why did she feel that she couldn't even enter into a discussion with him?

She carried Zach through to the bedroom. 'Here's your crib, right next to Mommy's bed. I'll be able to stick my hand through and hold your hand.' She held him up to look, but Zach just blinked.

Her attention was caught by something new. 'Wow, look at this.' She leaned over and touched the mobile hanging above the crib and turned on the music. The soft, multicoloured animals started to spin around to 'Nelly the Elephant'. 'Did you get this?' she asked Lincoln.

He nodded slowly, folding his arms and leaning against the doorpost. 'Colour and noise are supposed to stimulate babies.' That smile again. That smile that drew you in and held you there. Held you with those dark blue eyes.

Being around him was good. His easy way and infectious laugh made her feel comfortable. She'd fallen asleep in his arms several times over the last few weeks, resting in the chairs next to Zachary's crib in NICU, and woken to find her head on his chest and her arms wrapped around him.

The electricity between them was still there. He just wasn't acting on it.

And for some strange reason it hurt.

She knew it was all her fault. She hadn't reacted when he'd told her that he loved her. She'd stayed silent, and he must have been hurt by that. But what could she do? What could she offer him? A woman with an altered body? Someone who hadn't yet reached the golden 'five years cancer-free'? The chance to have no natural children of his own? Lincoln was a gorgeous, handsome man. He deserved to have a better future than the one she could offer him.

She already knew that he was becoming more attached to her and Zachary. If the last few weeks hadn't been so hard she might have got her act together and done something about it.

But she hadn't. And now here she was, in his apartment, with her baby son.

She felt an arm at her waist, but it was a casual movement, not an intimate one. Zachary's eyes were starting to close, so she pulled off his padded jacket and laid him down in his crib for the first time, leaning back against Lincoln to watch his eyelids finally flicker shut and his little body relax.

'It's been a big day.' His voice was warm, comforting, like a big blanket enveloping her.

'It has.' She sighed as she pressed the little nightlight next to the crib. His first night home from hospital. Should she really be feeling so terrified?

'Want me to make dinner?'

All of sudden she felt exhausted. She wanted to lie

down in the bed next to her son and watch him sleep. She wanted to watch his little chest rise and fall. She wanted to stretch her hand through the bars and let his little fingers wrap around her big one so they could hold each other while they slept. She shook her head. 'I'm not hungry, Linc. I just want to lie down.'

He gave her waist a little squeeze. 'You've got to keep your strength up. I have it on good authority that babies are hard work. How about I make you something light like scrambled eggs?' His hand lifted up and stroked the back of her neck in a soothing motion. 'It will take five minutes then you could soak in the bath if you wanted.'

A bath. A deep-filled bath overflowing with lavender scents and bubbles. That would be sheer bliss. She hadn't had a bath since she'd had Zachary. She always seemed to be racing in and out of the shower. It had seemed quicker, more convenient. This could be perfect.

She gave a little nod. 'Scrambled eggs would be good.' She stepped over towards the en suite bathroom and picked up the bottle of dark purple bubble bath, opening it, tipping a generous portion into the white roll-topped bath then turning the tap on full blast.

Ten minutes later, tummy full of scrambled eggs and a baby soundly sleeping, Amy stepped into the water and slid her body beneath the bubbles.

She would have a think about things tomorrow—sort everything out in her mind. Everything would seem clearer then and she would think about what to say to Lincoln. She could make plans about returning to Santa Maria and finding a paediatrician for her son. She would eventually have to think about childcare for Zachary—who would want to look after a baby that had been born premature? She would need childcare that could be flexible around her shifts. Would she be able to find anyone to do that? Maybe she should find a different job? Even the thoughts exhausted her. Tonight she just wanted to relax.

'Amy!'

The sharp knock on the door woke her with a jolt. Her brain took a few seconds to focus, obviously a few seconds too long because the door opened and Lincoln stuck his head through the gap. 'Is everything okay?'

Amy had sat bolt upright with the knock on the door, leaving her breast above the bubbled waterline and her flat side exposed. Her hands flew to her chest and she ducked beneath the bubbles again. 'Lincoln! Don't come in, I'm still in the bath!' Her cheeks flamed red. She must have dozed off as the water was now lukewarm. She leaned forward to grab a fluffy towel from beside the bath.

He must have seen her scar. He must have seen the empty side.

Lincoln pulled back. The panic on Amy's face was evident. He hadn't meant to embarrass her, he'd just wanted to check she was okay. Then he stopped. Took a deep breath, stepped into the bathroom and closed the door behind him.

'Lincoln! What are you doing?'

'Something I should have done weeks ago.'

He bent forward and picked up the towel she was grappling for, holding it open in front of him. 'Come on.'

Her flaming cheeks burned even harder. 'You've got to be joking.'

'No. I'm not.' His voice was firm and determined. He gestured with the towel once more. 'Come on, Amy.'

'No.' Her voice was sharp and to the point.

He stared at her.

'Don't, Lincoln. You're making me uncomfortable.'

He knelt down next to the bath so his face was level with hers. 'I'm not trying to make you uncomfortable, Amy. But this is an issue between us—you know it is. I'm not here to upset you. I'm your friend. I'm here to support you. Now, get out the bath so we can talk about this. Take the first step.' He held the towel out again.

Her bottom lip trembled. She didn't feel ready for this. She wanted to pull her knees up to her chest, tuck her chin on top and hide her body from the world. Why couldn't he be plain? Why couldn't he be ugly? Would that make it easier? Would it be easier to bare your blemished body to someone who didn't reek of perfection?

She bit her lip, a sheen across her eyes. *Take the first step.* How did he know exactly what to say? She had to be brave. He was right. He was getting right to the heart of the matter. It was an issue. She just didn't know if she could handle this.

There was only one way to do this. She had to try. She owed it to herself to try. She closed her eyes and stood upright, stepping out the bath almost simultaneously and moving across into the comfort of the white fluffy towel. He wrapped it around her and she caught the edges of it, pulling it closer and tucking it around her before she opened her eyes.

He gestured to the side of the bath. 'Sit down.' He picked up another towel and dried her bare legs. Had he even had a chance to get a proper look at her scarred body? What had he thought?

His arm went around her shoulders, escorting her from the bathroom and into his bedroom. *His bedroom.* She hadn't set foot in this room the whole time she'd been staying here. She felt the breath catch in her throat as he guided her over towards his bed, then her heart plummeted as he stood her in front of the free-standing, full-length mirror next to his bed. He raised his hand and pulled the cream blind at the window, plunging the room into semi-darkness, with some of the early evening sun still filtering through the blind.

All of a sudden she didn't feel so exhausted. Maybe the nap in the bath had revived her, but she didn't think so. Her blood was racing around her body. Why did this feel so natural? Why wasn't she terrified?

She'd been planning to leave. She'd been thinking about telling Lincoln a million reasons why she and Zachary shouldn't stay there. So why did this feel as though it should happen?

'Now.' He guided her in front of the mirror, standing behind her with his hands at her waist. 'What do you see?'

'What do you mean?'

His voice radiated calm. A man totally in control, who knew exactly what he was doing. 'I want you to look in the mirror and tell me what you see.'

She turned to face him. 'I can't. I don't want to do this any more.'

There it was on her face again. Panic. Put her in a situation out of her control and she floundered. He ran his finger down her cheek, the most delicate of touches. 'Yes, yes, you can.' He gently spun her around again. 'I'll tell you what I see.' His hands crept back around her waist, his tall body right behind hers, his strength and muscles running down the length of her body, his chin resting on her shoulder, staring at their joint reflections.

He smiled into the mirror and touched her hair. 'I

see a beautiful woman, with gorgeous red tresses and magical green eyes.' He ran his finger along the skin at her neck. 'I see pale skin and a tiny splash of freckles across her nose.' His chin swapped round to the other side of her body, as if he was appreciating her from all angles. 'And I like the pale skin—because it's different. Most women here could die a death from fake tan—or a death from a real tan. I like it that your skin is completely natural and untouched by the sun. You don't need a tan. Your pure beauty radiates from your skin.'

His words danced like a song over her. Rising and falling, causing her heart to flutter in her chest one moment and her clenched stomach to flip over the next.

She looked at the reflection in the mirror. The pale face stared back at her. The tired eyes, the washed-out face. Why couldn't she see what he did?

She leaned backwards a little, relaxing into his strength. In some ways she hated this, and in others she knew that the time was right and this was exactly what she needed. And Lincoln was right—it was easier doing this with a friend.

His hands reached in front of her body to where the towel was tucked in. She flinched. No! She could see the fear in her own face in the mirror, but she was intrigued by his reflection. His fingers were gently untucking the towel, loosening it and lifting the edges, dropping the white towel to the floor and leaving her naked body exposed in front of the mirror.

And his face didn't look shocked, didn't look disgusted and didn't look repulsed. In fact, he bent and kissed the skin at the bottom of her neck, wrapping one arm around her waist, keeping her close to him.

He lifted his head again, staring at her in the mirror. 'Don't be afraid,' he whispered, a comforting smile on his face. Her hands were trembling again, she couldn't help it—she'd never felt so exposed. And although the room was warm, goose-bumps appeared all over her pale flesh.

His hand came up on one side and cupped her full breast. There was nothing sexual in his touch. Her breast was working overtime feeding her son right now and even the slightest touch could make milk leak. On the other side his fingers traced a light line up from her hip bone to under her arm, pausing for only a second before running along the flat, pale, white line of her scar—where her breast should be.

Her eyes took in her reflection. Six weeks on from giving birth and her lower body had started to return to normal. Her stomach wasn't flat. It probably never would be again and there was a small, visible red scar running along her bikini line. But it was a neat scar, well healed and already starting to retreat into her body. In a few years' time it would be pale and virtually unnoticeable. Unlike the scar at her breast. A visible marker of something missing.

He kissed her neck again whilst his fingers danced along her skin. And he kept on kissing her as his hands gently caressed her. She was caught, watching the reflection in the mirror of a handsome man touching a lover's body. There was no shame. No horror. Like a slow movie scene, with romantic music playing. Only this time, instead of music, it was one word repeating itself over and over in her head. *Acceptance.*

The kisses reached the bottom of her throat. The hand left her full breast—as if he knew it was too sensitive for touch right now—and reached up to tangle in her red curls. He moved, lifting up her arm on her affected side and looping it around behind his neck. Then he watched in the mirror as he ran his fingers once more down her side. Another woman might have flinched at the light, tickling sensations. But for Amy it was different. It was all about acceptance. And it wasn't about his acceptance of her. It was about her acceptance of her changed body.

She was staring at the reflection in front of her. And the old sensations were gone. And she didn't see something to be ashamed of. She didn't see something she should hide from the world. This wasn't something she would ever share. But it was something that she didn't need to hide away from any more. For the first time in six years she could look at her naked body without feeling fear or repulsion. This was a woman who had the right to be loved.

Her hand moved from behind his neck to run through his hair. The movement caused her to lean backwards, exposing even more of the sensitive flesh at the base of her neck to his lips. She wasn't looking in the mirror any more. She was losing herself in the feelings.

'This is the body of the woman that I love. This is the body of a vibrant, healthy and whole woman.' His fingers went to her flat surface again. 'This is only a tiny part of Amy. And I don't care if you decide to have reconstruction surgery or not. I will take you however you come. If it matters to you then fine. But don't change anything for me, because I love you just the way you are.'

He spun her round, hands at her waist. He looked her straight in the eye. He moved forward, pressing himself against her. She was naked and he was still fully clothed. But she could feel his hard length through his jeans, pressing against her abdomen. A smile came across her lips.

He was hard. He was very hard. It didn't matter that she felt her body was disfigured. It didn't matter that she felt she had to hide. The proof was right in front of her—literally. She turned him on. He wanted her.

She felt twenty-five again. She felt young and whole. The way she used to feel when she'd danced around his cabin naked. Her fingers moved and unfastened the buttons on his jeans, releasing him into her hands.

For the first time in five years she felt powerful. She felt sexual. It was a glimmer of what she'd felt in that hospital room the last time they'd kissed. Control. She felt in control.

He was staring at her, with those sexy, half-shut eyes. Even if she'd been on the other side of the room, those eyes alone could have turned her on. But right now his fingers were moving lower. Going from one set of red curls to another. She moved closer. She wasn't going to flinch at his touch now. This was what she wanted. She was ready.

She'd had her six-week postnatal check. Everything was as it should be. There was no reason she couldn't have sex. And from the way her body was currently responding, it was telling her it was time.

He reached his hands up to either side of her head. His eyes fixed on hers. 'Are you sure?' he whispered. 'We only do this if you want to—you're in charge.' There was a glimmer in his eye. He knew exactly what he was doing. He was giving her all the control—and it was sexy as hell.

She tilted her head to one side, her eyes glancing down at the prize possession in her hands. 'I want to see what I'm getting.' She whipped his T-shirt up and pulled it over his head, revealing his muscular torso.

Her hands pressed against him. 'Not too shabby,' she whispered with a glint in her eye.

She pushed him backwards onto the bed, climbing above him. 'So *I'm* in charge?' she questioned.

His smile revealed his straight white teeth. 'Absolutely.'

'Good. Then this is what we're going to do…'

The early morning sunlight was filtering through the blind again. Amy had been up twice in the night to feed and change Zachary, and on each occasion he'd settled back down to sleep quickly.

It would have been nice to wake up in Lincoln's arms and feel his body heat next to hers, but the reality of a premature baby dictated how things would work out.

Last night had been cathartic for her. She'd finally got to the place she needed to. She'd felt desired, wanted, sexual. She'd felt loved. But the early morning light brought a whole new range of issues with it. Issues where she'd barely even scratched the surface. She threw back the white duvet and swung her legs out of the bed. Her feet padded across the dark wooden floor and she stopped in the doorway of Lincoln's room.

His long, lean naked body was entwined around his duvet cover. It looked like one of those ultra-trendy pictures you could buy in black and white and put on your wall. His chest was rising and falling and there was a dark shadow around his chin where the stubble was starting to appear. He was picture-perfect.

She moved in front of the free-standing mirror where he'd undressed her last night. She released the belt on the fluffy white dressing gown and let it fall open. She stared at her reflection. One round full breast and one flat white scar. Her finger traced along the line of the scar. Even now, after everything that had happened, it still made a little shiver go down her spine. Last night Lincoln had shown her acceptance. Acceptance for who she was now. She kept staring, her breathing and heart rate quickening. She didn't like the image in the mirror. She didn't like the person staring back at her. Lincoln may have shown her acceptance but in the cold light of day she couldn't accept herself. She couldn't accept the reflection in the mirror.

Last night may have been wonderful, but it was only the start of the journey for her.

She could hear his breathing behind her. It could be so easy if she could just push all this aside and forget about it. It would be so easy to climb into bed next to him and snuggle into his arms. But this was never going to go away.

What was wrong? Why did her life feel like sand running through her fingers on the beach? How could she explain that to him? How could she tell him that no matter how good he was to her and Zachary, right now she needed to be on her own. How could she tell him she had to leave?

This was killing her. She'd thought that the cancer might kill her and she'd beaten that. But this was causing her more pain than the cancer ever had. More pain than the surgery and more pain than the chemotherapy and radiotherapy put together. And the worst thing about this was that she was the only person who could feel it. She wanted to feel free, she wanted to feel easy with herself. More than anything she wanted to have a happy family life. And she knew without a shadow of a doubt that Lincoln loved Zachary as if he were his own.

That's what made this so hard.

She had to step away. She didn't want to hurt him, but if she stayed without facing her demons she couldn't predict their future.

She wanted to be with Lincoln because she loved him. Not because he was the easy way for her to deal with her past illness. It wasn't true to herself and it wasn't fair to him. If she tried to deal with how she felt while staying with Lincoln, it could cloud her judgement and influence her decisions. She needed to step away. And she needed to do it before he became even more attached to Zach.

What if he met someone else? Someone who could give him a family of his own? The thought made her stomach churn. It was a risk she had to take.

She wanted to love Lincoln with her whole heart, not just the little piece she hadn't locked away.

His eyelids flickered open and a lazy smile appeared across his face. He lifted the corner of the twisted duvet. 'Wanna come in?'

She shook her head, but walked over towards him and sat on the edge of the bed. 'Morning.' Her voice was cool.

He rested his head on his hand. 'What's up? Something wrong with Zachary?'

'No, he's fine.' She smoothed her hand along the bed, focusing on the crumpled sheet rather than his face. 'He's sleeping again.'

'So why don't you come back to bed?' There was a twinkle in his eye again and it pulled at her heartstrings. She didn't want to hurt him. He'd helped her in more ways than he could ever imagine.

She took a deep breath and stood up, turning to face him. She had to be calm, she had to be in control. 'I have to leave, Lincoln.'

The words came like a bolt out of the blue, causing him to sit upright and swing his legs out of the bed. So much for a lazy morning. 'What on earth are you talking about?'

'I can't stay here any more. You've been so kind, but I need some time—some space.'

Deep lines of utter confusion furrowed Lincoln's brow. 'We go from last night—to this? Did I do something wrong?'

She shook her head and touched his arm. 'No, Linc. You didn't. You did something wonderful. But that's what's wrong. I've spent five years avoiding this. I've spent five years not dealing with this. And I can't move on. I can't move on to the next stage of my life without dealing with this first.'

'So why can't we deal with it together?'

She sighed. 'Because there can't be an "us". There can't be a "together". I've got to take some time to learn to accept who I am and what I've been through. And I've got to do it on my own. I've got to do this on my own terms.'

'Why on earth do you think you've got to do this yourself? I told you last night that I was happy to take you the way you are.'

She sat down next to him. 'I know you did, Lincoln.' She looked down at the space where her breast should be. 'You're happy to take me the way I am...' she looked at him with tear-glazed eyes '...but I'm not. This isn't about you. It's about me.'

'Don't give me the "it's not you, it's me" speech. You owe me better than that.'

She bit her lip. 'I know I do, Linc. And I'm sorry. Ultimately, I truly want us to be together. I want us to be family. But I've got to be selfish about this because right now I know I'm not ready and I've got to look after me first.'

'And you think this is the way? You think this is the answer? To go away? Hell, Amy, you're just out of hospital with a premature baby—do you really think this is the time to find yourself?' He was pacing around the room now in his white jersey shorts, agitated. She had to pull her eyes away.

But he hadn't finished. 'I've spent six weeks—*six weeks*—helping look after your son. And now you're just going to take him away from me?' His pacing grew more frenetic. 'I'm the one who's spent the most time with him, and I know I don't have any rights to him, I know Zachary isn't mine. But he feels like mine. He *feels* like my son. I can't just let you walk away. Zach knows me, he recognises me—how can this be good for him?'

Amy could feel a tear trickle from the corner of her eye. This was harder than she'd ever imagined. Her heart was breaking. She'd never wanted this for Linc. She'd never wanted to hurt him. But that was exactly what she was doing. She'd come to him because she'd thought he'd be the best doctor for her son. But things had changed so much. This hadn't really been about healing her son, this had been about healing herself.

'This is about Zachary, Linc. This is all about Zachary. How can I be a good mother to him when I can't even look at my reflection in the mirror? How can I focus my time and attention on my son when this is hanging in the background? How can I even think about another relationship when I'm still not comfortable in my own skin?

'I want to be free to love you. I want to be free to watch you have a relationship with my son. But everything inside me is so screwed up. I need to go back home—home to Santa Maria and my friends. I need to learn to look after myself and Zach before I'm ready to do this. Don't you see what you've done for me? The best thing in the world. You've helped me realise I need to face up to my demons. I'm healthy, Linc. Physically, I'm healthy. And I hope that when I reach my five-year anniversary I'll be able to kiss my breast cancer goodbye completely. But inside?' She shook her head.

'I'm not quite there yet.' She lifted a finger and touched the side of his cheek—gently, tenderly. 'I need to take one last step. This is the final hurdle. The last thing I need to overcome. And you've given me the courage to do it. I want to have a relationship with you. I do. But right now I'm short-changing you. I'm not loving you the way I should. You need to let me go. You need to let me go and come back on my own terms.'

He stopped pacing and stared at her. She couldn't read his face. It was as if he was trying to make sense of her words. As if he was trying to rationalise what she was saying—trying to construct an argument against it. She could see the tension across the muscles in his shoulders and his abdomen. He was upset.

Then she saw his shoulders sag, his muscles relax. It was as if he'd resigned himself to the fact she wanted to leave. As if he understood her words and realised this was the only way.

And it caused her tears to flow even stronger.

He reached over and brushed a loose curl from her cheek, tucking it behind her ear. She could see a million thoughts in his eyes. He leaned forward. 'Sometimes the hardest bridge to cross is the one in your own mind.' His words were quiet, almost a whisper. 'I can't do this for you.'

'I know.' The words hung in the air between them, like a moment of suspended time.

He brushed a kiss to her cheek. 'If this is what you need, then I can't pretend to understand, but I'll always support you. You and Zach.'

He lifted his head. 'When do you want to go?' He hesitated. 'I want to say goodbye to Zach.'

She breathed a huge sigh of relief. It almost felt like a weight was lifting off her shoulders. She knew this would be killing him, but he was still giving her room to breathe, room to heal. 'I guess I should go today. I don't want to make this any more difficult.'

'Do you need a hand to move?' She could see the emotions on his face now. The pain she'd caused him bubbled beneath the surface. How could she do this to him?

'No. No, thanks. I'll make other arrangements.' She had to. She couldn't hurt him any more.

'Then let me say goodbye.' He picked up last nights discarded jeans from the floor and pulled them on. He grabbed a T-shirt from the cupboard and walked through to her bedroom. Through to where Zachary lay sleeping in his crib.

She watched as he bent over and stroked the side of Zachary's face, whispering to him for a few minutes. She had no idea what he was saying and she was glad, because her legs currently felt like jelly.

He turned to face her, striding briskly from the room but stopping just for a second beside her.

His dark-rimmed eyes caught hers. She wanted to tell him she loved him. She wanted to tell him that she ached for his touch. She wanted to tell him that she would never feel about anyone else the way she currently felt about him.

He hesitated, just for a second, as if trying to fathom if he should say the words circulating in his brain or not. Then he gave her a little smile. 'You were my One That Got Away, you know?'

'What?' His words confused her.

He moved closer. 'They say everyone has one. *The One That Got Away*. The one person that if you could turn back the clock and do something different for, you would. Anything that would have stopped them leaving. You were mine, Amy. And you always will be.'

His eyes met hers. 'Maybe this is right for us.' He glanced around him, his gaze sweeping over the apartment. 'There's something that I've wanted to do for a while—something I've been putting off. This might just give me the time to do that.' He looked thoughtful then reached over and squeezed her hand. 'Promise me you'll keep in touch.'

Her lips trembled. 'I promise,' she whispered as he kissed her cheek once more and walked out the door.

She stared down onto the San Francisco street and watched him walk briskly along the sidewalk. This was hard. Harder than she could ever have imagined.

But inside she knew it was right. She'd made a decision. Out there was the man she loved. She wanted to be with him with her whole heart.

She just needed to learn how to love herself first.

CHAPTER TEN

Amy drew a deep breath before climbing the stairs. She couldn't hide the tremble in her arm as she lifted her hand to ring the bell. It was a quiet, unassuming street, with trees lining the length of it, giving it an air of suburbia in the middle of the city. The gold plaque next to the door glistened in the sun. *Donna Kennedy, Counsellor.*

Normally she would have done this kind of thing by recommendation. Taking the word of a few reliable colleagues and friends. This time she'd made an appointment with the first counsellor she'd found in the *Yellow Pages* who would see her with a baby. She only hoped the warm friendly voice on the phone lived up to reputation she'd built in her head.

The door swung open. A small round woman with grey hair lifted Zachary straight out of her arms. 'Come in, come in.' She bustled Amy into a wooden-floored room that looked out over a wide garden filled with colourful flowers, pointing her in the direction of a comfortable leather armchair.

Everything about the place was friendly and inviting. The sunlit room was spacious enough to be comfortable but not sparse and clinical and looking like so many other office spaces. Amy could hear someone clattering around in the kitchen behind her, the smell of baking inviting her stomach to rumble. This was a home.

The woman settled herself in another chair, adjusting Zach in her arms as she chattered non-stop to him. Her smile lit up her face. 'It's been a long time since I got my hands on a baby.' She stuck her pudgy finger into Zach's little fist, waiting until his tiny fingers clenched hers.

Amy sank back into the chair. A pitcher of iced water and a couple of glasses sat on the small wooden table next to the chair. The windows to the back garden were open, letting the smell of cut grass and open blooms seep in through the air. She shifted in the chair. It was a little worn in patches, the leather thinning on the arms, but was obviously well used. Always a good sign.

She caught Donna's eyes on hers and instantly understood. This was a well-rehearsed routine. The easy, welcoming atmosphere. Taking the baby to allow her to relax, to focus on the reason she was here. She might look like a bustling grandmother, but this woman was wise.

A warm feeling swept over her. She'd come to the right place.

Donna gave Zach's head a little rub with her fingers, tracing them down his heavy eyelids—almost hypnotising him to sleep. Then, once she was satisfied with the outcome, she looked Amy straight in the eye. This woman was a professional through and through. 'So, Amy, tell me, how do you feel?'

No preamble. No 'explain why you are here'. Just straight to the point, 'how do you feel?'

Amy pressed her shoulders back into the armchair. Zach was quiet; he was sleeping. The sun was beating

down on the grass outside and she could see birds pecking at the berries on the bushes next to the window. She
took a deep breath. She could do this. This was easy.
Everything about this felt right. But more importantly,
for her, the time was right.

She looked Donna straight in the eye. 'I feel angry,'
she said.

The plane circled a few times. The rain was torren-
tial and was obviously affecting their ability to land.
Time after time they swept over the darkening green
rainforest as they waited for a suitable landing spot.
From here, if Lincoln strained his eyes in the distance
he could see the snaking Amazon, winding its way
through the forest.

Home to hundreds of potential patients.

He'd successfully negotiated a variation in his contract, allowing him some extra unpaid leave from San
Francisco to serve with the Amazon aid boat.

It hadn't been difficult. The hospital needed some
good publicity right now, so supporting one of their best
doctors on some aid missions had been an easy move
for them. It helped that as the President's doctor he was
still the darling of the media and could whip up some
support for the people out here.

He'd managed to persuade a few colleagues at other
hospitals to help out, assembling a team with a wide
range of skills. Some of the best surgeons in the country were taking a few weeks out of their vacation time
to come and do a series of operations on some seriously
ill children. The planning had been a logistical nightmare, but at the end of the day these children would get
what they needed. And the people of the world would

get to see their plight as a film crew had decided to tag along for the ride.

Normally Lincoln would have avoided filming at all costs but he knew that interest in him would soon wane so he wanted to make the most of the opportunity to show the world the healthcare needs in the Amazon. It might even attract a few more willing docs to join the service on a regular basis.

The staff at San Francisco had been great, helping him with fundraising activities and praising his humanitarian efforts.

But Lincoln wasn't really going to help the people of the Amazon. That had always been at the heart of his work, and had been the only reason he'd volunteered in the first place.

But this time was different. This time he was doing it for himself.

'Linc, it's your weekly call!'

Linc looked up from where he was finishing with the latest addition to their baby clinic. Alice, one of Linc and Amy's old colleagues on the boat, was brandishing the satellite phone and waving it at him furiously. He placed the newborn back in the cot and moved towards their communication room—probably the hottest room on the boat.

As usual the line was crackly. 'Hey, it's Linc,' he said as he flopped down into the nearest seat.

'Hi, Linc, how are you doing?' He leaned backwards in his chair. The weekly telephone calls from Amy had started a month after he'd started back on the boat, a few days after he'd received her letter telling him she was doing well.

'How's Zach?' He always asked about Zach first. He couldn't believe how much he missed the little guy.

'Zach's good. He was at the clinic last week. They thought he might be developing a bit of a squint, so they've referred him to an ophthalmologist.'

'Who?' The words caught his attention instantly and he leaned forward in the chair. It didn't matter that he was on the other side of the world. He wanted to know what was happening to Zach.

'Some woman called Fern Price. She specialises in kids and is supposed to be very good.'

He scribbled her name on a bit of loose paper he had in his pocket—he'd check up on her later.

'How's Alice's hair holding up?'

Lincoln laughed. Alice moaned about the state of her hair from the moment she got up until the moment she went back to bed. Lincoln leaned back in his chair and raised his voice. 'Be thankful you're on the other side of the planet, Amy.' He wrinkled his nose. 'Though looking at how frizzy Alice's hair is, I'm surprised you can't see it from there.'

'*What?*' The shriek came from the other room. 'I'll get you for that, Lincoln Adams.'

Lincoln smiled. That's why he was here. This was what he needed. Friendship. Companionship and a lot of distractions.

'I saw you on TV again last night.'

'What?'

'On TV. The reporters love you.'

'As long as they bring more funding I don't care. A few more recruits would be nice too.'

'I wish I was there.' Her voice sounded wistful.

He felt a tingle run down his spine. 'I wish you were

here too. but we both know an Amazon aid boat isn't the right place for Zach.'

He heard her take a deep breath. 'Are you coming back soon?'

He looked around at the battered boat, with its depleted medical supplies and too few staff.

'No,' he said firmly. 'I've still got work to do here.'

'I miss you, Linc. We miss you.' She hesitated a little. 'And I've got a surprise for you when you come back.'

'Really? What is it?'

'I've applied for a new job.'

'Really? Where?'

'In San Francisco.'

His heart stopped. She hadn't wanted to stay in San Francisco. She'd wanted to stay in Santa Maria and bring her child up in a community rather than a city. The hugeness of the step wasn't lost on him. The line crackled, a sure sign it was about to disconnect.

'Linc, speak to you next week,' he could hear her shouting.

'Sure,' he said as the line fizzled and died.

He stared at the satellite phone as the little red light flickered the cut-out.

'I've got a surprise for you too,' he whispered.

The weekly calls were hard—on both of them. But at least it was a starting point. Part of him wanted to go home right now, and part of him wanted to stay here in the Amazon, where he could hold on to his heart.

He pulled his wallet from his back pocket and found the dog-eared photo he was looking for. Zach, smiling and chewing on a toy. He smiled at it then peered closely at his eyes, looking for any sign of a squint. But there was nothing he could see. And what he really wanted to do right now was pull Zach onto his lap and look at him for himself.

He looked at the calendar. Three weeks. Another three weeks then he would head home. He'd tell her nearer the time. Until then his dreams would be haunted by a pale-skinned redhead.

'Linc, we need you!'

The voice stirred him from his thoughts as he saw people dashing about next door. Another emergency. Another life at stake.

Right now he was where he needed to be.

CHAPTER ELEVEN

THE bright lights were waiting for him at the airport—again.

Lincoln sighed. He'd just flown from Iquitos airport in Peru to Lima then Mexico City and on to San Francisco. He was exhausted. He'd been travelling for more than fifteen hours and all he wanted to do was collapse into bed.

He pasted a smile onto his face. In the last few months he'd gone from being the President's doctor to being the Amazon doctor and filmed for a US television series that was now beamed around the world. For some reason unknown to Linc, the people of the world seemed to love him. Television news crews followed his every move.

'Lincoln! Lincoln!'

A crowd of teenage girls were waiting at the arrivals gate for him, all wearing T-shirts adorned with his face and thrusting autograph books towards him. He swung his rucksack onto the floor—the rest of his luggage had gone missing at Lima airport, again. He smiled and posed for photos patiently. He could do this. It was all for a good cause.

An impatient TV reporter tapped him on the shoulder, flicking her dark hair and batting her eyelashes at him. 'Can you tell us, Dr Adams, are you going back to the Amazon?'

He'd just landed. He hadn't even had a chance to get his hands on an American hot dog yet and she wanted to know when he'd be going back.

He kept his smile carefully in place. 'I'm home to do some work at San Francisco's Children Hospital—where my regular day job is. I've got a list of surgeries that need to be scheduled for some kids in the Amazon, but I'll need to take a bit of time to try and organise that. A lot of the surgeons we require have very specialised fields and tight schedules so it could take a few months.'

The TV reporter flicked her hair again. 'Can't someone else do that for you?'

Lincoln shrugged his shoulders. 'Amazon Aid is trying to arrange a co-ordinator for me, but it has to be someone who understands the types of equipment and skills we require. It's a big job.' Despite his tiredness he shot her a beaming smile. 'I'm sure they'll find me someone soon, but in the meantime your viewers can donate to the charity or, if they've got a medical background, volunteer to help out on one of our missions.' He looked straight into the camera. He'd learned in the last few months that every piece of publicity helped. Applications for the Amazon aid boats had shot up since the television series had been screened. Some keen women had even tried to lie on their CVs about their qualifications—all in an attempt to get closer to him.

He had a whole pile of applications in his rucksack, along with some significant other paperwork that he'd had to come back to the States to sort out. It was amazing how things could change.

But more than that, something inside him had changed. Something deep inside. And whether he liked it or not, he'd Amy to thank for it. First Zach, and now another child with a pair of dark brown eyes, currently clouded by childhood cataracts, and a smile that could melt his heart. Another child pulling him in. With something he could cure. A kid whose parents had abandoned him on the boat, thinking his damaged eyes made him worthless. A kid he fully intended to bring home with him.

The reporter batted her eyelashes again. Did she have something in her eye? She was really beginning to annoy him.

She ran her hand up his arm, looking like a leopard about to pounce. 'So, Dr Adams, all work and no play makes Linc a dull boy. What do you plan on doing now you're home?'

The way she said his name grated. He felt as if a snake was currently crawling up his arm—and he'd seen enough of them recently.

His reply was curt and to the point. 'Sleep.' Interview over. He swung his backpack over his shoulder and headed towards the door.

But something caught his attention. A flash of a red jacket with the Amazon Aid sign, topped by a mane of red curls and a set of arms clutching a squirming toddler.

A hand caught his wrist. 'Lincoln. You're back. Great. Meet your new surgical co-ordinator.'

Brian Frew, the man behind the organisation of all the Amazon Aid expeditions, looked extremely pleased with himself. 'Lincoln, meet Amy. Amy, meet Lincoln.'

He froze. He'd never seen her wearing red before. It wasn't a colour normally associated with women with red hair. But Amy looked stunning. She gave him a wide smile. 'Told you I had a surprise for you.' She stretched her hand out towards him. 'Pleased to meet you, Dr Adams.'

His eyes fixed on Zach. Now approaching his first birthday, he was obviously developing well. He still had that lean look about him—common for babies born prematurely—and would probably never be a chunky toddler.

Amy had obviously been keeping hold of him in a vise-like grip and with one arm outstretched towards Lincoln Zach was currently making a break for freedom. Lincoln clasped Amy's outstretched hand and reached with the other for Zachary, who bounced over into his arms and started tugging at the leather thong around his neck.

'Hi, little guy. How are you?' he whispered. Green. His eyes were green now—just like his mother's. And they were straight. The patch he'd worn for a few months over one eye must have worked.

Amy cleared her throat. Brian was looking frantically from side to side, obviously wondering what was wrong. 'Can you give us a minute, please, Brian?' Amy's voice was strong and determined, with only the slightest waver. Brian nodded nervously and sloped off towards the door.

She stepped forward, into Lincoln's space, her face only inches from his.

'You're my co-ordinator?'

'I told you I'd applied for a new job in San Francisco. It almost seemed as if the job description was written for me. I decided it was time for me to show how much I wanted to be here. I left you a message on the satellite phone last week.'

He shook his head. 'I never got any messages. The satellite phone died last week, that's why I didn't phone to say I was on my way home.' She was right in front of him and he had Zachary in his arms. Ten long months he'd waited for this.

She smiled. A happy smile. A healthy smile. 'Well, now you're back in the country I intend to try and keep you here for a while.' There was a wicked glint in her eyes. This was the Amy he had known. A confident woman, who knew what she wanted.

The implication was clear.

He took a deep breath. It almost felt as if his life were flashing before his eyes. Was he dreaming this? At some point on the plane he'd drifted off and his dream had definitely resembled this one. Could he still be sleeping on the plane?

No. His plane dream would never have included that obnoxious reporter. He looked at the green eyes in front of him. They were sparkling. And they were definitely there—this wasn't wishful thinking. There was only one thing he could ask her. 'How are you, Amy?'

She moved even closer, sliding one arm around behind Zach's squirming body and the other palm flat on Lincoln's chest. His eyes drifted downwards. Her chest was pressing towards him. Both sides of her chest.

She followed his gaze downwards and smiled. 'I guess I should have said I had two surprises for you. I took the steps I needed to. I figured since you already didn't object to scar tissue, you could handle a little more. I'm healed. I'm whole.' She lifted her head, staring directly into his eyes. 'I have a wonderful counsellor—I'd like you to meet her. And I am now "officially"...' she gave a little curtsey '...five years cancer-free.'

He took a deep breath, his heart pounding in his chest. 'That's great news. I'm happy for you. But what does this mean for us?'

He watched her, waiting for her to speak. Hoping and praying she'd say the words he was looking for.

'I have some unfinished business.'

Not what he'd expected. It sounded so formal. But, then, she was Miss Unpredictable. Could he really live a life like this?

'Business? With me?' He raised his eyebrow at her.

She nodded. Her hand moved from his chest, around his waist and down to his behind. 'I've done everything I can. I've taken care of what I can. Physically, mentally, emotionally, I'm ready, Linc. I'm ready to start again. And I'm hoping you are too.' Her eyes held his. Her lips were trembling. Was she about to cry?

'I just need to ask you one question.'

'What's that?'

'Can you take me as I am? Can you live with only ever having one child? Can you live with a woman who can't give you any children? Are you ready to give me another chance? Because I can promise you I'll never hurt you again. You've given me a lot of time to think about things. Can you give me a chance again?'

He smiled. Little did she know what he held in his bag. The future he had already planned. He kissed her forehead, then her eyelids, then her cheeks. 'I think I can manage that,' he whispered. 'And I've got a little surprise for you too—one I'll tell you about later.'

She took a deep breath. 'Good.' She leaned in and wrapped her arms around his neck, with Zach between them. 'Well, in that case, I've come to get my One That Got Away.' The tears were gleaming in her eyes. 'Because it was always you, Linc.'

And this time the tears were in his eyes too.

* * * * *

A sneaky peek at next month...

Medical Romance™

CAPTIVATING MEDICAL DRAMA—WITH HEART

My wish list for next month's titles...

In stores from 1st June 2012:

☐ Sydney Harbour Hospital: Bella's Wishlist — Emily Forbes

& Doctor's Mile-High Fling — Tina Beckett

☐ Hers For One Night Only? — Carol Marinelli

& Unlocking the Surgeon's Heart — Jessica Matthews

☐ Marriage Miracle in Swallowbrook — Abigail Gordon

& Celebrity in Braxton Falls — Judy Campbell

Available at WHSmith, Tesco, Asda, Eason, Amazon and Apple

Just can't wait?

MILLS & BOON® Book Club   *2 Free Books!*

Get your free books now at
www.millsandboon.co.uk/freebookoffer

Or fill in the form below and post it back to us

THE MILLS & BOON® BOOK CLUB™ — HERE'S HOW IT WORKS: Accepting your free books places you under no obligation to buy anything. You may keep the books and return the despatch note marked 'Cancel'. If we do not hear from you, about a month later we'll send you 5 brand-new stories from the Medical™ series, including two 2-in-1 books priced at £5.49 each and a single book priced at £3.49*. There is no extra charge for post and packaging. You may cancel at any time, otherwise we will send you 5 stories a month which you may purchase or return to us — the choice is yours. *Terms and prices subject to change without notice. Offer valid in UK only. Applicants must be 18 or over. Offer expires 31st July 2012. **For full terms and conditions, please go to www.millsandboon.co.uk/freebookoffer**

Mrs/Miss/Ms/Mr (please circle)
_____

First Name
_____

Surname
_____

Address
_____

_____

                                        Postcode
_____

E-mail
_____

Send this completed page to: Mills & Boon Book Club, Free Book Offer, FREEPOST NAT 10298, Richmond, Surrey, TW9 1BR

Find out more at
www.millsandboon.co.uk/freebookoffer

Visit us Online

0112/M2XEA/REV

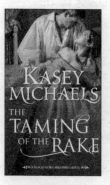

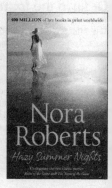